The School of Hard Knocks

WITH

P.D. NELSON

"I may not have gone where I intended to go, but I think I have ended up where I needed to be." —

Douglas Adams. *The Long Dark Tea-Time of the Soul*

"The secret of life, though, is to fall seven times and to get up eight times."—

Paulo Coelho

Chapter-1

THE GREAT DIVIDING RANGE is the backbone of the east coast of Australia, comprising a series of plateaus and low mountain ranges starting from Cape York Peninsula in Queensland's far north, spanning 3,680 kilometres south to the West Gipslands in southern Victoria.

The Snowy Mountains hydro-electric scheme took twenty-five years to build and was completed in 1974. Even before the scheme was finished, it was regarded it as one of the civil engineering feats in the modern era. It is one of the most complex integrated water and hydro-electric power schemes in the world, designed to collect and store water that would normally flow east to the coast and then divert it through trans-mountain tunnels and power stations before releasing the water into the Murray and Murrumbidgee Rivers for the purpose of irrigation.

Over one hundred thousand people from over thirty countries came to work in the mountains to make true a vision of diverting water to farms to feed a growing nation, and to build power stations to generate renewable electricity for homes and industries. Sixteen major dams, seven major power stations, a pumping station, one hundred forty kilometres of interconnected underground tunnels, and eighty kilometres of aqueducts were constructed.

Cooma was a town with a population of just over ten thousand people, and was regarded as the gateway to the Snowy Mountains, located virtually at the foot of Mt Kosciuszko; Australia's highest peak located less than one hundred kilometres to the west.

As a young boy growing up in the 'high country', it was almost a rite of passage to explore the many rivers, man-made lakes and dams, all virtually right at your front door. The crystal clear alpine waters of the Snowy, Numeralla and Murrumbidgee Rivers, all bursting with the run-off from the melting snow, full of both rainbow and brown trout, and only a short bike ride away. A young teenager with his fishing rod accompanied by his faithful dog, up at the crack of dawn and home again before the streetlights came on. It was meant to be a great upbringing for any young Australian kid, that's what the people from foster care said, and governments don't lie . . . do they?

The brand name Speedwell was almost indecipherable along the rusted frame. The two bike peddles weren't a match, and the slightly buckled rear wheel was salvaged from a wrecked Malvern Star. It was an inch bigger than the front, so the rear guard needed to be removed to make way for the extra height. At speed, a slight shimmy vibrated up through the handlebars, which just meant you needed to tighten your grip and hang on.

The last six months of this teenage boy's life had been spent rummaging through dump yards, jogging the five kilometres to the local tip and back, and scrounging off school friends all just to build what was now his pride and joy. A bitza, like a mongrel dog, this bicycle was painstakingly pieced together with his own hands, and like water off a duck's back, he merely shrugged off the snide remarks and smug comments as he arrived at the schoolyard each morning with a beaming smile.

With the Christmas school holidays in full swing, Phil Kelly looked towards the western horizon. He estimated he had two more hours before sunset. The greying clouds above were tightening, and the first haze of an incoming storm was his call to head back to the bridge that spanned the mighty Murrumbidgee River. He packed up his cane tackle box, secured the treble hook of his lure inside the butt guide of a two-piece rod, and started to hack his way back along the river's edge towards the pumping station another two kilometres downstream. Crashing through the acacias, mulgas and the skin-piercing thorn wattles that populated the banks of both sides of the river, Phil Kelly could just make out his bike leaning up against the south-side pylon. It was hidden from plain sight under the single-lane wooden bridge that separated government-owned property and the pain-in-the-arse Algansic family on the opposite bank who boasted one of the largest privately owned farm holdings in the region.

Kelly placed his tackle box on the rear bike rack, then tightened the octopus strap. He broke his rod down, then tied each piece off under the bike's horizontal frame with two old shoelaces. He pushed the bike out from under cover of the bridge to the edge of the road. With a rolling start, he swung his leg over the seat and found both peddles. He slid his peak cap down to ease the sting in his eyes as the rain set in, raised his body from the wet seat and began to press hard around the first bend in the road before the gradual incline indicated the start of what would be a forty-minute ride back home under an incoming southerly buster.

Frankie Algansic was regarded as the golden child. After his mother had previously given birth to six consecutive daughters, the weight of responsibility to produce a male heir had finally been lifted twenty-one years ago to the day. Today was day two of three days set aside to celebrate his 21st birthday. Seven empty kegs were stacked up in one corner of the woolshed, countless bourbon, vodka and tequila bottles lay scattered on the dirt floor. Drunken bodies were interspersed amongst the disarray, some inside the comfort of their swags, others curled up in the back of their ute's. The thumping sounds of Stevie Wright belting out *Evie*, parts one, two and three drowned out the roar of the V8 engines as a few local boys were showcasing their driving skills completing a series of figure-eight burnouts in an open paddock under a cloud of rising dust with a crowd of onlookers all cheering for more.

Maureen Benson was one of the few friends of Frankie's sisters to have lasted most of the night, and part of the next day. That was until she hit a brick wall around midday, and Frankie decided to lay her to rest inside the spacious cabin of his brand spanking new racing-black Ford *Bronco*. She was no looker, but beggars can't be choosers; she was a female with a decent pair of tits, and under Frankie's warped mythology, she was a willing participant.

Frankie downed the last two fingers of a near-empty Jim Beam bottle, then discarded it over his left shoulder. He stumbled over to his parked pickup with both hands cupped, then placed his head on the heavily tinted passenger window while he peered inside. Maureen was still curled up with her head resting on the centre console. The evidence from the previous day and a half of binge drinking was blatantly obvious. The hours of meticulously preparing herself for what had been ear-marked as the party of the year had now been replaced with the vulnerabilities of a girl with no defence.

Her hair hung loosely to one side. The off-the-shoulder party dress she'd saved up for looked dishevelled. The top part of her left breast was slightly exposed, with enough of her lacy blue bra on display to stir into action the next part of Frankie's plan. Even while in his current state of inebriation, Frankie needed to re-adjust his jeans as he felt a rising twitch below his leather cowboy belt. He felt for his keys, then looked over to see the rabbit's foot hanging loosely from the ignition. It was time to collect on a half-hearted promise made by a woman as high as a kite on bourbon and dope.

The 351-V8 fired up. Frankie shifted into first gear and picked his way through the minefield of glass and sleeping bodies. The high fives from two of his pissed as a fart mates was all the reassurance he needed as he headed away from the homestead to negotiate his way over the slight incline of the south paddock, past the old windmill, and ultimately towards the privacy offered under the Murrumbidgee River bridge. His favoured location for what was about to transpire.

Happy twenty-first, Frankie, he silently grinned from ear to ear.

Maureen sounded a confused grunt as her head bounced off the padded console while the vehicle negotiated a small wash-out. An overhanging willow tree that grew on the river bank slightly obscured the one and only gate Frankie needed to exit. He braked hard, slid out from the driver's seat, and swung it open. There was no livestock in this paddock so he left it swinging on the breeze until his return trip, which he hoped wouldn't be more than an hour at best. The sound of spitting gravel and rocks under the wheel arches was soon replaced with the quiet of the four 16-inch off-road tyres rolling over the sealed road surface. Frankie raised his knees to hold steady the wheel. He arched his back and struggled to undo his fly with his now rock-hard manhood itching to come out to play.

Maureen elbowed herself to a half-upright position while attempting to rub away the sleep in both eyes, with the inside of her mouth feeling like the bottom of a budgie cage. She looked and felt like shit. Frankie grabbed the wheel with his right hand while he finessed Maureen's head towards his exposed crotch. She needed something wet—anything to wash away the taste of booze, and too many cigarettes. She felt the force of Frankie's powerful arm, still disorientated, her open mouth suddenly filled with something stiff and flesh-like. Maureen gagged while resisting. She attempted to free herself from his grasp. She coughed and choked a second time. No force on earth would stop what happened next.

The sound of a projectile vomit was soon replaced with that unmistakable smell. A technicolour display of diced orange carrots, bright yellow corn kernels with cabbage and onions, lamb and pig roasted over a spit all mixed with beer and bourbon flowed unabated from her open gape like a mishandled fireman's hose covering Frankie's jeans while seeping down onto the driver's seat. She lifted her head to be startled by her own reflection in the rear-view mirror. She wanted to scream but couldn't as the gushing puke continued, rebounding off the top of the dash only to smear the windscreen with a haze of creamy, chunky disgorge.

Frankie didn't have the luxury of a cast-iron stomach. He placed his free hand to his own mouth as he dry-heaved, only to feel the first dribble of barf ooze through his fingers. He swapped hands and frantically wound down the window. With his head now leaning out through the open space, he let fly with his own retched version of hell-on-wheels while trying to slow the vehicle. He could see the northern entrance to the bridge fast approaching. The 'No passing - No overtaking' sign whizzed past as he turned the wheel slightly to his left. His face was now dripping with his own spew. The sound of loose planks underneath caused the *Bronco* to shudder slightly then the passenger front wheel collided with a low guard railing ripping the steering wheel from Frankie's hand. He grabbed it again and turned hard to the right, then felt and heard a loud *thump* noise from in front while he thought something may have glanced over the bonnet before hitting the windscreen so hard it cracked. The crunching sound of metal could be heard under the weight of rubber, then the lighter rear-end was flung into the air, lifting the empty two-tonne pickup clear off the ground.

Maureen's head flew forward and rebounded hard against the factory airbag warning label above the glove compartment with a wild side-to-side whiplash. She fell to one side causing the side of her head to collide with the window, then slumped to a brace position and remained dead still before slowly sliding to the floor. Frankie stepped hard on the brake pedal. The sound and smell of burning rubber mixed with the rancid reek of a cabin splattered with human puke were overpowering. Frankie needed to stiff-arm the wheel with both arms to break his forward momentum. The *Bronco* came to a sudden stop at an awkward angle with the bonnet pointing down over an embankment. Frankie felt for the door handle with half his breakfast, forming a slimy glove-like film over his fingers. His fingers slipped before he wiped both hands down the front of his T-shirt and pulled up hard on the door handle again while leaning into the frame. It flew open, and he launched his body to the freedom of the outside world. He emptied the remains of his stomach while coughing and struggling to breathe through his nose. In the back were some loose rags and an old used towel. He leaned over and retrieved anything that would ease the nightmare he was experiencing.

Frankie staggered to the front of the *Bronco*, and he felt a sense of dread overcome him in that instant. There was a distinct red smear of blood starting at the chrome grill over the bonnet, then continuing on to the windscreen. A broken headlight cover was evident, plus a wiper blade was bent out of shape. He made his way to the passenger door and opened it. Maureen was rolled up like a ball occupying the entire floor space. He placed both hands under each armpit and pulled her limp body clear and laid her back into the seat. His hands started to shake. Both legs felt like jelly as panic set in. Waves of nauseating despair engulfed his body as he searched for any signs of life. He sighed with a small respite of relief when she murmured a dribbling moan while a trail of her own blood leached down the side of her face onto her chin, then down over her throat from a gash above her left eye.

Frankie wiped her down the best he could with the towel, then buckled up her seatbelt before easing the door closed. He scrambled his way back to the roadside and looked back towards the southern exit to the bridge. Something out of place caught his eye. It was metal looking, but contorted and twisted. It wasn't until the distorted image reached the working parts of his drunken brain that he could see a wheel—a spoked wheel still spinning on its thin axle. He swallowed hard as he approached the mangled mess. His mind was sending discommoding messages.

He turned his head towards the sound of a barking dog. A border collie was head down near some tall grass on the verge farther up the road, away from the exit to the bridge. Frankie's mind was racing. He needed to think, but that wasn't remotely possible in his current state. Each step closer to what was left of the bike seemed like they were his last. Instinctively he looked to his right and then left for any other cars or people that may be in the vicinity. The rain was steadily increasing and looked like it was set to stay. He prayed that was the case.

Frankie picked up the two largest broken remains with both hands. He walked at a brisk pace back towards the bridge railing. This section of the river was over sixty feet wide, and he knew it was deep. With the melting snow combined with the recent rains, the river swept past at a steady rate with eddies and swirling whirlpools breaking the surface of the water as it disappeared around a gentle bend. Frankie searched his immediate surroundings one more time, and then simply let the bike fall from his grasp. Before the sound of the splash could be heard, he was heading back towards the barking dog.

He knew deep inside what to expect. Bicycles don't ride themselves?

A cane tackle box lay in the middle of the road. It was upturned with the contents spread out over the painted centre yellow lines. A single gumboot stood upright. The dog turned and snarled. Its hackles were raised with teeth gritted. Frankie picked up a loose rock and let it fly. It missed the dog, causing it to make a cautious step to one side with both eyes locked on to the man standing not five feet away. Frankie clapped both hands and yelled, "Scram. Go on, get outta here."

He kicked out with his crocodile skin boots while waving both arms wildly. Again, the dog stood its ground. Frankie remembered his .22 magnum strapped behind the driver's seat. He raced over and slid it out from its cover, then actioned the bolt. A shot rang out as a thunderclap roared loud in the distance. The dog flinched, realising the danger, stepping back and away. Frankie aimed and fired again. The border collie yelped while it stumbled to one side before hobbling away over the embankment, back towards the water's edge.

Frankie lay the rifle down in the pickup's rear tray. In a panic-stricken state, he bounded over to the long wet grass to see a body lying face down. The second gumboot was still on the left foot with the cuff of his jeans tucked in. It was scuffed and torn. A grey wet weather parka was shredded around one shoulder. Frankie's heart pounded inside. Through the driving rain, he sensed the tears of fear rolling down both his cheeks. He nudged the body with his boot. Nothing moved. He moved in closer and pushed harder. Still, no noises or sign of life.

The one saving grace, he thought, there was no blood evident. That was until he crouched down and rolled the body onto its back. He placed both hands to his face while facing the shifting blackened sky and screamed, "No fucking way. What have I done?"

The face of a young teenage boy looked back with closed eyes from under a well worn peaked cap. The back of his skull resembled a cracked egg. Time was ticking. Frankie shook the limp body with one cautious arm while placing an ear close to his mouth and listened for the slightest hint of life, only to be greeted by the sounds of silence. Half the lower lip was torn and hanging to one side, exposing the three bottom teeth like a rotting skeleton.

It was now or never, he thought. *Here—in this place right now, I'm totally exposed.*

He reacted without consideration, sliding both arms under the corpse, then lifted it to waist height. A bloodied and splintered bone had pierced a hole below the arm's left elbow. Again he looked back over both shoulders as he struggled under the extra weight back towards the railing a second time in as many minutes. Frankie fought back the urge to vomit again. The nauseating feeling inside his stomach was winning the inner battle of mind over matter. Without breaking stride, he launched the body over the top rail. It rolled in mid-flight before belly-flopping into the river below. Frankie placed both his bloodied hands on the railing and gazed at the spot of disturbed water for what felt like an eternity in morbid disbelief at what he had just been forced to do. The murk of fast-flowing water swallowed Kelly's body before he resurfaced face down as he continued floating into the teeth of what were kilometres of fast-flowing rapids and broken white water.

A young teenage boy's life had just been extinguished. Wiped out in a moment of insanity. Nothing would bring him back now.

Frankie turned and picked up the second gumboot, then just hurled it towards the river in frustration. Then he grabbed the upturned tackle box. With a loose hand, he brushed some strewn lures, two spare spools of line and a bone-handled filleting knife back inside before sweeping away with the soul of his boot the loose hooks and sinkers that lay scattered about indiscriminatingly. The top half of a fishing rod poked out from the damp overgrowth, so he grabbed that as well. Then he ran at pace back down to the river's edge, carefully placing all three items around a recently used campfire surrounded by river stones. "A tragic accident," he tried to convince himself. "Yeah—that'll work. An unfortunate fishing trip that resulted in a teenage boy drowning."

The end justifies the means scenario was repeating itself over and over inside Frankie's perturbed mind, and yet he knew it was a goddamn lie. The sounds of a woman wailing dragged him back to the reality of the situation. Like it or not, it was time to leave. There was nothing more he could do, and now he needed to deal with Maureen.

Chapter-2

THE ROYAL HOTEL in downtown Cooma was a traditional Australian pub built in 1858. It boasted a wrought iron wraparound lace verandah that encompassed the entire second-storey and was a popular one or two-night destination for the hordes of ski fanatics that passed through each season on their way to the ski fields of Perisher Valley, Selwyn Snowfields and Thredbo Village.

Nathan Blackwell was a stickler for routine. Each and every day that ended in y at precisely five o'clock, he would pull up the same barstool inside the long straight public bar that faced the Snowy Mountains Highway.

The current publican was a man that few people, sober or drunk, dared cross swords with. His adopted name of Banga stuck after he did exactly that with the heads of anyone that caused trouble while on his watch and was well deserved. His giant frame made the working area behind the otherwise generous bar look cramped as he moseyed up to a lone man seated on a barstool with his head slightly angled down. A single shot glass sat empty next to a half-drunk pint of beer. The phone in Banga's football-sized hands resembled a child's toy. He held the handset high in one hand and asked, "Nathan, got a call from the missus. You wanna take it?"

Blackwell raised his head and tapped the rim of his glass for another shot of Tullamore Dew, then nodded disconcertingly. Banga placed the phone down on an unused bar runner and left.

"Rose, is that you?" Nathan answered while he silently considered his wife's growing nervous Nellie demeanour.

"He's not home yet. It's been dark for over an hour now, and the rain is getting heavier. Plus the temperature is expected to drop to under ten degrees tonight. They're saying we may even get some hail." Her worry-wart tone only further caused Nathan to confirm his previous summation.

"I assume when you refer to 'him', you mean that smart-arse Kelly kid again?" Nathan answered with an edge of discontent.

"Yes, of course—who else? I checked the bedroom. All his clothes are still there. I don't think he's done a runner this time. I'm worried. We don't need any more trouble with the Department of Child Protection right now. Our next review is scheduled to coincide with the first term of school after the Christmas holidays end in February."

"Rose, calm down and let's not worry about DCP at this minute. He probably sought shelter under a tree somewhere dry to wait out the worst of the storm. Give it another thirty minutes, then call me back at seven-thirty."

Rose checked her immediate surroundings as she stood in the kitchen of her government subsidised home. All the remaining four foster children under their care were in the process of either showering or watching TV at the opposite end of the house. She eased the door closed anyway, and whispered in a harsh tone, "Remember, Father Bryant specifically asked to meet with him tonight—and in private."

Nathan shifted in his stool while turning his head towards the vacant end of the bar. He cupped his hands over the mouthpiece. "Well, if our boy is not home in time, offer him an alternative."

"Father Bryant was adamant he wanted *that* boy," Rose confirmed. "The good-looking one, I remembered him saying. God, it makes me feel ill inside just thinking about it. Religious induction... what a joke? Does he think we're all that naïve? I'm due to drop him off after evening mass."

Nathan asked, thinking he already knew the answer, "Did he go to his usual fishing spot near the bridge?"

"I don't know. I assume so. What will we do if Kelly doesn't show up in time? We can't piss off the bloody Church. Shit, Nathan, we're all in this together now."

"I'll finish my drink and drive the car down Mittagang Road all the way to the river and see if I can track him down. Has that bloody dog of his turned up?"

"I've not seen it hanging about. Mind you, I haven't looked either. You know the two are inseparable."

"I'll see you at home within the hour." Nathan was about to hang up.

"Yes, but what if he's gone missing again? This will raise questions about our duty of care, we may lose our accreditation."

"Like you said, Rose, we don't have to report him missing until our next review, so we have the rest of December and all of January to work through this problem. Don't panic, this is a good deal, and we can milk it for all its worth before we need to move on. Stay the course, Rose. Just remember the seven hundred twenty dollars he's worth to us every month."

Nathan hung up with rising anger threatening to spill over amongst the growing number of thirsty clientèle arriving at the end of a working week which was at the opposite end of the spectrum to the public profile he had so meticulously pieced together over the last ten years.

Chapter-3

KELLY'S BODY WAS ENGULFED by the ice-cold waters. It felt like death from a thousand paper cuts as the strength of the fast-moving river devoured his body. His internal instincts sprang into action as he was awoken from his unconscious saturation. Within a few short seconds, he felt himself sinking and floating away while being buffeted by the frothing swirl. He struggled mentally with his current surroundings, not even sure if his eyes and mouth were open or closed. His lips felt swollen and senseless. He started to extend his arms in a breaststroke action when a mind-numbing shot of pain flowed up his left arm. He wanted to scream.

Kelly's head broke the water's surface for the first time in a bobbing action like a snagged fishing float coming free. He was facing backwards with a clear view of the wooden bridge as it faded from sight when he caught the red glow from a set of brake lights heading south. He could see the tailgate of a dark pickup speeding away under the last rays of sunshine as it penetrated the forming tempest above. The increasing sounds of the upcoming rapids were like an alarm bell ringing loud inside his throbbing head.

Kelly raised his good arm, and felt his bottom lip flapping loosely against the flow. He inhaled a much needed lungful of precious air. With his body rolling and twisting, he knew his best chance to survive was to get himself into a feet-first position. Easier said than done. He extended his right arm and kicked with both legs until he finally turned. He reached over and placed his broken arm across his chest and out of harm's way. The Murrumbidgee takes on three distinct turns. Firstly to the left, then right, then back to the left before splitting into two separate tributaries. Kelly had fished this part of the river many times as far downriver as the cliffs which then denied any further land-based progress. He tried to steer left with no success as he accelerated into the waiting shallow broken rock.

He kept his body tight, grabbing a much-needed breath each time he was in clear air as he searched both sides of the river for some solid ground, a tree or even a flat rock to execute his exit. A bent willow offered a lazy overhang in the distance. He pushed his working arm clear to manoeuvre his body closer when the spine of his back shuddered as it struck a half-submerged granite boulder spinning him a full half-turn. Dazed and now face-down, he thought he heard the yelp from a dog in the distance. Was it real or just a cruel hoax? Images of his dog Santa flowed through his memory but nothing was making much sense.

Stay calm and think about your next breath, he reminded himself time after time.

Like any other drowning livestock, his battered body continued zigzagging around the exposed granite marble-shaped boulders while being pummelled with broken tree branches and busted limbs from all sides. The first drop off was the only a few feet high and he negotiated that without incident. The second he knew was double that followed by over one hundred feet of clear water before the last and final twenty-foot fall where the two parts of the river reconnected. Again, Kelly was sure he could hear a dog barking from behind. He wanted to turn his head, but there was no chance in hell of doing that anytime soon. He felt the floating sensation of his next free-fall. It was a small respite until a deep whirlpool from the swirling backwater swallowed him. Kelly's entire body spun like a loose windmill three times before being spat out the other side.

Santa was facing his own set of challenges. Headfirst, with his four legs churning in time below the angry white water, the border collie rode each rise and fall of the river without fear or concern. His ancestral reflexes moved him forward in search of his young master.

Kelly's momentum slowed. He took this short time to assess his injuries. Each breath drawn confirmed his ribcage was badly bruised, but he didn't think anything was broken. A blind man could see the splintered bone penetrating from his arm. He could feel the knock on the back of his head but had no idea how serious that was. The only silver lining to the excruciating pain was the anaesthetising effects of the freezing water. He tried to recall how he might have ended up in the river. He remembered peddling his bike around the first bend in the road with the rain stinging his face, and then it all went blank. His thoughts were suddenly interrupted by a paw slapping him on the top of his forehead. He almost shat himself while he screamed out loud, "Bloody hell." Then he saw the smiling eyes of his faithful dog.

The booming roar from the upcoming rapids instilled a sense of fear for both man and beast. The distance closed at a quickening pace. Resisting the urge to tense his body, Kelly remembered to relax his torso for the oncoming onslaught. And so it went on, a boy and his dog both at the total mercy of the powerful Murrumbidgee.

Kelly rested his working arm over Santa's back, careful not to exert any downward pressure. Together they were both jettisoned clear of the cascading avalanche of free-falling water. Kelly tried to hit the other side with his legs parted but sunk deep into the frothing swirl anyway. Santa ended up a good twenty metres in front. The dog had the nous to turn, and dog paddle headfirst back into the current to halt his forward progress. Kelly grappled with himself underwater trying to work out which way was up. His love of the water was all about being on it—not underneath it, his perforated left eardrum beat a dull ache under the increased pressure. He could feel himself letting go, sliding into a blackened world of nothingness, a sense of calm was knocking on his life door. He wanted to open it and step through, to ease the pain and finish the freeze creeping through each internal organ. He gasped for a clean breath with his eyes blinded by the mud and floating slime, splashing wildly with his mouth spitting out crap like a bilge pump until he felt the sodden fur of Santa once again. He clutched a hand around the dog's tail and held on for dear life.

A quietened calm replaced the chaos as the river began its slow crawling wind through kilometres of steep limestone and granite gorges carved out over the eternity of time. Kelly allowed the thoughts of sitting around a warm campfire cooking doughboys on the hot coals with his dog close by to warm his mind. A flare of false heat ran through his cooling veins. Santa kept up his steady pace with Kelly half hanging off his back until a faint glint from a rising moon broke through the dissipating cloud cover. That's when Kelly noticed the vertical cliff walls slowly being replaced with trees and a soiled riverbank. A silhouetted hillside rose up in the far distance. He urged the tiring dog on with some words of encouragement. Santa responded to the desperation in his tone. Working the water with his tiring limbs, Kelly relaxed his hold, allowing the dog to drag his weary body clear of the river. Kelly felt for the bottom with both feet. He stepped his way towards the edge while steadying himself by gripping some grassy undergrowth before he could crawl the last ten-metre stretch to the safety of the rain-soaked mud and grit.

Salted tears ran down the cheeks of his glaciated face with feelings of pure relief now playing havoc with his inner emotions. Santa shook his body from head to tail to dry off the excess wet then lay down by Kelly's side. He reached out with his hand and pulled his dog in close. Santa winced in pain. Kelly lifted his hand to see it covered in blood, and then just held him tight around his white collared markings. As the adrenalin levels subsided, his body began to shiver uncontrollably. Kelly reached inside his jacket and unzipped the pocket. As a kid growing up entrenched in the system of foster care, he'd spent many a lonely night alone in the bush while dodging the actions of people whose sole purpose was to offer children in their care a safe sanctuary. He pulled clear a plastic zip lock sandwich bag. Inside were the three essential items he never left home without; a lighter, his compass and a small flashlight. He placed a hand on his belt and felt for his leather pen knife holder. To survive tonight he needed to get warm, and for that he needed a fire.

Kelly placed his good hand on the ground to heave himself up to a standing position. He stood upright then swayed to one side. Instinctively he felt for something to hold on to, to help him just stay vertical. A rush of blood to his head made him feel dizzy. He stumbled forward, then backwards like a drunk man into the dark of night. He felt his legs go first which was soon followed by an ungainly fall back to solid ground where he lay shaking in an uncontrolled shiver completely exposed to the elements. Tonight would be a near-record-low temperature this close to Christmas Day.

Chapter·4

THE TRANSITION from a teenage boy to becoming a hardened stockman could be measured simply as time spent in the saddle for the folks that lived in the high country. For Luke Pender, the smoke from the thirteen candles on his birthday cake barely had time to disappear on the cool easterly breeze before his father marched him out through the swinging fly-wire kitchen door to be presented with his much-awaited birthday gift. His family gathered around as the saddle blanket was pulled clear. A Halfbred Stockman's Pride felt-lined leather saddle sat perched on the porch railing. For young Luke, it was not just about the gift itself. More importantly, this represented his rite of passage to accompany his father, uncle, and older brother on this year's muster.

Before the week's end, Luke's horse named Domino, which stood over fourteen hands high, was now half a mile in front of his family, and right now Luke Pender felt about ten foot tall with the responsibility as the lead rider. His job was to act as the first warning to any approaching vehicular traffic to the live hazard that followed behind. A mob of eight hundred sheep were becoming flighty as the smell of fresh water wafted on the hot, dry wind. To their rear, the open plains of Shannons Flat faded away under a cloud of dust and flies. The sheep had just crossed the Amaroo Fire Trail and were about to complete the twenty-mile-run following the dirt Outer Yaouk Road to a shallow river crossing before moving the mob south where the Murrumbidgee and Bredbo Rivers intersect to meet up with a team of shearers ready and waiting for the annual clip.

Luke unbuttoned his full-length Driza-Bone then pulled from the deep side pocket his hand-held two-way radio. He flicked the switch on as he approached the river's edge with a loose rein, allowing his horse to bend his neck to savour the sweet-tasting water.

The green LCD light showed three bars. He raised it to mouth level and pressed the *speak* button. "Dad, are you receiving? Over."

There was a slight pause before the familiar crackling noise sounded from the small speaker. "Copy that, Luke," his father responded. "Have you reached the river yet? Over."

"Just arrived at the Bidgee now. It all looks fine. We shouldn't have any problems crossing over. Just watering my horse now. Over."

"Okay, we'll see you soon. By the way, son, how's your rear-end? Do ya reckon you'll be able to sit down for grub tonight or you going to eat standing up again? Over." The sound of his uncle laughing could be heard in the background.

"You're a fair dinkum comedian, aren't you, old man? My backside is just fine," he lied. "Over."

Luke stood upright in both stirrups, straightened his back to ease the cramp, and hopefully some small relief from the realities of breaking in his new saddle. The sound of running water was always a welcome distraction from the monotony of moving a mob of sheep to the flatlands. He unclipped his canteen, ready to dismount when Domino suddenly shied sideways. The horse lifted his head with both ears pricked while facing upstream. Luke turned his upper body to search for the source of the disturbance with the knowledge that spooking a red-belly-black or brown snake while sunning itself on a smooth river stone was an all too often unwelcome encounter. The horse backed away, then stood calm—searching and listening.

Luke slid out of his saddle and grabbed both reins. He stepped back and away from the river before leading Domino forward towards an uprooted silver wattle laying half in–half out of the river; a victim from the last flood. The tops from a sway of grass moved in a parting action. Luke considered the possibility of bumping into an angry wild boar. His mother was adamant in refusing his initial request to allow her youngest son to carry a rifle. All he had was a skinning knife hanging from his belt.

A slight whimpering sound could be heard. That was followed by a muffled bark from what had to be a dog. Luke tied his horse off to a stripped tree branch. He stepped in closer with his senses on full alert while thrashing the ground in front. There was a small clearing on the other side of the tall grass. He crashed his way through to be greeted by a border collie crawling on all fours, leaving spots of blood in his wake along a trail of smooth pancake-shaped rocks. Luke bent down and eased the injured dog into his open arms. He lifted him clear, then turned to make his way back to higher ground. The dog seemed well fed and in peak condition. It wasn't a stray, Luke quickly decided. He wondered why it was out here all on its lonesome? He placed the dog gently down under the shade of a tall red river gum, then slid his hand clear to see it was covered in blood. Luke then nursed the dog to one side and noticed the bottom half of the dog's hind leg hung loosely by some damaged muscle tissue and loose skin. He'd seen the same wound many times on foxes and kangaroos after a badly aimed bullet missed its intended target. The dog looked him in the eye with a sort of knowing glint, then started to crawl away while in obvious pain. Luke fell to his knees and cradled it by the head.

"Come on boy, you need to stay still. I'll take care of you. My dad will be here soon. We can try to patch you up— or at least do *something*." He wasn't confident.

Santa mustered the energy to bark three times, causing the wound to leach more blood over the dog's filthy black and white undercoat. The dog whimpered while wagging his tail then dragged himself ten feet back towards the river. Luke straightened and followed in an increasingly distressed state.

Dogs were an integral part of every stockman's life; to be respected and adored. A good sheepdog was worth his weight in gold, he knew that. They had two red kelpies, and a blue heeler keeping the sheep in line on this very drove. Santa came to a stop on top of a small bank. Below was a mound of wet mud covered in some loose shrubs. If Luke didn't know better, it resembled a nest from a breeding crocodile, but that was an impossibility this far south. Then his heart skipped a beat when he noticed some movement at one end. A small blue-tongue lizard scurried away.

The dog barked again, and Luke just launched himself over the embankment, causing his boots to bury deep into the wet mud next to the strange shape. He bent down to one knee and started to brush to one side the foul-smelling mound of soil when a shoeless foot, complete with toes, appeared still attached to a leg in denim jeans. He moved to the opposite end, closer to the water and peeled back some loose lying green leaves and broken branches. A face appeared from underneath the muck. "Friggin' hell," he half-shouted while reeling backwards, causing him to fall clumsily onto his backside. He leaned forward and continued unearthing the human remains when he heard a gurgling sound. "Jesus bloody Christ," he shouted a second time. "This guy is still alive!" Things happened very quickly after that moment.

Firstly, Luke contacted his dad on the two-way to explain his find and convey his exact location. Both his father and Uncle Dave pushed hard through the mob of sheep. Jake Pender issued final instructions to his eldest boy to move the sheep across the shallow river crossing and water them down. Jacob whistled the dogs into action as Jake and Uncle Dave leaned forward into their saddles and galloped off down the dusty road towards the river.

Luke returned to the site of the body with his canteen. He filled it before trickling water over the young man's head while wiping it clean. Only now did he realise it was the face of a teenage boy, not much older than himself. He continued to clear away the mud and gunk, feeling the generated heat of nature's own blanket on his hands. Luke wasn't sure if he should try to move the body clear when he noticed a bone protruding from one arm. "Shit, that can't be good. You're in a real mess, aren't you, mate?"

Within minutes, the sounds of horses pounding over the sodden ground could be heard. Luke yelled out over his right shoulder, and his father was the first to arrive.

Luke stood up to make some room. "He's bloody-well alive, Dad. I heard him grunt before. Watch out for the arm, it's snapped clean through." His quivering tone mirrored the anguish he felt inside.

Jake Pender pulled his brass Zippo from a front pocket and held it close to the young man's mouth. A faint fog appeared on the polished surface. "Yeah, he's alive all right, but he's banged up pretty good. We gotta move him to higher ground, son." He stood and shouted out to his brother, "Dave, bring that silver bed sheet with you, and both our shovels." He turned to face his youngest son. "Luke, you and Dave dig out some clear ground so we can slide the blanket underneath and lift the body clear, okay. I'm gonna go and rustle up someone who will know what to do." Jake passed his brother Dave with both his arms full as he headed back to his horse. He grabbed his two-way to speak with his eldest son. "You on-air, Jacob? Over."

"Yeah, Dad, what's goin' on? Over."

"Listen carefully. It's time that so-called champion horse of yours earned its keep. I want you to head over to the Pritchard property on the other side of Flat Top Mountain. You know, Molly, the retired nurse? Over."

"Yeah, she patched me up once before after I got tossed from a crazy bronco at last year's rodeo. Over."

"That's the one. Now tell Molly to grab her medical kit and get over here in double time. We've got a young man suffering from hypothermia, and possible multiple fractures. Tell her he's definitely got a broken arm. She'll know what to do. You got that? Over."

"No worries, Dad, I hear you loud and clear. Over."

"By the way, Jacob, time is of the essence. A young boy's life may depend on it. Over and out."

There are some men born to ride a horse, the stockmen of the high country are in a class of their own, spending more time in the saddle than sleeping in their own beds. Man and his mountain-bred horse both working together as a single unit weaving their way over rugged terrain, dodging the many hidden rabbit warrens, wombat holes, flint-like granite rocks, and shifting ground underneath all the while at a blistering pace. Jake Pender could have easily invested in his own trophy cabinet to proudly display his many previous achievements. Instead, they sat gathering dust in the bottom of his wardrobe. He simply wasn't that type of man.

Jacob leaned forward to stroke the back of his horse's ears. "You hear that, Panic, we've got a job to do?" He felt the strength of his mount rise up through the hindquarters as he ran his hand down the length of Panic's powerful neck. Jacob grabbed a short rein and shifted in his saddle. His horse became acutely alert while raising himself up on his hind legs. All it took was one gentle nudge with both stirrups into the horse's girth, and both horse and rider were off like a twisting dust devil in a spray of dirt and flying stones.

Four and a half miles of flat ground lay ahead with three dry creek beds to negotiate. Panic vaulted over each one in a single leap and just kept galloping. There was a choice of two trails to tackle the mountain. One veered right and followed the base in a long half-circle. The second went straight up and over the steep incline and was shorter by a third. Jacob attacked the latter, knowing the ability of his mount. He leaned forward over the horse's neck while Panic powered his four hooves upwards, digging in, and not once did he break stride. The flattened mountaintop was a minefield of loose football-sized rocks that required a mindful prodding step. Slowly, both man and his trusty horse weaved their way through, ducking under the stringybarks, the low hung branches of the prickly thorns, and the windswept gum trees. A wrong footing could result in a twisted or broken ankle and mean a bullet to the head. Next was the decline and the most hazardous section. Jacob allowed a loose rein, giving the horse its head while leaning back over Panic's hindquarters with both stirrups sitting high and in front. The trick here was not to slow. A steady braking canter was the name of the game, and Panic took it in his stride. The final stretch was all dry, clean ground. Panic took off once more with a thick white lather forming over his white coat. Both ears were pinned back as the wind whistled past Jacob's Akubra rabbit-skin hat.

Molly Pritchard's homestead loomed large over a small ridge. Both horse and rider came to a screaming halt in a cloud of dust just short of a white picket fence lined with red roses. Jacob dismounted in one action and ran up the three stairs onto the wooden porch. The door flung open, and Molly stood captivated by the marvels of this boy's horse skills.

"What's your hurry, young man? I saw you coming in from over a mile away."

A short conversation followed. Molly picked up the phone to contact the one and only ambulance in Bredbo. Joan Ampt answered the call on the second ring. "Bredbo St John Ambulance base. What's the nature of your...?"

Molly cut her off mid-sentence. "Joan, this is Molly. Where's the ambulance right at this moment?"

"Molly, is everything all right? Your voice sounds urgent."

"Please, Joan—the ambo, is it available?"

"Well. . . not exactly, Molly. Pete's out on a call to pick up Dave Morgan's wife. She's having difficulties with a home birth. They think the baby may be breech. He's on his way to Cooma Hospital as we speak, and not due back on base for at least two hours."

"Shit, is that woman pregnant again, how many is that now?"

"This will be number nine, I think. What's your emergency?"

"Joan, I don't quite know as yet. I'll take my old Toyota and stick a mattress in the back. Jake Pender has sent his son to advise they've found a young boy down near the crossing. Apparently he's in a bad way. I'm leaving now. I'll call you on the two-way when I know some more. Gotta go, Joan. We'll talk soon. Bye."

Molly Pritchard first caught sight of smoke rising over the opposite side of the river. The mob of sheep were scattered about to her left. She pushed her old rusted Toyota J40 tray-back through the crossing, causing a decent size bow wave to wash over the opposite bank. The Pender family all turned in unison at the sound of a diesel motor bouncing over the small incline that indicates the road has finished and you are now entering an open paddock. Molly could see both Jake Pender and his brother gathered under the shade of a gum tree. She pumped the brake pedal three times and pulled to a stop less than ten feet away from a teenage boy laid out on a canvas swag while wrapped in a blanket close to a raging fire.

Molly made her way over and took one look at her new patient, then flew into action. She grabbed the mouthpiece in the cabin of the Toyota and pressed the *call* button. "Joan, do you read me? Over." A slight static noise could be heard coming from the dash-mounted speaker as Molly waited for a response. She lowered the mouthpiece and looked back down at the frail body laid out flat. Jake Pender caught her eye. She returned his concerned gaze. "Jake, this boy is in serious trouble. He needs a hospital *now* and will require surgery to fix that arm. It will take too long getting to Cooma by car, plus he's suffering from shock."

"Molly, is that you on-air? I read you loud and clear. Over."

"Hang on a minute, Jake." Molly raised the two-way back to her mouth. "Joan, use the landline and get onto the Royal Flying Doctors. Ask them how long until they can make an emergency extraction from this location then get back to me a.s.a.p. I'll do what I can while I wait. Joan, I'm switching to emergency channel ninety-eight. You got that? Over."

"I'm dialling the number in Wodonga as we speak. Hang in there, Molly. Switching to channel ninety-eight now. Over and out."

Molly dropped the mouthpiece onto the passenger's seat and unbuckled her bag, then knelt down on one knee. She placed a handheld thermometer to her patient's left earlobe and waited for a read. "I expected worse, ninety-nine point four. Not good but not critical."

"He was almost buried in mud and crap when I found him, Molly. Well—that was after the dog showed me the way," Luke wanted to explain.

All eyes turned to see the border collie spread out flat on one side panting with his tongue half exposed, hanging to one side, and now covered in loose dirt. "Well, I can tell you this much," Molly pointed out, "there is no way this kid could have done that himself—not in this shape. That's what probably kept him from freezing to death."

"It must have been the dog. It has to be this boy's dog for sure," Luke stated.

Molly asked, "Who's got a knife handy?"

Each man pulled his own skinning knife clear from its leather sheath and held it outstretched by the blade. "Stupid question, I suppose," Molly replied. "We need to cut his jeans, jacket and shirt away so I can do a full examination. Gently, remember he's not a cow ready for slaughter. And see if you can find some ID, a wallet or something?" she added.

Nurse Molly applied an anti-allergenic air splint to the broken arm. She'd just administered 5mg of morphine from a 10mg ampoule when the radio crackled to life. "This is pilot Shaky Merrit from the Royal Flying Doctors, calling Molly

Pritchard on emergency channel ninety-eight. Do you have a copy? Over."

Molly bolted over to the passenger's seat and picked up the mouthpiece. "Copy that RFDS. This is Molly Pritchard on-air. What's your current location? Over."

"Molly, the gods are smiling at you this day. We are currently one hundred ninety-nine kilometres south-west of your reported location en route back to our base in Wodonga. Can you confirm exactly where you are first? Then report in detail your medical emergency while we change course. Over."

Molly looked over towards Jake, and he answered the pilot's request. She repeated word for word. "Four miles south-east of Flat Top Mountain on the western side of the Murrumbidgee live-stock crossing. There is a mob of eight hundred fat Merino's grazing to our immediate north, so you can't miss us. Over."

"Copy that. If I remember right, Molly, we can put down on the Yaouk Road before it reaches the river? We only need half a mile of straight road. Can you confirm that is the case? Over."

Jake put up two fingers and nodded in the affirmative. "Yes, we can confirm well over a mile of good road as you approach from the west. Over."

"Okay, copy that. We'll need you to clear a strip of any loose debris, like rocks, branches, and livestock. Are you able to confirm that request? Over."

Jake and his older brother Dave were already mounting their horses. Jake pulled hard on the horse's bit and turned. "Luke, you stay with, Molly. She'll need a hand to get this kid on to the back of the Toyota. Then meet us over by the road."

"Happening as we speak, Shaky. Over," Molly happily acknowledged.

"Roger that. Our ETA is under thirty minutes. Give us a rundown of your patient's status, Molly. Over..."

Twenty-seven minutes later, two bright landing lights came into view over the north-eastern horizon as the RFDS King Air B200 completed a low-level flyover. The two Pratt and Whitney Canada PT6A turboprop engines roared past at low altitude as the pilot dipped his wings from port then back to starboard. The plane turned 180 degrees on a low arc and made its final approach, pulling to a complete stop about two hundred metres short of the river. The pilot cut both engines, and the door unfolded.

What happened next was like watching a bush ballet in full performance as the flight nurse together with the trained pilot weaved their magic. It took less than eight minutes to re-assess the patient, strap him onto a stretcher, then secure him back inside the flying hospital. This was just another day at the office for the dedicated team of the Royal Flying Doctor Service.

Within minutes after levelling out, and reaching their cruising speed of 270 knots, the flight nurse immediately discarded the decision to fly to Cooma Hospital. Next on the list was Canberra; the nation's capital. She then spoke with the emergency department over the plane's two-way to explain the extent of the patient's injuries in more detail. Her main concern was the possibility of internal bleeding plus clear signs of having suffered severe head trauma. After further deliberation, they made the decision to lay a flight plan directly into Sydney's RFDS Mascot base. From there, an ambulance would be waiting to deliver the patient to the Westmead Children's Hospital, where a team of experts would be prepped and at the ready to perform emergency surgery.

Chapter - 5

KELLY FOUGHT HARD to open one eye. A shimmering haze of blur hovered just out of arm's reach, blinking on, then off in relentless order. He attempted to raise one arm to sweep it away, only to feel the restriction of a human hand. The eyelid on his right eye was suddenly separated, and an intense light filled the darkness. He heard the sound of a man's voice. "Okay, that's a good sign. His pupils are both fully dilated and responsive," the doctor advised.

Both Kelly's eyes tried to focus on the shuffling images. He shifted his head from side-to-side. His mouth was bone dry, and his throat felt red raw. A woman's voice sounded calm, laced with kindness. "Well, welcome back to the land of the living, Sleeping Beauty. My name is Sandy and I will be your ICU nurse for the next eight hours. Come on then, let's prop your head up and see if we can get you comfortable, shall we?"

Kelly heard the electronic buzzing as his bedhead lifted. His eyes were now blinking rapidly to clear the gunk around his eyelids. It was like swimming underwater without goggles.

"The room has been kept dark until you can adjust to the natural light. Don't worry, it's all very normal until you become fully lucid and aware of your surroundings. You will find it difficult to talk for a few days. You've had a feeding tube down your throat for nearly eight weeks now," the soft voice explained.

Kelly took no notice.

A body shape started to form. Kelly could make out the smiling face that belonged to that soothing voice. He adjusted his arm to lift himself upright. He was in a hospital, but he didn't know why.

"Try to suck on this cube of ice for me," Nurse Sandy suggested before asking. "Do you know your name? Do you understand where you are, and how you ended up in the hospital?"

Kelly wanted to answer the first question and almost dry retched trying, so he nodded yes while sucking, and then no, with a blank stare.

The nurse then asked, "So you *do* know your name?"

Kelly nodded a second time.

"Can you write it down for me, because at this stage you are a complete mystery, young man," Nurse Sandy smiled back. She passed him a hand-held whiteboard with a non-permanent marker dangling by a string and waited. Kelly turned the board around for her to read.

"Just, Lucky Phil, is that right?"

Kelly nodded.

"How old are you then, Lucky Phil?"

Kelly scribbled the number sixteen.

"Where are you from; your home and family? God, they must be going out of their minds with worry."

Kelly grabbed the crayon a second time. 'No home - no family - no worries. Just me. Where's my dog?'

Nurse Sandy read the words with little reaction. She knew patients coming out of an induced coma often experience memory lapses. "All right, that's enough for now. You need to get some rest. I'll be back in a minute."

Kelly touched Sandy on the wrist, then indicated he wanted to write some more.

She looked at the whiteboard and responded, "Today's date is the twenty-first of February." Then she asked, "Why?"

He put a line through sixteen and re-wrote the number seventeen.

"Happy belated birthday. Keep sucking on the ice."

Christmas, New Year's and my birthday have come and gone? What the bloody hell happened?

Kelly was transferred late the following afternoon via the lift to the general ward on level three. The room was shared with seven other people, each separated by a thin blue curtain.

Another nurse arrived and introduced herself as Tricia. Soon another lady dressed in civilian clothes stood over the side of the bed. Her I.D. tag read: Department of Child Protection typed under the N.S.W State Government logo. "Hello. My name is Hillary Preston and I'm here to help."

A first warning bell rang loud inside Kelly's head. The first lie had been cast. The nurse puffed Kelly's pillow, and offered a cup still half full with melting ice cubes, then asked, "Are you able to speak now, Lucky Phil? Is there any discomfort?"

Kelly answered with a single, "Yes," in a gravel-like tone. The nurse stepped to one side, "Okay, I'll leave you two alone now."

Miss Hillary Preston adjusted her reading glasses and dragged a single chair close to the bed. "Young man, my job is to ascertain your current mental and physical wellbeing. Then based on my findings, I will be making some decisions relating to how we deal with you after you've been discharged from the hospital. Do you understand?"

Kelly nodded while swishing a mouthful of ice inside his mouth.

"All right then, let's get started. You say your seventeen, but you can't remember your full name—your family name. Is that correct?"

"I just remember being called, Lucky Phil," he lied.

"What day was your birthday, then?"

"January twenty-nine," Kelly answered truthfully.

"You can remember your birthday, but not your full name. Are you sure?" There was a slight pause while she looked deep into Kelly's eyes for a reaction. "They found you on the side of a riverbed near a town called Bredbo, and yet the local police have no record of a missing person who answers to your description. Why is that so? Where is your family? Where did you come from, and how did you end up in that river?"

Kelly allowed the soothing feel of the ice-cold water to slide down his throat. This whole situation was a blessing in disguise, and he needed to take full advantage of the unusual circumstances. It was time to change the status quo in his favour. He had been preparing himself for this type of interview for months now. Kelly shuffled inside the bed linen and fired his first shot. "Do I need to seek some legal advice? You know, to protect my legal rights and all that stuff?"

Hillary wrote something down in her precious file. "Can I call you, Phil?"

"Absolutely, Hillary," Kelly mocked.

"Why do you think you should have a lawyer present? Are you in some kind of trouble?"

"I'm under the age of eighteen. I should be represented by a third party who has my best interests at heart. Don't you agree? Are you refusing me legal aid, Miss Preston?"

The interview came to an immediate halt, and Miss Hillary Preston left the building.

Two days later Kelly's cast was removed from his arm, and he was strong enough to walk unassisted with the aid of just a single elbow crutch. He found a wrought-iron table and four chairs set up under a large fig tree that overlooked a fish pond. A man in his late twenties approached carrying a satchel style briefcase under one arm. He looked like he'd just finished celebrating his best friend's buck's party. His face looked ruddy, his shoulder-length hair was uncombed, and his nose was a road map of crimson veins. His suit looked like it had come straight from The Smith Family Shop and his socks didn't match. Kelly met his gaze as he approached in a slow-moving swagger.

"Are you the kid they call, Lucky Phil?"

"You have to be the lawyer," Kelly stated rather than asked. "Been a couple of rough days has it?"

"We all have to pay our dues, my friend. I'm from Legal Aid. Can I sit down?"

Kelly shifted his bottle of water. "Be my guest."

"Firstly, you have to appoint me officially. Since you can't remember your own name, signing anything would be a waste of time—or would it?" He let the words hang in the air like he knew what was going to happen next.

"Phil Kelly. Where do I sign?"

"My name is, Lawrence Inman, sign here and I'll fill in the rest later. Right now we need to talk."

Kelly asked, "So as of now everything I say is privileged. Is that right?"

"Right on, buddy. You've got your five minutes, so give me the whole spiel. I have been briefed on how some sheep farmers found you washed up on the banks of the Murrumbidgee River, and then up until the time you arrived at Westmead Hospital. So tell me, why do you need a lawyer?"

Kelly methodically stepped him through the last twelve years of his life. From the time he was left stranded on a church pew by a pregnant woman who he assumed to be his mother. The six toxic foster homes he'd suffered while still in Sydney until he was eventually transferred to a town called Cooma as part of a government-sponsored pilot program to assimilate disadvantaged teenagers with the opportunity of a fresh start in the country. "You know, fresh air and clean living, Lawrence," Kelly joked. "Four years I spent with that family until it became obvious I was being groomed as the next altar boy to receive his religious indoctrination. I'd witnessed on more than one occasion what that meant, and there was no way I would allow those fucking paedophiles to lay their grubby little hands of faith on me."

Lawrence Inman finished writing his notes, then looked long and hard at the young man seated opposite. "You're not lying, are you? I can always tell when someone is bullshitting."

"I'd like to say God's honour, but I don't think me and him are on talking terms at this moment. What's my legal status as far as being forced back into foster care?" Kelly asked.

"Phil, I've dealt with more than a few of these types of cases. At seventeen, you can offer a defence to refuse being forced back into the system only on the proviso you can provide evidence that you can support yourself. Like a job and a roof over your head. Attending school can ease the work problem, but you have no access to any financial help."

"I have some cash stashed back in Cooma. I was about to skip town when somehow I ended up in that river. I still don't know how that happened? One minute I was riding my bike back home, then poof, all of this…"

"How much cash you talking about?"

"Over five thousand stashed under an old cubby house near the horse corral at the rear of the house," Kelly answered.

"Seriously," Lawrence questioned, "five thousand dollars?"

"I've been saving for a long time. A dollar a rabbit, five bucks for a fox's tail. I was a fantastic shot, plus I had a paper run after school and odd jobs every weekend. I was highly motivated, let me tell you. The clock was ticking."

"That will help. Do you have someone you can trust to bag it and drop it off at a courier service in town?"

"Yeah, one person I trust with my life."

"Don't kid yourself, Phil. Trust no one, my man, life is a bitch—listen to a man that deals with the shitty end of town every day. Are you sure?"

"It's all good. Write down an address for me," Kelly assured him.

"I can apply for an Interim Order to place you in a safe house that I know from experience can be trusted. Mosman is an upmarket suburb with a decent high school. I deal with these people from time to time. Rich folks with a guilty conscience about how they carved out their fortunes. They offer a short-term stay for troubled teenagers as a means to cleanse their souls. But the school thing is a deal-breaker. We'll need to enrol you as a matter of urgency. Do you know what the word eccentric means?"

"Arr, not really. Why?"

"Well, you'll find out soon enough. Give me another week or two, Phil. First, I'll need to pull a copy of your birth certificate then check on the statutes regarding wards of the state. You say you were born in Sydney somewhere? Can you give me your mother's surname; married or otherwise, and what about a hospital?"

"I assume it was, Kelly, but I'm not sure. I know the hospital, though. It was Royal North Shore on Pacific..."

"It's okay, I know where it is. Right now, the safest place for you is right here in this hospital. Stay focused, don't talk to anyone, and just get better. Do you have a change of clothes when we leave?"

"I've got exactly what Paddy shot at. I arrived here in my birthday suit."

"Okay, I'll need to sort that out then I'll see you back here next Thursday."

Kelly wanted to ask, "What about this Miss Preston from DCP? Will I need to talk with her again, because I don't trust those bastards as far as I can throw 'em?"

"You won't be seeing her again. Trust me." Lawrence gathered up his loose papers and stuffed them back inside his satchel. He stood to leave. Kelly pushed out his chair and extended his good arm. The two men shook hands.

"As my lawyer, didn't you just advise me to trust no one?" Kelly gestured.

"You pick up quick, my boy. See you in a week or two."

Chapter-6

L AWRENCE INMAN was appointed by the Juvenile Court to deliver in person, Mr Phil Kelly, to the Sirius Cove Road address in the tree-lined suburb of Mosman at 4:00 P.M. His Jeep *Cherokee* slowed and pulled to a stop under a frangipani tree that hung low over the footpath at the front of a two-storey brick and tile home. A middle-aged woman smiled while looking like she was standing on a nest of butcher ants. She was dressed in a brightly coloured floral pants suit waiting at the bottom of a sweeping set of tiled steps that finished at a raised portico. Her hair was pinned tight in a bun with what looked like a couple of chopsticks poking out each side.

Both front car doors opened. Kelly slid out of the passenger's seat with just an overnight bag filled with some basic personable items in his right hand. He stepped in behind the court-appointed lawyer as they made their way across a manicured front lawn. A curtain from an upstairs room parted slightly revealing the face of an older distinguished-looking gentleman sporting a snow-white Colonel Sanders van-dyke beard and moustache.

The excited-looking woman took a couple of steps forward. "Hello, Lawrence, it's so good to see you again." She sidestepped the lawyer and made a beeline straight at Kelly. "Welcome to our home, young man. Please, come closer, and let me take a look at you. My name is, Shirley, as in Shirley Temple. I'll show you to your room if you like. You can freshen up then I'll introduce you to my husband, Lyle. Don't be shy, we're all friends here."

Kelly offered the hand of friendship, not sure of the correct protocol. Shirley almost fell forward and wrapped her arms around his neck in an unabated show of affection. Kelly wasn't prepared and instinctively retreated half a step backwards. This was foreign to him. Most times any person that came this close meant he was due for another beating. He dropped his bag, then reluctantly returned the kind gesture. She smelt magnificent. "Thank you for allowing me to stay in your beautiful home. My name is, Kelly—Phil Kelly." It was the only thing he could think of to say. He was nervous and felt apprehensive.

"Oh, we know all that. Lucky Phil? Tell me, is Phil short for, Philip?"

"I don't know, never got to ask."

"Right, yes... yes, of course. Well then, follow me. Your room is on ground level with its own private entry. We've only recently renovated the bathroom and shower, plus you have a separate toilet. You also have the use of a kitchenette. There's a gas cook-top, a microwave plus a sink with both hot and cold running water if you ever want to cook yourself something to eat. Both Lyle and I don't always eat at home, just so you know. There's a set of clean sheets and a fresh towel on the bed. Take your time to look around. I'll put the jug on, and you can meet us upstairs. Do you prefer tea or coffee?"

Kelly drank neither but opted for the tea. He spent the next twenty minutes under the hot shower head, cleansing his skin of all the usual hospital smells. He took the time to check out his body in the half-length mirror pinned to the back of the en suite door. His hair was still in the process of re-growth after the hospital haircut. It felt prickly as he ran his hand through to rinse the shampoo. The scar across the back of his skull was still tender to touch and slightly raised like a fleshy zipper. He dressed in the same new jeans and T-shirt he arrived in, the only clothing he owned at this point. Shopping will be the first priority over the weekend, he reminded himself. He counted out a set of sixteen stone steps that followed the side of the home, which finally opened up to a rear enclosed courtyard that included a below-ground saltwater pool complete with all the usual paraphernalia that goes with the lifestyle. A three-quarter size tennis court was hard to miss.

The rear door creaked open and out jumped Shirley for a second surprise hug. She was genuinely excited by the company. "Lyle," she yelled out over her shoulder, "come and meet our guest."

Lyle was tall. He looked to be about six-foot-four, a good couple of inches taller than Kelly. He grabbed both his hands and shook them as one. "Welcome to our humble abode, Phil. It's been a while since we've had a teenager in the house. Come on in and take a seat. There are a few things we must explain about your first week as our special guest."

The kettle whistled loudly in the background. Shirley went to work organising some afternoon tea. "Come, I'll give you a quick tour of the home. We've purchased everything you'll need for your first day at school. Shirley has two new uniforms for you to try on, plus shoes and socks. All the usual bits and pieces you'll need for a fresh start," Lyle explained.

Kelly studied the two uniforms laid out flat on a six-seater L-shaped sofa. There were two green and white striped school neckties neatly folded to one side. He'd never worn a tie before. He knew plenty of fishing knots, but a tie...? *This will be a first.*

Monday morning at 9:00 A.M., Shirley dropped Kelly off at the front gate. She shifted the stick into park, then switched off the engine. "Now, as I explained earlier, Lyle and I will be back by next Friday evening. Our flight arrives at Mascot around five P.M. Don't you worry about dinner, we'll all find a nice restaurant, okay. We've left some money on the kitchen table. Sorry about leaving you like this in your first week, but this trip is a must for Lyle and I don't like him to travel alone. You'll be fine. Anyway, it might be nice to have the house to yourself. You remember the rules? Any problems, you can talk to our neighbour across the road. Mrs McGrath is a good woman and can be trusted."

Kelly stepped out of the car, then bent down through the open window. "Yep, no problem. Thanks and have a great trip. See you on Friday." He turned as the Mercedes drove off, then took his first steps into a new life. Kelly felt good inside, like a pathway had been cleared, and all he needed to do was take the leap of faith. He was hoping his life was about to change, and hopefully for the better. Inside, his guts that never lied sensed an unknown danger. Let the games begin.

Mosman High School was located on Military Road in the 'hoity-toity' lower reaches of Sydney's North Shore. To Kelly, it looked bigger than some small towns he'd passed through while living in the country. His first stop was to meet with the school guidance counsellor at 9:15 A.M. to sort through his elective subjects, and no doubt run some off-the-cuff mental test to gauge his current state of mind. This woman would no doubt have some access to his otherwise locked juvenile file.

Starting the school year ten weeks into the first semester was equivalent to a sentence of forever being treated as 'the new guy'. A stranger cast aside by the already newly formed alliances forged from either primary school or past friendships. Cracking the ice in any new relationship was always going to be a tall mountain to climb for any new kid from the bush.

High school is a steep learning curve for any teenager, and for the seventeen-year-old, stone-faced, lanky-looking Phil Kelly, it was going to be a brutal lesson resulting in another one of life's valuable lessons. Fail here, and the ramifications could be life changing.

After two hours behind closed doors, they assigned Kelly a chaperone for his first day to show him the ropes while they introduced him to each department head. His name was Robert. His skin looked pasty with a set of teeth that went in every direction except the right one. Still yet to reach puberty, he looked like he might be bald before he reached twenty-one, and as Kelly was soon to find out, he suffered from epilepsy.

Recess had just finished, and the two boys walked towards the recently closed school canteen which opened up to a set of internal stairs that led to the first floor of the science building. They passed under a giant Moreton Bay fig tree. An ablution block was to their immediate right. Kelly could hear voices from inside, and the smell of smoke hung in the air.

Halfway up the first flight of stairs, Robert stopped and turned. He tried to speak, but instead of words, an incoherent mumble flowed from his bluish-coloured lips. His eyes rolled back into his head, and his tongue just sort of hung loosely to one side of his mouth. Then he eased himself to the ground in a controlled fall, like a trained stuntman. Robert's body convulsed and shudder violently as the seizure took control. His head slapped hard as he bounced down each step–*thud-thud,* one at a time. Kelly didn't know what to do, so he just yelled out to no one, "Help. Somebody help me. Something is wrong here."

He ran up the final eight stairs. The long corridor was void of any life, and the closest classroom was empty. He shouted again, "Help, anyone... please." Kelly's stomach was churning. He thought about running down the corridor when he heard a moaning sound from below. He looked over the railing. Robert's head was half hanging while sort of balancing on the bottom step. His nose was bleeding. Kelly took four long strides, three steps at a time to reach the bottom. He placed a hand on one shoulder and the boy's waist to slow down his convulsions. His body felt like an out-of-control jackhammer. "Bloody hell," Kelly shouted, and then he remembered the voices in the toilet block. He ran back towards the big tree and ventured inside. "Shit. Thank Christ you guys are here. I need help. This kid I'm with is chucking a fit. Where are all the bloody teachers?"

Three sets of eyes stared back through a haze of smoke. "Fuck off, idiot. Can't you see we're busy?"

"No, seriously," Kelly asked again, "this kid is in real trouble. He needs a doctor or something."

Three students were passing around a joint. The tallest one glanced over at the stranger. "Get lost, loser. Not our problem." His bottom jaw clicked as he blew a trail of smoke rings into Kelly's face. His own face was covered in freckles like hundreds and thousands on a child's birthday cake with a red birthmark down the left side of his neck.

Kelly returned a dagger's glare while the smell of marijuana filled the confined space. "Fucking dopers," he mumbled under his breath.

Freckles handed the two-paper joint over and took a threatening step forward. "What did you just say?"

"You heard me," Kelly spat back. The siren sounded for the start of the next period. Kelly heard a girl scream, so he turned and headed back outside. Three female students stood over the bouncing body. Suddenly a large woman from the canteen rushed over. She placed two fingers inside Robert's mouth and pulled his tongue clear. It was a deepening shade of blue now. His face had changed colour, and now he looked not from this planet. More students started to gather. Two teachers arrived in a slow jog and knelt down next to the convulsing body. The senior of the pair started issuing orders. "Someone run over and alert the deputy principal—*NOW*". He looked up towards another student and pointed, "You, get the school nurse. Tell her it's, Robert McEwan. She'll know what to do."

Within twenty minutes, Kelly's appointed chaperone was whisked away on a stretcher to a waiting ambulance. The last remaining teacher instructed all the straggling students to find their allotted classrooms. He turned to face Kelly, who was standing dead still. "What's your name, and which class should you be attending right now?"

"Good question. I was on my first-day orientation when this happened. Will Robert be okay? Looked pretty serious to me," Kelly asked.

"He'll be fine. We need to find a home for you until lunchtime. Then you can go see the deputy principal for a list of afternoon classes to attend. Follow me."

"Okay," Kelly answered.

The last two periods before lunch Kelly spent in a classroom labelled, 'Learn to speak an Asian language'.

"Indonesian?" Kelly remembered asking the Javanese exchange teacher, "I don't intend to live overseas any time real soon," he added with a sense of why.

The foreign exchange teacher asked, "Your name is, Phil Kelly, is that correct?"

Kelly nodded.

"Well, apparently because of recent events, you have two spare periods to be filled for today, and so Indonesian it is. Treat it as a cultural exchange," the teacher enjoyed sharing.

Kelly grabbed one of the many spare seats towards the rear of the room and prepared himself for his first lesson at Mosman High.

The lunch bell sounded, and each classroom began to empty, filling the corridors with the mixed sounds of laughter and muffled chit-chat. Kelly waited until the room emptied then asked Miss Asia, "Excuse me, can you please tell me where the deputy principal's office is?" Good manners and clean underwear, he remembered being drilled by one of his many bullshit parents from his disjointed childhood.

She walked him outside and pointed to a pair of glass doors in the opposite direction to where all the foot traffic was heading. "Straight down the corridor, turn right at the end. Exit this building, cross over to the admin block. The office you want is located third on the left. Mr Fraser is his name," she explained with a sexy accent.

"Thank you." Kelly made his way through the hustle and bustle of students heading for the canteen. He pushed open the glass door, then continued on towards the exit sign. He stepped outside, and in that instant, he was grabbed from behind with a full arm lock around his neck. A second pair of hands wrapped his tie in a tight fist. He felt it contracting against his Adams' apple. The skin on his face tightened while his eyes were almost squeezed shut, watering as he struggled for his next breath.

Within moments, any student within a fifty-metre radius started to look for any other place to be than right there. They scurried off in all directions like fleeing cockroaches. Two teachers on lunchtime roster duties turned their heads and focused their attention on anything 'but' the commotion happening less than thirty feet away. Kelly wondered why as he struggled to just stay upright, dropping his school backpack in the process. His mind was racing, trying to put two-and-two together.

This was to be his formal introduction to the school hierarchy that was affectionately nicknamed the 'Kangaroo Court'. A jury of four were formed, and a finding of guilty would lead to his sentence being carried out with extreme prejudice. No kid was ever innocent in this bully's courtroom. Without warning or justification, they hauled Kelly away in full daylight to the holding cell housed within the prison-like brick ablution block he'd visited previously, hidden from view behind the two-storey science building.

The self-appointed judge and jury held the confused teenager hard against the rough brick wall. The leader of the pack stood tall and grinned through pursed lips as he leant forward and shared his first words of wisdom. "So, you're the new kid, the one who pushed poor Robert down those stairs?" The four men laughed awkwardly at the joke.

Kelly inhaled a much-needed breath as they loosened his tie. Freckles' mouth was so close to his face, he could smell the dope on his breath. There were times for talking, and times for assertory action, but Kelly couldn't resist one quick barb. He always struggled to keep his mouth shut, which was why he ended up being smacked around so many times before. "Aren't you too old to be still attending school? Repeat a couple of years, did we?"

Patrick O'Finlay was caught off guard. The truth hurts. He could feel his cheeks burning and needed a quick response. He was occupying centre stage.

Kelly quickly decided that some affirmative action was his best chance to get out of this situation while he still had the element of surprise. He seized his only probable chance to inflict some damage of his own while he still could. With each arm tightly pinned behind his back by two strangers, he leant back into the cradle of their combined embrace and prepared for a counterattack. He looked deep into the oil-black eyes of his attacker and let fly with his right boot in a scissor-like kicking action. Kelly felt the softness of his leather shoe come into clean contact with Freckles' scrotum. Kelly watched his face squint. There were no more hundreds and thousands, just the unforgettable eye-watering feeling of his balls being repositioned somewhere inside his stomach.

The effect was instantaneous. The gurgled groan only a man can truly understand was a testament to his accuracy as his assailant crumpled to the floor while howling like a stricken animal. A combined gasp echoed through the stinking toilet block as the other three accomplices waited for the cloud of uneasiness to clear. Their grip tightened with the fear of repercussion. As the youngest son of a major Sydney crime family, Patrick O'Finlay was virtually untouchable... Or was he?

Freckles eased himself back up to a standing position. This was unprecedented, and he needed a show of strength to shore up his position as the tough guy of the school. He regained his breath, and some lost composure, then returned the ball-tickling gesture in spades. Kelly's body recoiled. He gagged and spewed up the contents of his stomach as the excruciating pain permeated throughout his groin. His shoulders sagged as he fought the body's urge to pass out. His head rocketed back with a full-frontal blow from the fist of a humiliated man with a one-track mind now focused firmly on seeking retribution.

Patrick O'Finlay's attention was drawn to the sound of a flushing toilet. He kicked open the first stall to see a boy of small stature attempting to pull up his trousers. "Kermit, you stinking greasy frog. Get the fuck out of here or you'll be next. Move it," he demanded. Kelly caught a fleeting glimpse of the retreating kid they called the Frog. His amphibious-looking facial features were an obvious derisory to his adopted schoolyard name. Kelly could only watch on as blood continued to spill over his scuffed shoes. Then he was stripped down to just his white Y-fronts. His feeble frame trembled in trepidation, enveloped with an uncontrollable fear behind the mask of a grimaced scowl at what may happen next. The frailty's of his underdeveloped body was not matched by the strength of his will to survive—at whatever the cost, no matter what that price may be.

He questioned the motives of his merciless attackers. *What was this treatment, and why am I their target?* Kelly knew he was on his own, alone, with nobody coming to his rescue. The four cretins all enjoyed a combined coward's laugh.

Now in a distraught state-of-mind, each of the culprits grabbed an arm or a leg. The dull ache in Kelly's groin started to dissipate. He wriggled and lashed out any way he could while yelling obscenities before being forced through a swinging door that hung at an awkward angle from a broken hinge before being dumped in the end vacant stall. The porcelain bowl had long been smashed with just the jagged bowl half-full with discoloured, clouded water. The young kid from the Snowy Mountains was grappled around his neck with his head forced down to the slime and filth that covered the cement floor. With his head facing the cracked toilet, the overhead chain was repeatedly yanked, flushing its load of brown-coloured excrement over his face with a force that made it imperative to keep both his eyes and mouth firmly shut. Each student unzipped their fly and belly laughed as they took their turn to urinate over Kelly's head and shoulders.

The warm, rancid-smelling liquid flowed over his exposed nakedness. The stench was putrid. He held his breath and dared not open his mouth, with his head bowed down. The fetid mellifluent dripped from his hair and ears. This was to be a final lesson in dehumanising their victim for no rhyme or reason other than they could. This was an initiation for the terrorised teenager as a welcome to their world—Patrick O'Finlay's world. With his underworld family connections, he was exempt from any form of repercussion.

The stark realisation that Kelly was in some serious trouble and at risk of maybe some permanent injuries was now a fading thought. He was held by his ankles and hauled out from the stall backwards, still face down.

The boy a select few knew as Lucky Phil was no longer aware of his surroundings. His body had transgressed into a state of shock. In a last-ditch effort to protect himself, he instinctively contracted into a foetal position against the premeditated onslaught. Next, in came the boots, two and three at a time into his ribs, shoulders and his exposed back. From all sides, he was being pulverised without fear or favour. Kelly buried his head in his open hands for futile protection. Again and again, they kicked and taunted the skinny corpse-like piece of disregarded human flesh as he cringed on the cold floor. His mind was drifting into another world—a tortured world full of pain.

Kelly silently pleaded in wasted hope. *Suck it up and somehow survive this day.*

The small toilet block became deathly quiet. A dripping tap and the smell of stale piss was a stark reminder of where he lay cowering alone. Kelly felt the rise and fall of his chest as he took time to inhale and expel his next breath. His entire body was burning in an agonisingly tormented ache. He was frozen in fear—inconsolable, knowing he had to get out of this hellhole any way he could. A dark blue and purple-coloured haze had already closed shut one eye. He straightened his back and moved his arms and legs individually to check for broken bones. Under duress, he felt an acute pain shooting through his chest like a red hot poker searing the inside of his ribcage, confirming a broken rib—or ribs. He'd been down this path before.

With the aid of a soiled washbasin, he hauled himself up to a standing position. A blurred reflection from a cracked and peeling mirror beamed back the image of a beaten youngster's body. He continued his slow breathing and took his first step as another piercing pang of pain swept through his entire upper body. He started a visual recon in search of his clothes, opening the remaining three closed swinging doors only to find they were all empty.

"Those bastards have dumped my uniform somewhere," he agonised through a mouth dripping with the taste of his own blood. With little or no choice, he splashed some water on his face with his bruised arm and prepared himself for the walk of shame. The school grounds were packed to the rafters during lunch. Kelly limped out of the secluded toilet block and turned right, needing to cross the open school grounds to find his way back to Military Road. He stumbled from the shade of the two-storey science building while a crowd of gathering onlookers started to notice the walking wounded first-day student in just his damp underwear. Some were shocked, others enjoyed a morbid fascination and giggled while pointing fingers.

Kelly focused all his attention on the fence separating him from what was ultimately his final humiliation, allowing him to be liberated from his distress and head for the relative calm of his safe house at least a mile and a half away.

He just wanted to escape the scene he was playing a starring role in as the curious crowd of bystanders gathered, not wanting to miss the show. All eyes were glued to the skinny, bruised and battered new kid as he crossed the open bitumen concourse. A female teacher came running to offer some aid. Kelly was scathing and merely brushed her aside while increasing his purposeful stride. A second male teacher attempted to place a jacket over the growing welts and discolouration forming on his emaciated body while trying to offer a caring arm around his bleeding shoulder. With a curt, "Fuck off," the relief teacher reeled back, unable to comprehend how this pupil could be in such a state. *Where are his clothes? Who is responsible for this hellish attack?*

And then the O'Finlay four referred to by some as the Fagan Gang smugly brushed past for one last piece of advice. "Bloody hell, you teachers need to start taking better care of the new kids, he looks kind of all bent out of shape—doesn't he boys?" Patrick O'Finlay patronised in a condescending tone while his three lackeys backed him up with a taunting sneer.

Kelly turned away from their combined focus with the freckled image of Patrick O'Finlay firmly imprinted inside his brain like a life-size sheet of carbon paper, then scaled the fence and started a quickening walk. As his joints loosened, his pace increased, and soon, he was jogging. This slowly transformed into a flat-out stride. Ignoring the pleas from his brain to slow down, the tenderness of his amassed pain was no barrier. It became obsolete as he hobbled in an uncontrolled canter to the sanctuary of his empty room.

He stripped off his one remaining piece of clothing and threw it into a bin, then lay down on his bed. His adrenalin levels subsided, and the reality of his situation became painfully obvious while still trembling in an uncontrolled body shake. It took almost an hour to shower and redress. Kelly found the keys to Lyle's car on Shirley's bedside table. He reversed from the garage, then headed towards North Sydney Hospital.

His initial refusal to answer questions from the hospital authorities about the cause of his injuries was put down to possible shock. He was treated in the emergency room until the results of his X-rays came back, showing previous bone breaks to his ribs and left arm. Add to that the evidence of multiple other yet to heal scar tissue, the hospital had no choice but to follow a strict set of protocols in dealing with any possible child abuse cases like this. DCP would need to be notified first thing in the morning. This new piece of legislation had only just been rushed through both houses of parliament and was now law after a recent bout of domestic violence cases involving spouses and children became both front-page news and the lead story on two of the four television stations late the previous year.

Kelly's two cracked ribs were strapped, and he received seven stitches above his right eye before being pumped full of morphine and moved to the general ward for overnight observation. He stirred from his drug-induced slumber half an hour before midnight. He needed to complete two simple tasks; take a piss and get the hell out of that hospital. He dangled both legs over the side of the bed under the gloom of restricted light and allowed himself to fall to the floor. Kelly swayed to one side, almost knocking over a plastic cup of water off a small personal locker that he knew held his clothes. He found the male toilets without too much fuss. It was the start of the midnight shift change, and the perfect opportunity to make his exit.

He drove Lyle's Range Rover to a place called Balmoral Beach that overlooked the entrance to Sydney Harbour and found a soft piece of grass. This was a time he needed to be alone, to search deep into his soul, to salvage some self-respect and dignity. He made two conscious decisions during this time of reflection. First, he'd decided school wasn't for the likes of him. The university of life would now provide his education on the streets, and as a lone soldier. Second, this was not to be the demise of this young man's hopes and dreams in a lucid shattering display of cowardice. This was a time to acknowledge and deal first hand with his innermost fears. Against all the odds, Lucky Phil knew he needed to tackle this problem head-on. Out of the depths of his despair, he would challenge himself to rise above the spineless acts of others and embark on a journey to seek his retribution. This debt needed to be settled on his terms and within his chosen time-frame. Today a few life-changing decisions would be put into the category of 'work in progress'. For the hunted to become the hunter, patience was the key. A virtue that was often said to be found in a woman, but never in a man—except a man on a mission.

Chapter-7

A MAN'S SALVATION is often said to be found in strange places. Kelly packed up his meagre belongings. A toothbrush, some gargle, two pairs of clean jocks, and the towel Shirley had given him only four days previously. He wrote a short goodbye note, shut the door behind him, and walked the two miles over the hill to Musgrave Street Wharf. The green and yellow ferry tied up at Circular Quay, and he jumped on a train to Town Hall Station. From there, it was only a short walk to the City Kawasaki dealership.

Kelly parted with just over half of his five thousand cash booty like it was Christmas morning without a tree. He strapped on his new Shoei helmet, fired up the four-cylinder engine, and eased his new Kawasaki GPZ 900R dream machine out of the showroom, and on to the streets of Sydney for the very first time. He needed to clock up at least two thousand kilometres running in the sixteen-valve liquid-cooled inline four-cylinder, 908cc engine. The M5 tollway heads north out of Sydney. Kelly cruised along at a comfortable 100 kph cruising the left-hand lane for the next sixty kilometres. Kelly slowed and followed the *left lane only* sign that leads to the small seaside town of Terrigal back towards the coast. He booked into a caravan park next to a place the locals called the Skillion, a high bluff that offered an unobstructed panoramic view back down to the Pacific Ocean. He spent the next two months recovering from his recent run in with the man he would never forget. Each day he would jog the beach from end to end, complete one hundred push-ups, then swim and body surf for an hour. He'd weaned himself off all his medication and was following a strict diet— pints of cold beer, and good old-fashioned pub food. The first of the winter weather rolled in from the east, and this was Kelly's call to execute his next move. He had a plan.

The bright neon lights of Kings Cross beamed like a lighthouse of lost hope to an ever-increasing number of street kids that were forced to roll the dice one last time. Transients, who through unforeseen circumstances, had suddenly found themselves thrust into the evil web of No-man's-land that followed its own set of rules. Bustling for a spot amongst the soup kitchens, shifting between half-way houses, hunkering down inside the few churches that opened their doors after 11:00 P.M. each night. This was a means to an end for a growing number of the lost generation, and in most cases, it usually wasn't a happy one.

Kings Cross enjoyed the added advantage of offering sanctuary because of the sheer number of curious people who wanted to experience personally how the other half lives. As long as a man could dodge the poofter bashers, evade the piss-heads and addicts who for the price of the loose change in your pocket would sell their souls for that next hit, surviving intact was a daily event that required forward planning and exact timing. The trick was not to put yourself in harm's way by being at the wrong place at *any* given time.

Kelly's bankroll was down to under a thousand dollars. He needed to go and find work somewhere, and for that, he needed a roof over his head. The time had come to test the bonds of a past, and sometimes warped foster home friendship that was probably the closest he would ever come to regarding someone like an older sister. He coasted to a stop outside a public phone booth, thinking how fortunate he was that this woman's surname wasn't Smith or Jones. The White Pages listed just seven Polands' in the Redfern area. The task became simplified with just three showing the initial J. He pencilled the three addresses on the back of a beer coaster.

Abercrombie Street was a stone's throw away from Sydney University, which made perfect sense. Terrace houses lined both sides of the street like Lego in a visual display of assorted colours, and each in a varying state of disrepair. A dumped car was angled parked, stripped clean of anything worth a buck while being supported by some discarded builders' bricks. Kelly could see a pair of legs poking out from underneath another vehicle that looked like it still had an engine. A pooling trail of used engine oil ran across the concrete street into a stormwater drain.

Kelly braked to a stop and checked the number 32 a second time. The front door was painted a deep ruby red colour behind a waist-high wrought-iron fence with a self-closing gate. He parked his bike on the footpath, pushed through, and knocked three times. No answer. Kelly hadn't slept for over twenty-four hours and was dog tired. He needed to rest. He followed a worn path to the back of the three-storey terrace house. A rear porch was home to an old couch which looked inviting as a possible place to crash. Kelly made his way back to his bike. He looked at the second address, flipped the side-stand up, and began coasting the short distance down the footpath towards the single rear side street when the loud roar of a twin-cylinder bike drowned out the noises of a few Aboriginal kids arguing over a football.

A Norton 850 *Commando* whizzed by, causing the kids to scatter. The ground almost shook as the bike flew past at speed, crossing through the oil slick. The next sound was the unmistakable noise of metal grinding on the gravel road. Kelly grabbed a handful of front brake and turned his head to follow the shower of sparks from the right-hand side chrome exhaust. The rider had enough smarts to let go as he took the full brunt of the fall on his left shoulder. The bike continued to spin into a parked car, wedging its frame firmly under the rear end. The rider's momentum came to an abrupt stop. He stood up and started brushing away the loose gravel from his full leathers.

Two more Japanese bikes entered the street, each with a pillion on the back. They both stopped on a dime, forcing the lone rider to back up against his bent-out-of-shape Commando. The two passengers jumped clear and took up a formation line. A third killed his ignition and pulled a large Bowie-style knife from his belt. The fourth hung back to keep a watchful eye on any stragglers. The sounds of doors and windows slamming shut was an ominous sign indicating this was not an unusual event in this trashy part of inner Sydney. With his arm outstretched, the knife-wielding man approached the bleeding rider with a look of fortitude. Kelly watched on as the rider grinned, revealing a set of big white teeth. He was wide across the shoulders and stood in defiance like an idling bulldozer. His one good arm poked out at an awkward angle from his massive chest like a big male silverback, while the other hung lazily with blood trickling from the ends of his fingers. His skin was dark with thick locks of unkempt black hair hanging down to the square of his back from underneath a half-face German *stahlhelm*-style helmet. He looked like a modern-day Geronimo without the war paint.

Kelly's ringside position offered an unobstructed view. He was about to sit back and watch the show when something inside triggered an emotional response. Just months earlier, he was in a similar position—alone and in trouble.

The rider slid off his helmet and swung it in an upward action, collecting the jaw of his first incoming attacker. The knife fell from his hand. The other three made the mistake of trainspotting the action. Geronimo stepped in, and power kicked the second man square in the chest, he was propelled back and landed heavily onto the road surface. The sound of flesh and bitumen coming together was enough of an incentive for the first and third man to make a combined run at the rider. The lookout guy pulled a handgun from under his jacket and started to wave it around. He fired off a wild shot which deflected off the parked car. It only took a single spark to ignite the flow of petrol from the bike's split tank. A blue flame shot high into the air, and then a dark cloud of stinking smoke formed a black screen behind the group of men.

Kelly started his bike. The purr of the four-into-one extractor was almost rhythmic. He kicked it into gear and fingered the throttle. The lone rider lashed out a third time with his one good arm. He was wide of the mark and stumbled forward, leaving his guard down. One attacker bent over to retrieve his dropped knife. The other swung a full roundhouse kick and connected a clean blow to the rider's jaw. Geronimo didn't even blink an eye. He grabbed the Asian man in a bear hug and barrel-rolled him to the ground. A second shot sounded as Kelly drew closer. The rider buckled to one knee as the bullet penetrated the fleshy part of his upper leg. Kelly accelerated before stepping on the rear brake while sliding the bike hard to his left. The single rear YSS gas shock absorber worked a treat as the rear end fishtailed and collided with the gunman. Kelly hit the gas hard and headed directly for the man with the knife. Then he popped the front wheel high into the air, causing the attacker to bounce off the bonnet of the burning car. Kelly looked at the rider, "Now might be a good time to get on, mate."

Geronimo bent down and grabbed the knife. He jimmied the Norton's rear number plate loose, then ripped it off with his bare hands before asking, "Which way you headed?"

Kelly lifted his visor, "Does it really matter? Maybe the hospital might be good for starters."

With a distinctive accent, he answered. "No hospitals. Who are you anyway?"

Kelly replied, "I'm nobody and no one. Last chance."

The rider turned to his left to see the guy who took the brunt of Kelly's rear-wheel scratching under the car for his lost gun. Geronimo steadied on his bad leg and let fly with his size-12 boot. The sound of a man's jaw separating from the rest of his face was a reminder not to ever put yourself in that position. He hobbled over and struggled to lift his leg over the back of the bike seat.

"You all right?" Kelly asked.

"Right as I'll ever be. Head down to the bottom of this street and chuck a left. From there, I'll tell you where to go."

The Kawasaki Ninja 900 was one of the quickest production bikes on the market over a quarter-mile. Clocked at 10.55 seconds, the two complete strangers covered the same distance in less than 14.

Not far from Darling Harbour between Chinatown and Paddy's Market was a little-known speck of Sydney known simply as: In Between Two Worlds. Kelly felt the tap on his right shoulder and began to slow as they entered Little Hay St. The sign at the front read: *Al Forno Montevideo Restaurant - the flavour of Uruguay* with a giant chilli in bright red neon flashing below. They cruised past, turned left, and pulled up to the rear of a building. His passenger slid off with a grunt of pain, shooting up his bleeding leg. He limped over to a six-foot-high wooden gate and entered in a four-digit pin code. The gate popped open. He turned to face Kelly, "Push that heap of shit inside and shut the gate. I'll tell my sister to give you a bucket of hot water and a scrubbing brush. There's a hose behind the garage. You can wash the blood off over there."

Kelly eased his bike inside and lifted it onto its centre-stand. Moments later, an attractive-looking Latino woman arrived with the bucket, dropped it to the ground and left, closing the rear door to the restaurant behind her. He scrubbed the bike from headlight to the rear number plate before the blood dried. At the back of the locked garage was a small lean-to. Kelly pushed the door open. Inside was a room with a tiny kitchenette and a bathroom. He stripped down to his jeans and cleaned himself up. A single bed in the corner looked clean and beckoned Kelly to come closer. He was in a deep sleep before his head hit the striped black & white pillow.

Chapter-8

THE HISTORY of Aboriginal Australians is thought to have spanned 50,000-75,000 years before the first European settlement in 1788. The first records of European mariners sailing into Australian waters occurred around 1606 and included in their observations the land known as *Terra Australis Incognito*: The unknown Great Southern Land. The first ship and crew to chart the Australian coast and meet with Aboriginal people were from the *Duyfken,* captained by Dutchman Willem Janszoon.

Between 1606 and 1770, an estimated fifty-four European ships from a range of nations made contact. Many of these merchant ships were from the Dutch East Indies Company.

In 1770, Englishman Lieutenant James Cook charted the Australian east coast on board his ship HM *Barque Endeavour.* Cook claimed the east coast under instruction from King George III of England on August 22, 1770, at Possession Island, naming eastern Australia, New South Wales. Captain Arthur Phillip and the First Fleet, comprising eleven ships and around 1,350 people, arrived at Botany Bay between January 18-20, 1788.

After the discovery of gold in 1851, over forty thousand Chinese immigrated to Australia, culminating in an unofficial 'white only policy' under the guise of the *Immigration Restriction Act of 1901.* In the year's post World War II, Australia promoted immigration with the catchphrase 'populate or perish' to replenish the countless citizens lost throughout the war. It negotiated agreements to accept over two million migrants and displaced people from Europe, offering assisted ten pound passages to Australia for over one million British migrants, and finally, in the 1970s, the federal government repealed the restrictive white-only Australia policy.

Australia is now a 'multi-cultural society' which translates to Sydney being divided amongst all these diverse ethnic groups vying for a piece of the action. The Chinese dominate Chinatown. The Italians controlled the eastern suburbs, and the Greeks ran the markets, the fruit & two veg stalls, delis and milk bars. The Russians owned most of the illegal gambling establishments and SP bookmaking in the western suburbs. The bikies controlled the flow of drugs and prostitution, with the Irish still ruling the roost over most of the North Shore. Sprinkled in amongst all that were the minority groups who made a comfortable living doing their own thing, all the while being careful not to step on the toes of another countryman's claim. Everyone made a buck and were all fully aware where the line in the sand was as far as who controls what. That was life, and those were the rules— like it or lump it.

The family Kelly was about to meet for the first time fell comfortably into this last category.

Kelly peeled himself off the bed while clearing the fog of his mind and tried to recall where he was while rubbing the sleep from both his eyelids. He could hear a continuous buzzing noise coming from the other side of the adjoining toilet wall as he zipped up his fly. He was interrupted by a *slap-slap* noise, then followed by some heavy panting. Kelly's mind created some alarming images.

He splashed some cold water about his face and smelt the armpits of his only shirt before pulling it back over his head. He stepped outside and shielded his eyes from the glare of a midday sun. His bike had been moved under some scant cover but was still on its stand, reminding him to feel for the key inside his front jeans pocket. The footpath followed the fence line past the garage he saw when he arrived earlier. The slapping became louder, and soon, undecipherable voices could be heard. He stopped at an open roller-door. Inside the garage was a three-quarter-size boxing ring. Dancing around on the raised canvas floor were two men. One with focus pads, the other with sparring gloves and headgear with both wrists heavily strapped. A glassed studio was over to the back and left. Inside was a flat-top padded table and a reclining dentist-like chair. A man resembling André the Giant was receiving some finishing touches to a neck tattoo. Kelly could see an image of the Grim Reaper riding a Harley. There was some text underneath, but he was too far away to read what it said.

A voice growled from the same general direction. "Who the fuck are you?"

Kelly propped. The room came to a silent standstill. Both men in the ring plus a group of three other spectators in full patched colours with the words, God's Garbage MC plastered across their backs all stopped and stared at the new arrival. A second voice from inside the ring broke the awkward void. "You need to wait outside. There's a bench seat on the other side of the clothesline," the trainer hollered while he casually checked out the stranger standing at his door. He removed his focus pads, and tossed them to one side then with just the one free hand, jumped over the top one-inch plastic-coated manila rope landing on the balls of his feet like he was like some weird kind of ninja.

Kelly eased into a slow turn, walked away while stepping under some rubber bar runners still dripping wet on the clothesline. The burnt-out remains of the crashed Norton lay on a wooden pallet near an old unused out-house.

Shit—they didn't waste any time?

The four patched gang members exited the garage in single file, probably in order of importance. The nominee opened the back gate while handshakes were exchanged with what looked like the Sergeant of Arms and the ninja. Kelly focused his attention anywhere but on the four men leaving. Not long after, the sound of four thumping Harley Davidson's thundering off down the single street was enough to awaken the dead.

The ninja guy approached Kelly with an extended hand, "My name is, Emmanuel. You can sleep better than my old lady after a good shag. What's your name, hombre?"

Kelly looked at his watch before answering. It was now Saturday, and he'd lost an entire day. "My friends call me, Lucky Phil."

"Lucky Phil? Well, I don't see any of your friends here right now. What do your enemies call you?"

"Whatever they like, hopefully just not to my face."

"Hope you're hungry?" Emmanuel smiled.

"Thanks, but I'll be moving on. Need to sort some personal crap out," Kelly replied as an uneasy silence hovered.

"Where do you come from? Not from around these parts?" Emmanuel asked.

"Like I told your friend earlier, I'm not important. A lone soldier. Thanks for the offer." Kelly pulled the key from his pocket. His helmet was still hanging loosely from his right-hand mirror. He grabbed it and unbuckled the clip while heading towards the closed gate.

He got about halfway when a familiar, heavily accented voice carried loud from an open door. "Get your scrawny-looking arse inside before I tell my two sisters you don't want to eat the food they have both spent the last few hours preparing just for you."

Kelly turned to see the lone rider leaning on a single crutch with his wide toothy grin on full display, standing in just a pair of boxers bandaged up like a mummy. Both his arms were covered in full-sleeved tattoos, and his back was no different. "Don't be a pussy. Can't you handle a bit of spicy hot food?" Emmanuel laughed and was soon joined by his worn-out trainee still towel drying his wet hair after showering.

"Okay, I'm game. It's been a while since I had a real decent feed," Kelly answered. "Don't want to disappoint your sisters."

"That's bloody right. My name is Fernando. Just call me Fanny." He outstretched his open palm. Kelly stepped in, and their two hands interlocked in the unspoken battle of a first-time man-shake. Both men locked eyes with that slight grin and applied the hand vice without looking obvious. Kelly had spent countless hours perfecting 'the handshake'. One, two, and three slow seconds ticked by, then both men smiled while releasing simultaneously.

Emmanuel stepped to one side, "And this is Julius, we're all brothers. The rest of the crew you can meet inside." It was done, the glue of friendship had been squeezed, and everyone could now breathe a little easier—but no one ever did.

After the doors were closed, the two sisters joined the table, and the entire family took up their allotted seats. Kelly quickly grabbed a spare plate, piling on some *choripán* or grilled chorizo, *fainá ñoqui*, the pasta known as gnocchi and some thin chickpea flour bread. Fanny's brother Julius handed him a stubby of pale lager called *Pilsen Bajo Cero*. Kelly flipped the top off and joined in the feast. He struggled to pronounce most of the menu items, and the Uruguayan flavours that permeated through each dish caused a hungry man's taste buds to dance inside his mouth. They filled the entire afternoon with laughter and good cheer.

After the table was cleared, and the last dishes cleaned and put away, the three brothers sat Kelly back down where shots of tequila were downed with salt and lemon, 'lip, sip & suck', and then followed soon after with a barrage of questions towards the only stranger seated at the table end.

Fanny started the ball rolling. "So, Lucky Phil, what's your story, then? How is it you happened to be in that part of

Redfern the exact same time those Chinese wanted a piece of my arse? Bloody fate, I say."

"Not everybody has a story to tell. When I bumped into you, I was looking for a place to stay before I start looking for a job."

"What sort of work you after?" Fanny asked.

"Anything that pays cash with no questions asked. I have no real working skills. The next full-time job will be my first. High school wasn't a big hit for me," Kelly answered back.

"Off the books and under the radar," Julius added.

"Pretty much hit the nail on the head."

Fanny and Emmanuel shared a brotherly sideways glance. Julius looked like he may not have been the sharpest tool in the shed, and he just kept smiling at nothing and everything while filling the four shot glasses.

Fanny leant forward on his crutch. "Never let it be said that the Uruguayan people aren't appreciative of another man's actions. We can offer you the job as a kitchen hand each Friday and Saturday night plus a free feed, and the room out the back is vacant until I say otherwise."

"And I might know a man that can keep you busy for the rest of the week. I'll check it out and let you know," Emmanuel explained.

Kelly raised his glass, "Well, we'll see, but I'll drink to the offer." Each man emptied his tequila. "Do you mind if I ask you a couple of questions?" Kelly prodded.

Fanny was the first to speak. "I guess we owe you that much, speaking personally of course, but the answers will depend on the questions. Go on, fire away."

"I'm gonna take a stab in the dark and say you all seem to be well connected with the Sydney scene. You ever heard of a family called the O'Finlay's? In particular, I'm interested in one man named Patrick—Patrick O'Finlay. I'm pretty sure he's Irish."

The three brothers made eye contact, which didn't go unnoticed. Fanny stood up. "Why do you want to know about this man... this family?"

Kelly hesitated before answering. "Let's just say I have a personal interest in catching up with an old friend before I can collect on an outstanding debt."

"He ain't no friend of yours, Lucky Phil, so you can cut the bullshit right now. Follow me, we need to find somewhere more private to talk," Fanny said. "Plus, our sisters need to set the restaurant up. We've got a full house again tonight."

They motioned for Kelly to follow through a side door. That led to a set of stone stairs following a basement below. Another small door was cracked open, and the four men ducked under. Julius flicked on a light switch that lit up a long arched walkway that smelt stale and musty. As they followed its uneven pathway, a rumbling sound could be heard and felt vibrating from above. Clouds of dust filled the damp and stale air. "The restaurant is an old police station, and this leads to what was once a magistrate's court before the turn of the century. Ironic that the same building is now our home," Fanny went on to explain.

The corresponding ascending stairs were made from cobblestone. Emmanuel unlocked the door with a key. To the left was another flight of internal stairs that led to a sliding glass door. This opened up to an outdoor balcony filled with huge pot plants. There was a wood-fired barbecue, which also doubled up as a pizza oven. A large Mexican *chimminy* occupied centre-stage and was chock-a-block full of freshly splintered kindling. Julius arrived with four fresh beers.

"Sit down, get comfortable, and I'll explain why you might want to rethink your proposal to catch up with, Patrick O'Finlay." Fanny's tone had changed considerably.

Emmanuel entered with a map of Sydney rolled up and tucked under his arm. He laid it out flat on a low table. Fanny limped over, and with his crutch, he placed the rubber end on the Sydney Harbour Bridge. He looked at Kelly, still seated, and nudged him with his crutch. "Pay attention, because this may save your life one day. This side of the bridge is the city and Kings Cross.," he started to explain while moving the crutch. "This is the eastern suburbs, including Bondi Beach, and this is all run by the Italians. Over here is Chinatown, and yes—it's full of Chinese. Nobody fucks with the Triads—well, not yet, anyway. Out west is Parramatta, and nobody really gives a rats-arse about that shit-hole except some uneducated small-time hoods and a few emerging bike gangs. Darling Harbour and the docks are run by the Unions with influence and money flowing in from the Russians." He moved his pointer to Luna Park, then all the way up to Hornsby in the north. "This is the end of the northern suburban train line. Beyond this is farming land with pigs and cows plus a growing number of small-timers trying their luck at growing marijuana crops in the national parks." Then he stopped at Avalon. "This is where the northern corridor stops, and from here all the way back to Manly are the northern beaches. Home to the rich and famous." Then he continued his march on to North Head, back towards Taronga Park Zoo, ending at Kirribilli House. "This is the Prime Minister's official residence," he pointed out before finishing at a spot in North Sydney. "You see all that, well that my friend is controlled by one woman, and you would have to be either a dimwit or just plain clueless if you hadn't at least *heard* the name, Ma O'Finlay. Some people refer to her as, Big Ma, just not within a five-kilometre radius of where she lives in the suburb of Crows Nest."

Kelly's ears pricked. "Crows Nest, where exactly?"

"Kershaw Lane, where the whole O'Finlay clan occupies the only three houses. It's like a bloody fortress. Big Ma O'Finlay is the matriarch and head of what was once Sydney's largest crime syndicate, a shrinking family business she rules with an iron fist."

Kelly shifted in his chair and knocked down the remains of his beer in one easy flow. "That's a big slice of pie for just one family."

Emmanuel nodded for Julius to refresh their beers, then took over the history lesson. "What you need to understand is there was a time her family had it all, that is her late brother, Sean. Back in the late 1950s and early 60s, the Irish crime syndicate ran most of the extortion, prostitution, illegal gambling, SP bookmaking and money laundering throughout most of Sydney. The Italians were next to arrive and first started gaining a foothold around 1965, and with their connections back home in the land of spaghetti and meatballs, this marked the first arrival of illegal narcotics to the white sandy shores of Sydney. The Irish never felt comfortable partaking in the peddling of any form of hard drugs. They viewed the selling of heroin as heinous. Most of them all had families with strong ties to the Church."

Fanny interrupted, "Rumour has it the Irish boys were made an offer they couldn't refuse."

"Never get between an Italian and a bag of money, they say," Kelly joked.

"The Italians took control of the city, Kings Cross and all the eastern suburbs. That left the Irish with the entire north side of the harbour, including the northern beaches," Emmanuel finished.

Fanny flipped the top of his beer with a cigarette lighter. "Her brother Sean O'Finlay was never happy with the deal, and he made his feelings known to the Italians. He ended up being executed from a shotgun blast, point-blank to the head back in 1973, while stopped at a set of traffic lights down near the beachside suburb of Curl Curl. Very messy and very public, and the shooter was never found."

"A red-letter day for the cops, and I'm guessing there was no love lost between the Irish and the Italians?" Kelly guessed correctly.

"Sean O'Finlay had no living brothers, courtesy of the heady days of the IRA," Fanny continued. "Survived by his wife, she saw the writing on the wall. This woman was never part of the criminal side of the family, but like a good wife, she toed the line—until that day. Soon after she grabbed her only child, reverted back to her maiden name, and just disappeared. After her husband's death, the responsibility of taking control of the family business fell solely upon a younger sister named, Margaret, or as most of Sydney's underworld refer to her—Big Ma. With the aid of Ma's three boys, the key player is her eldest son, Sean Jnr, named after his late dead uncle. From the time Sean could peddle his first pushbike, he had been groomed by his uncle, and now his own mother, to one day assume total control of the family business."

"And this only daughter of her dead brother," Kelly asked, "what happened to her?

Julius left the room and returned with a plastic squeeze container of talcum powder. He held it out front for Kelly to take a closer look. "You see that cute little baby face on this and about a billion others just like it?"

"There isn't a kid in Australia who hasn't seen that," Kelly answered.

"Yeah, well, that's the daughter," Julius almost shouted.

Kelly grabbed the container, "No shit."

"That's right," Fanny interrupted. "If you live on the north side, and follow the rugby league, well, you're either a Bears or if you only have half a brain, a Manly supporter. The North Sydney Bears play all their home games at North Sydney Oval. A sideline cameraman captured the spectacular one-handed winning try scored on the wing to seal the victory against the reigning premiers and arch-rivals, the silver-tailed Manly Sea Eagles. That photo became famous after appearing on the back page of the weekend edition of *The Sunday Telegraph.* Not because of the win, but the image of a toddler in the background under that huge Moreton Bay fig tree all decked out in the Bears colours with her hand held high in the air celebrating the win with those curly locks of strawberry blonde hair poking out from underneath her red and black hand-knitted beanie. An ad agency picked up on the photo, and within three months, she was the fresh new face for the Johnson & Johnson conglomerate."

"Happy days for, Mum and Dad," Kelly threw in.

"More than a few happy days—well, for Mum, anyway. She went on to appear in countless baby commercials, magazines, and as she grew older, the offers just kept rolling in right up until the time she and her mother fell off the face of the earth."

"So, money wasn't a problem when they shot through," Kelly added. "My guess is they would have headed back to the home of the four-leaf clover—the motherland."

"No shortage of family in Ireland, that's for sure—plus she'd be safe as houses over there," Julius said.

"And this prick, Patrick... where does he fit in?" Kelly asked.

"Patrick is the third and thankfully the last-born son, and let me tell you right now, he is a fucking lunatic. Don't make the same mistake as many others before you have and underestimate his cunning and tenacity."

Kelly shifted forward on the sofa. "He's nothing but a bully, and all bullies are cowards hiding behind the facade of wanting to portray being the tough guy. You get him alone, without the protection of his family . . ." Kelly stopped mid-sentence and turned to face Emmanuel. "That boxing technique I saw you teaching Julius earlier? I've never seen anything like that before—very impressive. Where does that originate?" Kelly wanted to set the tone for his next question.

Emmanuel answered by asking his own question. "Have you ever travelled throughout South East Asia?"

Kelly almost laughed at the idea of travelling overseas. "I've never even been out of the state."

"The Thais call it Muay Thai. Basically, it's a form of boxing where each part of the body is used to form an attack. Hands, elbows, knees and feet. No head butting. Mine is a version of that with some subtle taekwondo variations thrown in to adapt to survive outside the ring. Street fighting," he explained like a proud father.

"I practised a fair bit of self defence growing up as a kid, and I've been told I've got a head as hard as a coconut."

"You're going to get yourself killed chasing a rainbow that never sets. That pot of gold you search for will put you in an early grave," Emmanuel wanted to say.

"Not if you can do *your* job. I'm a real quick learner," Kelly answered.

"My client list is a closed shop. There is no sign out the front advertising what I do."

"I just figured if there ever *was* a time to ask, it would be now. Where I come from, a good deed doesn't go unrewarded." Kelly wanted to test the waters.

Fanny asked, "And where exactly do you come from?"

"From a place where a man is only as good as his handshake."

"The best I can do is offer you some casual work on the weekends—as a token of my thanks."

Kelly sat in silence for a few seconds. "I'm about to turn eighteen in a few months, and in all that time I can still count the friends I trust on the one hand. To add three more to the mix in just two days—I think I'll just say thanks but no thanks."

"It's just a job, man. I'm not asking to date your sister," Fanny fired back.

Kelly placed his empty stubby on the low table and eased himself up from the cushioned sofa. "If it's all the same, I'll be heading off now. Thanks for the feed. One last question—those three Chinese; why a bullet in the leg from ten feet? If they wanted you dead, you'd be exactly that. Looks like they wanted to send you a message."

"Perhaps it was just the opposite. Maybe we were firing the first salvo across their Chinese bow."

"Remind me never to go sailing with you," Kelly joked.

Emmanuel stepped over and stood close to Kelly. "Come on, I'll see you out."

Kelly stopped in front of a stack of electronic gear. Two huge Cerwin Vega speakers sat to one side with their front dust covers removed. "Nice stereo," he smiled back at Fanny.

"That all belongs to Julius—plus a heap more. He might look a bit simple, but when it comes to all the new high-end tech gear becoming available—well, the man has a gift," Fanny answered.

Emmanuel headed for the door, with Kelly following closely behind. Both men entered the rear yard a second time. Kelly removed the key from his pocket, then grabbed his helmet. He pushed the bike back off its centre-stand and rolled backwards. Emmanuel opened the back gate. Kelly fired up the Ninja 900R and kicked it into first gear. As he prepared to edge through the gate into the lane-way, Emmanuel placed a hand on his right arm. "My brother can be a hard-nose sometimes—no, make that all the time. Here, take this."

He slid a card into Kelly's top pocket, then held out an open hand. Inside was a blood-red marble. "Hand this to the man whose name appears on that card, he'll understand. Tomorrow morning at five A.M., park your bike inside the green garage two doors down. A onetime pin-code is scribbled on the back of the card. I'll give you ten minutes in the ring, and we'll see what you're made of after that. That's the best I can do."

Kelly heard the sound of the gate locking. He looked at the card: JC. Crumpernickel 684. On the reverse side were the numbers 6069. He shifted in his seat while accelerating past the green door and headed for Kings Cross with the North Star burning bright over his left shoulder.

Chapter-9

M A O'FINLAY was a big-framed woman—huge, in fact. She moved like a pregnant hippopotamus and spent most days with her giant backside firmly planted into her favourite lounge chair where she monitored all her family's interests and issued orders like a modern-day female Caesar.

Sean Jnr was in his thirties. He was Ma's first lieutenant and right-hand man. His mother's second set of eyes and ears, her back-stop and confidante. With an analytical brain, Sean was responsible for the meticulous planning of any new business that fell under the umbrella of 'the family wants this, so we're going to take it'. He was the family enforcer, and he revelled in all its collective glory. He delighted in the simple fact that he held this enormous power in the palm of his hand, and could exercise it with a free will, to anyone, with the full knowledge of the protection provided by both the family and the endless supply of corrupt cops, politicians and judges they had on their payroll.

Sean was highly intelligent and was said to be an avid student of the five P's principle, courtesy of his Uncle Sean's genes: '**P**erfect **P**reparation **P**revents **P**oor **P**erformance'. He was the mastermind, and probably the only reason he had never done *any* hard time as a guest of Her Majesty's Long Bay Prison.

The second son was Dean, he was twenty-seven and an introvert. Very quiet, he kept to himself most times but was a real sneaky little bastard. He detested violence and was basically a coward. The rumour mill suggested he may have batted for the other side but would never be proven. He watched everyone and everything and then reported it all back to Sean. He absolutely idolised his older brother, which only helped to fuel the resentment felt towards Dean by his younger sibling.

Patrick O'Finlay was an entity unto himself. He was one of those troubled kids who would have enjoyed plucking the wings off a butterfly and then sitting back and watching it slowly die, or terrorising the dog and cat population on fireworks night. Death to him was simply a means to an end. He wasn't mentally capable of showing empathy or remorse. Emotionally he was stunted, entrenched in his own mental quagmire with no simple directions to find his way clear. Patrick was a loner with no social skills, subject to violent and unpredictable outbursts, with his favoured weapon—a trusty flick knife as his constant companion. Yet to turn twenty, he was almost certifiable, and a constant burden on his mother. As the firstborn son, Sean was often left to clean up and make 'disappear' the evidence of his deranged younger brother's alcohol and drug-infused antics. Sean knew he was a threat to not just himself, but the entire family.

Patrick harboured a deep secret, a conspiracy so sensitive, if revealed to his family, he would pay the ultimate price. He was tormented between his unquenchable thirst for more power, respect amongst the underworld fraternity, and his proclivity to drag the O'Finlay empire into the 21st century. As the youngest of the three sons, he was constantly reminded by his mother, "Patrick, you're still earning your stripes in this business, patience my boy, your time will come," she said many times. He didn't have any patience. Patrick was greedy and cunning, mixed with a burning ambition to control the family business, and he was a very dangerous man to be around. He wanted more... much more, and he wanted it now.

Patrick could never understand his family's strict stance on the 'no drugs policy' adopted by his late dead uncle, all those years ago. The O'Finlay family was into just about everything else illegal, but never dealt with, or was involved in the sale of narcotics. Patrick was right in his thinking that the profits to be made were insurmountable. He just lacked the foresight, and the maturity to fully understand the associated risks that came with the territory.

With his three lunatic associates that made up the Fagan Gang in total, Tommy, Deso and Whacka, Patrick had laid down a strategy to change that policy. He intended to take the family business in a whole new direction, and he didn't give a second thought to who stood in his way. The first step was set to take place the following Friday night.

The Triumph *Stag* was an English-built vehicle designed by an Italian named Giovanni Michelotti. The convertible 3.0-litre fuel injected PI-V8 sports tourer boasted a five-speed manual gearbox with electronic overdrive, full leather interior with a wood grain dash. They were a beautifully styled sports car, and a chick magnet to boot. The mustard-coloured *Stag* looked out-of-place while parked one block north of what was once a nightclub called the Venus Room, made famous by the man known as 'Mr Sin'. Abe Saffron was once king-of-the-hill, and back in the '70s, not much happened in Kings Cross without his approval.

No-18 Orwell St was now a legitimate backpackers' hostel except for one sectioned off area located on the ground floor known as the Hot Room. Each Friday night five men with direct family links to Sicily would gather in the Hot Room at around 10:00 P.M. The rules were simple: No weapons were *ever* permitted inside, and a bankroll of $25,000 was the minimum price of entry. The second part of the equation wasn't a problem. It was a time to blow off a bit of steam, clear the cobwebs while drinking some expensive cognac, smoke some Cuban cigars, and whinge about the women in their lives.

The game was seven-card stud. Three two-hour-sessions with three thirty-minute breaks. The two Costa brothers, Vincenzo and Antonio, were usually first to arrive, and tonight was no different. Their now-deceased father, Salvatore Costa, was the first member of the Australian-based La Cosa Nostra to be given the title of *caporegime*, a captain in charge of his own crew, answering only to the *Capo Bastone*; the Underboss, after his handy work with a sawn-off shotgun to dispose of the Paddy problem back in the '70s. Even though the title did not pass on to his sons, it gave them bragging rights that would never be questioned.

Their driver pulled over, and both men exited the vehicle. The outside lookout man acknowledged their arrival with a simple nod of the head. There were no strangers here this night. He gestured for the two brothers to enter the tiled foyer. Inside, both men handed over their handguns, then stood and watched the pieces being locked away inside a wall-mounted key-lock safe. The second doorman turned and slid free the white plastic cover of a light switch. Behind was a black button which he pressed with his index finger. The electronic door lock released, and they entered the card room. Inside, the green felt table was a permanent fixture in the room's centre. In one corner was a fully stocked bar, and the door to the en suite was located on the opposite wall. The only other exit was a steel reinforced door that could only be opened from the inside. That led to a cellar below, which gave access to a secluded side street. It was for emergencies only, and to date, had never been tested.

The next to arrive were Frank Morello and Dominick Strollo. Both of these men were born in Palermo. The fifth and final player was Mario Salerno from Catania. Each man followed the exacting routine as they had done so many times previously. Together these four families represented the entirety of the illegal Italian business interests in Sydney's underworld.

Patrick O'Finlay sat in the front passenger seat. The time was just after midnight. He wound down the window and flicked the final remains of a joint out into the gutter before finishing the last two fingers from a near-empty bottle of Jack Daniels, then turned to face the designated driver before issuing final instructions. "Whacka, you stay in the car with the engine and lights off. When you see the two of us exit the front door, get your arse into gear and be ready to get the hell outta here. There's a security camera above the front steps, and I want to make sure it gets a real good look at this car—including the license plate. So you drive past slowly, you got that?"

"No problems, piece of piss," Whacka replied, with no clue as to why.

"There's no such thing, you idiot," Patrick growled. "Just stay alert and be ready to roll. You *do* know the quickest way back out of the Cross, don't you?" Patrick's tone underlined the uneasiness felt inside the parked *Stag*. He turned towards the rear seat. "Roxanne, you're the weak link in this chain, but I know you're a pro. Nice and easy, you know the deal. Just get the outside guy's attention focused in the other direction, and Tommy and I will do the rest."

"I want my money upfront," Roxanne pushed.

"Yeah, and I promise I won't cum in your mouth. You ever hear that before? You'll get paid when I have what I came for in my sweet little hand. Don't get cute with me, Roxanne," Patrick threatened.

Tommy placed a hand on her black fishnet stockings, well above the knee. "Maybe you can throw in a freebie, Roxy. You know, for old time's sake." Tommy was only half-serious and knew the answer already. Roxanne was an absolute knockout with a long list of high paying clientèle, which is the exact reason she was there on this night.

"In your dreams, drop-kick. I like a man with at least eight inches. That means you'd need to bang me twice," Roxanne responded with her typical quick wit through a lipstick smile. Tommy withdrew his hand and decided he had no chance of matching words with the high-class hooker.

Patrick sucked in a deep breath. "Right then, you all ready? Remember, you and me, Tommy, in and out, real quick. Okay, Roxy, you're up."

Patrick exited then folded the front seat forward, and with one shapely leg at a time Roxy squeezed out onto the footpath. She rearranged her body-hugging skirt, then placed both hands under each bra cup and pushed up. She fumbled in her bag for a cigarette. "How do I look?"

Patrick answered in his normal smart-arse fashion. "Like a girl who needs some action." He patted Roxanne on the backside, "Go get 'em, baby."

Roxanne turned the corner with the sound of her three-inch heels fading away with each step. It was time to roll the first hand-grenade through the Italian's front door.

Tommy bent over the open boot. He pulled out a sawn-off shotgun and handed it to Patrick. He then slid a .45 calibre Glock 41 down the back of his jeans before reaching into the bag one last time and grabbing a hand-held Taser before handing it over to his boss. Patrick counted to ten and then poked his head around the corner of the building. He could see Roxanne propped about five feet past the doorway. The flashing from her empty lighter highlighted her heavy make-up.

"Jesus Christ, a girl can't catch a bloody break these days." Roxanne bemoaned while she slowly turned to face the doorman. He was in a suit, standing rigid with both hands cupped in front with a coiled wire hanging from his left air. His eyes were already locked onto her seductive figure. Roxanne dropped her cigarette and then crouched down to pick it up. Her healthy cleavage was on full display. "You got a light?"

"Don't smoke," the goon replied.

"Well, good for you, but I bloody-well do, and this crappy lighter has just given up the ghost. Maybe you can weave some man magic for me? All you guys are good at that stuff—aren't you?" She took two steps closer, stopped, and continued flicking the flint. Her thumb was starting to feel numb. "I'll make it worth your while," she added as a teaser while licking her full lips.

The second man-brain below his belt woke up with a slight wink. He looked at his watch. It was still a good hour before the first break was due. "Give us a bloody look then." He stepped down to street level with a smirk on his face. In a sleazy swagger, he made his way over to where Roxanne had both feet firmly planted. She wasn't about to move, he needed to come all the way to her chalked spot.

Patrick and Tommy turned the corner. They had about fifty feet to cover before they would pull down their hoods and leap into action. Roxanne handed over the lighter. The suit flicked it a couple of times without really trying. "It's fucked, darling, might be a good time to give 'em up."

"Hang on, I might have another one in my bag." She placed her hand inside and felt for her vibrator. "Here, hang onto this for me, will you? I know I had another lighter in here the other day."

The suit stood there with the jelly-like sex toy wobbling in his closed hand. "Nothing like the real thing, sweetheart," was the best he could offer, it didn't really matter.

He felt a sting in his right shoulder, then another. The two dart-like electrodes were both firmly embedded while delivering their 50,000-volt load. His body started to shake and convulse in short spasms. Roxanne had a free hand on her pepper spray and was an excellent shot. The suit fell to one knee. Patrick kept his finger on the trigger, and the goon gradually fell to the ground while trying to rub the spray from his eyes. Tommy arrived from behind and delivered the final blow with the butt of the shotgun. The two men shot up the stairs, then stopped. Patrick eased the door open. The second suit was sitting in a chair reading a magazine. Patrick nodded towards Roxanne.

"Help, somebody help. There's a dead man on the footpath," she screamed. Patrick laid the nylon cord across the second step. He and Tommy each grabbed an end, took two steps back, and held on tight. The door pushed open with force. All the second lookout man could see was his backup man lying face-down with a woman freaking out. He ran down the first two steps, then tripped face first onto the footpath. Patrick jumped from his spot then clubbed him with a truncheon twice, and one for good luck. His body went limp. They dragged both bodies and dumped them behind two industrial waste bins.

"Tommy, go through his pockets and find those keys." Patrick turned to face Roxanne, "Time to split, Roxy. Get the fuck out of here, and I'll see you tomorrow where we agreed. You did good tonight, now disappear." She didn't need to be told twice.

"I've got 'em, boss." Tommy rejoiced by dangling two keys on a plastic key ring.

"Quick, follow me, the easy parts over," Patrick half-whispered. They entered the foyer, and all was as it should be—very quiet. Patrick inserted the first key, and the safe door swung open. Inside were five handguns, but only one was a Beretta M9 with a custom-made pearl handle. Patrick held it in his hand and smiled before whispering while pointing. "Got you now, you bastard. Wait here, Tommy, and keep an eye out on that door."

Patrick was gone in a second back out to the street. His mindset was telling him to run, but his stride remained controlled with a casual air, not wanting to attract any unwanted attention. He turned the corner while Whacka popped the boot a second time.

Patrick looked to his right, then left. The street looked desolate. Tucked into one corner of the boot was a polyurethane icebox sitting on two telephone books. He lifted the lid. Inside was half a slaughtered pig cut into two equal pieces and stacked like pancakes while immersed in a slurry of iced water. He snapped off the safety, pulled the slide portion back and chambered a single round. Then he slapped the rear quarter panel. Whacka kicked over the engine and let it idle, then turned to face his boss. Silently, Patrick went through the countdown on the one hand, *three, two, one...* Whacka gave the accelerator two gentle flicks with his foot. The Zenith-Stromberg CDSE carburettors whispered a throaty growl as fuel and aspirated air were forced into the 3.0-litre engine. Patrick fired two rounds through a sofa-sized cushion. Two muffled *thuds* were no louder than a car backfiring. He eased the boot closed, and as he made his way back to the front door, he wiped the gun clean just for good measure. Tommy looked like he was dancing on a bed of hot coals. Patrick replaced the Beretta, shut the safe, and quietly closed the door behind him. Tommy raised his hand. Two headlights lit up the darkened street, followed by the noise of the engine firing back up. Patrick slipped the keys back into the jacket pocket of the lookout guy who was still in fairyland. Because he'd failed his driver's licence written test on three different occasions now, Patrick took up his usual passenger's seat position after Tommy slid into the back seat, and the *Stag* headed up Macleay St, turned right into Darlinghurst Road, and headed back towards the Sydney Harbour Bridge.

Patrick turned to face his wheelman as Whacka started to increase speed while approaching the northbound exit. "What are ya doing?"

Whacka flipped the indicator left as he prepared to change lanes. "The Department of Main Roads has just installed six new speed cameras. A mate of mine reckons if you hug the inside lane nearest the train line, the cameras can't pick up the number plate. Watch, and I'll show you. Fucking thieving bastards." The Triumph continued accelerating, 100, then 120 kph. When they reached 140, Tommy pushed his extended arm out through the driver's window while offering a one-finger salute. As the vehicle sped past, a blinding flash of light lit up the lane like a bolt of lightning from above.

Patrick instinctively ducked for cover by laying his head down onto both knees. "You got any other bright ideas? Seriously, are you fucking brain dead or what?"

Whacka turned his head to face his disgruntled boss, "Lying piece of shit. Wait till I see Nugget again." He eased his foot off the pedal and allowed the car to slow while blending back into the reduced flow of early morning traffic.

"Keep driving. The fine won't be coming to me anyway," Patrick explained while shaking his head.

Chapter-10

ON THE LAST SUNDAY of each month, the four controlling members of the O'Finlay family were duty-bound to attend a scheduled meeting in the privacy of Ma's home to discuss in detail their exhaustive business interests, and calculate any possible future threats to their livelihoods. Theirs was no different to any other legitimate run company, business was business, and it was a cut-throat game played for keeps by people that would shake your hand while inching the spike of an ice pick into the square of your back. Everything and everybody was an unspoken open-slather in the ongoing battle for supremacy.

Sean was always the first to arrive and gave his mother a polite one shoulder embrace while she was still talking on the phone. He sauntered over to the fridge to grab a bottle of water. Big Ma hung up the phone with repressed anger in her tone. "You're not going to believe what I have just learnt from Detective O'Sullivan—off the record? I've just about had it up to here with that boy."

Sean unscrewed the cap and asked before taking his first mouthful, "What's goin' on, not bloody Patrick again—surely?"

"O'Sullivan has just finished explaining, two-weeks ago some idiots attempted to take down a private game of cards at the old Venus Room."

Sean almost choked on his water. "That's owned by the Costa family. The Mafia boys play cards there every Friday night. Who in their right mind would attempt to fuck with them? That's suicide. Not even Patrick is that fucking thick." He wiped his chin clean with the back of his sleeve. "You said attempted, so... are they all dead now?"

"The cops aren't sure what happened. Whoever was involved managed to take down both foot soldiers before they were found by a Good Samaritan who then rang triple zero."

"So why do you think Patrick was involved, and where is he anyway?"

Ma pulled out a chair. "Because the cops pulled a partial plate from a Triumph Stag, leaving the scene of the crime. Then they matched that to the same car that was picked up by a speed camera on the northbound bridge exit fifteen minutes later. The photo shows an arm hanging out the driver's side window with the tattoo, Broky – 78-79-80..."

"And . . . I don't follow?" Sean queried.

"The name was spelt, Broky. Peter Brock's three Bathurst wins from 1978 to 1980... ring any bells?" Ma asked, already knowing the answer.

"You mean that idiot, Tommy?" Sean shouted.

"But it gets better," Ma wanted to explain further. "The car in question is registered to a Miss Madeleine O'Hara."

There was a slight pause before Sean remembered the name of his own cousin. "Madeleine, are you serious? That's impossible. Is she even old enough to drive a car?"

"She just celebrated her twenty-first birthday," Ma answered. "You should know by now, Sean, there is no such thing as *impossible* when it comes to your youngest brother. O'Sullivan said they ran her name through Interpol, and without digging deeper, they *think* she is still in Ireland."

"Think!" Sean shouted again. "She either is, or she isn't. How do you register a car in Australia while you're ten thousand miles away? You need to attend in person—don't you?"

"I don't know, but two things I do need to know are: we need to track down Madeleine *and* this mystery car, and second: we need to have a serious talk with, Patrick. The Costa family? If they get wind that an O'Finlay is trying to mess with them...? Well, that spells trouble with a capital T."

"No one has seen nor heard from Madeleine's side of the family since Uncle Sean died," Sean thought to be the case.

Ma walked over to the kitchen bench to heat up the kettle. "Well, that's not *quite* true." The sound of the front door opening was Dean arriving. He sensed the tension in the room, so he decided to pull up a chair and sit.

"You were saying Ma . . ." Sean's words lingered.

"She sends me a card on my birthday and Christmas. Her mother passed away a few years back. She has been working in London and parts of Europe. She travels all over the place, so, no—I don't know where she is right now, and I don't have a contact number. Just an address near Dublin."

Patrick ambled in from the rear of the house with his 'I don't give a shit attitude' with a cold beer in his hand. "Don't know where who is? I thought the entire family was supposed to be involved in these little monthly get-togethers. Apparently, I was wrong."

Both Sean and Ma had reached an impasse, and Patrick sensed that all was not well on the home front as he had expected. In a calm, low, composed murmur, Sean ordered his youngest brother to be seated.

Ma looked Patrick square in the eye with a seething alienation, "Patrick, this is no time for any of your bullshit. What do you know about a midnight visit to the old Venus Room? I want to know if you had anything to do with what went down that night? Do you have any idea what the ramifications could be, not just to yourself, but also to this entire family?"

Patrick returned a dumber than dumb look. "What are ya talking about? Are you referring to those two sleazeballs Vincenzo and Antonio? You know they prefer to be called just Vince and Tony these days. What a fucking joke." Patrick locked eyes with his mother. "They still are, and always will be, the sons of the man that whacked your own brother—our uncle. And these Italians all gloat while hiding behind the walls of their marble mansions, still pissing themselves with laughter every day. Ma, if I wanted to take those sons-of-bitches out—they would both be dead as we speak. I heard it was a failed snatch 'n grab for the cash. I hear those boys play with some serious dosh," Patrick smirked.

Sean spoke next, cracking the knuckles in both hands as he stalked the kitchen in full stride while he contemplated his next move. He lifted Tommy's tattooed arm into the air. "UN-fucking-believable. Broky. Get the fuck out of here, Tommy, before I throw you out. This is a family meeting."

Tommy left without hesitation. Sean refocused his anger back towards his delusional brother. "What do you know about this bloody Triumph that's apparently registered in our cousin's name, Patrick? The cops have made the car, and it will just be a matter of time before they find it."

"What car—and a cousin? Where the fuck you going with all this?" Patrick had practised his expression in the mirror many times.

Ma sat down next to Dean with a fresh pot of tea. "What have you heard, Dean? I know you won't lie to your own mother." She glared at Patrick while he returned his own steely gaze directed straight at Dean.

"Same as Patrick, Ma. Word on the street is most likely like a bungled robbery. Probably just as well, if you ask me."

The room fell silent while Ma poured a cup through a small wire strainer. "Patrick, either way, the Costa family will make their own assumptions. Right or wrong, they will point a finger squarely back to this family. We can't afford a turf war right now, or any other time for that matter. We've got that big job planned and don't need any distractions. I'm putting you on ice for a while. Sending you back to Ireland."

Patrick kicked his chair backwards and jumped up. "What the hell are you talking about—Ireland?" This was going better than even he imagined.

"I want you to track down, Madeleine. She goes under her mother's name now of O'Hara. Madeleine O'Hara. I need to know if she is where she's supposed to be. For all we know, or don't know, she might be in Australia right now, and if so—why? Plus, I want you out of the picture until this incident at the Cross cools down. You might be in danger."

"Madeleine?" Patrick feigned shock. "What's she got to do with all this?"

"That's exactly what we need to find out. My mind's made up. You leave tomorrow. Dean, make the call to, Astrid, then tell her to book the first flight out tomorrow." She looked at Patrick again, and he was less than impressed. "Dean, tell her business class." Ma returned her glare back to her youngest boy, "There, you happy now?"

"Ma, in case you've forgotten, the job planned for this Sunday is mine. A job I bought to the table and planned. This is my fucking job," he remonstrated.

Sean pulled out a chair and positioned himself opposite his younger brother. His teeth were grinding like a whacked-out meth-head. "You don't need to worry about the job you, dip-wit. Dean and I can handle that. This won't be our first, you idiot. I think we'll manage without your hot head getting in the way. Maybe this is a blessing in disguise. You need to lie low somewhere now until we can sort through this bloody shambles created by your misconceived ideas on how the family business is conducted. It's time you accepted responsibility *and* the ramifications of your reckless actions. You have one simple job. Go to Ireland, find Madeleine, and with the family connections wiping your arse, even *you* should be able to handle that." Sean's tone was condescending. He knew it drove Patrick crazy inside, but that was the price of incompetence.

Liam, who was a close and trusted member of the family, was tasked with the job of escorting young Patrick to the international terminal the following afternoon. Ma's instructions were explicit. "Watch him like a hawk until he walks on to that bloody plane," she spelt out in simple, plain Irish-English.

Patrick asked Liam to drop him at the terminal entrance. "No can do, Patrick. My instructions are explicit. Sorry," Liam answered.

After checking in and with his boarding pass in hand, Patrick grabbed his carry-on and shook Liam's hand before joining the queue and passing through the final security and hand luggage checks. Patrick placed his bag on the X-ray roller then stepped through the security scanner. He was waved up and down with the magic wand then allowed to proceed to the escalator and continue on, reaching the final boarding lounge on the next floor. Satisfied that his job was done, Liam left and found his car. As he pulled back out into the line of traffic, Patrick tracked down a public telephone and made a call to his mate Tommy.

"Patrick, is that you?" Tommy answered, surprised by the unexpected call.

"Yes you dope, who else rings you on this number? Come and pick me up from outside the QANTAS terminal right now. I'll be waiting out the front, leave straight away, all right."

"The QANTAS terminal, what are you doing there?"

"Don't worry, Tommy. I'm already one step ahead of the play, old mate. Just get your skinny backside over here and pick me up."

Patrick found a vacant bench seat outside the terminal entrance, still smarting at the ease in which he steered his own mother into handing him the perfect alibi. My day will come, he promised, thinking about the long road ahead he and Tommy were about to negotiate. "Fuck my family," Patrick spat from his venomous mouth.

Chapter-11

THE GOGGOMOBIL was a series of micro-cars produced by Hans Glas GmbH in the Bavarian town of Dingolfling between 1955 and 1969. Glas produced three models on the Goggomobil platform. The Goggomobil T-sedan, the Goggomobil TS-coupé and the Goggomobil TL-van. The engine was an air-cooled, two-stroke, two-cylinder unit originally displacing 250cc, but was later available in increased sizes of 300cc and 400cc. It had an electric pre-selective transmission and a manual clutch. The engine sat behind the rear wheels. It also boasted an independent all-round suspension using coil springs with swing axles.

Between 1957 and 1961, some seven hundred sports cars called Goggomobil *Darts* were imported by Buckle Motors whose dealership showrooms were located in the Sydney suburb of Brookvale. They also produced other Goggomobil models under licence, including the saloon, coupé-convertible and some light van variants. These were fitted with Australian produced fibreglass bodies based on the Sunbeam *Alpine* in place of the steel bodies of their German counterparts. Australian production totalled approximately five thousand units.

Gassan Allamadin was born to a typical family of Armenian Gypsies. At the tender young age of two years and five months, he was first introduced to their strange business world. His travelling family of twelve included cousins, aunties, uncles, both grandparents and his own parents in a scam that included Gassan partaking in his newly adopted role while passing through a town called Aragats located on the Arpacay River which made up the western border of Turkey.

The best-laid plans are simple, and this plan was supposedly full-proof—until this one day. The location would be carefully chosen: any busy marketplace frequented by Western tourists. The modus operandi never changed because it was a winner every time. A toddler would be strategically left alone on the sidewalk in a brand-new sailor's outfit, complete with expensive shoes, and a cap to match. It was only a one hundred lira investment that would pay a healthy dividend. Next, his father would give him a gentle nudge in the backside with a sharp object to start the tears rolling down his cute rosy-red cheeks until a caring tourist would inevitably come to a sudden stop. The heart wants what the heart needs, and within minutes, the young Gassan was being consoled in the loving arms of some poor unsuspecting visitor enjoying a well-deserved holiday.

Next to arrive on the gathering scene of concerned onlookers would be a cousin, dressed in her soiled and shredded Gypsy attire with a hairstyle that hadn't seen a bottle of shampoo or a hairbrush for weeks, demanding for all to hear that her baby be returned from the thieving Westerners. When a woman has a child held close to her chest, the urge to nurture that child is a paternal instinct. Who in their right mind is just going to hand a baby over to a strange woman who obviously does not share the same socioeconomic circumstances?

This couple were from Spain, and rightfully were demanding some valid proof, while hoping a policeman would arrive to sort this mess out. Conveniently, that is exactly what happens next. Now the distraught mother is crying and upset, so to prove she is the child's mother, she rips open her shirt to showcase a full set of firm breasts, "Look, you see my milk? I am still breastfeeding," she screams. The crowd is shocked, and soon it doubles in size with many men now taking more than a passing interest.

Now it's time for the rest of the family to arrive—albeit one by one from different directions, and soon the pick-pocketing begins in earnest. The final part of the scam was the visit to the police station by Gassan's real mother, with proof that he was in fact her child with three hundred lire tucked into her shirt sleeve. On this day, there was no policeman, and there was no Gassan. His disappearance was never reported, and he never saw his real parents or any of his family again. He was a disposable asset and easily replaced.

Today he was celebrating his 18th birthday and was excited to be picking up his new Goggomobil TS-convertible with a bright lipstick-red paint job. At just a few inches over five feet tall, he would have made a great jockey except he was scared of horses. Once a thief, always a thief, plus he had another problem. This one started out costing about thirty dollars a week, now his habit was chewing up ten times that amount. He needed a decent score, and after a month of careful planning, and many a lonely night spent completing surveillance duties, tonight was the night. After trolling the streets dotted with wealthy harbourside mansions, he had narrowed his hit list down to four individual properties.

With the roof retracted, and the wind blowing in his bloodshot eyes he followed Spit Road passing over the Spit Bridge, drawing strange stares and pointed fingers from the increasing flow of traffic while behind the wheel of what can be best described as a Tonka Toy on steroids. While stopped at the red traffic lights at Spit Junction, with the last of the daylight hours dropping behind the man-made skyline, a group of ex-Mosman High School students were crossing the lights. One of them stopped on the median strip and turned his head to the right. "Hey, Frog, is that you? Check this out, guys? The Frog has picked himself up a new ride."

The Frog just smiled and took a generous toke on his joint, then blew the smoke out over the sun visor. "Seeing is believing, baby. Minip-minip," he enjoyed sharing. The traffic lights changed to green, he revved the two-stroke motor which sounded like a ride-on lawnmower with a set of extractors and dropped the clutch only to stall the 400cc engine before he eventually coasted through the intersection while turning the ignition a second time, then headed left for a meet with his dealer.

For there you have been - so it is there you shall return. The Frog's dealer handed him what he boasted as being the best shit to hit the streets in the last twelve months. These trips were called black dots and were a breakthrough from the all-too-familiar tiles that often caused severe stomach cramps. His dealer suggested he cut the tiny pill-shaped trip in half with a razor blade and spread the mental holiday into the light-fantastic over two separate occasions. The Frog pondered that for about half a second, then decided; where's the fun in that? He popped the entire black dot down his open throat and headed for a place he liked to spend some time alone before heading off to work.

Taronga Park Zoo is located at the end of Bradley's Head Road in Mosman, home to over 4,000 animals spread out over the entire headland of the harbour peninsula occupying over sixty-nine acres of land. The break in the barbed wire fence was only a short walk from the end of Whiting Beach Road. The Frog scaled the limestone wall with ease, which would bring him out next to the recently constructed Birds of Paradise enclosure. From experience, Gassan assumed wrongly, he'd have at least thirty to forty minutes before the first effects of the acid would take him to a place where he could separate himself from the realities that were his mundane and droll life.

He ducked under the first CCTV camera to reacquaint himself with his furry ape friends. He watched on as the kaleidoscope of colours opened up a whole new world. Within the hour, he was playing the role of *Dr Dolittle* with the ability to converse with anything that moved or made a sound—and he did this in many languages. He was totally immersed in his animal kingdom, except this time the monkeys and apes were sharing their ancestral history in a haze of bright orange, shimmering reds and greens, and his favourite colour pink. The lions boasted an irradiated yellow mane like a burning ring of fire. The giraffes he thought would make an interesting riding companion, but he didn't have a ladder handy, and it wasn't until he found himself halfway up a paperbark tree that offered a nice overhang into the brown bear enclosure he decided it might be a good time to find a safe haven. Then he got hopelessly lost.

To the zoo's immediate left is Sydney Harbour National Park, which is skirted by Taylors Bay. There is a popular jogging path known as Taylors Bay Walking Track that eventually brings you out to a place called Chowder Bay Bushland. It took most of the remaining night, but Gassan eventually found his way to a point where he was presented with another familiar-looking limestone wall, so he scaled that too. After hacking his way through years of neglected flower beds, hanging vines, trees, and anything else that grows in the humid Sydney climate, he stumbled across an abandoned house. All the windows and doors were nailed up tight with solid wood timbers. His only way in was to climb an exterior galvanised iron downpipe, remove some old clay tiles covered in years of moss, and drop down through the roof. That's when his black dot really cut in, and he spent the remainder of the morning hours plus most of that day in an alternative world that defied belief. He knew if he left this hidden treasure trove in his current state, he would never find his way back, so he stayed-and-played until it was safe to reemerge back into the material world. That proved to be more difficult than he realised when he found the entire staircase had been removed, and the only way back down was to retrace his original steps, which turned out to be anything but easy.

That next day, the Frog revisited the mysterious home he'd lucked upon. He parked his Goggomobil in a popular picnic area and jogged the last three hundred metres back along Illuka Road, then stopped at the front gates. It was a two-storey circa 1920s Manor House surrounded by a high wrought-iron fence, overgrown with thick vegetation, and occupying an entire corner block at the very end of the street. It was almost totally private with just one recently built, three-tiered modern style eyesore separated by a small slice of land that was owned by the army. The whole area of Ashton Park was dotted with old WWII bunkers that offered a direct line of fire to the Sydney Harbour Heads in the hope of surprising any Japanese Navy ships that wanted to try their luck during the Second World War. More importantly, after completing a title search in the city, the Frog had discovered the previous owner was listed as an Italian antique dealer named Stefano Elia Paolo Costa. Then he checked the N.S.W Registry for Births, Deaths and Marriages, and soon learnt this same man had died over sixteen years ago. Most people assumed correctly it was a deceased estate and one day would be either sold or demolished. The Frog, like most people, wrongly assumed it to be empty. They would be only half right.

Two nights later he was climbing to the first floor, via the same external downpipe with the tools of his trade inside his backpack. This time he smashed a small window, popped open the locked sash and entered a vacant room with his torch beam pointing the way. Beads of perspiration ran down his temples with anticipation while he repeatedly swallowed to moisten the inside of his mouth. Opening the first door revealed a long hallway which led to a pair of finely detailed elegant-looking wooden doors. Sliding one of the doors to the left, it opened onto another much larger room. This room was huge. It looked like it may have been an old ballroom with a parquetry dance floor in the room's centre. The twelve-foot-high ceilings showcased intricately designed ceiling roses and crystal chandeliers plus three solid marble fireplaces with matching mirrored mantels. There were wooden crates full of white boned China crockery, silverware and candelabras scattered about the floor.

It looked like all that once made this house a home had been meticulously packed away before being carefully placed in the upstairs area for safekeeping.

The next thing the Frog remembered were two full suits of armour proudly standing together in a far corner. With the aid of some light, the Frog could now clearly make out the helm, breast and back plates were all intact with gauntlets still attached. The closest one was holding a long battle axe, angled forward in the left hand, the other had both hands folded over an intricately decorated double-handled sword.

There were countless items of furniture, solid oak roll-top desks, Queen Anne oak dressers with chiffonier all covered in dust covers. There were over a dozen old tea chests stacked two-high in one corner, each one containing what looked like ladies' clothing. Opening the three doors of a free-standing clothes dresser, it was full of men's suits accompanied by matching hats with canes, some casual, some very formal. The ladies' dresses looked to be from around the time of the American Reconstruction era, full of lace and hoops. There were ball gowns, long jackets with rows of heeled dress shoes lining the floors of each cupboard.

Scanning the room with his flashlight, the Frog noticed another cupboard, this one differed from the others. Each of the four doors was fronted with stained glass and separate locks. He jimmied the locked doors open with his screwdriver, stood back and stared inside with dumbstruck bewilderment. It almost took his breath away.

Hanging side-by-side, all covered in clear plastic, were three American Union officers' uniforms. Comprising frock coats, shell jackets, cloak coats with an officer's sash, dress shirts, officer's buttons and cravat. Proudly hanging on a single bronze clothes hook was a field officer's sword, still inside its own decorated scabbard.

Hidden in the corner was a large trunk with a padlock still attached to the clasp. Sliding it out, it felt heavy. He placed it on a small table and went to work on the lock. The trunk had four brass reinforced corners and matching hinges. There was a plate above the lock with an inscription engraved spelling out the name 'Captain Joseph H. Martin'.

The rusted padlock broke in two, and he slowly pried the lid open. Inside was a personal diary, leather-bound and sealed with a red ribbon. The captain's name was inscribed on the front cover in raised lettering. A leather satchel contained a copy of the Bible and what looked like an old title deed and two birth certificates. The Frog read the names out loud. "Luca Angelo Costa, born Augusta, Sicily, 11:29 P.M., March 21, 1976, and Vincenzo Salvatore Costa, born Augusta, Sicily, 11:37 P.M., March 21, 1976. Eight minutes apart. Twins?"

The Frog retrieved an inscribed presentation 14k gold Civil War pocket-watch with a signed cabinet card. Two pairs of neatly folded white gloves were placed on an officer's hat bearing a captain's insignia and a Coat of Arms. He picked up a leather holster with obvious signs of where its matching revolver once rested inside.

With exacting precision, he started removing each piece, eventually revealing another smaller wooden box. Lifting this out was the source of the weight. He placed the box next to the other items. It was secured with a swinging brass clasp. The Frog opened the box and stood frozen in a stunned paralysis as dollar signs floated through his Gypsy brain.

Inside was Captain Joseph H. Martin's personal firearm. A Colt Army Model 1860, .44 calibre revolver. Lifting it out from its red velvet casing, he noted the hinged loading lever. It boasted a rounded barrel about eight inches long with a navy battle scene inscribed down one side. He placed it in the palm of his hand and raised his arm to a firing position. Stretched out horizontally, he stood still momentarily and placed himself in the shoes of the captain. With the weight of this firearm, he wandered, in the heat of battle, holding a gun like this, and at arm's length, how the hell a man could maintain his balance on the back of a galloping horse while coming under enemy fire?

The Frog's attention was interrupted by the left-to-right sweep from a set of headlights entering the adjoining vacant block of land. He stood on the windowsill to see two men exit a parked car under the reflection of a waxing gibbous moon. Within seconds they both disappeared over a fence. The Frog paid it little attention; he was a patient man. Tonight's exercise was simply to catalogue the pieces he thought were saleable, snap some photos, then do his homework to first place an estimated value on each item, and then source a buyer. It was always about the money, nothing else.

Chapter-12

A T THE RIPE OLD AGE OF SIXTEEN, Wayne Curran was nominated as the 'Rip Curl Rising Star' in the prestigious surf magazine, *A Surfers' Paradise,* after having just taken out one of the top-ranking world surfers by winning the state-sponsored competition at the Sydney beachside suburb of Palm Beach. The surfing media were in a frenzy and were quoting his big splash into the surfing world as someone to 'keep your eye on folks' and Wayne was milking it for all it was worth.

He was basking in the glory of his newfound fame. His aspiration from an age as young as fourteen was to augment his ranking points while still attending his last years as a student enrolled at the prestigious North Sydney Boys Grammar, nicknamed 'The Factory'. More like a well-honed production line than a secondary school, North Sydney Boys Grammar had a sole purpose, and that was simply to groom students for a seamless entry into one of Sydney's top three universities, which they did like sausages sliding off a meat grinder. Wayne's single ambition was to turn pro and head off overseas to wallow in the lofty heights of the world surfing tour.

His wealthy father refused any financial assistance. He wished only to waylay his only son's pipe dreams, recommending instead that he follow in the safe and orchestrated footsteps predetermined by his steadfast parents. They were both adamant that their son would attend university and follow a well-laid-out ancestral path, gaining his Bachelor's Degree of Economics, then working his way through the business world to secure his place on the corporate ladder.

Now nineteen, and living on the Gold Coast in Coolangatta, Wayne's short career had reached an impasse.

Owen Peterson was a childhood friend and a long-time surfing buddy. Wayne remembered, like a recurring nightmare, Owen explaining his decision to quit full-time employment, deciding to dedicate the next two years of his life to 'having a crack' at professional surfing. He had now won three of the last four competitions, including the jewel in the crown of the Australian surfing calendar, the famous Bells Beach Classic.

Wayne had now slipped from being the number one ranked surfer on the east coast of Australia and was in danger of losing the pot of gold at the end of his surfing rainbow—an exemption for five of the top seven competitions at the commencement of next year's World Tour.

Wayne delved into his conniving brain for answers. His dream was fast becoming a distant anamnesis. He was resentful and appetent for a solution, spending sleepless nights searching for a final solution. He was haunted by the unabated media hype following Owen like a swarm of bees. All were jointly quoting: 'Owen Peterson, the next best thing in the surfing world'.

Wayne had started on a plan to address both his cash-flow problem and a way to rid himself of Owen out of his floundering life forever, clearing his rightful path to surfing fame and fortune.

Kill two birds with one stone. The end will always justify the means, Wayne rationalised his warped methodology.

Wayne knew Owen had an Achilles' heel; women and a sexual addiction to cocaine. He wasn't hooked or an addict, but Owen liked to party and participate in binge sessions on cocaine or speed, then enjoy long sex orgies with expensive, high-class call girls.

Ever since he was a young nipper, Wayne recalled that Owen's parents would spend the Australian winters holidaying in Europe. With the offer of some quick cash, and a night on the booze and hooch, he convinced his long-time friend to use the vacant house for a pre-arranged exchange of cash for cocaine. Wayne and Owen grew up together on the same street. As his best mate, he was familiar with the house which was necessary to pull off his masterful sting.

Brad Stevenson's star also burnt bright, as the main supplier of recreational drugs on the Sunshine Coast. These were the play-fields of the wealthy and famous, all with an insatiable craving for some fun in the sun. This was his primary place of business.

Brad was a likable lad with an inexhaustible throng of appetent clientèle. He first introduced himself to Wayne after witnessing him flaunt yet another surfing trophy high above his head after winning the Burleigh Heads Single Fin Competition. As the then number-one ranked surfer, Wayne attracted horded of groupies wanting to share in his limelight. Brad was looking for a big score. It was an election year, and the supply of both cocaine and speed along the Gold Coast had all but dried up. He was becoming desperate to resupply himself and not risk breaking the cycle of trust he had built up over the last few years with his list of wealthy users. Like a Messiah spreading the spoken word, Wayne offered Brad an answer to all his problems.

The second part of his plan required some serious muscle. Wayne was fully aware of Patrick O'Finlay's family connections from the first two years he spent attending Mosman High. Patrick was a perfect patsy for what he had in mind. His greed and unwavering covetousness in wanting to see himself as a reincarnation of an Irish version of the *Peaky Blinders* would be the allurement Wayne would use to bring Patrick O'Finlay to the foray. After their recent meeting in Bondi, and as planned, with the smell of sharing a big haul of cash and drugs, it was a simple task to engage his required skill-set.

After signing some autographs, Wayne left the Four-Leaf Clover Restaurant located on the foreshore of Bondi

Beach, content that he had laid enough trailing seeds of greed, and now it was just a matter of time before he would reap the rewards of his well mapped-out plan.

Chapter-13

WAYNE CURRAN ARRIVED at Owen Peterson's parent's home in the harbourside suburb of Clifton Gardens around 2:00 A.M. He needed this time to perform his own private switch before the sellers arrived in about two hours time. After driving down from the Gold Coast, Brad Stevenson turned up at the same address an hour later with an aluminium briefcase full of cash. Owen met him at the front door and showed him to the upstairs games room. Wayne greeted his long-time cohort with a smiling handshake and a nervous swallow from a mouth that was feeling like he'd eaten some road kill, knowing what he was attempting to pull off over the next few hours. Everything was set, and it was a green light to go. Soon he would be financially secure and on a plane to the USA, and the O'Finlay family would walk away with a haul of cocaine worth over half a million dollars on the drug-hungry streets of Sydney. *A means to an end*, he kept convincing himself.

After checking the contents of the case, Wayne suggested Brad leave the cash behind the bar, out of sight, while they enjoyed a few beers and some Kelly pool while watching a replay of last year's ARL Grand Final between the Balmain Tigers and the Canterbury Bulldogs on the big-screen TV. Wayne knew both men were one-eyed Doggy supporters.

Owen was in seventh heaven, looking forward to a night of alcohol, cocaine and women—and in that order. Being in the media spotlight was inhibiting his own private life. Coming to Sydney with his long-time friend Wayne was a well-earned distraction. Time to blow off some steam, he reassured himself constantly. He had already arranged for some 'Top of the Town', high-class girls of disrepute to be dropped off at the house after 5:00 A.M. He knew his father had many mistresses and liked to record them repeatedly watch his own sexual exploits. Being a chip off the old man's block, Owen walked downstairs and entered his father's private office.

Owen knew his promiscuous father had only recently installed, at considerable expense to himself, the latest and greatest in digital recording equipment from his recent trip to the States. None of this high-end technology was even available for sale in Australia, Owen remembered his wealthy old-man proudly stating. He stepped over to his unfaithful father's imported Italian office desk and opened the second drawer. Inside he kept a set of ten round discs with the brand name TDK VIDEO DVD RW, then removed the top disc. Finding a black felt pen, he wrote OP self-porn on the label, then bent down and activated a hidden switch to reveal a room designed for self-gratification. Owen opened up the recording device and inserted the shiny silver disc then pressed the red button labelled *record,* satisfied in the fact he would have access to endless hours of his own, self-starring pornographic movies before returning upstairs to rejoin the party.

Wayne gathered up the growing pile of empty stubbies and placed them in the bin behind the bar. He looked over at the wall-mounted big screen TV and shouted to the other two men, "Guys, you gotta watch this," pointing while Terry Lamb commenced his game-winning twenty-five-metre sprint, sidestepping the fullback to score under the posts, and seal the grand final victory 24-12.

While all eyes were firmly fixed on the giant TV, Wayne knelt down and started filling the fridge with the last two six-packs of beer. As the three men started cheering and celebrating the Bulldogs miraculous win, he quietly opened the aluminium case and stashed the cash inside the empty carton. Then he quickly replaced the contents with some cut newspapers he had previously left on the shelf, before squeezing a few drops of Superglue into both locks before casually stepping out from behind the bar.

With the carton overflowing with empty stubbies held in full view under his arm, he joined in cheering for the Doggies before explaining to Owen, "I'll just go and throw these empties in the recycle bin outside. Be back in a minute, okay."

"Yeah mate, no worries, your shout when you get back," Owen cheered loudly, still rejoicing in the result as they replayed the winning try.

Wayne hurried to the downstairs office, using the exterior stairs located at the end of an outside balcony, cursing himself for stepping through a muddy shallow puddle of pool water before he entered the office he knew so well. Wayne placed the cash inside a soft sports bag before stashing it inside a room that only three people even knew of its very existence. On his return trip, he emptied the box into the outside recycling bin and returned to refresh each person's beer. His heart pounded inside with both palms, forming a sweaty film of perspiration. He was so close to the end, he could almost taste it.

Sean O'Finlay was always a subscriber to the theory that if you're not early for an appointment, then you're late. Like most men, he hated to be kept waiting. Patience was a virtue he refused to subscribe to.

An individual who went by the single name of Kojak reversed the stolen SUV down Ma's rear lane-way and was met by a grunt, standing guard at her back gate with a second set of plates at the ready. The two men went through the ritual of who looks like the toughest guy and shared a hog-like snort while Kojak swept through the rear yard and into the 'belly of the beast'.

Kojak was a practising Warlock, right into all that devil worship and witchcraft hocus pocus. He was almost looked upon with a cult status while haunting the streets of Sydney in his favourite long flowing black and red velvet cape. His claim to fame, apparently witnessed by a large group of party revellers, was while being involved in a verbal altercation with a loud-mouthed young rapper, a gold chain hanging from the teenager's neck depicting Jesus Christ nailed to the cross came into contact with Kojak's left hand, leaving a burnt imprint on his palm. Witnesses swear you could smell the pungent odour of smouldering flesh as the devil reincarnated quickly left the scene and disappeared into the night.

Big Ma's reinforced back door resembled something you might expect to see in the American president's private bunker. It looked to be fireproof, bulletproof, and would probably have withstood a nuclear explosion. You almost risked an injury just trying to open it. Kojak followed a hallway that led to a private office and joined the remaining three members of the crew. Dean was hovering around his older brother like a bad smell, and Liam, as part of the O'Finlay family inner-circle, acknowledged Kojak's on-time arrival with a curt nod of the head.

Sean gathered the four people around a pool table. With a laid out sketch of a house showing the internal layout, he started to map out the plan.

Sean, Liam and Kojak were all decked out in swanky three-piece suits, dressed to impersonate three Drug Squad detectives, with real police ID's and badges to match. They planned to take down a predawn exchange between a dealer and his supplier. Sean closely scanned each person's face and started laying down the law.

"You're all aware this job was Patrick's brainchild. Unfortunately, he won't be with us tonight, but the plan is set in motion, and nothing changes."

Each person nodded in acknowledgement. Sean continued, pointing towards Kojak. "You drive to the location. I'll give you the address on the way. Patrick's inside man is ready and waiting. After we arrive, Kojak, you circle the block twice, then reverse the car into the driveway. Dean, you come around the back of the house with me. I'll enter through the unlocked rear door. You follow me in, and then wait at the bottom of the stairs for my signal, okay. I don't want you anywhere near that room upstairs until we have the cash well and truly secured. Keep your eyes peeled for anyone coming or trying to leave, and I mean *anyone*. When you see all of us returning, get ready to move—no piss-farting around, you got that?"

Dean nodded while Sean placed one hand on the mud map. "I'll open the front door for both, Liam and Kojak. Then the three of us will make our way up the stairs, follow the hallway left to the last room on the right, and make our surprise entry. Inside this room will be five people. Only one person has a connection to the property. The buyer is a nobody from up Surfers Paradise way somewhere. This is his first big score in Sydney, and he shouldn't give us any grief. The two sellers we don't know a lot about. It won't matter. The element of surprise is on our side. Everyone will be nervous. This will be to our advantage. All clear so far?"

Everyone nodded in the affirmative.

"This is a big house people," Sean continued, "but very secluded, at the end of a cul-de-sac with no nosey neighbours to worry too much about. After we have the cash, I'll place it in the hallway then call you upstairs Dean to come and grab it. Do not come up those stairs until I give you the all-clear. Got it?"

"Yeah, I get it, Sean," he replied like a scorned child.

"The two hundred fifty thousand will be in a locked aluminium suitcase. We keep the cash and, as Ma has pointed out, leave the cocaine as a trade-off for their undivided cooperation. This is all about the cash and a quick snatch 'n grab. We know from Patrick's source the only other people packing any hardware will be us, but we'll pat 'em down just in case. So we go in, do a number on these guys, and then get the fuck out of there. I don't want to be inside that house for more than ten to fifteen minutes—tops. They're all rank amateurs with no Mob connections. They'll all shit 'emselves at the sight of three members of the Drug Squad crashing their little party while praying for us to spare them any jail time with the sellers happy to be left with the case full of shit. We have rehearsed this, and we all know what to say and do... *right*?"

Again, each person nodded, then confirmed with a disjointed, "Yeah, no worries. It's all good."

"Is everyone up to speed, then? Because I don't need anyone screwing this up tonight. Are there any final questions?" Sean asked.

The room remained silent. Sean turned and threw Kojak the keys. "Go and check if Wes has changed the plates. Start the car, and we'll be there in a minute."

This was going to be an old-fashioned sting by supposed corrupt detectives, which was a prerequisite to promotion along the North Shore of Sydney. Kojak slipped on his gloves and waited in the SUV. The rear compartment door opened. Sean threw in two bags, and the four of them headed off, with Liam sitting in the front left seat.

The black cruiser melted into the flow of traffic and sat just above the speed limit, then passed through Spit Junction and headed down Bradleys Head Road towards Clifton Gardens. There was no chatter or friendly banter. Kojak thought about turning the radio on. A bit of rock 'n roll might break the monotony, but he was sure Sean wasn't a lover of music.

He overheard Sean mumble some words to his brother. Dean leaned over the back seat and retrieved one of the bags. The sound of a zipper opening was soon followed by the familiar smell of gun oil wafting from the back seat that was synonymous with all firearms, while both Liam and Kojak were handed a .38 police-issue Smith & Wesson.

Sean started barking out directions, left here, second right, then left again. Kojak made some mental notes of the area, landmarks and street names. He needed to remember how to get back out of here, hopefully without some very pissed-off people chasing them in a hail of bullets. They took their first run past the house. The cruiser didn't slow. It all looked as it should as the dashboard clock neared 4:01 A.M. The house was a large modern style with an elevated driveway snaking its way up to a set of stairs that led to a pillared front entrance, almost in total darkness apart from a dim light from an upstairs room. A dark sedan was parked to one side near the front stairs.

Approaching for the second time, Kojak flicked the headlights off, slowly reversed up the drive and parked the car to the side of the house, obscured from the main entry. Everyone exited the vehicle. It was time to light the rocket.

Dean followed his brother to the rear of the house. They both entered while Sean gestured with a hand signal for Dean to take up his designated position at the bottom stair. Sean placed a small-calibre pistol in his hand and whispered, "This is only a precautionary measure, just in case", and then cracked open the front door from the inside.

Dean slid the gun into the front of his jeans. The reflection of a flickering television could be seen coming from an adjoining lounge room. Dean's nerves were on edge as the three men crept their way up the sweeping staircase in single file. He tried listening to anything that might help paint a picture in his mind about the shit-storm that was about to take place upstairs.

Patrick and Tommy had previously taken up a position in an outdoor gazebo that over-looked a below-ground saltwater pool, waiting patiently since 3:30 A.M. Nerves were being tested as they counted down the thirty-minute time clock.

Patrick motioned for Tommy to follow his lead while they each methodically checked both spare magazines were loaded with their full six-round capacity. The Glock G-43 was a favoured weapon among the criminal fraternity. Tommy remembered Patrick would often joke that if the bullet didn't kill you, the resulting fall back to earth would.

Both men's eyes were glued to the room upstairs, Patrick heard car doors slamming shut from the front of the house. He glanced down at his watch. It read 3:43 A.M. The sellers had just arrived. The two dealers entered the upstairs room and swapped the customary drug dealers' shifty, suspicious scowl with each person. They were well acquainted with Wayne, exchanging friendly shoulder nudges. A tall and heavyset man that looked like he could handle himself was carrying the case full of cocaine. He found a seat on a comfortable white lounge and looked at his gold Rolex while placing the locked case on a small coffee table, ready to get down to business.

The longest eighteen minutes of Patrick's life ticked away until the sound of a second vehicle arriving forced the hairs on his neck to stand up. He slowed his breathing while he watched Sean and Dean enter the back door.

Tommy could see shadows through the slated upstairs curtains with the sounds of muffled voices filtering down from above. The sliding door opened, and a single man walked to the end of the L-shaped balcony. The glow of a lighter highlighted his shoulder-length surfie-blond hair as he sucked away on a joint.

Patrick tapped Tommy on the shoulder and whispered, "Get your act together, mate. It's time for the shit to hit the fan." They each inserted a full mag, racked the slide and felt the trigger safety. The otherwise quiet neighbourhood was about to erupt.

Patrick could feel the adrenalin pumping through his veins. Like a junkie, he was on a high to nothing, immersed in a feeling of euphoria. His perceived alternate reality had kicked in, a virtual world that existed only in his clouded, drug-altered-mind. The final obstacle of living in his brother's shadow, blocking his rise to the ranks of the head of the family was about to be eliminated in an ultimate show of strength that he knew would reverberate throughout the criminal world bestowing upon him the respect he so rightfully felt was his alone.

Patrick and Tommy counted down the final seconds, before making their move, edging their way up a set of outside corkscrew designed steel stairs leading to a balcony that ran the full length of the entire second-storey.

Patrick could see Wayne, standing with his back towards him, leaning against the hand railing. It looked and smelt like he was puffing away on a joint. He and Tommy both heard Kojak and Sean enter the room only metres away, yelling and demanding complete and total cooperation. Kojak was screaming indecipherable words at the top of his lungs with his badge held up high for all to see. It was his tone, shock and awe—the element of total surprise that was their weapon to create a scene of utter confusion.

The hysteria of seeing the cops come barging in had the desired effect. Liam walked around the pool table in the room's centre with his firearm raised and menacing. Sean announced their official arrival. "This is the Drug Squad, everybody, down on the floor *NOW*, and get your hands where we can see them. This is a bust."

Chaos reigned supreme as each person tried to comprehend what was precisely happening. Sean seized the initiative and quickly surveyed the room, then noticed a man standing on the balcony outside. He stepped through the large glass sliding door to drag him back into the organised confusion. Patrick's chest felt like it was about to burst open. His gun arm trembled as he took aim and fired two shots into the square of Sean's back. *It's done, my God, I actually did it,* surprising even himself at how effortless it was to murder his own brother in cold blood.

Both Sean's feet lifted from the slip-safe balcony deck as his body was flung forward in an out-of-control oscillation of arms and legs. Sean tried grasping at the railing in an attempt to halt his unrestrained momentum, before finally plunging over the edge. Like a mistimed dive from the high board, Sean's body landed belly-first in the pool below, face-down and floating. A slick of crimson leached from the two new craters in his back.

Wayne flinched at the sound of gunfire. Startled, he turned and faced Patrick, looking totally stupefied. He was numb with a terrorised fear of what he'd just witnessed. "Fuck me, no way," he screamed with a stretching shriek of horror. "Are you fucking kidding me? Jesus, Patrick—what the hell are you doing, you idiot? This wasn't part of the plan, you were..." Two quick *thud-thud* noises spewed from Patrick's self-attached Osprey muzzle suppressor. Wayne's open Hawaiian shirt rippled, his breastbone shattered, leaving two gaping holes you could almost see the light of day through.

"New plan, Wayne. Sorry, mate. Didn't we tell you?" Patrick smirked. This was becoming all too easy. He remained motionless in a gunman's stance, feet apart with a smoke trail spiralling from the end of his barrel. The warped smile and parted lips of a bloodthirsty killer was the final image Wayne would take to his grave as he was catapulted backwards, crashing against the rear railing and falling with the unrestrained *thump* of his head to the wooden decking.

Tommy rushed inside with his Glock firing randomly at anything or anyone that moved—it made no difference. Both Kojak and Liam were caught totally off guard by the unexpected gunfire.

"What the fuck is goin' on?" Kojak howled as he recognised Tommy's face with no time to form a defence against the point-blank fire from his powerful firearm. Tommy emptied three shots into Kojak's general direction. How could he miss—he was that close. The force of the 9mm slugs catapulted Kojak's body up and away. He resembled a reversing parachutist as he became airborne, his back slamming into a carved wooden-framed print hanging off a wall. His muted body slowly slid to the floor, leaving a bloodied reddish smear in its wake like a bad hand-painted canvas.

Liam turned towards the sounds of gunfire and just kept squeezing the trigger on his .38 police special. Bullets flew in all directions as he sprayed the room. One caught Tommy on his non-gun arm, while another shattered the large window adjoining the glass sliding door. The remaining four cartridges were wasted, and now he needed to reload. He paused when he saw the familiar face of Patrick. It took a couple of seconds to register, which was a few too many. Patrick soon entered in an unrestrained canter. Stepping over the broken glass, he took aim at Liam and just kept squeezing the trigger until his magazine emptied. Both Liam's legs and upper torso wobbled like a life-size Gumby Bear with the impact of the potent Glock. Liam's eyes were trying to focus on the man standing in front of him. His stare was soon replaced by sheer revulsion as the lizard-like grin of Patrick ogled back at him. Patrick slapped in a second magazine, and then casually raised the 9mm to shoulder height. "You had your chance, Liam. Out with the old and in with the new, old friend. You just chose the wrong side."

He squeezed the trigger one more time and watched the side of his family friend's face disappear in a red-hot fireball of brass and copper. Liam rocketed back onto the felt surface of the pool table, arms and legs spread-eagle. His own mother would have struggled to recognise his pulverised face.

Owen was in a state of suffocating panic—shell-shocked. He stood rigid on the hardwood floor like a shop mannequin. He was witnessing what looked and smelt like a war zone. His brain was struggling to deal with the carnage unfolding only a matter of a few feet away. He decided to make a break for it and ran towards the door. Reaching the top stair, his eyes were locked on the front entrance and his only chance of survival.

Dean was at first confused by the shots coming from upstairs, then he was overcome with trembling fear. He knew enough about firearms to confirm they weren't all from a .38. Something much more powerful. He wanted to run up the stairs like a modern-day John Wayne and save the day for the good guys. *Who am I kidding?* he argued with himself. Dean remained crouched in a holding position, waiting for his mind to release its mental constraints. He detested violence in all shapes and forms. Dean's attention was drawn to the top rung of stairs. He noticed the hysterical face of a man ranting and raving while looking past him towards the slightly open front door.

"They're all dying, everyone is being murdered... blood, too much blood," Owen babbled in a state of dribbling incoherency.

Owen was oblivious to the presence of another man, even when Dean yelled at him to stop while stalking the staircase, one step at a time. Owen was freaking out. His instincts were begging for him to just get out of there any way he could. As he attempted to brush past, Dean fired his revolver as an instinctive move. Owen took two bullets to the chest and stomach. He cart-wheeled down the remainder of the stairs and landed heavily on the carpeted floor below, bleeding out while a guttural moan gurgled from his mouth.

As all hell broke loose around him, the dealer seated in the lounge knew calm would prevail. He had instinctively already grabbed his case full of cocaine, now crouching behind the sofa. His body baulked at the sound of each shot fired. Frantically, he reached into his jacket pocket and retrieved his Colt .45. His fingers fumbled for the trigger as bullets peppered the room.

Patrick was in the zone, a killing frenzy that showed no signs of relenting. He knew he had five rounds left when a head popped up from behind the couch with the wrong end of a handgun slowly coming into view. As easy as shooting ducks at the Royal Show, he casually emptied one clean shot into the top of the crouching dealer's forehead, then stood over the corpse and fired a second round into his right shoulder before picking up the case. Careful not to soil it from the pool of blood now spreading over a large portion of the pool table, he deposited it next to Liam's dead body before turning to find his next whipping boy.

Tommy's bleeding arm was becoming a burden. He walked into a small bathroom next to a bar to search for a towel. He was in the process of wrapping his arm when he heard the sound of a man sobbing. A dark shape could be seen grovelling inside the shower recess. He slid open the door, aimed his Glock and fired. He heard the sound of the firing pin against an empty chamber. Tommy released his spent mag and inserted a fresh one, then aimed and fired a single shot into the hand attempting to cover his own trembling face. A spray of red smeared the frosted glass shower screen and open swinging door, soon to be followed by a meandering trail of blood trickling its way into the drain. Fully clothed, the dealer's mouth would forever remain open in a silent scream of anguish. His final expression had a look of certitude, almost like today was his rostered-day-on only to die a merciless death. Tommy kicked the door close.

Patrick walked behind the bar to find a man in a praying position, pleading for his life while holding an aluminium briefcase with both arms close to his chest. Like firing a water pistol on a hot summer's day, Patrick emptied two clean rounds into the visible part of Brad Stevenson's manicured head of hair. He watched as the top of his skull spread like an exploding mushroom, scattering brain matter over the door of a small bar fridge.

As Patrick bent over to retrieve his second prize, Dean came scampering down the hallway and entered the last room on the right. Initially he just saw scattered bodies lying randomly on the floor. A corpse lay awkwardly on a pool table. He struggled to recognise Liam's pulverised facial features while inching closer, just in case. He couldn't see Sean, then panicked. Searching in vain, he asked, "Sean, what the fuck? Where you are? What's happening?" he screamed like a banshee, confused and terrified at the same time. His hand was shaking as tears began rolling down his petrified face.

Patrick's upper body slowly rose from his concealed position behind the bar with the briefcase gripped tightly in his left hand. Dean was initially startled and turned, struggling to comprehend the impudent face of his younger brother. At first Dean was mollified to see Patrick. Some sense could now be made from a nonsensical, macabre scene that surrounded him like a bad dream. Dean's relief soon turned into a look of unbridled delirium. He was totally floored and stumped as to why his younger brother was standing in this very room—with his arm raised and pointing. *What's that in his hand?*

"You're supposed to be in Ireland," was all he said. His eyes emptied of his life force. Inside, his heart was pining for his mother. His brain refused to comprehend the distorted image of his own shared flesh and blood—now aiming a gun directly at his head. None of this made sense. His mind was messaging him with flashes from his past—a past spent with the boy standing only feet away. Playing soccer in the back lane and learning how to crack their first safe with Uncle Sean. He recalled the treasured memories of his brothers all growing up together mimicking The Three Musketeers, all for one and one for all. His firearm fell from his drooping hand and bounced on the hardwood floor.

Dean extended both his arms in a final plea for common sense to prevail. "Patrick . . . What the fuck are you doing? I'm your bro..."

Boom! Like a full broadside, the barrel of Patrick's Glock interrupted his final plea for clemency. The 9mm slug is designed to kill up to a range of fifty metres. At just over fifty inches, the damage was unimaginable. A neat entry hole rimmed his brother's forehead. As the bullet exited the rear, his skull separated into three sundered pieces and flew off in random directions. Bone matter mixed with soft brain tissue—tainted with blood and amniotic fluids followed three points of the compass. Dean was thrust backwards like being shot out of a cannon, landing neatly on a centre cushion as part of a three-seater white lounge setting. His incapacitated body looked like he was waiting for his favourite movie to start, only spoilt by a trickle of blood filling his left ear as his head slanted slightly to that side.

Tommy was momentarily perturbed but not surprised as he looked at Patrick void of any remorse or mercy while Dean's lifeless body sat there with half the back of his head missing. *Jesus, Patrick, your own brothers . . . Scary bastard.*

Both men stood and surveyed the annihilation they had just inflicted. Satisfied with their work, Patrick told Tommy to check the contents of each case before cleaning up. Opening the first case, it was packed with plastic bags of white powder. Tommy smiled and then cheered. "Eureka baby." He was unable to conceal his excitement. He then tried to force open the locks on the second case, but they refused to move. Tommy fiddled with the two release buttons—still nothing. He asked Patrick to take a look.

"I'll be stuffed," Patrick remarked. "Someone has poured some shit into the locks." He reversed the Glock held in his hand, and with the butt-end, he bashed each lock to smithereens until the case fell open, causing its worthless contents to flutter back to the floor like a kaleidoscope of sliced newspaper butterflies. "Where's the bloody cash, Tommy?" Patrick's pea-sized brain was trying to analyse what it was he was looking at. Picking the case up from the floor, he hurled it at the wall, causing a framed picture of a scantily dressed Jayne Mansfield to fall to the floor. He started to scream in a fit of rage while kicking the worthless case around the room. "Fucking dirty rotten double-crossing pricks, where the fuck is my money?" he screamed towards Tommy.

Tommy picked up the empty case and shook it, still not believing they had somehow both been scammed.

Still visibly distraught, realising someone had swindled them, Patrick started to fire a string of questions at Tommy. "How could this have happened? Someone obviously switched the money before we got to it. Who else could it be— it had to be that surfie wanker, Wayne? I knew he couldn't be trusted, Tommy. That son of a bitch had to be responsible for this," he continued in a fit of fury, both glad *and* disappointed at the same time Wayne was now lying dead on that balcony. "Dead men tell no lies, Tommy."

"Yeah, dead men tell you sweet fuck all, and he sure as hell is dead, Patrick. At least we still have the case full of cocaine to offload, that's something."

"Yeah, something but not everything," Patrick replied, still chagrined at being duped and made to look like the fool he never contemplated he was.

"Shit, Patrick, check this out." Tommy was almost nose up against the dusty outline of where the fallen picture of the well endowed Hollywood starlet once hung.

"Tommy, we don't have time for any sight-seeing. I'm trying to think, mate."

"No, what I mean is, it looks like a miniature sensor is embedded into the wall."

"A bloody what?" Patrick sidled up to Tommy's shoulder and joined in the inquisitive squint.

"Maybe it's for an alarm or something? We need to find out where that prick has stashed the cash, Tommy. You check all the rooms up here, and I'll do the same downstairs."

A defunctive aura hung in the air. The smell of gunpowder was ubiquitous. Patrick glanced over at Dean's body slumped on the couch with a hole in his head, but he felt no guilt. Patrick reached into his front pocket and pulled out a small plastic sandwich bag. Inside was a single spent shell cartridge plus the slug he dug out from the pig's leg. He searched the room for a spot that was not too obvious but was assured to be found. "A little bombshell, Tommy, for our Italian friends. The cops won't miss this."

Tommy looked on, then suggested, "What about the pool table?"

Patrick smiled, "Sometimes Tommy you're an absolute genius. I know that Italian prick is fastidious about cleaning that bloody Beretta every week, including all his clips, so I'm hoping there's a print." He unclipped the bag and watched the shell roll down the middle pocket ball return. "At some stage, the cops will want to remove the felt, and then... bingo! But just in case, we have one final surprise." Patrick wandered over to where the body was lying behind the white sofa. The gold Rolex was tempting, but Patrick resisted the urge. He knelt down and unbuttoned the dead man's jacket and saturn shirt. With his gloved hand, he felt for the hole in the corpse's right shoulder. He knew this because he put it there for this very reason. Patrick prodded with a pair of long-nose pliers inside the wound until he felt the metal-on-metal of his own 9mm slug. He pressed hard with both fingers, then eased it back out, emptied the slug from the bag, and forced it inside the torn muscle like a carpetbag steak.

Tommy walked past the bar and exited the room while Patrick scaled the stairs, stepping over the bleeding corpse of Owen on the way. To his left looked like a dining room, and maybe some ground floor bedrooms. He went the other way towards the sound of a TV. He followed a small passageway past an open-plan kitchen. To his right was another open door. It was someone's private office.

A large oak desk with an expensive-looking executive chair faced a bay window. He switched on the light and started to empty some cupboards and filing cabinets, scattering their contents over the teak-stained floor. Then he stepped around to the business side of the desk, pulled a pencil-thin torch from his back pocket and scanned the contents of each drawer. As he rolled the chair out of the way, his torch fell to the floor and ended up under the desk, coming to rest on a large Persian rug. He knelt down to pick it up and then noticed a fresh, damp mud stain from the sole of someone's shoe.

Shining his torch, there was a second fainter stain facing a large matching wooden cabinet opposite, with frame-mounted pictures of men holding fish and some golfing photos. Patrick stepped closer while focusing on the wood panelling. He noticed another half shoe print under the cabinet. He considered the very real prospect of an inbuilt safe hidden behind. He tried moving the wall unit, but it didn't budge. A closer inspection with his flashlight showed a slight gap running vertically from the top back to the floor.

"Somehow, this whole section is designed to swing open." Patrick murmured while he stepped back and looked again at the first shoe stain. Placing his own shoes next to the same spot, he reenacted the last person's stance. "Someone stood right here in this exact spot?" Pointing the flashlight, he asked himself, "Why?"

The only other piece of furniture close by was the desk. Patrick crouched and blindly felt with his hand for anything out of the ordinary. "Oh yeah, baby—come to daddy," he rejoiced.

Pressing a cleverly concealed switch, the sound of an electronic lock opening from inside the wall was like Aladdin's cave cracking open, resulting in one whole section of the cabinet shifting to reveal a small hidden room built in to the recessed wall behind.

Patrick stepped in. The room was dark with LCD diodes blinking back at him like city lights off a rack of electronic equipment. A blue and red Puma sports bag sat on the floor. Patrick bent over and pulled the zip half-open. "You sneaky little bastard, Wayne. Thought you could rip me off. I don't think so. To the victor goes the spoils," Patrick gleaned a satisfied simper as he fanned a stack of bound banknotes with his thumb. Patrick could hear Tommy's boots coming down the stairs. "Down here in the office," he yelled over his shoulder.

Tommy shunted into the small hidden recess, "Jesus, Patrick, what are all these flashing lights?"

"Mate, don't bloody worry about that, look what I found."

Patrick held open the bag, and Tommy's eyes opened wide. He quickly counted forty neatly bundled folds of fifty-dollar notes and twenty-five of the same in twenties. "Whoa, you bloody beauty. Good job," Tommy shouted.

"Yeah, and with the cocaine, we can start to set up our own dealer network along the entire stretch of the eastern seaboard. And then we'll start up our own supply chain, Tommy. After that, it's the big time and happy days. My obstinate old mother, after hearing the news of her two dead boys, she won't be long before I convince her to retire and hand over the reins to her only surviving son—good old, Patrick O'Finlay," he celebrated.

"Come on then," Tommy said. "We've got what we came for. Let's get out of here before someone calls the cops."

They both left the closet-sized room designed for sexual pleasure and headed through a rear laundry door that led to the outdoor entertaining area. Patrick placed the points of his boots over the pool's bull-nose limestone paving and watched with a morbid fascination at the sight of Sean's floating body. "You had your time in the limelight. Progress brother—it's a bitch," Patrick voiced in a slow drawn out monotone, convincing himself the deaths of both his siblings were not only justified, but an absolute necessity for the long-term future of his family's empire-in-waiting. He asked Tommy, "How's your arm by the way?"

Tommy rotated his arm, revealing his favourite tattoo that started at the wrist and continued to the inside of his elbow. "Bloody sore. What do you reckon, I just got shot?"

Patrick grabbed Tommy's arm and laughed at the irony caused by the stray bullet. "At least now you can't see that stupid spelling error any more, Tommy. Come on, we'll swap over the cash and shit into the two duffel bags I got in the car, then dump the briefcases with both the Glock's on the way back to your house. Remember also, you're gonna have to stay out of sight for a few weeks, you understand? Might look a bit dodgy if you're seen walking around with a bloody great big bullet scrape on your arm." Both men shared the humour with a clangour of a laugh.

After the exchange was complete, Patrick placed all four cases into the back of the ute and tied down the tarp. Tommy allowed his car to just roll away down the slight incline under the constrict of just his parking lights until he found the hard bitumen. He entered the street and fired up the 308-V8 engine, then drove around the first corner before switching on the headlights. Following each street in reverse order, he found the intersection that led back to Bradleys Head Road.

"Take the next right, Tommy," Patrick ordered.

Tommy returned a quizzical stare and asked, "Why?"

"Every cop-shop in Sydney has cameras positioned at the front entrance. The one at Mosman covers the car park, but it also picks up part of Military Road. This bloody car stands out like a fucking lighthouse on wheels. Turn right," Patrick repeated. "We can take the back road to Balmoral Beach, and there we can ditch the guns plus the two aluminium cases."

Tommy stopped at the front of a harbourside restaurant. He tossed both the cases into one of two commercial bins that are emptied each morning. Patrick grabbed both Glock's and ditched them down a stormwater drain. The drive back to Tommy's house in Frenchs Forest would take over fifty-five minutes. Patrick started playing out in his head the well-rehearsed starring role he would need to play out as the only surviving son of the O'Finlay family.

Patrick had the urge for a cigarette and a shot of tequila, which would have to wait. The dashboard clock read

4:37 A.M. All that killing took less than forty minutes. It felt like hours had passed. His heart was still beating wildly. The inside of his mouth felt like he'd been chewing on a handful of stale Sao biscuits.

The Frog looked at his watch—the time read 4:07 A.M., and he'd been hard at it for almost two-and-a-half hours. The Frog pulled a hip flask of Wild Turkey from the exterior pocket of his backpack and headed for the top-storey loft to blow his last joint. He sat sideways with his feet up on a large window seat and gazed out the lead-light-glass with his thoughts consumed by the challenges he will face in trying to empty this house of all its treasures without detection. He continued blowing smoke rings at his own reflection, then stubbed out the remains of his joint on the floor, stood and yawned. A flash of light, soon followed by a second and third, like a small firecracker, appeared in quick succession from across the vacant property.

Curiosity killed the cat, and the Frog's inquisitive Gypsy mind jumped into another gear. In his line of business, opportunity knocks in the strangest ways. He negotiated the small staircase back to the floor below, pulled clear a dust cover and wrapped his tools inside, then stashed them in a safe place. The Frog unbuckled the two fasteners on his backpack and slid in the vintage mahogany wooden presentation case holding the Colt, the leather satchel plus the pocket watch, and then prepared to leave the same way he came. He dropped to the ground and pushed his way through the dense growth. A bougainvillaea bush was all that separated him and a bird's-eye view of what was happening on the other side of the six-foot-high rear wall. Its prickly thorns ran havoc over the exposed parts of his hands and face as he brushed over the top. The Frog covered the distance between the two properties and found a part of the fence shadowed by some loose scrub. He noticed a cut-down tree trunk and pulled himself up to a position that offered an unencumbered view over an outside pool and directly into an upstairs room. The Frog was transfixed at what he was witnessing.

He felt his inner-self tremble. A sickening feeling consumed his entire body, and the urge to throw-up was something he could ill-afford. Shots were being fired. Bodies were falling—slaughtered in plain sight. "What the fuck?" he whispered under his breath. The dark silhouette from a floating body bobbed up and down against the suction of the skimmer box, and still more gunfire filled the room. He was close enough to hear the silenced thud with each yellow muzzle flash. He wanted to get as far away from this place but was too scared to move in case he exposed himself.

He slipped back down below the fence line and crouched with his back pressed hard against the bricks. The Frog was about to make a mad dash across the open block when the voices of two men put an end to that idea. He heard footsteps approaching his position and crawled into the natural cover of the waist-high branches and leaves on offer. First one man, then two cases, followed by his accomplice, all came flying over the wall. Two car doors closed, and the park lights came on. The Frog stayed perfectly still while silently spelling out the personalised number plate TURBO T. The car rolled away down the slight incline, then the unmistakable sound of a V8 engine firing up broke the early morning silence as it shifted through each gear.

It was now or never—the quick or the dead, and he could be very quick. The urge to take a look was overpowering. The Frog allowed his backpack to fall to the ground and scaled the fence. He eased his way up a set of spiral stairs. That's when he got his first close-up of the body floating face down in the pool below. The smell of potassium nitrate, charcoal, and sulphur hung in the still night air. He stepped around shards of broken glass and counted three bodies in plain sight. An arm lay exposed from behind a sofa. All Gassan could see was a gold Rolex waiting for a new owner. It was a classic risk versus reward situation, and it was time to collect. He bent down and unclasped the band, then slid it over the limp hand.

The sound of a downstairs door banging against its strike plate prompted him to head back downstairs. The Frog couldn't help himself and pushed the swinging door open. The first room to his left was an office with the overhead light revealing loose papers, some files and books strewn about the floor. A wooden wall unit had somehow been shifted from its normal stationary position. He stepped in closer and soon realised it was specifically designed to conceal a small built-in cubby space. The Frog poked his head inside, thinking there has to be something worth stealing in here or why would someone bother going to all that trouble? He risked turning on his flashlight. "Hello, hello. What do we have here, then?"

The blinking lights were like neon dollar signs when the sudden sound of the phone ringing caused Gassan to tighten his arse cheeks. "Bloody hell," he half-shouted. The sound of multiple car doors closing through the slightly open front door told him he needed to move fast.

Four high-class hookers stepped out of a people carrier designed to carry seven. The minder slid out from behind the wheel and walked towards the front door.

The Frog quickly identified a surge protector. The word *record* blinked from a button on the front of another electronic component he had never seen before. *This looks like some type of recording device?* He reached over and started pulling power plugs from their wall sockets. The flashing word *record* went blank. He wrapped the loose cords around a couple of times and tucked the unit under one arm. The chime of a doorbell could be heard as he fast-tracked it back out the rear door, scaled the fence, picked up his pack and got the hell out of there in double-quick time sprinting towards his parked Goggomobil.

He retraced his route back down Military Road where two marked cop cars were pulling out from the Mosman

Police Station car park with lights flashing and sirens blaring. "I bet they're not going for Pizza," the Frog joked.

Chapter-14

SENIOR SERGEANT Detective Brian O'Sullivan was not the first to enter the house that still reeked of death and human faeces with an almost visible pungent aura that hung foul in the air. The confronting scenes of multiple deaths reminded him of the first major crime scene he attended as a detective. The Milperra Father's Day bikie war between both the Comancheros and the Bandidos in September 1984 racked up seven victims. He completed a walk-through of the entire upstairs area, struggling to come to grips with the reasons why Dean O'Finlay and two of the family's known accomplices were now all sprawled about the room showing the bloody proof of an exchange of gunfire.

He recognised Kojak slumped to the floor. O'Sullivan crouched down next to the body. One uniformed officer was stationed at the door, the second looked like he was about to heave his breakfast all over the crime scene. O'Sullivan peeled open the fingers on Kojak's left hand and removed a police badge. He slid it into his jacket pocket while asking himself. *Where the fuck is, Sean?*

He silently considered the phone call to Big Ma, something he was not looking forward to. A swarm of uniformed police were still in the throes of setting up a perimeter while forensics prepared to methodically document the entire house—inside and out. Tomorrow's headlines would later describe the massacre in their normal hype and over-exaggerated versions of the truth:

SYDNEY GANGLAND MASSACRE

NINE DEAD: POLICE HAVE NO CLUES

LOCK UP YOUR CHILDREN

ARE THE STREETS OF SYDNEY SAFE?

The tight snap in the voice of Probationary Constable Nigel Andrews from outside meant only one thing. The first-year detective yelled towards the upstairs room "Sarge, we got another one down here in the pool, you better come and take a look."

Detective O'Sullivan was careful not to disturb the shattered glass as he stepped onto the balcony and cast a view at the discoloured water surrounding a floating body. With the aid of the forensic unit, the constable helped drag the corpse clear and laid it down, face-up.

O'Sullivan hushed the words under his breath, "Well, that answers that question. What the hell happened here tonight?" He regained some composure, then yelled out another order. "Check the remaining rooms downstairs for any more surprises. Oh, and Andrews, find me a phone that works."

Constable Andrews reentered the house through the rear door, and the first room to his left was the office. He stepped over some scattered files and loose papers to a large L-shaped desk and picked up the phone to check for a dial tone. Andrews heard the sound of shoes descending the stairs from the end of the hallway. "Sarge," he yelled over his shoulder, "the phone in here is good to go."

"Fine, give me the room, Constable, and then go and see if the Coroner has arrived." Senior Sergeant Brian O'Sullivan watched as Andrews left the room. He raced outside to get a closer look at Sean's body when he noticed the second badge lying on the bottom of the pool. *Shit.* O'Sullivan turned to face a second uniformed officer setting up some stripping around the pool area. He yelled over to where he was free wheeling the yellow and black roll of tape, "Go out the front and let me know if any media have turned up yet then report straight back to me."

"Yes, sir."

O'Sullivan needed to work fast. He found a long-handled scoop net and dragged it along the bottom of the pool towards the bottom three steps. Dropping the net, he knelt down on all fours and pocketed the second badge. O'Sullivan walked back inside and closed the office door, then dialled a number he knew from memory while trying to prepare himself for the expected wrath from Big Ma.

Ma O'Finlay's family home was no different from the many other similar properties that were typical of Sydney's inner suburbs. She shunned the trappings of wealth, always remembering her poor upbringing in poverty-stricken Ireland, and wanted the same level headiness to trickle down to all her children. A mixture of semi-detached and free-standing double brick and tile houses were all fronted by a small grassed verge with deciduous trees lining the streets, smack bang in the middle of suburban Crows Nest.

Rear lane-ways intersected most of the housing in this typical Sydney suburb, giving a private access point without the complications of nosey neighbours sniffing around. You could roll a Sherman Tank through Ma's solid steel back gate, and nobody would be the wiser. To a casual passer-by, the only notable difference was that three houses in a row were all hidden behind eight-foot-high brick walls with huge wrought-iron gates protecting the entrance to each driveway. They were all occupied by members of the O'Finlay clan, less the two that now lay dead in Clifton Gardens.

The sound of the phone ringing in the kitchen woke Ma from a restless sleep. She looked at the time on her bedside clock. It read 6:15 A.M. She shuffled her massive body to the wall-mounted phone, all the while fuming at the early interruption.

Ma listened to the familiar voice of the family-friendly and well-compensated Detective Brian O'Sullivan. She started to tremble in an uncontrollable quiver. Her face became ashen as her obese 120kg chassis slid slowly to the floor. She felt numb, begging and praying she would wake up any second still in the comfort of her own bed. It wasn't to be. She let out a wretched cry. The rising shrill of a mother's scream echoed through the empty house.

It wasn't until she remembered her youngest son was safe in Ireland that she could break the vice-like grasp from the depths of her despair. She then allowed the phone to drop from her open hand. "Sweet mother of God, thank The Lord you are still alive, Patrick," she cried through a mother's broken heart.

Within minutes of receiving that call from Detective O'Sullivan, Ma's house was soon fast-filling with the extended members of the O'Finlay family. Ma wanted answers. She was directing her uncontrollable anger at no one person in particular, but the reality was she wanted all and sundry to know she was deadly serious.

"I need to know what the hell happened inside that house earlier this morning? Who were the shooters? I want to ID all the dead, and who, if anyone, is still alive?"

Pointing her finger at Davey, she let fly with a fire breathing rage in a manner suggesting she was about to rip someone's head off, "Ring our other police contacts and tell them Ma O'Finlay needs to know *right now*. I want names."

She then turned to face two other second-tier family members, trembling in fear they listened to each word launched from Ma's raging mouth as if their own lives depended on it. "Wes, you and Shane drive to the address in Clifton Gardens. I want you to go and sniff around. Find out any information you can. Go, *go now*," she yelled.

Ma ordered another Irish member of her household to pick up the phone, still lying on the floor. "Connor, ring this number." As the young man dialled the international code for Ireland, he handed the phone to Ma. The phone rang three times, then picked up.

"Terry, is that you?" Ma snapped.

"Yeah, is that you, Ma?"

"Terry, listen carefully, I need to talk with, Patrick. Something unimaginable has happened, and I need Patrick back here in Sydney urgently. Is he there with you?"

Terry paused for a few seconds before answering. "Ma, he's down the boozer," he lied. "Do you want me to get him?" Terri was cringing as he waited for an answer.

"Terry, you tell him now to book the next plane back to Australia, you got that?"

"Sure, Ma, I'll go now." He thought he better ask. "Is everything okay? What happened?"

"Just do as I say *now*, Terry," Ma screamed before slamming down the phone so hard it cracked the outer casing.

Terry slowly and methodically cradled his handset. "Shit might happen to some people, but not to me," he promised. He wasn't prepared to take a bullet for his idiot of a second cousin. He went to the fridge and pulled out another cold beer before returning to make a collect call to Australia.

Bloody hell, Patrick, this better not blow up in my face you little shit.

Terry was already regretting being coerced into helping out his distant relation on the other side of the world. He dialled the number in Sydney.

Patrick took the phone from Tommy's outstretched hand and listened to Terry explain his mother's recent call to Ireland. "Calm the fuck down, Terry," Patrick replied. "It's all under control, okay. Don't worry, I will sort it all out."

Walking back to his lounge chair, Terry had deep reservations about Patrick's ability to sort his own washing, let alone his enraged mother. They were both walking on eggshells now.

Chapter·15

THE CRUMPERNICKEL 684 turned out to be a two-storey pool hall on George St in the middle of the city with every latest and greatest coin-operated gaming machine ever invented occupying the entire ground floor. The upstairs mezzanine area was restricted to 'men only' of legal drinking age because of a Special Facility Liquor License allowing BYO grog with a small corkage fee attached. There was a wall of Alley machines that fell into the category of legalised gambling with the ability to cash in your credits. There were also four full-size snooker tables, each partitioned into its own private gaming room with bar facilities available for hire, payable by the hour.

Kelly soon found out JC was short for Jesus Christ. Almost like a reincarnation, he was a dead ringer with his long straight thinning hair, and a wispy, slightly greying beard. His office was also on the upper floor with a small self-contained unit you needed to access through a locked private entry.

The blood-red marble was a private joke between JC and Emmanuel, but it opened a door which Kelly ran through with both eyes firmly closed. Ignorance was bliss, and a job is a job. His working day started at seven P.M. each night until JC said it was time to knock off, usually between five and six A.M. the following morning in time to catch up for another workout with Emmanuel. Kelly kept his nose clean and avoided any trouble with the regular clientèle that definitely did *not* include any of Sydney's upper class. Soon he gained the man's trust, and JC started to groom him for something bigger with better financial rewards, delivering packages all over Sydney on his bike. A man didn't need to be a rocket scientist to guess what was inside. Kelly never asked and was never told.

This was his formal introduction to the seedy world of recreational drugs. Everybody was smoking dope. You could buy a pound of marijuana anywhere between three and four hundred dollars. A weighted ounce sold for fifty dollars, sixteen ounces to the pound. A brick of one hundred Thai Buddha sticks cost six to eight dollars each and sold for between twelve to fifteen bucks a pop. A single house-brick-size block of hashes could reap over a thousand dollars in profit alone, and thanks to some clever university chemistry students, acid or LSD, the new kid on the block, and everybody was into it. Drop a trip costing less than a few pints of beer then enjoy your mental pillage into the rarely opened parts of your brain on a private technicolour tour jam-packed with its own individual private coloured hallucinations.

It was the time after Woodstock, flower-power and free love. The sexual revolution. Icons like Janis Joplin and Jimi Hendrix had set the tone for an alternative lifestyle, Led Zeppelin and the Stones were in full swing. ACDC was setting the world stages on fire, and Queen, with Freddy Mercury, were showcasing their unique musical talents. It was a great time to be young and alive.

They say all good things come to an end, and this all came to a very abrupt end late one afternoon in an underground Sydney car park less than a kilometre from the Crumpernickel 684.

Apart from the many patched bike gangs in Sydney, there were also the skinheads and the sharpies. Between all these different groups of social misfits and sometimes maniacal driven people, they all fought for the same thing; money and control of Sydney's illicit drug trade. The Crumpernickel was well patronised by the sharpies, easily identified by their short-cropped hair on top with a long oily mane hanging down past shoulder length.

Tensions among these three groups had been building for some months, with the odd skirmish flaring on different occasions. Basically, they all hated each other's guts, and at some stage, there was going to be a moment of truth, a show of strength, with a clear winner at the end. The day it all came to a head was a Saturday afternoon, the time and the place were agreed upon by all the riff-raff involved. That evening will be forever firmly imprinted into the mind of an eighteen-year-old teenager from the Snowy Mountains.

JC closed up shop at around 5:00 P.M. that afternoon. He wasn't party to what was about to transpire, but he wanted to safeguard his business interests. JC and Kelly left through the rear fire escape door with JC's trusty Winchester lever-action rifle by his side. At first, JC insisted that the young Kelly stay behind, but there was no way he was going to miss out on what was about to go down only a hop, skip, and a jump away. The two men both took up a position on level-one of an underground city car park located at the cnr of Pitt and Goulburn Streets. Looking down, there were no parked vehicles to be seen anywhere on the lower ground floor. An educated guess would put the number of people already gathered at well over one hundred.

The numbers were swelling with each group already beginning to set up a forward guard in three separate locations, all brandishing their own individual personal weapons of choice. Some had chains and baseball bats, there were knives and swords of all shapes and varying sizes. Knuckle dusters were a popular choice. Woman-folk were scattered amongst the growing masses—at the ready to back their man as the hostilities heightened and the battle lines were established. There were no firearms—not visible, anyway. This was to be a street brawl, not a killing spree. The tension in that basement was palpable, propagating as the verbal exchanges intensified. The warring assemblage was ready to engage. Someone had to make the first move, and it was God's Garbage who stepped up to the plate.

They established a semi-circle and started forging ahead, person to person, side by side, chains circling above their heads like the rotating blades of a helicopter with baseball bats and machetes held out in front. Their women following at the ready, a safe distance behind—for now. The sharpies and skinheads were sizing each other up, but this was a fight between three gangs. The skinheads made the next move. They broke stride as one, both men and woman together, running into the line of patched bikies. The sharpies followed soon after, cracking the heads of a few skinheads on the way. All three groups met as one in the middle of the subterranean make-shift field of battle. The main event was about to take centre stage.

This was a monumental gathering of hundreds of street-hardened maniacal gang members. Sydney was about to put on a spectacle, an inaugural one-night-show with no encores. It was survival of the fittest with each tribe's future at stake. There would be no post-battle negotiations. The last man or woman standing would walk away with the ultimate prize: money and power.

From their first-level vantage point, JC and Kelly had an unrestricted view of the whole bloodbath. Neither of them had ever witnessed anything resembling this level of violence before and probably never would again.

Kelly's body started to tremble. A bead of perspiration formed on his pate. The fear he felt was for the vanquished below. But like watching that impending train wreck as it derailed, he couldn't peel his eyes away from the devastating spectacle taking place here on this otherwise quiet Saturday afternoon.

The average man in the street wasn't meant to witness scenes like this. This was all too real, not some make-believe movie set. The sound of sharpened steel and human flesh coming together with chilling accuracy was almost nightmarish as body parts were being sliced open with every blow. Bones and internal organs became exposed for all to see. People were screaming and howling—some for motivation—some as they lay bleeding out on the cement floor. There was nowhere to hide on this day, everybody and everything was fair game. Bodies were dropping like flies in a Mortein factory, only to be bashed some more by the trailing woman. They were to be the final solution, cleaning up the dregs as the line of combatants moved forward. They were merciless, callous and unrelenting.

It was hard to make out who was who; everyone was wearing leathers. Kelly could see the bald heads of the skinheads, but as volumes of blood spilt indiscriminately, it all blended into one great bloody mass. Suddenly a lone soldier with a bow and arrow emerged from the butchery. What was he thinking? Hi—I'm William Tell, did anyone bring an apple? This was close-quarters combat in its murderous finale.

Not everyone will survive this day—it was a no-brainer, Kelly needed little convincing. There would be casualties, and some of them fatal. He knew there would be no cops involved—just not yet. They would have realised, or at the very least, have been tipped off by a snitch or an informer. As far as the boys in blue were concerned, 'box on you bastards'. They would eventually be tasked with the gruesome job of cleaning up the bloody carnage only after the undaunted had all fallen.

The orchestrated massacre continued unabated. The numbers were dwindling, but this was a long way from over. Mutilated bodies were interspersed around the car park floor. Some were being helped, but that meant being exposed and possibly ending your day—maybe even your life. People were slipping over in the pools of blood and guts. It looked like God's Garbage were gaining the upper hand.

Kelly stood behind a waist-high steel railing. JC was to his immediate left with the Winchester firmly in his grasp. Out of sight, but at the ready. Both men were fixated on the scenes playing out directly in front at ground zero. It was like being treated to a private box at Her Majesty's Theatre, which was only a short stroll away.

A dark shape stepped out from the shadow of a support pillar directly behind JC and Kelly's position. Both men were oblivious to this new arrival, and why wouldn't they be? Kelly heard a muffled *thud*. JC flinched, causing the Winchester to fall from his grasp with a clanging sound as it bounced on the cement. Kelly's first reaction was to turn towards the source. He caught the bright muzzle flash of another silent shot, then felt a stinging feeling in his right upper leg. He baulked while shifting his open palm to the spot on his leg, only to feel the warmth of his own blood. A second man stepped out from behind a parked SUV with a pump-action shotgun held horizontally, and out in front with just one hand. The reflection of an overhead fluorescent light highlighted a face full of freckles. Kelly instantly recognised the grin.

JC bent down to grab his rifle, Patrick O'Finlay placed the barrel of his shotgun on the side of his neck and gestured with his free hand for JC to stand erect. Tommy moved from his left-side position and cracked his handgun over the back of Kelly's head. Kelly buckled to one knee and fought off the body's desire to just close up shop. He tried to control his breathing while slowly easing himself on to his one good leg.

Patrick grabbed JC by the neck and pushed him forward to the edge of the railing. He balanced the barrel of his shotgun over JC's left shoulder, angled it down, then found his target.

A thundering *boom* echoed throughout the vast expanse of the underground car park. Kelly's body recoiled to what sounded like a clap of thunder not more than three feet away. His eardrums were screaming with a piercing high-pitched ring. The second blast exploded as it too resonated through the entire basement area. The sound of the pump-action was all the warning Kelly needed to shift to his right. Neither Patrick nor Tommy noticed.

Kelly silently repeated the words Emmanuel had hammered into his head each and every training session. *He who hesitates loses.* Kelly seized the moment.

He grabbed the railing with both hands, allowed his weight to transfer to his arms, then sprang up from his haunches while swinging his good leg in a sweeping action. Tommy's two legs left the ground, and the sound of a limp body hitting the hard surface soon followed. Patrick was in the throes of firing a third round. He whipped around, then head-butted JC on the bridge of his nose. Blood started pissing out all over the front of his shirt. Kelly propped then let fly with the best right-hand haymaker he could summon towards Patrick's smirking face. He felt his nose cartilage explode under the force of a tightly clenched fist. Kelly wanted more, but that opportunity was cruelly ripped away as Tommy's flexing truncheon dug deep into his kidneys. A tidal wave of pain engulfed him in that instant, and again, he fell to all fours, struggling to breathe. With his head bowed down, both his eyes were watering as he fought the urge to blow his lunch.

Patrick handed his shotgun to Tommy as he bent down and grabbed a handful of Kelly's blond hair, then lifted him back up to an upright position. In a terse whisper, he lent into Kelly's right ear. "If I didn't need two dump-fucks like you to take the fall for getting rid of another rival, you'd be both dead right now. Until next time, and rest assured—there will be a next time, Lucky Phil. You didn't think I would remember, did you? Running through the school grounds in just your whity-tighty's." Patrick laughed while so close to Kelly's face, he could almost taste his foul breath.

"Come on, Patrick, we need to get the fuck out of here, and now," Tommy hissed through clenched teeth. Patrick kneed Kelly in the balls, then let him drop to the ground. The sound of tyres turning on the smooth concrete surface was the last sound Kelly heard. He popped his head over the railing, and about a hundred sets of eyes were scouring the upper floor for the shooter. Kelly could see three bodies bleeding out below with women hovering about while screaming and wailing. That's when he noticed the Grim Reaper tattoo. The shrinking crowd started to round up their wounded and split the scene like an army of retreating ants. Kelly could see a group of patched God's Garbage members heading for the stairwell which thankfully was on the opposite side of the car park. He looked over at JC, who was starting to reenter this century. Kelly was fighting fit. He lifted JC and wrapped his arm around under shoulder. "Hang on tight, old man, we need to split—and right now," Kelly let him know in a voice laced with the desperation of the moment.

"Wait," JC struggled while wiping clean the blood trail flowing from his nose. "I need the Winchester." Kelly bent both knees. JC extended his wounded arm, grabbed the stock with his bloodied hand, and he and Kelly hobbled back to the stairwell door. It was time for a quick exit and get the hell out of Dodge.

They made their way back to the Crumpernickel 684 through the same rear fire exit. JC screamed at Kelly to head upstairs. He didn't need to be told a second time and made his way to the office, then slammed the door shut. There was an underlying sense of terror in JC's voice he had never witnessed before. This man was usually a very relaxed and laid back dude, but right now he was horror-struck and for a very good reason.

JC then took up a position at the front of the Crumpernickel's main street-front window facing George Street. The double door entrance was to his right and still locked. He placed his Winchester against the wall, out of sight but loaded with the safety off. The shopping public could be seen casually walking the sidewalks, oblivious to the events that had just taken place less than two hundred metres away.

A group of sharpies were the first to arrive and gathered outside shortly after. The wounded and bleeding were being helped by their comrades. They were searching out a safe haven. You can't just start walking the streets of Sydney displaying the aftermath of a gang war. A few gathering crowd were howling—men included. Others were screaming out instructions on how best to deal with the wounded. Their leader was remonstrating with JC to open the door through the glassed window front. Vehicles were slowing down along George Street while mums and dads were amassing on the footpath and began to stare in a warped, paralysed intrigue.

JC grabbed the Winchester and aimed it at the self-appointed chieftain, telling him politely to, "Fuck off, this place is closed." The embattled sharpies began to swell, like an angry lynch mob. They started hammering away at the window with their bare fists. From a rear position, a steel council garbage bin came crashing through the plate-glass shop front. The window exploded, covering JC with shards of broken glass. He fired a shot into the air, and then made his way up the stairs as best he could—two at a time, and almost ripped the door off its hinges as he made his hastened entry. Kelly finished tying off a piece of ripped bath towel around his bleeding leg then he stood firm in a state of dismay, all the while wondering what to do next.

The rampaging sounds of the hordes of desperate people barging through the broken window consumed the gaming floor below. JC dragged Kelly into the office and kicked shut the door. "That won't hold them for long. Here, give us a hand with this," he asked the only other man in the room. Together they managed to topple a tall cupboard. It fell to the floor, revealing an old unused window hidden behind. Forcing it open, JC then literally lifted Kelly's body and threw him headfirst into the small crawl space. Head to tail - one at a time, they both slow-poked their way down a short passageway on all fours. There was a half-size loft door at the end. On the other side was the roof of the adjoining building with a set of steel spiralling fire stairs, which they negotiated at a frenetic pace under the circumstances, and both made their way back to street level with JC on Kelly's six. He stopped and waited. JC placed a hand in his pocket and pulled out a wad of folded fifty-dollar notes, then pushed it firmly into Kelly's open palm. He pointed at the bullet hole in his jeans. "You need to get that taken care of, but not at any hospital. Do you have someone?" Kelly looked down at his bleeding leg and nodded. "All right, then. Make your way to where your bike is stashed and never come back here again. Don't run—just walk."

Kelly tried to fabricate a casual mindset, while he glanced back over his shoulder, only to see JC dispose of the Winchester into a large food scraps bin, and head off around the corner in the opposite direction. That was the last time Kelly would ever lay eyes on JC again.

Kelly walked towards Town Hall. His wounded leg felt almost numb except for the shaking while still in a fretful state of bewilderment at what he had just witnessed, struggling to digest all that he'd seen. And now the scowls of hundreds of lunatics hell-bent on exacting revenge was firmly entrenched in his memory. "They recognised my face," he tried to pacify himself. "They know who I am—shit!"

Kelly crossed George Street and headed past the street-level subway entrance to Town Hall Station, imitating a man who may have had one too many at the nearest pub. He turned the next corner, and the crowds of foot traffic thinned out considerably. For an ounce of dope each month, he stored his Kawasaki in a single lockable garage not far from Town Hall. He unlocked the door and left the key inside, rolled his bike out, pulled down the roller-door, and headed to a place in Manly called the Purple Door.

Chapter-16

THE DECADE of overindulgence, where greed was good, and money fell from every tree. The late '80s was a time for many to relive the teenage memories of the '60s and '70s, but now with the added advantage of being cashed up to the eyeballs. The stigma of a drug addict slipping down a dark alley and sharing a joint with a bunch of unemployed deadheads and no-hopers had been replaced with a new emerging market—the young executive. The '80s produced a new wave of players. Up and comers in the corporate world. They worked smart, played hard, made bucket loads of cash and loved to party all night long.

Defined by their labelled wardrobes, expensive cars and the three-hour tax deductible lunches, the long hours and the late nights of wining and dining were difficult to sustain and even harder to conceal. Enter the world of heroin, speed, cocaine and the much cheaper crack cocaine. That little piece of rock candy to take the edge off the pressures of a lifestyle that was an era of sexual enlightenment, where anything and everything was not only acceptable but expected, and could separate a person from the hippie, pot smoking street slum. Give me a bourbon & coke, with the coke on the side, please. Let's party, baby!

The corporate boardrooms were awash with lines of white powder. It was cool, almost a prerequisite to being accepted as being part of the 'in-crowd' to indulge yourself in the torrent of recreational drugs sweeping through the population like an incoming tsunami.

Patrick O'Finlay knew from his Irish ancestors the inherent problems with farming the land, and that's what basically he had become. Since the timely deaths of his two older brothers, his first hands-on experiences upon entering the world of a drug dealer was like a university education. The first semester started with him purchasing pounds of marijuana, Thai Buddha sticks and bricks of hashes to repackage and sell at street level. That soon changed when he ventured out and leased some small farming land bordering the Namoi River twenty kilometres out from a small town called Narrabri in northwest N.S.W., where he planted open fields of his own crops. But, no different to any other farmer, this was inherent with the problems of needing to set up intricate reticulation systems, warding off natural and human predators, and playing the game of kicking the political football.

With a State election due, the incumbent premier of N.S.W needed a platform for reelection. The media had whipped the voters into a frenzy, and were now demanding to see some results in curbing the rising scourge of drugs infiltrating into the community, affecting children and teenagers, eroding away the very essence of what some headlines would quote as the: 'BREAKDOWN OF THE FAMILY NUCLEUS'. Nothing short of some affirmative action would quell the publics' thirst for results. The N.S.W State cops were instructed by the premier to deliver him a bust to bolster the sagging polls, but the Federal Police were not on the O'Finlay payroll. A tug of war between the competing federal and state forces ended with the N.S.W Police receiving a tip-off from their federal counterparts, resulting in over fifty acres of privately owned land becoming front-page news with the largest haul of illegal contraband in Australia's history presenting the ideal photo opportunities. The election was in the bag, and Patrick was now out-of-pocket over $200,000 in expenses, which would equate to a street value of over $1.2 million.

Patrick took the loss in his stride, knowing he was a pawn in a business model that played by a different set of rules. There was no respite available, and it was time to move on to bigger and better opportunities. He was on a steep learning curve, a camber with a single outcome in mind.

His newly acquired empire was now firmly entrenched in the rapid growth of recreational drugs that didn't require any farming skills, was easily managed, and the profits were tenfold. In his search for new markets to peddle his poison, he needed to continually seek out new suppliers to satisfy his growing list of dealers. While his old-fashioned mother refused to deviate from her old ways, Patrick was going full steam ahead. He had set up a network of drug mules throughout the eastern seaboard of Queensland, N.S.W. and Victoria, with a common distribution point in his hometown of Sydney. He was now in a position to shift double the kilos of juice, subject to a supplier being able to guarantee a constant cache. That guarantee was to be provided by his own well-thought-out initiatives. Cutting out the middleman and going straight to the source was a masterly stroke, but it had taken time to procure a trusting relationship with his overseas contacts.

Ma O'Finlay sat in solitude at her kitchen table, still a shattered woman in mourning. In her hand, she held two framed photos of Sean Jnr and Dean that only a few short months ago sat atop their coffins during the heart-wrenching funeral service. Tears flowed down the side of her cheeks on a face that was struggling to conceal the strain of her inner torment. She studied the faces of her two dead sons, lost in her own private world of despair and disbelief at the indiscriminate cold-hearted executions of her two boys, despite that, she was none the wiser who would have the gall with the most to gain in pulling off a double-cross of this magnitude. She hid behind the facade of a crime boss in total control of the family business. The reality was something entirely different.

Her two sons had been buried in a private ceremony, attended by the immediate family and one selected member of the other prominent Sydney-based criminal families. There were protocols to follow. Unwritten rules needed to be adhered to at all times amongst the underworld fraternity. As the matriarch of the O'Finlay family, and with Sean Jnr now permanently removed as the next head of the business empire, Ma had been around long enough to understand that this time of transition represented a period of uncertainty. The family business was vulnerable to an aggressive takeover from the other competing rabble, who, once the dust settled on the graves of her dead boys, they would stop at nothing to add Sydney's North Shore to their own expanding interests.

Ma considered the blind luck that had intervened with her one remaining offspring being spared his life. The mere thought that Patrick may have also fallen victim on that godforsaken night of bloodshed and murder sent a chill down the curve of her ageing spine. She harboured deep concerns about her last surviving son and his inability to deal with the responsibilities that would be thrust upon him when the time eventually arrived to take the bull by the horns. His involvement will now need to be fast-tracked, and that was a never-ending dilemma.

The sound of the rear gate opening prompted Ma to clear the trail of tears from her bloodshot eyes. She lifted her large frame from the comfort of her chair and lumbered her way over to put the kettle on. Detective O'Sullivan was escorted inside the house to conduct his fortnightly update on the police findings thus far. He gave Ma a respectful embrace. Both he and a young Margaret O'Finlay had shared the same rear lane-way as kids growing up in Blanchardstown, not far from the city of Dublin.

"Tough times, Ma," O'Sullivan offered. "How you coping?"

"How do you think I'm coping, Brian? We both feel the burden of grief when loved ones are lost. Shit, Sean looked up to you like an older brother back home during those early years. What have you got for me that has you so wound up and couldn't be discussed over the phone?"

Detective O'Sullivan turned and cringed at the sight of Patrick arriving through the front door with his lapdog friend Tommy obediently following close behind.

"I asked for Patrick to meet us here. I want him to hear what you have to say," Ma explained.

"Good morning, Ma." Patrick cast a suspicious eye over their unwelcome guest. "Detective, what do we owe the pleasure of your company today?" His condescending tone was meant to be obvious. Once a cop - always a cop.

O'Sullivan returned a curt nod, "Patrick." Tommy's presence didn't rate a mention.

Patrick leant in and offered his mother an awkward embrace. "You feeling better today, you look tired, Ma? You should consider taking it easy for a while. Tommy and I can take care of things in the meantime—no dramas, hey Tommy."

"I'll take some time off, Patrick, when you grow up." Ma knew her son was putting the screws on her to relinquish some day-to-day control. *Not yet, my boy.*

Tommy remained quiet and sat down at the opposite end of the table with his long-sleeved shirt buttoned to the wrists, while Patrick helped himself to a couple of beers from a bar fridge on the back landing.

Detective O'Sullivan placed on the table a captured still photo printed on A4 paper. Ma walked over and looked closely at the scratchy image. "What's this?" She was leaning over with her glasses balancing on the tip of her nose, still straining to make out the shadowy image of a body lying face down in what looked like a local tip. She stood erect, "I don't understand, who is that supposed to be?"

Patrick returned and flipped the tops of both beers, then passed one over to Tommy. He picked up the photo image. "Who's the unlucky stiff?"

"As I was about to explain to your mother, at first, forensics didn't connect the dots, that was until this turned up." O'Sullivan floated a second photo onto the table, showing a magnified shell casing. "The John Doe you see in this photo turned up three months ago with a single bullet hole to the head, and another in the heart. All his fingerprints had been burnt off with hydrochloric acid. No ID, and no leads, but we did retrieve both bullets. We ran those through the federal database, but no match—that was until now. You remember that bungled raid at the Venus Room?" O'Sullivan allowed the question to linger while observing Patrick's body language.

Ma glanced over at Patrick. Tommy took a long swig from his stubby, then looked up at Patrick. He offered a quick wink with a straight face.

"Yes, go on," Ma replied, her curiosity sparked.

"Well, the local cops who attended the triple zero call had no idea who was inside playing cards at the time of the assault. The game was wrapped up, and the five Italians prepared to leave. As Vincenzo Costa was handed his Beretta by one of his own henchmen, a uniformed cop, fresh out of the academy, insisted each man provide evidence of a current permit. By law, any firearms licence must accompany the weapon at all times. I mean, who carries a bloody permit with them? Anyway, they temporarily seized all five weapons until each person could provide a valid State permit at the Kings Cross Station House within seven days. The detectives from the Major Crimes Squad heard of the windfall and turned up with some paperwork signed by a judge allowing forensics to fire off a sample round from each weapon and run each one through all the cold case files. The slug we pulled from one of the corpses at Clifton Gardens matches his gun."

"Matches whose gun—which one of the five?" Ma yelled.

"Vincenzo Costa, the firstborn son, and heir to the position as head of the family. It was a perfect match for his pearl-handled Beretta. The jury is still out as to whether we can use it in court, fruit from the poisonous tree and all that legal bullshit. But now we know he, or at least his Beretta, was there on the night Sean and Dean were murdered, Ma."

"Are you sure about all this, Brian? What I mean is, did you get this information directly or through another source?"

"This comes straight from the forensics unit in the city. There is no mistaking the match. It's his own gun," O'Sullivan stressed. "But there's more, Ma."

Patrick glanced over at Tommy. He was commending himself on his own genius. He wanted Tommy to silently acknowledge the same.

"Spit it out, Brian. What else?" Ma demanded. Her rage was building as she contemplated her response.

"What you need to understand Ma is this case fell into the lap of the newly formed MCS."

Ma's expression was self-explanatory. "The bloody who?"

"The Major Crime Squad," O'Sullivan explained. "They work alone and definitely do not share information or evidence unless it's for the sole purpose of moving the investigation forward. It was never made public, but forensics uncovered three wireless cameras at the crime scene in Clifton Gardens, installed in the upstairs room on two separate walls, and one in the ceiling. They turned the house upside down, looking for the matching components, but nothing ever turned up. When the Peterson family returned home from Europe, it wasn't until after the funeral service of their son Owen that the husband, after taking legal advice from their family lawyer, decided to share his knowledge of the secret room with the MCS."

"Secret room... what secret room? Why am I only hearing about this now? What am I paying you to do, just sit on your lazy arse and wait to see what unfolds?" Ma was spitting nails.

"Above my pay grade, Ma. The husband apparently liked to record his own sexual conquests, and not with his wife, in a room built into his downstairs office. Both parties agreed to keep his wife in the dark on the proviso they could have access to the recording equipment. I mean, the Major Crimes boys were doing somersaults thinking they might crack this case wide open. The room contained a floor safe. Accompanied by his family lawyer and two detectives, he opened the safe to find the contents were untouched. But... the recording device he'd previously purchased from America . . . Well, that was missing."

Patrick looked like he'd just been gut-punched in the solar plexus. "Recording device? he struggled to get out. "What fucking recording device?"

Tommy wanted to say, I told you so, but he cherished his life.

"It's not a continuous loop system," O'Sullivan continued like he was some kind of expert. "It needs to be manually turned on, then set to record with a digital disc installed. They call it a Compact Disc or CD. It enables up to eight hours of recording time."

"Yeah, yeah. Nobody gives a shit about the technical jargon. What about this disc, then? Do you know if someone set it to record? Is there a bloody disc or not?" Patrick fired his questions off, one after the other. His life force was seeping from his body, and the only person who may have any answers was the corrupt pig standing in his mother's kitchen.

"Something is not right here," Ma broke in. "I can sense it. Why would the Costa family take out one of its own suppliers? Business is business, and you don't just suddenly start popping off your own customers. And my family, my two boys..." Ma stopped mid-sentence to compose herself. She sipped on her tea, then turned back towards O'Sullivan. "What else do you have? Any more bombshells I should know about? World war three is about to erupt between my family and those bloody Italians if I find out they're involved. I need the complete picture before that happens. If there is such a disc—I want it found. Someone has to pay for what's been perpetrated against this family, I swear on my own brother's grave," Ma let fly from her toxic mouth like a spitting cobra.

Patrick swallowed hard while trying to regain some level of calm. "Fuck me! I can't believe this. Why are we only finding out about this now?" His anger was squarely pointed at the off-duty detective standing only feet away.

"My department only got wind of this information yesterday. I'm telling you now aren't I," O'Sullivan fired back. "There is one other small piece of information that also surfaced. So far it hasn't led to anything, but the MCS won't leave any stone unturned. Most of 'em have university degrees and are yet to turn thirty. We call them the schoolies—above and beyond reproach, corruption-free the police commissioner wants the public to believe."

"Get to the fucking point," Patrick cried out.

"The local uniformed boys were tasked with canvassing every house between Clifton Gardens and Military Road for any home CCTV footage facing the road. The coroner puts the time of death at between four and five A.M. A brown Holden ute was identified turning off Bradleys Head Road heading towards Balmoral Beach at 4:42 A.M. Unfortunately, we can't ID a plate, and tracking down this popular model of car is almost an impossibility. And the only other vehicle of interest was picked up as it passed a house in Thompson Street, and again as it cruised past the car park camera installed at the Mosman Police Station. This car is unique, and only a few thousand were ever sold in the Sydney area. It's called a Goggomobil *Dart*, red in fact. A Microcar. I've never heard of them before."

Patrick's ears were burning. He turned towards Tommy with shifting eyes before addressing both Ma and O'Sullivan. "I need to go talk with someone." Patrick almost left a dust trail in his wake as he flew out the back door with

Tommy hot on his heels. Tommy kicked over the engine of his chocolate-brown V8 ute. Patrick secured the clasp of his seatbelt. "Time to get rid of this car, Tommy, and I mean tomorrow. But, my old friend, as luck would have it, I know who happens to own a bright red Goggomobil. Let's go and find out where the Frog hangs out these days."

Chapter-17

KELLY MANAGED to jag the green light at the bottom of the Sydney Road hill that leads into Manly. The local cop shop and courthouse were located about a hundred metres to his right on Belgrave St. He continued straight towards the beach as the last daylight hours disappeared behind him over the western horizon. He turned left into Whistler St and followed that until it ended at the corner of Pine St. This was where the Drug Referral Centre simply known as the Purple Door was located one street back from the second most famous beach in Australia.

The post World War ll mansion formed part of a deceased estate left by a retired judge who in his thirty years presiding over the Manly Magistrate's Court, witnessed with a hidden anger the rising scourge of drug addiction inundate the community like a malignant tumour. A simple restrictive covenant attached to the transfer of title stated that the home was to be used for a community-based service. It sat vacant for years until the Manly Warringah Shire in their infinite wisdom finally agreed upon a plan for its future.

Two-thirds of the home, which included four double bedrooms, a country-style kitchen, two bathrooms and three toilets, were converted into treatment rooms for the increasing number of overdose victims in the Manly area. The remaining residence was sectioned off, and would be offered on a 'rent-free' basis by any person or persons currently studying a university-level degree in psychology or medicine, and willing to donate their weekends in dealing with the ever-increasing drug problem. It was regarded as a safe destination. A halfway house free from police intervention which offered a no-questions-asked pathway to either a hospital or government-funded rehabilitation.

The first time Kelly had met the two ladies who currently filled both these positions was after he dragged a hysterical naked woman from the surf at North Steyne in the middle of the night while nursing a serious hangover under a blanket on the beach. She was off her face on some new mind-altering drug called angel dust. She proved to be a real handful, and the only nearby help he could think of was this Purple Door he'd heard of previously. After delivering his kicking and screaming patient, still in his dripping clothes, the couple that ran the place offered him a hot shower to wash and dry his clothes, and a bed for the night in exchange for some home maintenance the next day. Kelly was a jack of all trades, and master of none, but could turn his hand to just about anything in or around the house.

A giant Norfolk pine dwarfed the enclosed backyard. Kelly struggled to clear his leg over the seat, and the tourniquet he'd wrapped around the wound an hour earlier was now soaked through. He was about to knock on the private door to the residence when it flew open. Kirsty was about to offer her normal bear hug of a welcome when she couldn't help but notice the blood trail. "Oh, my God, what happened to you?" Then she asked like an angry mother, "Did you come off your bike again?" She yelled out over her shoulder, "Jemma, quickly. I need a hand here." She grabbed Kelly by the shoulder before he collapsed. Jemma came flying down the long jarrah wooden hallway and took a position under his other shoulder. Together they laid Kelly out on a massage table, then cut his jeans away with some dress scissors. Kelly was feeling light-headed with a nauseating feeling of unwell slowly filtering through every part of his body. He wanted a drink of water but struggled to speak clearly. The last voice he heard was Jemma asking Kirsty to go fetch her student's medical bag.

Kelly spent the next three days under strict orders not to leave the house while the ladies attended university on the other side of Sydney. He was confined to just their own personal quarters plus the fully fenced private backyard. On the fourth day, he showered and was well enough to walk. Kelly thought he'd leave it another couple of days before he would try to get on his bike again. Meantime, Manly has a lot to offer. Why not? He was going stir crazy anyway, Kelly convinced himself without much trouble as he closed the rear gate, and limped his way to the closest pub.

Chapter-18

THE MANLY CORSO was laid out in 1854-55 by Henry Gilbert Smith, originally built as a boardwalk for early tourists to cross the sand spit between the beach and the harbour pier. The Corso remains the focal point of Manly as a part-pedestrian mall, lined with popular surf shops, pubs, cafés, galleries and street entertainment. Most of this street has no vehicular traffic, making it a broad pedestrian precinct for shoppers and visitors, and it is the quickest route from Manly Beach to the ferry and hydrofoil terminals.

The South Steyne Hotel boasted a half-decent beer garden. Kelly ordered a pint of cider then found a vacant table that overlooked the deep blue that was the Pacific Ocean on one side and on the opposite was the Corso. The outside temperature right now was a comfortable twenty-eight degrees Celsius, but inside things were definitely about to heat up.

Kelly emptied his pint, then walked through to the TAB that backed onto a sports bar on the opposite side of the hotel. He looked up towards a wall of mounted screens to view the latest odds when a stranger's voice spoke from behind. "What do you like in the next race?"

Kelly turned and thought he was dreaming. "Huh," was the best he could offer on such short notice. This woman was an absolute bombshell.

"The next race, who do think will win? I like the green and red colours—that's number seven," she added.

"My lucky number," Kelly told her, "but the nine should romp it in."

"The nine heh... we'll see. Let's make a deal, then. If I win, you buy me a drink, but if you win, you can still buy me that drink."

"Yeah, right?" he questioned. *That never happens!* "Your accent is Irish, isn't it? You might need to find a little Leprechaun to accept that bet—unless, of course, I wanted to just buy you a drink which at this stage might be a little preemptive," Kelly added with a comical tone.

"Arr yes, but a bet is a bet," she said.

"To be sure – to be sure," Kelly couldn't resist the crack at the accent. He tried to fight the urge to lower his eyes as this stunning woman stood in front of the terminal operator and slid in her betting ticket. He was always a bum man. She had a perfectly shaped behind tucked into a tight-fitting pair of Levis with a body-hugging white T-shirt displaying the logo of a southern right whale under the title: 'The Australian National Maritime Museum', that was slightly hidden from view with the V-shape cut of her strawberry blonde hair hanging freely down to the middle of her back.

Whoa, that is a whole lot of woman right there, Kelly sighed as she walked back to a table filled with a crowd of hip-looking people drinking and celebrating. He smelt the distinctive wafting scent of *Giorgio Beverly Hills* perfume drift on by in her wake.

Kelly placed his own bet and found a vacant spot at the bar under a TV with the next race at Randwick about to jump. A few of the crowd quietened as their focus shifted. "Come on, number nine."

The race caller's voice rose to a fever pitch as the sixteen thoroughbreds headed down the back straight.

"It's Irish Mist and the Shonky Barman neck and neck, Irish Mist—the Shonky Barman, five lengths to go and you can't separate them, punters, hold on to your tickets, everyone. The Shonky Barman has eased ahead, the jockey's bringing out the whip, and Irish Mist responds—wait—waaait—waaaait it's a photo for first and second, and I think third will be number

three, Distance Peaks. Oh, what a finish for this year's Governor's Cup . . ."

Kelly grinned and put the winning ticket in his top pocket until correct-weight was called all the while his thoughts were cluttered with the sweet images of this mystery woman. After spending way too much time convalescing his beaten body in different hospitals, a bit of female company might be just what the doctor ordered. He didn't need much convincing as his second brain, the one that lives and breathes below a man's belt-line, suddenly came to life with a reminding growth spurt. He was about to go and collect his winnings when the two-legged goddess just casually waltzed on over and asked Kelly what he was drinking.

Kelly's heart was pounding. His cheeks glowed with a feeling of flushing warmth, and all of a sudden, both his throat and mouth felt like he'd just swallowed a mouthful of Vegimite. He was anxious about making a memorable first impression, and about a hundred different thoughts flashed through his one-track mind. Only on the one previous occasion had the opportunity to get up close and personal with a person of the opposite sex ever presented itself which was on his 16th birthday, and that turned out to be a fumbling first-up disaster that never reached the finishing post. He needed to calm down and take stock of himself before the one and possibly his only moment might pass him by, vanishing in the blink of an eye. He took a couple of steps backwards to gather his senses. Thanks to an indoor pot plant strategically placed right behind him, he fell arse-over-head in a display of flying arms and legs, scattering a group of unsuspecting diners. Kelly cringed while silently cursing himself. *What just happened?*

Springing to his feet while still brushing away the remnants of someone's leftover lunch, Kelly's mind was working feverishly, trying to conjure a way of regaining a slither of dignity. His pride had taken a direct hit, shot to pieces. *Good job, you clown—smooth as silk.*

He tried to think of a witty comment, but his mind drew a blank. He could hear the young sex bomb chuckling quietly, humoured, as she rushed over and offered a helping hand to brush away some loose scraps of grilled coral trout and salad. She was asking Kelly, with a genuine look of concern on her face, "Are you okay? Wow, did you hurt yourself? I've never seen anyone do that before."

Kelly gathered his thoughts, "I drink cider, but since I won, please, it's my shout," he replied, trying to sound suave like a modern-day Cary Grant.

"Pint of Coopers Pale Ale for me," she said with a consoling smile. "I'll grab a vacant outside table overlooking the beach. Away from the crowds where you'll be safe—is that okay with you?"

Oh yeah, more than all right with me, Kelly silently applauded. He nodded and left to order the round, then returned and gently placed both full glasses down on two coasters, careful not to spill a drop. He could feel the eyes of every man and his dog in the beer garden burning an envious hole into the middle of his broad shoulders.

She stood up and offered her hand, "Most people just call me, Maddy."

Kelly felt a firm grip on a soft hand and hesitated for a split second, "Arr, Phil—Lucky Phil, nice to meet you."

They spent two easy hours over lunch. Maddy had a healthy appetite, perusing the predominantly seafood menu, choosing her three dishes carefully. Time was not the enemy today. Socially, Kelly was not a recluse, but he kept his private life exactly that—private. He had no time for small-talk or the endless rhetoric that dribbled from a world full of 'would be if they could be' stereotypes. Talking with Maddy was a breeze. He felt relaxed and at ease. With the warmth of the afternoon sun, the rows of Norfolk pines towering into the sky along the paved foreshore with the sand and the surf as a picture-perfect backdrop, you could be forgiven for thinking that you were on a resort island hideaway. It was almost too good to be true.

Kelly returned with a third round of drinks. *This Maddy certainly enjoys a drink on a hot day*, Kelly was fast coming to realise. He knew from personal experience that most women who fall into the nine and a half out of ten category are usually full of themselves and tend to be a bit narky. Getting hit on by every bloke you bump into more than likely takes its toll, he considered, but this woman seemed quite different. He instantly liked her, and by the way she was smiling back, his man radar was telling him the feeling might be mutual.

Maddy finished her crayfish salad and took the time to discreetly check out the more than interesting prospect sitting opposite. With his deep cobalt blue eyes and fading blond hair with a suntan to match, he was a really hot-looking guy, she thought. To Maddy, his strong physical presence told her that he kept himself in better-than-average shape. He exuded a friendly and sometimes shy persona, but spoke with a confidence that reflected a self-belief without being arrogant. *This Lucky Phil character was someone I could spend some time getting to know better*, she told herself. *A bit of business mixed with pleasure is never a bad thing*. Maddy's womanly instincts were relaying a good vibe. She was enjoying Kelly's laid-back conversation and easy-going company.

"What's with the limp?" she asked in that romantic Irish twang.

"Came off the bike in the wet. Just a few scrapes and bruises." Kelly then asked, "The T-shirt—what's that all about?"

"I'm currently in town, winding up a three-day photo shoot for a TV commercial to promote the Fremantle Maritime Museum over in Western Australia. The seventeenth-century wreck of the *Batavia* discovered at the Abrolhos Islands, what they managed to salvage is due to open for public display in Perth late January next year." She finished her drink. "So, why do they call you, Lucky Phil?" Maddy was lining up the killer blow with a women's precision.

"Well, I'm sitting here today with a view to die for while in the company of a beautiful woman. How much luck does a man need to be deemed as lucky?" Kelly answered with a casual smile.

Maddy looked at her watch, "Unfortunately, I need to head back for some work commitments later today. We have a wind-up dinner tonight with all the major stakeholders. How about we meet again and find a nice restaurant somewhere?" She slipped a card from her purse and pushed it over the table. "This is the hotel all the crew are booked into. It's not far. Do you know where it is?"

"I will soon enough," Kelly replied. "To be honest, I was hoping you may be able to help me out with a small problem before you leave?"

"Oh, really," Maddy smiled provocatively. "And what might that be?"

"I need to expand my wardrobe, but I know nothing about men's fashion. I was hoping..."

"Say no more. You're asking a woman if she wants to go shopping?"

"Well... yes, I suppose—shopping for me. Is that the same?"

"Close enough. Drink up. I know a great shop to get started. We can walk from here."

An hour later, Kelly exited the last of five different menswear shops weighed down with shopping bags. Maddy laughed, "Seriously, you have actually never done this before—have you?"

"Absolutely not, and I think I know why," Kelly replied, glad it was over.

"Where are you staying? I have a car parked close by. I can give you a lift. All those bags and a crook leg..."

"Lead the way." They exited the Corso at the beach end, then turned right. Maddy approached her parked car as a parking inspector was copying the number plate down.

"Oh, shit. Wait here a sec, I'll need to do this alone," Maddy smiled. She flicked her hair back while rubbing both hands down the front of her tight T-shirt, causing both her nipples to stand erect. "Oh, dear, I'm so sorry. Did the meter run out?"

The brown bomber turned and immediately stopped writing the ticket. "Are you the owner of this vehicle?"

"Yes." She dropped her keys, then took her time to bend over and pick them up. The mere male ran his eyes up and down each womanly curve. "Sometimes I just lose track of time, but still, that's no excuse. I know you have an important job to do," Maddy continued weaving her female magic.

"Are you about to leave?"

"Yes, I'm on my way to pick up my sick mother from Manly Hospital. She wanted me to fill a script, but the local chemist wasn't able to help. I'll need to find another one on the way to the hospital. How much will this ticket cost me, officer?"

He then asked, "Do you come to Manly often?"

"I'm here every Thursday night with a couple of girlfriends. We like the open mic night at the New Brighton Hotel. Do you sing at all? Maybe you could come on down and belt out a few tunes. It's so much fun."

"Well, perhaps we can let you off this one time with a warning."

"Oh, officer, will you get into trouble? I don't want to be responsible for..."

"No, no, it's okay," he interrupted. "We have discretionary powers, you know. The burden of responsibility is something we are trained to manage."

"Okay, thank you for your kind understanding. Maybe I'll see you again..."

"Thursday's heh?"

Maddy opened her door and slid in behind the wheel while smiling back at the gullible idiot standing on the footpath with an ounce of false hope scrambling his man brain. She turned the ignition and pulled out into traffic, then slowed to a stop while winding down the passenger-side window. Struggling to keep a straight face, Maddy chuckled through a perfect set of teeth. "Are you heading my way, I can give you a lift if you wish?"

Kelly answered while shaking his head at the ease in which a man will succumb to a cracking-looking woman. "How many times have you pulled that one off?"

"If the shoe fits..."

"That's a powerful tool to have in your arsenal. Just keep following the beach, and I'll tell you when to turn left. Nice car, by the way."

Maddy pushed a button on the dash, and the roof slid open. "It's too nice a day to miss out on a bit of sunshine. This is my first visit to Manly," she lied. The words flowed from her mouth with practised ease. She veered the Triumph *Stag* sharply and angled parked into a vacant bay next to a long boardwalk overlooking the ocean. "The beaches in Australia are just magnificent. I want to stop and take a photo." She jumped out and snapped a few shots of the rolling waves and the chalk-white sands. "Why don't you lean against the bonnet and I'll get a shot of you. My friends back in Ireland won't believe I'm spending the afternoon with a real Australian man otherwise."

Kelly obliged with an unseen reluctance.

"Jump in behind the wheel. It'll be a great photo." Kelly eased into the driver's seat. "Okay, good to go," Maddy said. "I've taken up enough of your time. Let's get you back home, shall we?"

"That's fine, I can walk from here. What time tomorrow night, then?"

"Let's say eight o'clock, just ask for me at the front desk."

Kelly crossed the road and turned left. A strange-looking pint-sized red car was parked on the grassed verge. Kelly stopped to check it out, slowly pronouncing the badge on the front grill. "Gog-go-mobil *Dart*. Never heard of it."

The main entrance to the Purple Door was a set of double-stained glass and wooden doors set back onto a raised verandah that surrounded three sides of the house. To the left was a white cane table with four matching chairs. A man stood up and almost bunny-hopped down the four steps. Kelly turned and recognised the face of the jockey-sized schoolboy he only knew as the Frog, and he didn't look well.

"You're, Phil Kelly, aren't you? I remember seeing you that day in the toilet block. My name is, Gassan. Is there someplace safe we can talk?" His demeanour was that of a desperate man.

Kelly paused a moment, "Mosman High, that was you...?"

"Yes, unfortunately. I heard what those pigs did to you. I'm in real trouble, and if there is one person I think will understand, I reckon it has to be you."

"Okay, follow me." Kelly headed for the lane-way that leads to the private residence behind.

"I need to get my car off the street. It's like a bloody great big bullseye sitting out here in the open."

"There's a garage out the back. I'll go pull up the roller door," Kelly offered, not sure why that was a problem.

Gassan shut off the engine. Kelly closed the door behind him, then put down his bags and ushered the Frog to an outside bench seat. "How did you know I was here?"

"I've been a regular visitor at the Door for years now. They do a great job. You know—bad habits and all that. I was visiting a friend drying out inside when he told me about a mystery man staying with, Jemma and Kirsty. I peered over the fence while puffing on a fag and recognised your bike. Can you help me?"

"Depends on what the problem is first?" Kelly replied.

"That fuckwit Patrick O'Finlay is the problem."

"All right, now you have my attention. What's goin' on?"

"He's looking for me. Late last night, I turned into my street, and I noticed a strange car parked opposite with a lone man asleep behind the wheel. I know all the cars in my street, and so I drove straight past. Fuck me if I didn't recognise the plate, so I just kept driving. The next morning I parked a street back then followed a bicycle path to the rear entrance of the boarding house where I rent a room. The fucking car was still there. A brown Holden ute. It belongs to that nutcase they call, Turbo Tommy, O'Finlay's personal bum boy."

"Why would he be looking for you?"

"I stumbled onto something really bad. I'm still not sure what it was or who was involved. Now I need some cash to get out of town for a while. That guy you work for in the city, he must know a fence? I've got a couple of things I think maybe worth something. Can you set up a meet or what?"

"Show me what you've got first?" Kelly asked.

The Frog pulled a pocket watch from his fanny pack. He handed it over. "Plus, there's more in the boot. I know collectors pay big money for this kind of shit." The Frog walked over to his toy car and popped the front boot. He grabbed a plastic bin liner, then placed the contents on the bench table.

Kelly picked up the wooden case holding the Colt, then flipped the catch open. He felt the weight of the pistol in his hand. "Bloody hell, Gassan, how did you get your hands on this? I'll be fucked, this is awesome." He waved the long barrel in the air, then looked closely at the inscription down one side. "Pawnshops are no good. They'll ask questions and insist on some form of ID."

"No shit, man," Gassan answered. "That's why I need a fence, someone with connections."

Kelly opened the satchel. The two birth certificates fell out with another official-looking document tucked in between. Kelly shuffled through the three certificates. "What's all this, then?"

"These are obviously someone's birth certificates—but this other one—go figure? I thought it might be a title deed to some property. Might look cool framed and hanging on my wall."

Kelly read the first line, "It says here it's a promissory note, and relates to a piece of property."

The Frog was a man blessed with street-smarts, but intellect took a sharp downward turn after that, "I told you so."

Kelly pointed to what was some sort of electronic device. "And this..."

"I'm not sure. Initially, I thought it may have been some type of alarm system. I've never seen one before. It says right here - Sony CDP-101."

Kelly paused for a moment. "Look, I may know a guy who can tell us what this is. He's a bit of an electronics expert. But the gun and this old timepiece...? How much money do you need to skip town?"

The Frog replied, "As much as I can get my hands on. What do you think they're all worth?"

"How the hell would I know? As much as someone's willing to pay, which is usually sweet fuck all. How soon do you wanna shoot through?"

"Like, right now would be good. Those guys are too fucking serious for me. I'm a dead man walking if they know what I think they know. You got any cash on you?"

Kelly pulled his wallet from a back pocket. "All I have on me right now is three hundred dollars. If I find out this shit is worth more, I'll go you halves in anything over a thousand. Best I can do. You happy with that?"

Gassan looked at his shaking hands. "I need more, eight hundred sounds a hell of a lot better."

"I bet it does, four hundred—that's my final offer. Take it or leave it."

Kelly pulled close the garage door. He leaned into Gassan's driver's side window. "A last piece of advice. Ditch the car somewhere, catch a taxi to Central then buy a ticket on the next train leaving Sydney. Keep an eye on the papers. You'll know when it's safe to show your face again in public."

"Tell me something I don't know. Thanks, and remember, you still owe me," the Frog voiced out the window as the Goggomobil turned into the street.

A single motorcycle was parked on the opposite side of the same street. Its rider sat patiently with his full-face helmet concealing his watchful gaze. Sitting on the bike side-saddle, he admired the small red car as it powered up the hill, leaving a trail of two-stroke smoke in its wake. Whacka straddled his ride, hit the ignition, and executed a fast 180-degree turn in heavy traffic. A few cars honked their horns and waved an angry fist at the loose rider. He powered up the hill, catching the red car in less than thirty seconds where he slowed and followed as ordered.

Kelly placed all three items inside a sports bag, zipped it tight, then stashed it under the seat of his bike. Jemma and Kirsty were due home within a couple of hours. He wrote a short note and left a twenty-dollar bill. 'My shout for takeaway, be back by seven'. He pushed his bike out to the street, struggling to slide his leg over the seat. He fired up the 900cc engine, then headed towards the Cahil Expressway and back to his old stomping ground in the city.

The name of the man Kelly rented the private garage from for a bag of dope each month was a Pakistani named

Faisal, and he did own a pawnshop. He and his four brothers enjoyed mixing a few crushed heads in their hookah while sipping on espresso.

Kelly parked his bike on the footpath directly behind the rear door to the City Pawnshop. He entered through the unlocked rear door, waving at one of the brothers working in a rear jeweller's room, and entered the main shop floor. He spotted Faisal and headed his way. "Got something here I think you'll be more than interested in, Faisal."

"Show me, please."

Placing the pocket watch on the counter, Faisal looked through his eyepiece, then popped open the back, slowly reading out the small inscription with a heavy northern Pakistan accent. "Appleton Tracy and Co. Waltham, Mass 36851. John Wilkinson, C.S.S. R.E. Lee - 1862."

Kelly thought Faisal was going to pee his pants. He started asking questions, too many in fact, and he looked nervous in a very exhilarated way. He wanted to know how Kelly came to be in possession of such a rare timepiece in near-mint condition. Kelly spun him a yarn about his dead grandfather, then asked for an estimated value. Faisal fetched a book from under the counter. Turning the pages, he stopped and pointed at a photo. "This, Mr Lucky, is that same timepiece". He would never have made a good poker player. He was doing a lousy job at bluffing his impassioned interest.

Looking underneath the photo, there was a short monetary reference: Value - US $2,500-$3,000 [est only]. Faisal lifted his head to face Kelly. The negotiations were about to start. "That price is based on an estimated auction value. It does not represent a street value," he wanted to explain.

"Bottom line, Faisal," Kelly prompted. He didn't have the luxury of time while in the heart of what was now enemy territory. Faisal slid off his glasses, then scratched the side of his head. He was an expert at this stuff and needed to play out the whole routine. It was like a play.

"Off the books with no paperwork, I'm assuming?"

"You assume right," Kelly answered.

"Best price, three hundred." Faisal did not blink an eye.

Kelly smirked. "Is that US dollars like the book says?"

Faisal smiled back. "OK, five hundred then—Australian. This very good price."

"Halve it, and then halve it again, Faisal. That works out to be around nine hundred factoring in the exchange rate."

"My final offer is six hundred."

"You mean seven-fifty don't you, do we have a deal? Take another look if you like."

"I should offer you a job, seven hundred—that's all I can pay."

Kelly offered his hand, and the deal was sealed.

Faisal counted out the notes then asked, "Mr Lucky, does your grandfather have any other such items?"

Kelly pocketed the cash, "You'll be the first to know, Faisal."

"And what about our other monthly arrangement...?"

"Those days are over, my friend. Sorry, mate, need to keep moving now. Be good, and say hello to your family for me," and then he left through the same back door.

Kelly pulled out onto George Street. The old Crumpernickel's front street window was still boarded up with advertising slogans pasted all over and looked dead in the water. He headed towards Chinatown, cruised past the Al Forno Montevideo Restaurant to see Fanny's two sisters setting up inside. He quickly honked on his horn twice. Augustina popped her head out the front door. Kelly lifted his visor, "Is Julius around today?"

"Sorry, I did not recognise you under the helmet. My three brothers are all gone for the afternoon. I do not know what time they come back. You wish to come in and eat?"

"No, that's fine. I'll come back again later. Thanks, Augustina." Kelly powered away and headed back to the Purple Door. His leg was killing him, and he needed a painkiller.

Chapter-19

THE TAXI DROPPED KELLY at the front entrance to the Cabbage Tree Bay Hotel ten minutes early. He paid the driver, then approached the main reception. The uniformed front office manager buzzed room 602 and waited. A short conversation took place before she ended the call. She motioned with a waving hand for a porter to come forward. "Follow me, sir." Kelly followed him to the lift doors. "Sixth floor, follow the corridor left. Enjoy your evening."

The lift door slid open, and Kelly stepped in.

Maddy's door was slightly ajar. "Come on in," she yelled from inside. Kelly closed the door behind him. He walked into the lounge area that opened up to an expansive balcony with a view over Manly Wharf and the harbour. Madeleine was sitting on the edge of a huge bed talking on the phone. "Grab a Heineken from the bar fridge. I'll join you in a minute, the view is magnificent," she said between conversations.

Kelly placed both elbows on the balcony rail and took in the view. He swallowed a mouthful of beer and began mentally processing the layout of the suite. Scattered randomly over the plush carpeted floor were some large cushions with two candles flickering on a mantelpiece. A platter of canapés, cheese and biscuits, fruit, olives, pate, salami and the like with two champagne flutes placed as a centrepiece on an engraved crystal platter raised a few mental questions. Kelly stood there and digested the ambience of the room. The awakening feeling in his pants had now turned into something more serious. He tried in earnest not to eavesdrop on the phone chatter as he attempted to clear the sexual images filling his aroused mind.

Maddy hung up the phone and met Kelly on the balcony. "I've cancelled tonight's dinner plans, and if it's okay with you, we can just order room service."

"Yeah, fine by me." Kelly almost cheered. He wanted to jump for joy.

"There's a bottle of champagne in the fridge, you do the honours, and I'll just go and freshen up."

The sound of a cork popping soon filled the spacious suite. Just then the door to the bathroom swung open, and Maddy reentered. Kelly was rendered speechless. She was wearing a near-invisible purple negligee that only just partially covered a matching pair of G-strings. Her firm breasts were clearly visible through the sheer lace material, and both her nipples were pointing straight at Kelly's bulging eyes like a set of headlights on high beam. *Oh, my God!* His jeans felt like a piece of hardwood was trying to force its way out. There was no use hiding it any longer. No force in nature was going to stop him now, except the word no. He had passed the point of no return, and Maddy knew it.

She pointed at the growing appendage in the front of his jeans, "Why don't you get comfortable and let me take care of that for you before you do yourself some harm? We can eat later."

I may never eat again.

Maddy walked over in a relaxed and provocative manner, and then gestured for Kelly to remove his shirt while she unbuckled his belt, dropping his jeans to the floor. "I think I know now why they call you, Lucky Phil!" She slid off his jocks. "Wow, maybe I'm the lucky one tonight." Then she eased herself down onto both knees and parted her full lips, taking him into her moistened, open mouth.

Surely this can't be happening... can it?

Kelly needed to draw on all his willpower not to release his pent-up load before he could reach second and third base. *Think of something else and do it NOW!* His own mother's face was never going to work. *Someone's grandmother—anything.* She expertly devoured his rock-hard wood for what felt like an eternity before eventually gesturing him onto the king-size bed while guiding his face with her two hands towards her moist vagina. She moaned in pleasure and quivered with groans of blissfulness as she relayed instructions to her enthusiastic partner. Kelly's mouth and tongue were on an adventure he didn't think was possible. Maddy's body writhed and stiffened as she screamed in the throes of ecstasy.

The couple moved as one into the middle of the bed. Maddy directed Kelly's stiffened rod of pleasure into her velvet mound, while she raised her legs high into the air and pulled the luckiest man alive, deep into her infused honey pot. Her breasts were perfectly shaped, and her hardened nipples tasted like first season cherries.

I hope this moment never ends, Kelly moaned in sexual glee. Backwards and forwards, they moved seamlessly together while he impaled her with his rigid shaft. Kelly braced himself and erupted, screaming a low, drawn-out groan, and emptied his bottled-up erotica into her dripping pudenda, then collapsed onto her chest. She gently ran her long painted nails along his back, feeling the strength and beauty of a fit young man's slightly blemished body.

Kelly eventually slowed down his trembling to restore some control over his legs long enough to stand and stuff his mouth with food. Maddy placed both her manicured hands on each side of his face, then gave him a longer than expected kiss on his lips. Her mouth tasted sweeter than a fruit tingle, and the essence of sexual secretion was stirring into action, another rising awakening.

That evening would forever rekindle a teenager's fantasy that waxed into a sexual realism. A moment in time Kelly would remember for the rest of his days on planet Earth. The time he was gently and skilfully led through the pearly gates of sexual jubilation and shown how to gratify a woman in ways, he could only dream of as an adolescent.

"Thank you, Lucky Phil. Now we both share a special moment," Maddy said with a glint in her eye that reflected a satisfied woman. "Tell me a little about you?" she prodded.

"Not much to tell really," he replied.

"What about your family, do you have any sisters or brothers?"

"I was a foster child from the time I turned four. There may be a younger brother or sister. I'll probably never find out."

"Oh, that's terrible. I'm sorry. I didn't mean to pry," Maddy offered sympathetically. "Did you grow up in Sydney?"

"Mostly, until I was about twelve, when I was shifted to a town called Cooma."

"Oh, I know Cooma. It's on the way to the snowfields."

"So I've been told. Never made it that far myself."

The two lovers swapped small talk until the first hint of daylight lit up the eastern ocean horizon. Kelly's awakening into the world of making love to a woman was equally matched by Maddy's willingness to indulge in what would be a night Kelly would never forget. Tonight he had truly shaken the embarrassing virgin tag—once and for all.

The squeaking sounds of the housemaid's wheeling cart from the outside hallway stirred Kelly to a slumbered awakening. He stretched his satiated body while still in a state of appeased gratification, remembering the previous night's strenuous activities. Kelly felt a warm glow flow through his six-foot-two-inch frame like a soothing river of contentment. He propped himself up on one arm with a single intention in his lustful mind, only to find the crumpled evidence of where Maddy slept. A handwritten note was sitting ominously on the vacant side of the bed with a red lipstick mark and a flower resting to one side. He picked it up and read on with a shrinking disappointment:

Lucky Phil - I think I really am the lucky one—I can barely walk!

You looked way too comfortable to wake lover boy, and after your efforts last night, I can only assume you needed the time to rest.

I rarely fool around like that on a first date, but I'm glad we did.

Sorry about my early departure, but I have a 9:00 A.M. flight booked to Perth.

This is a number I can be reached on back in Sydney after the weekend - 02–901-2679. Don't become a stranger.

XX Maddy ♥.

Kelly found the remote and turned on the TV. He slid out from under the dishevelled sheets and washed off the aura of sex in the shower. By now he had worked up a man-sized hunger that needed to be addressed. He found his discarded clothes strewn in all directions over the floor. He dressed and was about to close the door when the image of a Goggomobil *Dart* on the screen caught his attention. A female news reporter was filing a story from the eastern suburbs in Watson's Bay. She was filming in front of an ocean cliff on the South Head peninsula called The Gap. A popular spot for people who assumed suicide was the only option available. Kelly turned up the volume and sat at the end of the bed while listening to the reporter.

"*State Emergency Services are currently scouring the bottom of the cliff face known as The Gap while the Water Police continue their search for a possible missing person along the coast. This car parked behind me is called a Goggomobil* Dart. *Police have confirmed a suicide note was found on the passenger's seat. I have been told the owner of the car is known to authorities, but until relatives have been notified, this person's name will not be made public. For many years now The Gap has been a favoured...*"

Kelly pressed the *off* button and sat in silence. He felt a sickness inside that was only matched by his growing anger. "Those fucking pricks got to him. Fuck this O'Finlay arsehole." Kelly knew if Gassan was dead, that only meant one thing. Whatever information Patrick O'Finlay wanted—he had. And that meant he would be next in line for a bit of one-on-one time. What small piece of information the Frog had in his possession was important enough to cost him his life.

The housemaid's trolley almost tripped Kelly up as he headed for the lift and a much-anticipated appointment with Julius.

Chapter-20

THE RETURN FLIGHT from Perth to Sydney takes about forty minutes less due to the counterclockwise prograde motion of the Earth's rotation. Madeleine O'Hara used the ladies' room, then negotiated her way down the final set of escalators and was met by a uniformed QANTAS staffer displaying her name on a hand-written sign. "Miss O'Hara? I would like to direct you to the free shuttle bus service that will drop you at the international terminal. It's only a short fifteen-minute commute where you can connect with your scheduled flight to London."

Madeleine politely declined the offer, explaining she was spending the three-hour layover catching up with some Australian friends. She immediately exited the domestic terminal and waited in the taxi queue with just the two pieces of carry-on luggage. A taxi pulled into the pick up zone and popped the boot while a young testosterone-fuelled teenage porter sprinted over to lift her bag into the boot with a smile this woman had become accustom to. It always starts with the father, showering his cute little daughter with gifts, then the doting uncles, and soon it's the boyfriends all bending over backwards to gain the attention of a beautiful woman.

Madeleine passed the driver a hand-written address in the suburb of Chatswood. The taxi headed for the city by-pass. In close pursuit, tagging three cars behind was a 308-V8 L-34 Torona with the private plates: TURBO T.

Madeleine had previously organised a house swap after answering an ad in the local rag from an Australian exchange student who earned herself a twelve-month scholarship to study at the London College of Music. Rather than booking a hotel this way, she would not be required to supply her passport details. She could fly under the radar.

The deal included the upkeep of the gardens, which suited her fine. As an avid gardener and a keen grower of herbal tonics for natural and healthy medicinal remedies, Madeleine treated her model body as a temple, the vessel that nurtures her soul and therefore shall be treated accordingly—the same body that now earned a six-figure income since the day she turned sixteen. Her interest originally started as a hobby back in Ireland, but soon after she realised she had a knack for the wonderments offered by nature's call.

She was busy tending to a vast array of pots and herbs growing in the greenhouse when the small bell rang inside the shed, indicating someone had just entered the front gate. She waited for the front doorbell to sound but instead heard only the sounds of feeding myna birds and magpies from the eucalyptus tree that offered some cooling shade on the quarter-acre block.

Maddy removed her soiled gloves and began to walk towards the rear kitchen door when she heard the distinctive sound of a man's heavy shoe walking down the polished wood hallway. She glanced through the curtained window and was met with the dumb look of her arrogant nephew helping himself to the fridge.

Madeleine was well prepared for this second clandestine meeting with her idiot of a cousin, but was in no mood for any of Patrick's antics today, or any other day for that matter. She entered the outside laundry and removed a compact Glock G19 with no serial number from an overhead cupboard given to her by a man she planned to marry one day. She felt the weight of the fully loaded seventeen shot magazine in her hand, then slid it muzzle first into the front pocket of her smock.

Patrick greeted his cousin with a satirical arrogance that was an extension of his personality. "Madeleine, it's always good to catch up with family again. It's time to collect. You still own me four grand for the car. Nice ride, though."

She pulled an envelope from her bag sitting on the kitchen table. "Hello, Patrick . . . Let yourself in, why don't you? Don't bother knocking," she answered while handing over the cash.

"Arr, come on Madeleine the door was unlocked, and I knew you were alone. Or maybe Tommy and I should check the bedroom, just in case? Never know who might be hiding under the bed if you're as good as I think you are, Cus."

Tommy snickered under his breath from a safe distance.

"I want you to know, Patrick, this is a onetime deal as a favour to my grieving auntie. I am no longer connected to the family."

"Yeah-yeah, blah-blah-blah. This is all about finding out who is responsible for what happened to Sean and Dean. Blood is thicker than water. So, what did you uncover about our lover boy, then?"

Madeleine replied, "Why do you think he could be possibly involved in any of this? He didn't strike me as the kind of man to get mixed up in your grubby little world."

Patrick opened the silver two-door fridge a second time, then began stuffing his face with some Chinese leftovers. Madeleine loved verbally sparring with her less than an intelligent cousin. He wore the dunce's cap with an undiscovered ignorance.

"Do I detect romance blossoming on the near horizon? You think you're a real clever bitch now you've been tagged as some sort of fucking superstar, don't you? Always taking the high ground, but in reality, you're no better than any other street tramp hanging off the coat-tails of your dead father. I'm in no mood for any of your crap today. I need to find a way into this Kelly man's life. He may not even be aware he's in possession of a disc, and I need to get my hands on it before that happens. I don't want to hurt him, we just need to talk, and for that, I need him to come to me."

"A disc? I can sense the fear in your voice, Patrick. Maybe because he stood up to you like a real man? That must be a first for you, but probably not the last."

"Stop piss-farting around, Madeleine." Patrick's impatience was wearing thin.

"He told me he was in foster care for most of his life, but he may have a younger sister or brother," Madeleine shared.

"Madeleine, I'm not stuffing around here. I haven't got time for any of your quick-witted lip, all right. He may? Which one is it... he either does or he doesn't?"

"Calm down, for God's sake, Patrick. You'll need to put the screws on someone in Child Protection Services to unlock his juvenile record, or alternatively access information from one of the adoption information registrars like FIND. If someone from his family has reached out to him, there will be a record."

Patrick hung on every word while Madeleine explained his possible next move. She smiled at the paradox about to confront her disgruntled cousin. Madeleine looked at Patrick and started to laugh, which only added to his heightened anger, "You know the irony of all this, Patrick? You're saying the same person who put that crease on your nose is possibly now in possession of your precious disc. I have no idea of Lucky Phil's whereabouts at this moment. Isn't life wonderful?"

Patrick took a moment to digest what he'd just heard. "He wasn't born with the name, Lucky Phil. His name is, Kelly—Phil Kelly."

"Yes," Madeleine answered. She already knew that. "Now I want you to leave. Our business is done here. *Get out.*" Her own patience was wavering.

Patrick was becoming enraged. The fact another blood relative didn't respect the position he held within the family irked him no end. He took a step forward and clamped his hand tightly around Madeleine's throat, forcing her back against the fridge. Madeleine instinctively kneed him in the groin, then slapped him hard across the face. She might be a woman, but when you are burdened with the natural assets she possessed, learning how to deal with overzealous men was par for the course. She knew how to take care of herself, and Patrick held no fear for her—whatsoever.

Patrick was taken completely by surprise. Even he didn't expect this, especially from her. He stumbled backwards and instinctively felt for the flick-knife he carried with him at all times. He was beyond contempt now as he forced himself back to an upright position to face his intransigent cousin. Madeleine withdrew her small pistol and aimed it point-blank at Patrick's leather-black eyes. She pressed the short barrel into his forehead and pushed him back towards the wall opposite, leaving a neat round imprint on the surface of his skin. Maddy then stepped back and lowered the weapon below Patrick's belt buckle.

"I won't ask you again, Patrick," Madeleine demanded in a cool, calm and collected sonority. "Get the hell out of this house . . . *Now.*"

Patrick wanted to bend forward and relieve the pain he felt throbbing from his crown jewels. Staring at the barrel angled downward, with a smug smirk, he started slowly stepping backwards with alacrity. Both his arms were half-raised in the air. "You think you can just point a gun at me and get away with it? You know who you're dealing with here, Madeleine. This won't be the end of this, not by a long shot, I can assure you of that, you crazy bitch."

Madeleine feathered the trigger safety. "Yes, Patrick, I know *exactly* who I'm dealing with. Now move your arse before I blow both your balls back to the hole you crawled out from."

Patrick hobbled back down the hallway. While feeling his crooked nose, he recalled with contemptuous displeasure the last time he'd stumbled upon the disrespectful Lucky Phil. "Once I get my hands on this Kelly bloke, Madeleine, not even Ma will be able to protect you. I will be back, and that's a promise."

Madeleine slammed the door shut and watched through the drawn curtain as both Patrick and Tommy left through the gate. She walked back to the kitchen and dialled a number in Vaucluse, on the east side of Sydney. The phone picked up. "Tell your boss the lure has been cast, and the fish are on the bite," then she hung up.

Chapter-21

SUSSEX STREET leads you past the entrance to Paddy's Market. Kelly indicated with his blinker to turn right into Fanny's rear lane-way. An old Pontiac *Firebird* with a shitty-looking paint job was parked in a tow-away zone. Two men wearing dark sunglasses, long hair, and an attitude both looked to their left like clowns at the Royal Show while the tall white guy on the bike cruised past. Kelly checked the quarter panel window for a local-residence-only parking sticker, and the penny dropped.

He kicked the Kawasaki back down a gear. The smell of burning rubber filled the tight lane-way as he sped away. He wound out second then third gear before braking hard and made a sharp right back into Little Hay St. The speedometer edged past 100 kph, then 140, at 160 the end of the road fast approached. Kelly applied both front and back brakes. He could hear the four tyres from the chasing Pontiac screaming for grip as it rolled into the corner. The Emperors Court Chinese Restaurant came and went in the blink of an eye. He had just entered Chinatown and was now in unknown territory. He turned hard left into Sussex St, then right into Goulburn. That led to George St and towards The Metro Theatre. The entire complex was surrounded by bollards spaced one metre apart with a brick-paved pedestrian-only mall filling with enthusiastic music lovers making their way to the multiple entry points. Kelly lifted the front wheel. He raised his body as the rear-end pig-rooted over the gutter. A single gunshot popped from the vehicle's passenger side. Kelly aimed for the gap. He honked his horn, foot traffic started to scatter. The roar of the big V8 was another warning bell. Kelly slowed as a second pop whistled past his helmet.

He weaved in-between two bollards and accelerated again. The Pontiac came to a screeching halt. The passenger opened his door, placed a steadying arm across the roof, and took aim once more. He was too late, and slid back into the front vinyl bench seat, slamming his door shut. The God's Garbage boys drove off at speed and were soon lost among the hustle of Sydney's inner-city traffic snarl.

Kelly reentered the legal flow of traffic. He needed a Plan B. He found an underground car park and chained his bike to a pillar before grabbing the bag still safely under his seat. The escalators opened onto the Plaza Arcade. Kelly purchased a peaked cap, and a chequered red and black lumber jacket. He walked through the Chinese Garden of Friendship and hailed a taxi. On the first drive-by, both Fanny's sisters could be seen setting up the restaurant. Kelly instructed the driver to do a full circle around the block, then drop him one hundred metres north of the big red neon chilli sign.

Kelly tapped on the window. Juliette was the younger of the two sisters. She turned her head towards the noise, then spoke to her older sister. Augustina put down her cutlery basket and walked over to the locked front door. Her English was basic at best. "Mr Lucky, it's not safe here. Please, you must go. They look for you." She was waving her arms about like she was trying to shoo a fly away.

"Where is, Julius? Please, I just need to see him—short time," Kelly asked in slow English. Just then, the familiar voice of Julius called out, "Fuck me, what are you doing here? You're in deep shit! There are people..."

Kelly cut him off. "I know all that, Julius. Come and take a look at this, will you?" Kelly stepped inside, away from the glassed entry. He unzipped the bag. "You ever see one of these before? For some reason Julius whatever I have here cost someone their life."

Julius poked around inside the bag. "I'm gonna regret this. Quick, come with me."

The two men followed the same underground path to another part of the house opposite. Kelly could hear the sound of pool balls. Then he heard Fanny and Emmanuel arguing over some rules. Fanny was chalking his cue, "Lucky bloody Phil. Tell my obstinate brother it's two shots for any foul off the break."

"One shot, Fanny."

Emmanuel turned with a look of anguish, "You can't be here. You need to fuck off right now. Why would you bring him here, Julius?" He wasn't mucking around.

Kelly limped around the table. He stopped in front of Emmanuel. "I walked in off the street. No one saw me come in. I know the place is being watched. I just need to see what that is." He pointed over to where Julius had walked back into the room with a bunch of cords under one arm.

"It's a Sony CDP-101, and I'm hoping if I can find a compatible cable we can find out if there's a CD inside," Julius said.

Kelly asked, "What's a CD?"

"A compact disc. For storing digital media files. Like an updated version of the about to be defunct VCR."

Fanny caught Kelly's eye, "They think you and JC shot those three men. The Sergeant of Arms is dead and so will you be soon. The God's Garbage boys remember your face from the time you dropped me back here. You're in serious shit, my friend, and we can't be seen to be helping you, okay."

Emmanuel and Fernando swapped some harsh words in their native tongue. Fanny then picked up the phone and dialled 1. Kelly heard Augustina's name mentioned. He hung up and faced Kelly once more. "You have bought yourself five minutes. That's it, then you need to disappear, and you can't come back here again, you got that?"

Emmanuel opened the polished wooden presentation box housing the Army Colt. He let out a long, under-the-breath whistle, "Whoa man, where did you get your hands on this piece?"

Kelly answered back, "That might come in real handy later."

Emmanuel then asked, "You don't think it still works, do you?"

"It may, but I'm not risking a couple of fingers trying to find out," Kelly replied.

Julius stopped cursing in the background. "I think I may have got it working, hang on a minute." He pressed the *eject* button, and a drawer slid open. Then Julius popped out a shiny silver disc before reading out the hand-written label, "OP self-porn." He turned to face Kelly with a mischievous smile. "What you got here then, Lucky?"

"I wish I knew."

The room fell strangely silent. Fanny and Emmanuel put down their cues and found a seat. Each man watched with growing intrigue as the open drawer swallowed the disc. Julius hit *play*, and the 24-inch TV came to life. They all sat in anticipated stillness. Emmanuel stood up, grabbed a round of beers plus a bottle of *Sauza Tres Generaciones Añejo* with four Villeroy & Boch - American straight shot glasses. He filled each glass. "Can't watch a girly flick without a drink."

The old PYE TV suddenly came to life with an elderly gentleman in the throes of getting a head-job from two women while lying on a pool table. The screen went snowy. Now the same green felt top could be seen with two men playing pool while another man held an empty carton of beer.

Fanny yelled at his brother, "Turn it up, Julius. Bloody hell, we need some audio."

Emmanuel shot Kelly a passing glance, "I've seen this room before somewhere."

"Where do you reckon?" Fanny asked.

"Let's watch and see, it'll come to me in a minute."

The live-action rolled on. Suddenly Emmanuel jumped up from his seat, knocking over a full shot glass. "Fucking hell, this is that bloody house in Clifton Gardens. Shit, it was on the six o'clock news that often I'd recognise that room anywhere. How did you get your hands on this?"

"Blind luck—or maybe bad luck for some," Kelly replied honestly.

The first twenty minutes was pretty non-eventful with two men playing kelly pool for money while watching a game of football. "Hey, that's that famous surfer, Wayne Curran," Julius spat out. "I've seen his face on the cover of heaps of magazines." The time clock read 03:43 A.M. Two more men entered the room.

"The fucking dead dealers," Emanuelle cried out.

The time clock reached 04:03 A.M. Suddenly a man's voice could be heard barking out orders. "This is the Drug Squad, everybody, down on the floor NOW, and get your hands where we can see them. This is a bust."

Emmanuel craned his neck forward, "You have got to be kidding me? That's Sean fucking O'Finlay! And that's Kojak with that Irish bloke, Liam. I'll be fucked," he screamed. "They're not buying or selling cocaine—they're running a fucking scam impersonating the Drug Squad. I'll bet the cops had no idea about this?"

Four sets of eyes were glued to the action like it was the best reality porn film they had ever seen. The sound of gunfire and total pandemonium filled the screen. Bodies were dropping like nine-pins. "Je...sus bloody Christ," Fanny yelled. "It's Patrick . . . Sean and Dean's brother—their own flesh and blood."

"And look, there's that bum sniffing little prick, Tommy. This is un-fucking-believable," Kelly shouted.

No one dared to move, mesmerised by the images on the small screen. Soon after, Patrick and Tommy left the room filled with dead bodies carrying two cases. A short time later, another small man entered and slipped a watch off one body.

Kelly stood to get a good look at the face. "The Frog, that's what he stumbled onto, and that's why he's dead. Poor bastard."

Fanny asked, "Who is the Frog?"

"Only met him twice. It doesn't matter much now. Fuck me. This Patrick O'Finlay is a fucking psychopath, just like you said, Fanny. Who takes out two of their own brothers like they're shooting rabbits?"

All four men remained silent, trying to absorb the enormity of what they had all just witnessed. The screen suddenly went blank, and Julius pressed *stop*.

"Man, you're sitting on a big keg of dynamite right here, old friend. Like my favourite cartoon character Wile E. Coyote and the Roadrunner, you need to tread carefully, Lucky," Fanny stated the obvious.

"He knows I've got the proof. Well, he knows I have the CD player, and he has to assume there is a recording of his handy work. He'll be coming after me now. That's what I would do. I need to sort this clown out. One of us is going to die, and it ain't going to be me," Kelly promised.

Fanny stood, and downed his shot of tequila then asked Kelly, "Are you telling me that Patrick knows? How?"

Kelly paused for a second. "The answer to that lies at the bottom of Watsons Bay Gap. Somehow, I need to see his mother, big Ma O'Finlay. She has to be filled in, and then, and maybe only then, would she be willing to sanction someone to wipe this scum out once and for all. Fuck me, what a dog's breakfast."

"How the fuck are you going to set up a meet with one of the biggest mobsters in Sydney? Just knock on her door and say, hello?" Fanny asked with his arms spread wide.

"Maybe it's that simple," Kelly replied. "I need another shot of that tequila, Emmanuel."

"I think you may need more than that, my friend. Let's all just take a deep breath and work our way through the available scenarios. Cool heads need to prevail here today."

Kelly swallowed his shot. He paced the room, then addressed all three brothers as one. "Right now, as I stand here in your home, I've managed to piss off God's Garbage, the skinheads, and the sharpies. Christ, they all know I worked with JC at the Crumpernickel. And now Patrick is hot on my heels with only one thing in mind. I need some time alone, to think this whole thing through—some time-out. Don't worry, I have an old friend I need to check on until I can figure out a solution. Julius, can you pack the CD player inside a cardboard box? I'm taking that with me. It may be my only ticket out of this mess."

Kelly shared a handshaking shoulder nudge with each of the brothers while standing in the backyard. He placed a piece of paper inside Fanny's large palm. "If you need to contact me, leave a message at this number, and I'll get back to you the same day. Keep a spare seat for me at the dinner table, Fanny. You never know, we may cross paths one more time? Take care." He pulled down his cap, slipped on the heavy-set jacket, and grabbed his bag while Julius opened the back gate. Kelly tentatively stepped out to the lane, looked right, then to his left, and slipped out of sight with his head facing down.

Chapter-22

THE RIGHT HONOURABLE Anthony Roberts was the Local Member for Lane Cove on the North Shore of Sydney. As the Leader of the House, he also had taken on three front bench ministerial portfolios. He was the Special Minister of the State, the Minister for Social Services, and the Minister for Mental Health. He was regarded as a shooting star in the world of politics and had been earmarked as a possible deputy leader in the upcoming State Election.

Parliament House is located on Macquarie Street. Roberts sat behind his office desk with a feeling of angst threatening to consume him like an infectious disease. He knew this day would arrive when his one vulnerability would come back to bite him on the arse, and today was the day he would feel the pain of his own lust. Today he would now need to take that final step into the grubby world of political reality—today it was time to pay the ferryman, and that man's name was Patrick O'Finlay.

His private secretary buzzed his phone. "Sir, your three o'clock appointment has just arrived."

"Thank you, Rosemary. Please ask Jenny to show him into conference room B. I'll be there in a minute." Roberts gathered up the contents of a folder he had been scrutinising for the past hour. He needed a clue as to why the man in this file was of interest to the likes of Patrick O'Finlay. He was still none the wiser. Roberts pushed it inside a second folder titled Department of Child Protection, then stood up. He slipped on his suit jacket, deciding to take the two flights of stairs back down to ground level. Roberts needed time to breathe. He felt noxious and just wanted this meeting to be over. He passed the main Parliament House information desk. Jenny met his glance with a look of concern etched across her naïve face. "Minister, do you want me to notify security? Perhaps they can casually pass on by, you know, just in case. This man.... he looked at me funny. It gave me the absolute creeps."

"No, it's okay, Jenny. I'll be fine."

The door was open. Roberts walked in to see the back of Patrick O'Finlay's head gazing out a large window towards the Botanic Gardens and Mrs Macquarie's Chair. "Mr O'Finlay, please be seated. I have an extremely tight schedule today."

Patrick turned with a smug smile, "I bet you do, Anthony. Seems to me you're a *very* busy man. Did you get your hands on the file I asked to see?"

"What guarantees do I have that you will destroy all the copies of those photos?"

"You have none, Minister. And even if I offered you some line of bullshit, you wouldn't believe me anyway, so let's just cut the crap and get down to the business at hand, shall we?"

"These files cannot leave Parliament House. Do you understand? They are digitally encrypted and will sound off a couple of hundred different alarm bells if you attempt to leave this building. They're protected by law. Severe penalties apply if ever found in the wrong hands."

"Are those the same laws that say a respected man of the community shall not sodomise an underage boy, Minister?"

"You bastard." Roberts placed a file down on the boardroom table marked KELLY Phil.

Patrick opened it. Inside, watermarked in big red letters were the words *For Ministers Eyes Only*. Patrick sat down and flicked through the first few pages. "So, what am I looking at here?"

"It's the complete locked juvenile record on the individual in question," the minister answered.

Patrick read two names out loud. "Mrs Gillian Hartman [nee Kelly] and Miss Serena Elizabeth Kelly. Is this the mother, then?"

"Both mother and daughter. The mother remarried, but the husband passed away some years ago. The daughter changed her name back to her paternal father's name only recently."

"It says here she divorced her first husband under the battered wife legislation."

"Yes, she left her first husband with her four-year-old son while she was eight months pregnant. The divorce came later."

"And this says it was a joint application to reach out to her abandoned son."

"That's correct. If you read the complete file, the application was at the insistence of the daughter, but as a juvenile, she still needed her mother's written permission to file the Order."

"How can you be sure the son she searches for is this, Phil Kelly?"

"She left a sum of money with a written note at the church. It's the same person, there is no doubt."

Patrick was intrigued as to how all this works. "What happens after that?"

"Well, they apply for the Order. Then it's up to the other party to come forward before the reunification can take place. It's not a simple process. It takes a long time to enact. There are many pitfalls, and each party needs to be protected."

"So basically, the mother dumped her own kid, left him sucking his thumb inside a church, and now she wants him back."

"Nobody knows the actual circumstances relating to why she did what she did. Desperate times call for desperate measures. Drawing conclusions would be wrong. Are we done here? I'm expected somewhere in fifteen minutes."

Patrick then asked, "The address that's written down here, how recent is that?"

"It's current. That's where both mother and daughter reside. Serena Kelly is almost fourteen now."

Patrick pulled out a pocket notepad and a pen. He copied down all the information he needed. "A private school education? I see old Mum came good. Husband number two must have done all right?" Patrick stood up and flicked a small thumb drive at the minister. "Catch. This is your special photo album. It's the only copy. I don't think it would take too much effort to fill another album, you sick fuck. Stay in touch, Minister, and keep up the good work. Maybe my family can make a sizeable contribution to your next election campaign. I mean, that is how all this works—isn't it?" Patrick shouldered the minister as he swept past.

Tommy was feeding the meter when Patrick arrived back at the car. "Don't worry about that, mate, we've got some surveillance work to take care of."

Chapter-23

BALMORAL BEACH sits on the foreshore of Middle Harbour, looking directly out to the picturesque Sydney Harbour Heads. Queenwood Private Girls' College was named after the now-defunct Queenwood Ladies' College at Eastbourne, in East Sussex, on the south coast of England. The site at Mandalong Road was chosen because of its north-easterly aspect that overlooked Rocky Point Island located about halfway along a three-kilometre stretch of what is regarded as a family-friendly beachside location.

The school siren sounded at 3:15 P.M. to end the final period of the day, and this being a Friday, Serena Kelly unpacked her school-issued backpack, tossed her textbooks into her locker and hurried out to meet with her best friend Helen standing at the front gates. Normally she would wait with the hundreds of other students and catch the school bus provided that dropped her one street back from her home, but today was different. Both girls were eager to discuss the details of their much-anticipated long weekend away and needed the extra forty minutes saved by using public transport.

Both Serena and Helen crossed over The Esplanade that followed the harbourside pathway. They strolled past the old boathouse towards the public bus stop and sat down to wait for the 272. The two young teenagers were both excited *and* nervous about the upcoming scam they were attempting to pull off. For two weeks now, each girl had been busy laying down a smokescreen to dupe both Helen's parents and Serena's mother. Serena's mother was under the impression the girls were to spend the holiday weekend at Helen's parents' banana passion-fruit farm located a two-hour drive south of Sydney on the outskirts of Bega, a small town made famous for its cheese. In a visa-versa sting, Helen's mum and dad, who *were* actually spending the weekend at the farm, assumed their youngest daughter would be under the safe guardianship and the ultimate responsibility of her nineteen-year-old sister, Liz. Who just quietly did not give a brass razoo where her younger sibling spent the next three days as long as she was back before 4:00 P.M. on Monday afternoon. She had made her own plans, and they certainly did not include her pain-in-the-bum little sister hanging around.

Saturday night was the big bash party, the 'must be seen at event' of the school year at a small town called Wisemans Ferry, located about seventy-five kilometres north-west of Sydney. Located on the banks of the Hawkesbury River, and with transport already provided courtesy of two older boys they liked from the nearby Cremorne Boys High School, all the details had been carefully mapped out with the exacting precision only a teenage girl can devise. The simple fact that Ray Arigo was old enough to have his P plates, and also owned a half-decent car, was the difference between another drab weekend and one full of promise based on a pack of lies. Oh, to be so young, and yet still have all the answers.

Serena and Helen swapped stories about their last clandestine meeting with Ray and his good-looking friend Evan. They talked about their first kiss. Both boys also had part-time jobs, which also meant they had money. They discussed make-up choices, shoes, and checked their rehearsed stories to get them out of the house and free from the clutches of their overprotective mothers. The two teenagers shared a combined thrill of expectation that this could be 'the weekend' while the second bus slowed as it approached the Spit Bridge. The 190 came to a full stop, and both girls hurried off with a flurry of expectation. They had almost a full free hour up their sleeve now to discuss all the details before Helen's brother would meet Serena at Parrawi Head with a small 12-foot runabout. The span of water to

Clontarf Reserve was less than a mile wide, and even though the open parkland was surrounded by native bushlands, Serena's home was only a brisk ten-minute walk on the opposite side.

Her heart was pounding with anticipation as she visualised her wardrobe, working out what she would wear to the big party this Saturday night, which any person that mattered was all talking about. She was totally unaware of the forces of evil that were working against her.

The next morning, Serena kissed her mother goodbye on the cheek and raced down the front stairs, two at a time with her over-night bag packed. "Are you sure I can't drop you off at Helen's? It's no bother, really," her mother called out.

"It's okay, Mum. Helen and her brother are meeting me at the marina. It's quicker this way. It will take you a good thirty minutes by the time you cross the bridge, do a U-turn, then come home. I'm fine."

"Okay, ring me darling when you get to Helen's farm. Have a good time. I love you."

"Love you too, Mum. Bye."

Her feet almost didn't touch the ground as she negotiated the limestone and granite stairs to Clontarf Reserve. People were walking their dogs, Some kids were trying to fly a kite with little success. None of that mattered now. She was on her way to what may be the most important weekend of her life. To be a teenager and still be a virgin was considered very uncool. Serena took her first step towards changing that by following Sandy Bay Road, instead of crossing the open reserve. She could see the bus stand ahead where she looked for Ray's car. She knew the model, and she was also over ten minutes early.

A dark-coloured Ford *Transit* van slowed. She took no notice until it pulled up suddenly right in front of where she stood while nervously tapping both feet. The door slid open, and a man jumped out. Before Serena realised what was happening, she was being forced to the mattress that covered the entire rear loading bay with a cloth held firm to her mouth. Serena was a strong girl. She bucked and lashed out with both fists clenched in a frenzy of punches. The smell of chloroform was making her feel sick. She thrashed her head about from side-to-side, lifting her knees into the air trying to make solid contact in the spot her two older brothers had told her many times will render a man to the category of pretty much useless creating enough time to make a possible escape.

She felt her strength waning, her eyes began to fade, and her body became limp. The van sped off towards a dirt track that was a shortcut to Peronne Ave. That connected to Heaton Ave, which eventually would bring them out onto the four-lane Spit Road, and to a place unknown but for her two captors.

"Is she out yet, Patrick? Fuck, do you reckon anyone was watching?" Tommy was glancing over his left shoulder while he kept both hands on the wheel.

"Shut up and just keep driving. And what did I tell you about using names?" *Idiot.*

Ten minutes later, right on the tick of nine A.M., Ray pulled over to the small drop off bay at the top of Sandy Bay Road and turned off the ignition. The two horny teenage boys waited patiently for over fifteen minutes. "Sorry, buddy," Ray said to his anxious passenger, "looks like you're not getting any action this weekend—loser." He was laughing as he spoke just to rub it in that Evan's girl must have become spooked and pulled out.

"Plenty more fish in the sea, Ray. Don't you worry about that, I'll still score," Evan replied smugly, wanting to protect his unbeaten record of six consecutive weekends inserting tab A into slot B.

Chapter-24

KELLY RODE throughout the night, passing through Campbelltown while following the Hume Hwy south.

Reaching Goulburn, he deviated slightly to the south-west along the M23 which heads straight into Canberra. He followed the sign that read: Cooma - 128 kilometres. The Monaro Hwy cuts straight through the town of Bredbo about thirty kilometres to the north.

The first warming rays of the rising sun could be felt through Kelly's swag. He pulled the zip down and wriggled out. He took a leak near the river and tasted the cool country air fill both his lungs. It had a unique smell to it. There was enough loose firewood to build a warming fire, and soon he was seated on a river stone with a steel mug of hot instant Ovaltine warming the blood in both hands. He rinsed his cup, tipping the remaining water on the last of the hot coals, then kicked in enough dirt to render it safe. His next stop was St John's Ambulance, located in the heart of Bredbo.

Kelly eased his bike onto its side-stand. He pushed open a glass door and approached an elderly-looking woman seated behind a desk.

"Hello, young man. Another beautiful crisp morning. Please, come on inside. What can I do for you?"

"Good morning. My name is, Phil Kelly. I'm looking for a lady named, Molly. Sorry, that's all I have, but I've been told she's a nurse," he explained.

"She sure is, or at least was. Molly is unofficially retired now. Well, that's what she likes people to think. Are you a friend?"

"Apparently she saved my life. I just wanted to say thank you."

"Oh, my God, you're that kid Jake's young boy found in the river, aren't you? Look at you now, all well and in one piece. There might be a few young ladies happy to see the likes of you in town?"

Kelly's felt his cheeks blush. "So, Molly—do you know where I can find her?"

The well-rounded lady stood up from behind her desk. She walked past a small counter. "My name is, Joan. Follow me, please." She stopped in the middle of the main street with her arm raised. There was no traffic to worry about. "Can you see the church steeple over there? Turn right, and then you'll come across the showrooms of Hender & Sons' Tractors. Turn left down Jarangle Road until you come to Connolly's Gap. There's an old beat-up Ford ute sitting high up in a gum tree. Follow the dirt road until you see a white-painted weatherboard house. That's where Molly lives. You can't miss it. She grows roses—lots of them."

Molly's front yard looked like a mini version of the Botanical Garden. Brightly coloured reds, yellows and whites showcased the pathway to her front porch. The unfamiliar sound of a bike engine caused Molly to turn as she watered some flowering hanging baskets. She turned off the hose and stared at the man on his motorbike. Molly remained rigid as the stranger removed his gloves and lifted his dust-covered helmet clear. Kelly felt a warm sensation flow through his veins. Goosebumps popped up all over his body like mosquito bites. He allowed his old bomber jacket to slide off both his shoulders before laying it over the bike's seat and pushed the gate open.

Molly let out a small gasp. "Well, aren't you a sight for sore eyes? It's nice to see you with a bit of colour in your cheeks. Come over here and give me a hug, young man."

Kelly's legs felt wobbly, and he didn't think it was from the long ride. He stumbled forward and fell into Molly's open arms. Salted tears ran down both his cheeks. No words were spoken—they weren't necessary. It was a moment of joy to be shared by two people who knew why. Molly eased clear from their combined embrace. She held Kelly at arm's length. "Just let me take a good look at what you have become? A tall, handsome, strapping young man. All of Bredbo were rooting for you to pull through, you know. You were the main topic of conversation on everyone's lips down at the pub."

"Maybe I can return the favour and buy them all a round of drinks. My shout, I reckon. Molly, can you tell me what happened? Where did you find me?"

"Come on inside. I'll make you something to eat, and we can talk."

Kelly listened on as Molly filled in all the details. She slid a plate across the table with a one-inch thick T-Bone steak surrounded with baked potatoes, carrots and broccoli. "Feed the man meat, my husband used to say. It looks like you could do with a bit of fattening up?"

Kelly swallowed the last mouthful. He rubbed his full stomach, now resembling that of the smiling fat Buddha. A black-and-white photo hung on one wall of two men in uniform. Kelly asked the question. "Are they your sons?"

Molly paused as she looked up. "Raymond and Steven. Both gone now. One killed, the other MIA during Vietnam. A shitty time for all of us. Bredbo gave up five sons during that war."

"I'm so sorry for your loss." Kelly wandered if this feeling he had was the same a person might feel towards a grandmother.

Molly stood over the sink. Kelly walked over and grabbed a spare tea-towel. She handed him a dripping plate. "I just remembered something. I can't believe it slipped my mind. Did you own a dog?"

Kelly stopped drying, "Santa, my border collie. That's the other reason I came back. Did you see him?"

"See him! If it weren't for that dog, you wouldn't be standing in my kitchen, let me just say."

"Is Santa okay? Did he survive, where is he now?" Kelly fired each question, one after the other.

"Go and park that bloody great big bike of yours in the shed out back. Take a shower because I can smell you from here, and then we'll go for a drive."

Molly's old Toyota waded through the Murrumbidgee River live-stock crossing. She braked to a stop and pointed across Kelly's chest. "Over there. You see that fallen tree, that's where young Luke Pender found your dog. You were half-buried down closer to the bank. Do you want to take a closer look?"

"Na, one part of the river is the same as the next. I really want to go see me dog, Molly."

They passed the Amaroo Fire Trail, covered the miles of open plains while following the dirt road across Shannons Flat. Molly slowed, then pulled to a stop. "You're on gate duty today."

Kelly unclipped the chain and pushed it open. The name read: 'Crackenback Ridge Downs–J. Pender' burnt with a branding iron into an old creosote-impregnated railway sleeper. The natural landscape started to change drastically as the flat-lands became a diminishing reflection in the rear-view mirror, and the road continued to carve its way towards the foothills of the high country.

"Not long now, Phil," Molly pointed from behind the wheel. "Just over that next rise."

The farmhouse looked majestic, built well above the one-hundred-year flood lines of a bent creek with the blue haze of the distant mountains forming a bushranger's backdrop. Kelly estimated that over thirty people were gathered around a wide verandah under a green-painted aluminium bull-nosed roof. "Who are all these people?" he needed to ask.

"There are no secrets up here, word travels fast around these parts," Molly answered.

Kelly looked over at Molly with a look of the unknown. "Word... what word?"

"You're a bit of a celebrity, Phil. Don't worry, I hope you've got your drinking boots on. I have known Jake Pender to enjoy a beer on a hot day if you get my drift. I expect we won't be pulling up stumps until tomorrow sometime," she added with a wry smile.

The number was more like fifty. People kept drifting out from inside the house. A group of men were breaking in some fresh brumbies in a nearby corral. They all stopped and made their way over. Kelly opened his door, then walked to the front of the vehicle.

Jake Pender was your quintessential Australian stockman. He stood tall in a pair of scuffed riding boots, wearing a pair of cream chino pants with a red and white chequered dress shirt. Both sleeves were rolled up to his elbows, his stained and holed hat tipped slightly to one side. He strode over with a single purpose. His leather-like skin was lined with creases of dirt from years of hard yakka. His easy-going smile looked out of place. Kelly first thought his persona would fit more with that of a gunslinger. Jake extended his giant hand. Kelly pressed hard against his vice-like grip. Then Jake slapped him affectionately on the back, like he would against the rump of a good horse. Kelly needed to brace himself from being rocketed forward and ending up flat on his face.

"Welcome to Crackenback, Phil. I think you may have left something behind, mate." Jake whistled then yelled over his shoulder, "Luke, you can open that door now." Jake looked back at Kelly. "He's been scratching to get out for over twenty minutes now. He knows what's goin' on."

Kelly looked past Jake's broad shoulders towards the end of the verandah. Santa's black and white face came hobbling out on three legs, with his tail wagging like a hummingbird's wings. "We tried hard to save the leg, but it was too far gone. We didn't know what you called him, so we named him, Hopalong. He's a bloody good dog. You should be proud. Hard to break that bond between a man and his dog."

Kelly allowed his body to float back down to ground level. The border collie launched himself at his young master, landing squarely in his lap. Kelly held him tight to his chest. "His name is, Santa. The only worthwhile Christmas present I ever got." Tears were easy to hide behind a slapping tongue going every which way over his face.

Jake Pender wiped his shirtsleeve across his brow then yelled, "Someone please grab this man a bloody beer. Can't you see he's thirsty?" And that's when the party kicked into full swing. Luke turned up in a flash with an icy cold big brown bottle of Resch's Dinner Ale, and there were plenty more to go around.

The two young men shook hands. "You must be, Luke?" Kelly asked. "Molly tells me I owe my life to you. Just wanted to say a big thank you. For both the dog and me."

"Yeah, it was one hell of a day. One I won't forget in a hurry."

As day turned into night, three fires were lit inside 44-gallon drums. Two whole sheep and a fattened pig were roasted over a slow-turning rotisserie, powered by an old washing machine motor. Utes and 4wd's kept turning up with back-slapping strangers keen to shake the hand of the mysterious lost teenage boy from the Murrumbidgee River. They all wanted to share the yarn, adding their own versions of what did, or may have happened, and so the legend grew.

Jake pulled Kelly to one side about midnight, "You got a minute?"

"Yeah, sure," he said.

"Follow me." And so he did, towards the barn.

"Pull up a stump," Jake said. "I want to share a story with you." He pulled out a tin of tobacco. "You smoke?"

"No, but give us one, anyway."

Jake lit both rollies with his Zippo. "After they flew you out by the Royal Flying Doctor, I wanted to put your dog down. He was in pain, lost a lot of blood, and he was exhausted after your trip down the river. Luke wouldn't have a bar of it. We ended up arguing. He takes after his mother, that boy. In the end, he wrapped him up in a blanket and rode into Bredbo to see the vet. He agreed with me. Sometimes you got to be cruel to be kind. Anyway, Luke convinced him to operate. The vet was sure the dog wouldn't wake from the anaesthetic, but he did. Luke drove him home three days later and nursed him back to health. Hand fed him, carried him outside to do his business for ten days." Jake pointed to his left. "Right over there in that horse stall, in fact. When the dog was strong enough to move around on three legs, you know what he did?"

Kelly just shook his head.

"Well, he headed for that ridge up there to the north-east. If you were to draw a straight line to the spot we found you, that would be a good enough starting point. One hell of a dog. For the next month, he just sat on top of that hill and waited—waiting for you. Luke would have to ride up each afternoon and bring him back down for his tucker."

Kelly needed to wipe away the tears. Jake dragged on his smoke, "Don't worry about that, Phil. A good dog is worth more than a few tears to any man worth his weight."

"Luke is pretty attached, I can see that," Kelly said.

"Yeah, but at the end of the day Santa is your dog."

"Hopalong. Call him, Hopalong. It suits him. To be honest, my short life hasn't turned out the way I thought, Jake."

"Are you in trouble?"

"You could say that. I've pissed-off a lot of dangerous people, but I got myself into it, so I need to find my own way clear."

"We have a saying in the high country, Phil. If a man comes at you with a lump of wood, you find a bigger one. If he attacks you with a knife, you shoot him. If he's got a handgun, you find a shotgun and shoot first. If it breathes, we can kill it. If it's dead, it's dead forever."

"I wish it were that easy," Kelly said.

"It's the law of the land in the bush. You need to look your demons square in the eye Phil and then deal with 'em head-on."

"I envy the life you have up here. True friends that always have your back... plus your family."

"The only thing that makes a man worthwhile is his word and a clear conscience. At the end of the day, you'll need to decide. Right or wrong, it doesn't matter. You gotta take the leap of faith, eventually."

Kelly stubbed out his smoke. "I'm happy for Hopalong to stay on here, Jake, if that's all right with you? A sheepdog belongs with the sheep, even if it's from a distance. This is a good life, better than I can offer at the moment, that's for sure. I'll be heading back to Sydney some time tomorrow or when the beer runs out—whatever comes first? There's a man I need to face up to, and it can't wait any longer."

"I'll let Luke know about your decision, and good luck up north. Don't be a stranger. You're always welcome back at Crackenback Downs."

"I have a favour to ask before I go?"

"Ask away."

"I would love to take one of your horses for a ride. Be silly to pass up the chance while I'm here."

"Have you ever been on the back of a horse before?"

"No, but I've seen John Wayne do it. How hard can it be?"

Jake laughed out loud. "Only one way to answer that. Sunup, meet me at the corral, and I'll see if we can't find you a nice gentle filly."

"Cheers for that, Jake. How's your drink?"

"Bloody empty."

Chapter-25

MOLLY PULLED into her backyard. "Go straight on in, we don't need to lock houses around here."

Kelly opened the door. There was a hand-written note lying on the kitchen table. The door slammed against its stopper a second time. Kelly turned to face Molly. "This was on the table when I walked in."

Molly picked it up. "It says here that Joan received a message for *you* to ring someone."

Kelly remembered his final talk with Fanny.

"But she didn't leave a phone number," Molly added. "I'll ring Joan now. She's become more and more forgetful these days."

The phone picked up. Soon Molly was waving her hand at Kelly to grab a pen and paper. "Okay, Joan. What was it again? 02 869 2301. Thanks, Joan, talk to you tomorrow. Goodbye." Molly held the phone out in her outstretched hand, "I'm guessing you want to use this?"

Kelly rang the number. The sound of Fanny's voice answered in a deep, low, "Hello."

"Fanny, it's me. I just got your message. What's up?"

"Lucky, today when Juliette was clearing the lunch dishes, there was an envelope left on a table with my name on it. I opened it when I got home earlier today..."

"Yeah, go on," Kelly prompted.

"Well, it's just that there is a photo with a message written on the back."

"Fanny, why are you stalling? A photo of what?"

"It's not a what, it's more a who. The photo is of a teenage girl gagged while strapped to a bed, and she doesn't look happy if you get my drift."

"A girl!—What girl?"

"I'll read out the note exactly as it's written, okay. Phil Kelly, your mother's name is Gillian, and the photo is your fourteen-year-old sister, Serena. Meet me at the Pearl King - Sunday at 2:00 pm. Don't come empty-handed. It would be a shame to let the boys enjoy a bit of slap and tickle on such a young sweet piece of pussy. It has to be, O'Finlay," Fanny explained.

Kelly stood frozen in Molly's kitchen. His mind was racing. "I don't understand. How would he know about my mother? And a sister? What does she look like, Fanny?"

"A female version of you, Lucky. I'm not kidding, the resemblance is uncanny, man."

"I need to see that photo."

"You can't come here, you're too hot."

"Liverpool train station near the lockers." Kelly felt the key in his front pocket as a force of habit. "Can you meet me there, then drive my bike back to Sydney, and park it somewhere safe?"

Fanny only asked one question. "What time?"

Kelly looked at his watch. It was 9:40 A.M., and it was now Monday. He remembered checking his odometer when he arrived in Bredbo. Sydney was just over 340 kilometres away. "I'll be there by one o'clock. I'm leaving now."

"Okay, one o'clock it is."

Kelly hung up the phone and caught Molly's worrying stare. "I need to go, Molly. Sorry, but something has come up."

"Did I hear you mention your mother—and a sister?"

"Yep, you heard right. Sounds like bullshit to me, but I have to make sure. I know why you people choose to live in the country. The cities are full of idiots. I reckon when the time comes to settle down, it won't be in bloody Sydney," Kelly's tone suggested he was deadly serious.

Kelly made just the single fuel stop at a roadhouse outside of Goulburn. He arrived at the Liverpool Station car park with twenty minutes to spare. He grabbed a coffee, then inserted his key into a security locker and emptied the contents. Then he found a spare seat and waited for Fanny to arrive on the next train from the city.

Fanny turned up dressed in his riding gear. Kelly ushered him away from the hustle and bustle of the commuting crowds. "Show me the photo," he asked.

Fanny pulled the envelope from inside his leather jacket. Kelly slid the photo out and just stared at it.

"You see what I mean, a dead ringer," Fanny said.

"Yeah, maybe . . . I'm still not convinced. Either way, whoever this young girl is, she looks bloody terrified. I don't need any more excuses to take this prick out. He's already pressed my button one too many times. Time to face the enemy. Fanny, I need some hardware and not the kind you buy from Bunnings. Do you know anyone?"

"You need to see, Jimmy Four Fingers."

Kelly looked at Fanny with a quizzical stare, "Jimmy who?"

"Jimmy Four Fingers. He sold his old gun shop in the city, and now he runs a small fuel and mechanical workshop up on the banks of the Hawkesbury River in Brooklyn, but he'll have what you want, no doubt about it." Fanny tapped Kelly on the shoulder. "Follow me." He walked inside a newsagent, moved up and down the three short isles until he found a deck of playing cards. He paid the shopkeeper and stepped outside, then fanned the deck and slipped out the ace of spades before writing an address on the front of the card. "Here, give him this when you see him, he'll understand."

"I need to find where Patrick might be holding this girl. It will be somewhere close, not his home, but a place he can access easily without bringing any attention to himself," Kelly asked.

"Emanuelle wanted me to give you this." Fanny handed him two addresses. "Patrick uses a couple of safe houses. One is in Allambie Heights, and the other is hidden away in the Garigal National Park, up near where the Wakehurst Parkway ends in Frenchs Forest. He's drawn you a mud-map."

"Fanny, where do Patrick and Tommy live?"

"Patrick at one time lived two doors up from, Big Ma, but after his brothers died—sorry, I mean murdered, I've got no idea where either of 'em lives now."

Kelly then asked, "This, Jimmy Four Fingers, is he a lover of antique firearms, let's say American Civil War era?"

"Why would you ask that?"

"It's the only real currency I've got to trade."

"He's a good guy. Just go and see him, I'm sure he'll work something out. I'll need your full-face helmet as well. I can't risk being seen riding a piece of Jap-crap like this. I have a reputation to protect."

The two men shook hands and parted company. Kelly boarded the 1:45 P.M. city-bound train. The last stop was Central. He stepped out onto the long platform, exited through the main entrance, then walked until he found a multi-storey department store on the opposite side of the street. Twenty minutes later he was in the back of a Black & White taxi with a white knee-length overcoat, a blue, red and black ballpoint pen set plus a clipboard with some old sales receipts he fished out of a bin all stuffed into a paper Myers shopping bag complete with logo. The cab dropped him on Oxford Street, a block south of the massive government-owned Telecom Public Works Depot.

He slipped on his coat, and with the clipboard in hand, he strode into the grounds like he'd worked there for years and searched out the Vehicle Service Department. The cavernous workshop was where every Telecom work van was serviced each month and recorded in a logbook. Inside, a team of mechanics were busy changing out the oils, replacing tyres and any other general maintenance required on the hundreds of passenger cars, vans and light trucks. It was like being let loose inside a lolly shop, and it was a carjackers paradise. Kelly walked towards three Toyota *Hiace* linesman vans, complete with ladders, tools, hard hats and overalls waiting to be put back into service. Van no-323 had everything he would need, so Kelly entered the rear glassed office.

"Good afternoon," he addressed the young female clerk while flipping through the papers on his clipboard. "Tony in admin tells me van three-two-three is finished and ready to roll off the line, is that right?"

The young office receptionist looked up from behind her desk under a pair of black-rimmed glasses. "Excuse me?"

"Vehicle three-two-three, have you got the keys handy, there's a crew waiting now? They're ready to attend an emergency call out. Apparently, some clown has driven straight into a sub-station and has knocked out the entire phone network from Brookvale all the way back to Narrabeen," Kelly explained.

"I don't have that . . ."

Kelly interrupted, "What's your name? I'll need to ring your manager and let him know why there's a delay. Can I use this office phone?"

"Sorry, which van did you say again? Communications around here can really suck sometimes," she reluctantly offered as a defence.

"Yeah, don't I know it? Van number three-two-three." A minute later, Kelly grinned and walked away, jingling the keys in his hand.

Jimmy Four Fingers was an enigma, a bygone relic from the Provincial Irish Republican Army—the IRA. With over seventy-six confirmed kills between 1970 and 1977, he was the IRA's number one hit-man, holding almost hero status during his seven years of terrorising the Royal Ulster Constabulary. He was eventually arrested and jailed in 1978. After two years behind bars awaiting trial, the IRA paid a substantial sum of money to organise his escape and resettlement in Australia.

With his new identity in the chosen name of Aiden O'Shanassey, he enjoyed a relatively obscure new life running his small mechanical and fuel business on the upper reaches of the tranquil setting that was the Hawkesbury River, never forgetting the life debt he owed to his Australian connections of the IRA.

The tubed rubber air-line that stretched across both fuel lanes let out a short gurgled bell sound from inside a duel car-bay workshop. Dropping a spanner back to the floor, the ageing mechanic backed out from under the gearbox and wiped clean his oiled hands before leaving the confines of his workspace. He was approaching the single Shell fuel bowser only to find a Telecom worker approaching from a parked work van.

"Gooday, are you, Jimmy? A friend of mine said to give you this." Kelly handed over the ace of spades while counting the fingers on each hand. It was easy to see how he earned his name.

Jimmy Four Fingers' lips parted, and he smiled at the stranger. "Did that crazy Indian tell you why—the ace?"

"Na, but I reckon he can't play poker for shit," Kelly replied.

"Huh, it was a bet," he chuckled. "A fifty-dollar note for a clean shot through the spade from two hundred fifty metres. He didn't believe it could be done."

"Who won?" Kelly asked, interested in the answer.

"Fanny came second. Follow me."

Jimmy pulled to a grinding close, three old concertina doors, deciding it was a good enough time to pull the pin on today as far as work went. Kelly followed him to the other side of the relatively clean and well laid out working area. Jimmy mumbled something under his Irish breath and motioned with a nod of his head at a calendar nailed to a wall. An ace of spades was pinned over a date with a perfectly neat rounded hole in the dead centre of the spadille.

"I guess you well and truly won the bet, nice shot," Kelly commented.

"Thanks. What are you after?"

"Short-range, under five hundred metres, Special Ball 7.62 NATO. Muzzle suppressor with an optical scope, plus a sidearm."

Jimmy walked over to a half-stripped-down EH Holden sitting idle over a second sump pit. "Give us a hand with this, will ya?"

Together they pushed the vehicle forward about five feet. Kelly followed him down six steps into the pit. Jimmy slid back a metal panel to reveal a pin-pad. He punched in the letters IRA, followed by the numbers seven and six. A concealed door hissed open to reveal his personal cache of the tools of his old trade.

There was an old saying often shared amongst the small fraternity of single-shot people killers. 'Old assassins' will one day die, but their weapons will live forever'. The individual choice of an assassins' rifle was more important than choosing a wife. It needed to meet strict criteria and pass an endless test of technical capabilities. Upon the eventuality of death, it was an accepted fact that the authorities would eventually track down an old snipers' personal choice of weapons. To the chosen ones who accepted this as their life trade, this was like lifting your skirt and showing off your lacy underwear. No dropper wanted to be seen with a pair of granny's old knickers—only the latest-and-greatest would be accepted as a genuine pass.

Jimmy Four Fingers always enjoyed the few times he had cause to open this direct link to his glorious past. Inside was his own personal assassin's version of his résumé. He looked at his original AWC PM L96A1 sniper rifle with its matching 10×42 Hensoldt telescopic sight responsible for his claim to fame all those years ago. It always rekindled an enormous sense of pride, just looking at it in all its glory, but time stands still for no man with the rapid advancements in firearm technology.

"You familiar with this model?" Jimmy searched the young man's face for an answer.

Kelly leaned forward and removed the SIG-Sauer-SSG-3000. He screwed the Birdsong Black-T TacOps suppressor to the barrel end, then slid a single round of 7.62 x 51mm NATO ammunition into the seven-shot magazine and expertly inserted the clip with the under-slap of his hand. He eased the ATACR 4-16x42mm F1 scope with a MIL-R reticle from its protective hold and secured it to the steel 20 MOA canted base mount, then clipped the two o-rings closed. He lifted the rifle, laying the stock into the flat of his open left palm with the butt firmly embedded into his right shoulder, scanned the room, back and forth, then proceeded to dismantle the rifle in reverse order, all in under a minute.

"Pretty much answers that question," Jimmy had to agree. "How does a kid as young as you know how to handle a rifle like that?"

"No pesky parents to worry about," Kelly answered, while he remembered the old bushman he befriended known to the few as just Bunyan.

The old Irish legend opened up a sliding drawer, then uncovered from its dust cover, a Heckler & Koch MK-23 .45 calibre handgun, complete with laser sight and silencer. "Are you okay with this? It was always a favourite of mine."

"That'll be fine," Kelly smiled. "All right, then. What's all this worth?"

"You want to buy or rent?"

"Buy. These will all be going for a swim when I'm done."

"You're looking at four thousand for the lot. Plus, I'll throw in two boxes of ammo for nothing."

Kelly lifted his backpack then slid out the wooden box. He placed it on a bench top. "Open that and tell me what you reckon."

Jimmy lifted it off the bench, "Heavy little sucker, whatever it is." He opened the clasp. "Holy shit, is this what I think it is?"

"I don't know. What are you thinking?"

"I think if you want a straight swap, then we have a deal, but let me tell you this, you're selling yourself short. This is probably worth over ten thousand dollars." Jimmy held the pistol at arm's length while he ran his expert eye down the eight-inch barrel.

"By the look in your eye, I don't think you're thinking of selling."

Jimmy winked with a knowing eye.

Kelly packed up his new toys, hid them under some cabling in the back of the van, and made his way back down the M1 to a date with destiny.

Chapter-26

THE TELECOM VAN slowed as Kelly entered the Pacific Hwy heading south. He turned off at Falcon St which becomes Military Road and crossed the Spit Bridge towards the first of Patrick's safe houses he uses to package all his gear for redistribution to his network of dealers. Which just quietly were about to become anything but *safe* places to be caught hanging about in the foreseeable not too distant future.

The Allambie Heights property turned out to be closer to Manly Dam. Which made sense because it was secluded with a choice of escape routes if the cops ever upset the status quo and actually did the job they were entrusted with by the general public. *What a joke?* No-11 Maroa Crescent was located at the very end of a small dead end spur road that bordered a barbed-wire cyclone perimeter fence. A big two posted warning sign advised any misguided dog walkers they were barking up the wrong path.

Private Property

U.N.S.W. Water Research Laboratory

Trespassers Will Be Prosecuted.

Kelly parked the Telecom van, stepped out dressed in his new work overalls, boots and hardhat, and slid open the side door. He set up a mock workstation on the footpath with a couple of well-placed witches' hats before lifting a steel kerbside cable access door, all the while scrutinising the exterior of the house at number 11. The building was an old pre-federation weatherboard construction typical of the era. The front yard was overgrown with wilting weeds, with a side carport offering rear access to the backyard. He grabbed a small toolbox with a portable orange round-faced service phone and knocked on the door. A dog started to bark and scratch the inside of the closed door.

Bloody great.

The door cracked open to a gap just wide enough for the female occupant to slur, "Yea-ah, what do-oo ya wa-ant?" The house reeked of dope, and even her breath was enough to get you dancing with the fairies.

"Good afternoon. I'm from Telecom and here to check your phone line is still okay, we've had some reports of outages in this area."

"We don't have a phone, idiot. Fuck off." *Slam.* The door almost rocked off its hinges.

Strike one. Kelly crossed what was once lawn and followed the cracker-dust driveway to the rear of the property. He opened a side gate and checked the inside of a 12 x 12-ft garden shed. The girl in the photo could be held in any number of places, and they all needed to be ticked off. It was time to get inside. Kelly felt the rear doorknob and turned it slowly. *Click.* The laundry was small and smelt of mildew. He whistled the dog, who responded at a rate of knots, sliding to a slow drift on the slippery floor tiles. Kelly stepped from behind the door and slammed it shut.

"Who's that?" a voice shouted from another room.

"Santa Claus," Kelly replied. A long-haired hippie dressed in a multi-coloured caftan and a pair of ripped jocks flew up off a ramshackle couch. Kelly delivered a perfect right-hand jab to the point of his jaw, and he ended back where he started without too much fuss. Miss World waltzed in holding a stained bong in her hand with smoke still billowing from her mouth and nostrils. "Hey man, you're back? I told you before, we . . . Huh, what are you doing, let me go?"

Kelly left her with her bong banging away with both fists from the inside of a hallway walk-in linen press with a chair backed up against the doorknob. He started turning the house over. *If this Serena was a smart girl, and if she had been inside this house while she was conscious, she might have left a sign—something—anything?*

The sound of a distant voice echoed through the near-dilapidated house. "Someone let me outta here." *Bang!–Bang!*

The spare bedrooms were both almost void of furniture bar a soiled mattress lying on the floor. The main bedroom's ripped lino floor was covered with just a single clear plastic sheet, a set of scales, some containers full with clear sandwich bags, and a collection of flat-pack cardboard boxes were stacked in one corner. *Definitely the tools of a drug trafficker.* Kelly tossed the room anyway to find it was clean.

"Seriously, come on. I want outta here, please," the muffled voice of reason pleaded a second time.

The kitchen didn't look like a meal had been cooked or eaten there since the North Sydney Bears won their last flag back in 1922. Before leaving, Kelly pushed open the toilet door. He leaned over to lift the lid and noticed a piece of blue cloth poking out from the hollow cardboard centre of the toilet roll. He pulled it clear and read what he thought to be a fashion label. "Sweet-Sexy & Sixteen - size eight." *Could be— clever girl?*

The bong-head yelled again from inside the closet, "Hey . . . Mr Telecom dude, come on. I promise I'll give you a blow-job you if you let me out. Please, I'm claustrophobic."

Kelly cringed at the thought, wishing he could delete that disturbing image from his brain as he closed the front door behind him.

They call it Allambie Heights for a very good reason. The second safe house was located at the highest point of this natural peak that overlooked a golf course. It backed onto some open parkland called Jindabyne Reserve. A brick and tile home was set back off the road on a quarter-acre block. Kelly reconnoitred the exterior in his role as the helpful Telecom man, but it looked vacant. He kicked in a back door and checked out each room, anyway. The house seemed to be ready for demolition. There was nothing there of any interest. It was time to meet with the mother fox and update her on the nasty habits of her youngest cub.

All three houses in Kershaw Lane were devoid of any obvious human activity from Kelly's vantage point where he'd been busily repairing a non-existent phone line problem on the opposite side of the road. With the family being culled from within, it was no surprise. After an hour, he made the decision to find a way inside and wait. He walked up to the front door with his toolbox in hand and knocked. There was no answer. He made his way back to the van and drove around to the rear of the house, then parked next to the eight-foot-high perimeter wall. No problems there with a Telecom ladder at the ready. He laid his tools down at the back door and knocked one more time for good measure. All was quiet inside. Kelly used a woodshed to scale the corrugated iron garage roof, then simply stepped onto the tiled roof. He lifted six tiles and dropped down onto the ceiling rafters. He swung his flashlight from left to right until he located the manhole. Once inside, he opened the back door, collected his toolbox, and went about setting up the CD player, following Julius' instructions word-for-word. He made himself a pot of tea, sat on the couch with the Heckler & Koch sitting by his side looking at the photos of Sean and Dean sitting on the mantle.

Kelly checked his watch. It read 5:15 P.M. when the creak of the front gate opening alerted him that someone had arrived. The sound of a car accelerating away in the distance could be heard. He pulled a curtain to one side to see Big Ma lumbering her way up the front steps with a handful of mail in one hand. She was alone. The sound of a key sliding into the lock was followed by the door swinging open. Kelly stood to one side, hidden from view behind a tall wall unit. Ma closed the door, and Kelly stepped out with his gun arm raised.

"Who I am doesn't matter, what I'm about to show you will change your life forever, there will be no going back, but you have a right to know the truth," was Kelly's rehearsed opening line.

"Who the hell are you, and why are you in my home? Are you insane, young man—do you know who you're fucking with here? Are you are on a death wish? Save your life and get out now."

"Yes, I do know who you are, and I'm also well acquainted with your son, Patrick. I've made a pot of tea. I think it would be wise to sit down?"

"A pot of fucking tea, and how do you know, Patrick?" Ma looked down to her left and pointed. "What's that on the floor?"

Kelly was about to lower his firearm when he heard the back door open. A female voice shouted from the next room, "Auntie Ma, why is there a Telecom ladder leaning against your rear wall?"

Kelly thought for a fleeting second he recognised the voice, but that was ridiculous.

Ma then shouted out, "Madeleine, he's got a gun. Run."

"Who's got a gun?" Her head turned the corner, and she just stood in the one spot with both hands on hips. "What are *you* doing here?"

Kelly was dumbfounded. He needed to catch his thoughts, slow down the brain and rationalise. "Who the hell *are* you? Is this your auntie? You're Ma O'Finlay's niece? Fuck me. Seriously, I don't believe this is happening. What's going on here, Maddy? So, Patrick is your fucking cousin?"

"I never lied to you. Everything you say is true, but it doesn't change anything. Please . . . now let me ask you . . . why are you in my auntie's home with a gun pointed at her? That's the real burning question."

"I don't have the time to sort through all this bullshit right now." Kelly waved the gun, "Both of you sit down . . . *now.*" Kelly's tone achieved the desired result. "Right, look at the TV, and prepare yourself for something beyond bad."

"Phil, what is it, you're scaring me?" Maddy cried wolf.

Ma turned her thick neck toward her niece. "Do you two know each other? Is there something you want to share with me, Madeleine?"

"Not right now, Ma."

"That's right. There is something more important at play right now. Watch, listen and learn," Kelly said. He pressed *play* on the CD player, sat down on a spare seat and finished his tea.

Forty minutes later, Kelly stood up from the comfort of his cushioned chair and pressed *stop*. Ma's lounge room remained shrouded in a vexed silence. A feeling of loathing and betrayal hung in the air. Madeleine was sobbing uncontrollably. Both women sat and stared vacantly into each other's eyes, probing the other for a reaction. Tears of treachery were rolling down Ma's face. Her puckered face resembled a crumpled piece of discarded tissue paper, and Maddy noticed her hands were shaking more so than their normal uneasy rhythm.

Ma was rocked to the bones. She was gasping for air and started to gag. Thinking her auntie may be about to suffer a heart attack, Maddy rushed to the kitchen to get some water and a damp cloth. She patted down the perspiration streaming down Big Ma's forehead. She looked liked she'd just aged ten years. Her hair seemed to have turned a lighter shade of grey in a matter of minutes. Maddy was considering phoning an ambulance. She seriously didn't think that Ma, in her current state, was capable of overcoming the shock of what she had just seen with her motherly eyes.

Kelly bent down and ejected the CD. "I'm sorry you had to see that, Ma. Nothing anyone can say or do will ever replace the grief you feel for the loss of your boys. Now, at least you know the truth, and as insignificant as that may feel at this tragic time, it's better this way. I'm asking for your permission to go after Patrick and find this young girl." Kelly floated the photo onto a small coffee table. Madeleine leaned forward and picked it up. She looked at the young teenager, and then she looked back at Kelly for more than a few seconds. "Is this your sister?"

"I can't be sure. Either way, a yes or a no from you, I will not rest until I hunt him down, and I think you know that."

"What if this is your sister?" Maddy choked through the tears of her despair.

"She is only fourteen. Patrick wants this disc, and now we *all* know why."

"You have my blessing. I am sanctioning you to go and find your sister and to use whatever force is necessary to do just that."

Kelly looked down at Ma for some sign of confirmation. Her face looked cadaverous, lifeless and drained of human colour. Madeleine stood in the centre of the room, resolute with an air of authority. "I represent the O'Finlay name tonight, and I am telling you on my family's blood oath, there will be no retribution from anyone within this or any of the other families."

"Where does he live?" Kelly asked.

"He's not at his home now; I know that because today is his birthday. Tonight he will be at the Crows Nest Hotel. He plays in the pool comp every week."

Kelly disconnected the Sony and prepared to leave. He turned to face Madeleine. "That night you and I shared, what was that all about, then?" He almost regretted asking before the words left his mouth. He already knew the answer.

"I can't talk about that right now. Look at my auntie. Oh, my God. What have we just witnessed? I need to stay with, Ma. I'm not leaving her alone in this state," Madeleine replied through a vindictive, vengeful face. "Finish the job, Lucky Phil. Finish off that murdering bastard once and for all," she added.

"I have to go, Maddy. I just wanted to say before I do, some of life's lessons can be cruel and painful, and that includes the one you dished out from that seductive weapon between your legs. I thank you for being my first. I won't forget that in a hurry, even if it meant nothing to you." Kelly was deadly serious. He turned to leave.

"Hang on a second, young man," Ma struggled to speak through her quivering lips. "I want you to pass on a message from a mother to a son that never was. Come closer, please."

Kelly leaned in close and listened to her words like they might be the last. Then he left through the back door. He continued walking past the parked mustard-coloured Triumph *Stag* in the driveway.

Madeleine followed him outside, "Wait—please, just hang on for one second. You owe me that much."

Kelly stopped without turning. He thought he'd experienced every possible type of pain, but this hurt was something he'd never felt before.

"What are you going to do if you find, Patrick?"

Kelly turned slowly. "It's not a matter of *if*, just when. I don't think it will end well for one of us if that's what you're asking? Which team are you rooting for, Madeleine?" The words were laced with the betrayal Kelly felt at that moment.

"It's not what you think, Lucky Phil."

"It never is," Kelly fired back.

"I will need confirmation of Patrick's death."

"That might be difficult if I've got a bloody great big bullet hole in the back of my head, Maddy dear."

"Don't make this any more complicated than it already is. I have relinquished all business ties to the family, but they're still blood. God, my auntie just buried her two sons— and now this—with Patrick? What was I supposed to do, just abandon Ma in her hour of need?"

"Madeleine, you used me. I shared intimate details with you while we swapped pillow talk about a possible younger sibling. I was vulnerable, and you pounced. Now I hold in my hand a photo of a young girl being held against her will. Coincidence? I don't think so somehow."

"Please, take this. It's the home phone number where I'm staying in Sydney. I'm booked on a flight back to London next week, after that you won't ever see me again. I have to know the outcome. There will be arrangements that need to be taken care of. Family from Ireland will need to be notified. There are protocols in place to protect Ma and her interests from the other Sydney families."

Kelly looked down at the number in his hand. "If I find this young girl—sister or not—if she has been harmed in any way . . . It would be wise for you not to step foot back in this country, Madeleine," Kelly answered.

"I'll be at this house until I leave. Good luck and I am sorry—about you and me."

"You were my first, so that will stay with me forever, but only that." Kelly left the rear castle gate open.

The sound of the Telecom van leaving down the rear lane-way prompted Madeleine to walk at a steady pace to her car. She opened up the passenger's door and fumbled under the seat blindly until she felt the cold of steel on her fingertips. She dragged out the Glock G19 and held it in her hand while walking towards the rear door. Madeleine could overhear Big Ma sobbing, still sitting at an awkward angle, slowly sliding into a world of oblivion.

Ma forced her head up as her niece came closer. "Well, darling, the O'Finlay business interests rest firmly on your shoulders now. You'll just have to step up to the plate from here on. I hope you're up to the task?" Ma looked up at the two photos of Sean and Dean sitting proudly on her mantelpiece.

Madeleine raised her right arm while she stood on her auntie's blindside. Ma's head was facing up toward the photos of her murdered sons. "I know about your betrayal of my father," Madeleine hissed.

Her auntie turned to see the wrong end of a gun inches away from her face. "What are you talking about? Put that away, girl. This is . . ."

"Shut the fuck up. I have an inside contact with the Costa family. The only two people who knew my father would visit his mistress that night in Curl Curl was my mother and my father's sister. Dear old, Auntie Margaret. Goodbye."

Madeleine pulled the trigger twice and watched the side of her auntie's face being splattered all over the remaining two sofa cushions. Ma's obese body slid slowly to one side. Madeleine stood resolute, her hand was trembling slightly. "The O'Finlay interests surely do rest with me now. You can count on it, Auntie Margaret. Money in the bank, Ma—money in my bank," she repeated before stepping over to the phone and dialled the same Vaucluse number.

This time Luca Costa was waiting for the call. He picked up on the second ring. "What happened, tell me, did it all go as planned?"

Maddy answered in a matter-of-fact tone. "Better than we could ever have imagined. Bitter-sweet revenge for both our families is within our grasp. I've done my part. The rest is up to you now. Just like the old days when my father controlled all of Sydney. The time is near when we both can claim our natural birthright. Together, Luca, our two families will reign supreme."

". . . And this Kelly guy, did he take the bait?"

"Like a lovesick puppy. It's so much easier when someone else does our own wet work. After that . . . Well, the dye has been cast. It's time to make the onetime-offer to, Emmanuel. He won't have a choice. He made a blood oath to God's Garbage that can't be broken."

"I'm already onto that. I knew there was a reason I fell in love with you, Madelaine O'Hara. You are always one step ahead of the game."

"You better believe it, my lover. See you tomorrow, bright and early."

"Don't worry, both my brothers will be there." Luca hung up the phone. He looked over at a heavily tattooed man sitting opposite. "The time has come, Emmanuel, to make the call. Your own family's future rests solely on your shoulders. Life is always about choices, you have chosen wisely, my friend."

"We will never be friends, Luca," Emmanuel wanted to clarify.

"We don't have to be. Business is business. Mutual respect is all I ask."

Chapter-27

KELLY CHECKED HIS WATCH as he crawled along at a snail's pace through level-two of a three-storey Wilson car park. He remembered Madeleine explaining, "Tommy's car will stick out like a set of swollen dog's balls."

The van tyres squealed on the smooth cement surface as he pulled down hard on the wheel to negotiate the tight turn. Groups of people were walking down the stairwell or heading for the lift doors. Crows Nest was an entertainment and restaurant hub of choice for the nouveau rich North Shore jet-setting crowd of Sydney. Kelly suddenly slammed his foot down hard on the brake. A sharp screech of rubber echoed inside the undercover parking area. He cast his eyes over the parked vehicle, thinking Madeleine was spot on. He found an empty bay close by, reversed in and relaxed into his seat to prepare for the hardest part—the wait. It was 8:43 P.M.

Sixteen names were randomly drawn from an old two-litre bucket of cooking oil courtesy of the pool-friendly sous chef. The bar manager shouted out each name over the ambient buzz of the busy sports bar. A man everyone called, Crackers, who ran the pool comp each week like an Aussie version of the colourful Colonel Klink chalked the call onto the wall-mounted blackboard next to the cue rack under a cracked-glass framed copy of the N.S.W. State Rules of Pool.

Patrick cast an approving eye towards Tommy slouched into his barstool after hearing his own name called in the second half of the draw. They were both knocking back pints of beer like there was no tomorrow. Thursday's were always 'Parmy and Pint Night', a chicken parmigiana and your choice of the fourteen draft ales, lagers or stouts available on tap for the price of a single five-dollar note together with a gold coin donation to the local Crows Nest Junior Football Club.

A row of twelve, six-seater booths lined the opposite wall and were fast-filling with mostly the Crows Nest C-grade football side and their girlfriends, after the twice-weekly training sessions down the road at North Sydney no-2 oval. The expansive dining room was well patronised with a family-orientated atmosphere, all sharing in the culinary delights offered from a well-structured pub menu.

Ken Ingles was a Scotsman, who, standing in just his socks, stood no more than a little over five and a half foot tall. He resembled a Scottish version of Charlie Chaplin without the moustache, and as the publican, he always made it a priority to complete his customary eleven o'clock walk-through, checking each of the three bars before he called it a night and handed over the keys to his bar manager. All looked as it should on this busy night, and everything seemed to be running smoothly.

With only the final two players remaining in the pool comp, Patrick swayed as his eyes squinted while focusing on the black ball. He chalked the tip of his cue, leaned into the shot and called it like he was Eddie Charlton, "Eight ball in the middle pocket."

The muffled noises of the black ball bouncing from cushion to cushion followed the sound of phenolic polyester and acrylic resin smacking together. The shot lipped out and slowed to a stop, now sitting as an easy pot in the opposite pocket. The young teenage competitor grinned and potted the ball, then raised both arms high above his head, cheering loudly as he celebrated his unexpected win with unbridled exuberance. "Yee-hah, you bloody little rip-snorter," he shouted across the table while he offered a belittling farewell comment to his stunned opposite, "Fucking loser."

A drunken sneer on Patrick's lizard-like mouth was always the first sign of trouble. Like a red rag to a bull, Patrick's internal crazy switch flicked on, he just flipped out in an uncontrolled inner rage, and soon the challenge was on in a contest of who's got the biggest set of balls and the least amount of brains. Patrick was a front-runner in the latter every time. He staggered around the pool table and casually addressed the young lad, still gloating to his less than an enthusiastic girlfriend. "Hey, fuck-knuckle, that's not very respectful is it, carrying on like a bloody pork chop?"

The startled young man sized up the inebriated stranger with the bent nose on a face sprinkled with a thousand freckles and replied with a smug look, "Piss off, numb-nuts". He then turned to gauge the reaction from his hopefully impressed girlfriend. Patrick swept the white ball from the green felt top, palmed it into his clasped hand and let fly with a sideway, right to left sweeping action, connecting with the back of the unsuspecting youngster's scone in a sickening sound, then he pulled another pool cue from the rack and side-swiped the front of the boy's dumbfounded face. The startled teenager's legs buckled from under him, then he just keeled over and collapsed in a heap on the carpeted floor.

A group of diners gathered their belongings and fled from some adjoining tables. The stricken boy's girlfriend screamed in a terrorised shriek and stood motionless as blood gushed from the open crack in her boyfriend's skull while it formed a pooling stain on the carpet's chequered patterning. "Someone—call security. And call an ambulance, for God's sake. Please... anyone, call the cops." She fell to the young man's side and cradled his head in her hands. The evidence of the attack spilt over both her shaking hands, feeling the ooze of his blood only caused her to further fall into a hysterical state of disbelief. She was struggling to control her emotions, and she cringed in panic-stricken fear.

Two bouncers raced over and immediately recognised Patrick O'Finlay. They knew the drill well, ushering him back to the bar while the bar manager dealt with the bloodied mess lying underneath his pool table. The publican was quickly alerted and calmed Patrick down while whisking him away from the turmoil created with his own hand. He knew Patrick was a loose cannon. Unfortunately, his mother owned a bigger cannon and lots of them. Diplomacy was a delicate matter, but dealing with the likes of the O'Finlay family came with the territory. Crows Nest was their patch of ground, and this home patch belonged well and truly to Big Ma. With the offer of some complimentary takeaways from the bottle-shop, the publican soon convinced both men it was a good deal, and they eventually left before causing any further damage.

Patrick visited the men's room before picking up his free carton of beer, agreeing to meet Tommy in the adjacent shopping centre car park. A favourite parking spot for the locals in avoiding the cops who liked to troll the streets bordering the pub in their endeavours to fill their nightly D-D charge sheets.

Tommy stubbed out his cigarette, and while gripping both railings, he staggered his way up the short concrete stairwell, trying to remember where he parked his new car all those hours ago. He fumbled in his pocket for a set of keys and opened the driver's door on the third attempt, then inserted the key into the ignition and waited for his pissed mate.

Patrick flipped the top off a cold stubby into a stormwater drain and stumbled around aimlessly until he eventually remembered Tommy had only recently purchased a new second-hand souped-up vehicle that would have been at home competing at the Bathurst 1000. The 5.0-litre V8-powered SLR 5000 SS Hatchback included the A9X option and was like a travelling billboard as far as the highway patrol was concerned. Tommy was probably the luckiest embryo ever to complete that first swim in life, and he and Patrick drip-fed from the same bucket.

Patrick found Tommy wilting in the driver's seat, struggling to roll a joint as he drooped behind the wheel. Tommy's newly acquired vehicle finally exited the second level of the car park and headed east on Falcon Street with the throaty roar of the V8 rebounding off the buildings lining both sides of this straight stretch of road. With a trail of smoke wafting from the passenger window in their wake,

Kelly followed close on their heels. The high-performance V8 barely would need to shift past third gear. Almost idling through the oil-dangerous Neutral Bay S-bends and then passing by the Big Bear 24-hour fast-food hub before continuing down Military Road. From there the car crossed over the Spit Bridge, then followed the Wakehurst Parkway to Tommy's home, in a secluded street shared with just two other homes in an isolated part of Frenchs Forest.

Kelly extinguished his headlights, killed the engine and continued rolling down the slight incline. He parked the van under a planted line of cedar pines that bordered Trefoil Creek. The sound of a thousand croaking frogs filled the night under a glittering array of stars that burnt a pathless enamel of scintillating whites and iridescent blues. Kelly watched as the garage roller door closed before the two men disappeared from sight. He leaned over into the rear of the Telecom van and pulled out his scope, scanning in a slow wide sweep through the half-open passenger window. The rest of the street was void of any activity and was cloaked in total darkness. The low *thump* from a bass speaker soon cranked loud, and Kelly waited with a good enough view through the vertical shades.

"That's it, boys, keep drinking," he spoke under his breath, with one eye glued to his scope and the other closed tight. Kelly exited the driver's seat and stepped into the rear of the van. He felt a calming influence engulf him as he loaded another six rounds into the spring-loaded magazine, then reached over and cradled the SIG-Sauer in his arms like holding a newborn baby and inserted the clip with supreme authority. Kelly checked the scope was secured and raised it to check for line of sight and clearance. He needed to check the minute of angle and set the correct distance between the two datum points. The wind was moving at approximately 3-5 knots from the north-east. He stored the details in his memory bank and continued to wait—always looking until he had his confirmation.

"Patience, Kelly," he whispered in a low hush. "Always in a woman, but never in a man. Except for the man about to aim a rifle dead-centre of your beady little eyes, Freckles."

Patrick stood with the fridge door open, and shouted over the stereo towards the lounge room down the end of the hallway, "You want a beer or bourbon, Tommy?"

Tommy entered the kitchen. "What?"

"Beer or bloody bourbon, I said."

"Oh, beer first, then we'll roll another joint."

"You do that, and I'll check on our guest downstairs, make sure she's *really* comfortable," Patrick sneered. He followed the hallway and turned on a light at the top of a set of internal stairs that led to a room on the ground floor that at one time was used as a wine cellar. Patrick unlocked the door with the key from his front pocket. The smell of stale air and rising damp was overpowering. Patrick felt for the light switch blindly along the wall and flipped it on. The room lit up. In the corner was a single bunk bed and on that bed was the tousled body of Serena Kelly, still dressed in the clothes she wore from the time she was abducted the previous day.

Serena's ankles were both bound, and her shoulders ached with her wrists zip locked behind her back. She was cold, hungry and very pissed off. Her confusion had turned into anger, and then into fear before terror gripped her with each scenario she played out in her young virginal mind. The thought of being raped was foremost in her thoughts, always conscious of keeping her short dress in order, originally designed to attract the attention of Evan. Now the opposite was the truth.

Patrick took a swig of his beer and looked down at the dishevelled hair and face of their hostage. "You better hope the Indian can locate that fucking brother of yours real soon."

Serena felt her hands and pushed herself up to the edge of the bed. "My brother? Which one, what's going on, who are you, and what do you want with me? . . . And I need to use the bathroom you pig."

Patrick kicked a steel trash can. "If you can find this in the dark, use it, otherwise piss in your pants for all I care. You're not on holiday now, Miss Queenwood fucking Girls' School."

"I want to go home and see my mother. Does anyone know I've been kidnapped? She will be worried sick. Let me go, you bastard," Serena shrieked in frustration and burst into tears. Her bowel was at the point of bursting. "I need to use the toilet, and now, what sort of animal are you? I really have to go, or I'll pee my bloody pants, and I mean this very moment," Serena persisted.

Patrick threw his empty beer in the trash can, leaned over and dragged Serena by her shoulder-length mousy blonde hair to a standing position. Serena instinctively let out a short-pitched cry. Patrick cut the ties around her ankles and marched her out the door to a single downstairs toilet, then pushed her into the darkness. "You've got two minutes, and I'll be standing right out here."

Serena entered the cramped toilet and shut the door with her foot then shuffled one way with her hands still bound then turned to her left where she felt the wall with her chin until she found a light switch. With baby steps, she inched backwards until the cold of the porcelain toilet made contact with the backs of her knees. She angled her body and fell back onto the seat and relieved the building pain inside her bladder. The paper roll was empty. It didn't matter, and she was beyond caring, anyway. An aberrant affirm brushed over her as she contemplated her current dilemma. She felt a presence lost to her—not since the day she and her mother signed the final forms with the FIND agency had she been subjected to the same feelings of salubrity.

Kelly noticed a downstairs light come to life. His heart fluttered. He moved his night scope to the left and down. A small window was alight to the right of the garage. *Who might this be down there, I wander?* Suddenly a shadow could be seen through the frosted glass. The only clear view was from the top three inches of a small air vent covered with thin fly-wire to keep the mosquitoes out. Kelly held steady at this exact spot. The shadow stood up and started bobbing around. *Come on. Give us a look at who you are, just one quick peek?* Then in an instant, the face of a teenager appeared in the small gap, and just as quickly, it disappeared. *Good girl.*

Patrick opened the toilet door and dragged Serena by the shoulder. He steered her back to the cellar, then snapped the lock shut.

Kelly slid the side door slightly open, leaving a six-inch gap, and propped himself against some internal shelving. He eased the stock onto a four-high-stack of boxed new telephones and checked his line of sight through the illuminated reticule.

Kelly actioned one round into the empty chamber, then began the exacting routine he'd spent years practising while under the watchful eye from the old retired army sergeant named Bunyan. He slowed down his breathing to a controlled, steady rhythm.

"Distance - one hundred twenty metres." He turned the left dial twice. "Wind five, right to left. Okay."

Tommy was standing in front of his wall-mounted stereo looking through a collection of LP's. Kelly lined the crosshairs up with Tommy's right shoulder, and then he slowly moved the SIG-Sauer a few millimetres to the left until the illuminated centre highlighted a point square in the back of his target's scrawny little neck. The tiny LCD turned green when it hit 120m. Kelly inhaled and exhaled twice, and on the lull of his third breath, he gently squeezed the trigger.

A slight *poof* sound followed by a waft of cordite was the only evidence a shot had been fired in the middle of suburbia. The 7.62 NATO round entered the indent at the top of Tommy's vertebrae. His head thrust violently forward, and a perfect hole appeared at the bottom of his hairline. The projectile exited the point above the bridge of his nose, causing the top portion of his head, mixed with a mixture of brain matter and bits of skull bone, to smear the wall in a splattering disgorge of blood and other gunk. His body collapsed to the floor like a discarded string puppet.

Patrick was unaware of what had just transpired only fifteen feet away. He crouched down while feeling blindly in the bottom of the fridge for another can of beer before he reentered the lounge to the voice of Bon Scott sharing his– 'dirty deeds'.

He initially took little notice of Tommy lying on the floor with his head obscured by a beanbag. He often crashed early after a night on the beer and gear. Patrick placed his full can on the low coffee table and gestured for Tommy to get up. "Come on, you're as weak as piss, Tommy. Get your arse over here, ya clown. We're going to party hard tonight, you wanker. It's my birthday." Tommy remained in a sedate dissimulated state.

Patrick grabbed his beer and swallowed another long mouthful as his hips swivelled to the building crescendo of ACDC, and only then did he notice a trickling, reddish stain on the wall. His inebriated brain was trying to diffuse what it could be until he stepped closer and looked hard at Tommy, now with half his face missing. "What the fuck?" He instinctively turned towards the window.

Like a deflating balloon, Kelly drained the last breath of air from his lungs. He remembered a mother's final request to a walking, breathing corpse that was spawned from her own loins. Kelly lined up the crosshairs a second time. Patrick's owl-sized eyes filled the scope's lens. *One - two - remember me!*

This was not to be the kill shot—not yet anyway, but merely meant to disable and maim. Kelly watched on as Patrick's body was flung to the floor and obscured from his line of sight. He broke down the rifle before placing it back inside its aluminium case, shut the sliding door, and grabbed the MK-23 handgun. He skirted the tree-lined driveway. Slowly, he screwed on the silencer, then braced before crash tackling his way through a back door before racing up the stairs to deal, first with Patrick, and then to rescue what may be his younger sister.

Kelly stepped over the mess that was Tommy's old face. He turned the corner of the L-shaped lounge room to be greeted by a blood splatter over the carpet. Patrick was nowhere to be seen. *With half his shoulder missing he won't have gone far,* Kelly reassured himself.

The door to the kitchen was to his immediate left. He pushed his back hard against the wall, hesitated for a split second, then crouched and entered with the muzzle end of the silencer scanning the empty space. Kelly turned and started opening doors. A sickening thought suddenly flashed a disturbing image—*Serena?*

A trail of blood droplets was an ominous sign on the steel balustrade. Kelly cleared the stairs in two strides and remained frozen with ears pricked. The downstairs double garage and workshop were dark, with just a hint of ambient moonlight shining through the only window high on the wall facing the street. The bright yellow muzzle flash came from the adjoining garage—then another. A wooden rafter suddenly splintered from behind Kelly's shoulder before he could duck. Then a third shot smashed into some crumbling limestone, which created a forming cloud of fine dust. Tommy's racing car provided some decent cover. Kelly took refuge behind a free-standing Rheem gas hot water tank while blinking and wiping the lime dust from his eyes.

"I've got your little sister by the throat with the barrel aimed at her pretty little face, arsehole," Patrick yelled through the discomfort of his injured shoulder.

Kelly remained still. "That disc? You've been a busy boy, haven't you? Climbing your way up the family tree with your Glock. You want that disc, Patrick, I've got it right here—why don't you come and get it?"

Kelly heard a muffled sob emanating from behind the parked car. "Hang in there, Serena. This will be over quicker than you can count to ten," he shouted.

"Slide the CD over, and this *will* be over real quick," Patrick replied with his hand pressed tight over the young girl's mouth.

Kelly shouted out, "Serena, do you remember what they teach all the girls at school about how to defend yourself against over-exuberant boys?" The words hung in the air. Serena recalled those exact lessons from her two older brothers.

Kelly pointed the MK-23 to a vacant spot on the opposite side of what was Tommy's man cave. He fumbled for the Picatinny rail-mounted laser, then pressed hard with his thumb. A green LED danced in the darkness like a firefly over the stained wall. He moved the laser light in a slow and methodical sweeping action through the double garage with just the filtered light from outside. There were some boxes stacked in one corner. A surfboard leant against a rough brick wall, and a folded lawnmower was parked next to that. A whipper-snipper could be seen hanging off the adjacent wall. Starting at the rear mag wheel, Kelly bent down and placed his head an inch from the floor, searching the underside of the car through his clearing vision. Before he reached the Bridgestone logo on the front tyre, he stopped. The green laser dot was focused on the blue denim crease of a bent knee. Kelly steadied and spoke in a controlled tone loud enough for Patrick to hear. "I spy with my little eye, something that begins with P—*Patrick*." Kelly fired a single round. The reduced pressure being uncorked from the end of the silencer was the only sound heard as the bullet split the vacant air, making a slight whizzing noise. A rising shriek soon followed that while he watched Patrick's knee being ripped apart. "You're fucking history, scumbag." Patrick swayed to an uneasy stance while balancing on his one intact kneecap. Serena bit down hard on Patrick's hand. He released his grip, giving her enough time to turn and knee him hard in the groin.

The noise of a body collapsing into an assortment of rakes and shovels could be heard. That was all the confirmation Kelly needed. He stood and walked past the front of the parked car, feeling the warmth of the bonnet. Patrick lay sprawled amongst the garden tools. Kelly stood over him and looked into the eyes of a deranged killer, staring back like the coward he was. "Every dog has its day, Patrick. This is a message from your mother." Kelly pulled the disc from his back pocket and threw it at the quaking body. Patrick was attempting to slide away on his backside, grovelling as he pissed his pants, just as his many schoolyard victims had done so many times before this day. His head was frantically turning from left to right, searching for his dropped weapon. Kelly remained in the one spot, and spoke in a low single syllable voice, highlighting each word for effect, the last wishes directed to a dead man cringing in fear, directly from the mouth of the bereaved Big Ma O'Finlay.

"Patrick, this is a gift from your two dead but not forgotten brothers, Sean and Dean, and a special treat from a mother to a son that never was, and could never be. I liken you to an incurable, lingering cancer, Patrick, and today your mother has just found a cure. Goodbye."

Patrick scrambled to his left to retrieve his discarded weapon lying near the rear tyre. He was about to open his foul mouth and let fly with a barrage of profanities when a .45 calibre bullet entered the spot dead centre of his two snake-like, bloodshot eyes.

From the slime and filth of a high school toilet floor where a murderous drug-dealing lunatic conducted his private Kangaroo Court to a garage located in the leafy suburb of Frenchs Forest—it was finally over.

Serena stepped out from the shadow of Kelly's shoulders with both bare feet frozen to the cold cement floor.

Kelly policed the two spent cartridges as a force of habit and slid the Heckler & Koch down the back of his jeans. He grabbed a half-full jerry can of fuel and splashed the contents around the garage, covering Tommy's dream on wheels, then dropped the can to the ground. He was about to fly back up the stairs.

Serena turned to face the strange man. "Do you want to cut my hands free before you run away?"

"Shit, sorry." He found a rusted chisel on a workbench. "Stick both your arms out towards me." He sliced through the plastic ties, then turned and headed back towards the stairs a second time.

"And my bag? I need my bag," Serena barked her second order.

Kelly stopped in mid-flight, "Your bag?"

"It's got all my make-up, a pair of brand new shoes which I haven't even worn yet plus a beautiful off-the-shoulder dress I bought just for this long weekend."

Kelly was speechless, "You can't be serious?"

"Typical man. I last saw it in the lounge room before I was dragged downstairs to that stinking room."

Kelly made his way back upstairs, still shaking his head. The all-important bag was where Serena said it would be. He entered the kitchen and turned on all three gas knobs, then found an old newspaper, folded it tight, stuffed it into a toaster and pushed the lever down. The smell of LPG started to fill the room as he negotiated the stairs again, this time with the all-important bag hanging over his left shoulder. He handed it over to Serena's open arms.

"Thank you," she offered while giving Kelly the once-over.

"Come on, we need to get the hell out of here—now." Kelly activated the remote door, and the two complete strangers left.

Kelly opened the passenger door. "Get in."

"Do I know you from somewhere? Do you work for Telecom?" Serena asked as the van negotiated a sharp U-turn.

"Just casually. Are you okay, did either of those creeps lay a hand on you—are you hurt?"

"Do I look okay to you? Christ—who were those two lunatics?"

"The ghosts of a time best forgotten. Let's just let sleeping dogs lie."

"Oh, really, just like that?" Serena almost screamed. "You think you can mumble a few words and expect this will all just conveniently go away? What kind of person just turns up out of the blue and does all that, anyway?" She was waving her arms in the air like she was being buzzed by a swarm of bees. "Who are you—some kind of avenging vigilante or something?"

Less than a block clear, a thunderous inferno erupted with a raging blue and yellow conflagration illuminating the inert night sky. Serena flinched from the safety of the passenger's seat. "Holy shit, what was that?" She turned her head and looked out the window to see smoke and debris flying about like falling black snowflakes.

"That, Serena—is a chapter of my life that has just been erased forever, never to be opened again. Which brings me to my next point . . . Tell me about your family?" Kelly asked.

"My family, why do you want to know about them? No one is going to believe any of this, anyway—especially my family."

"You mean your mother," Kelly prodded a second time.

"Yeah, her, and my two older brothers and sister."

"Whoa, hang on a minute. You have other brothers and *another* sister?"

"Yes, of course, I do." She glanced at Kelly with a look that said, who is this nut-case?

Kelly asked, "Is there anyone else?"

"What do you mean—anyone else?"

"I mean, do you have any more siblings that are not part of the family unit?"

There was a difficult pause. Serena drew a long breath. "All right, this is getting weird now. How would you know about my lost brother? It's only something both Mum and I have recently been able to discuss in an open conversation."

Kelly's eyes lit up, "So there is someone, then?"

"Yes, there is another brother, but for some unknown reason, which my mother refuses to talk about, he was adopted out as a small child. I started a search for him last year, but no one has come forward as yet. I know he's out there—somewhere."

"How old would this lost brother be now?"

His birthday is on January twenty-nine. He would have just turned eighteen."

Kelly swallowed hard. His hands started to perspire inside his gloves. "What else do you know about this other brother?"

"Mum says he has a birthmark near his belly button. She cries when she talks about it."

Kelly pulled the van over under a streetlight, turned off the ignition and flicked the interior light on. He turned to face what was fast looking like his younger sister. He was struggling to control his speech. "Serena, did your mother ever tell you where she left this boy?"

"She doesn't like to talk about it. Let's just say she was forced to give him up for adoption."

"Yeah, like being left alone on a church pew with a note and some cash. Is that the adoption she was referring to?"

"Stop right there. It took my mother almost a full year of therapy to divulge that snippet of information. How is it that a perfect stranger would know that private detail? Not even the people at the agency are privy to that."

"Think about it for a second. Who is the only other person who *would* know?"

"Are you all there in the head? Look, I am grateful you came in like you did and saved the day for the good guys. Right now, I just want to go home and take a long shower. Take me home, I want to go home now."

Nothing was said as each person filtered the rapid-fire of discovered information. Serena finally turned and looked past the face. A strange feeling of peculiar familiarity stirred inside. At no time had she ever felt threatened by this man. In fact, she felt quite at ease, even when talking about the family skeleton tucked conveniently away in their mother's closet that had plagued both her brothers and sister for many years. Like the elephant in the room, no one ever really spoke about the gap in their lives until Serena turned thirteen, at which time she had been relentless in prying open those closed doors.

"Look into my eyes, tell me what you see?" Kelly asked. The question was followed by a noisy silence. The look in Serena's eyes slowly started to change. They were becoming softer, searching out for the part of her life that was lost due to the actions of her own mother.

"Oh, my God. Turn and face me square on," she almost demanded.

Kelly undid his seatbelt and shifted in his seat.

"Please, explain to me what's happening here? I don't understand," she whimpered through clouding eyes. "You look the same as my mother. Is this some kind of sick joke? Who are you? Surely it can't be . . ." Serena started sobbing. Both her eyes were welling up.

"I don't know. I'm trying to wade through all this myself. My birthday is on January twenty-nine. I just turned eighteen. I've lived in foster homes since I was four or five, plus I have a birthmark near my belly button. Look, I'll show you." Kelly popped open the press-studs on his overalls then lifted his T-shirt clear, and that was it for Serena. She opened the door and spilt out onto the footpath. Then she yelled at Kelly, "Get out. Sorry, I mean, please, can you step out and let me look at you in the light? Holy shit-a-brick, I can't believe this is happening for real."

The sounds of sirens could be heard echoing through the hills. Kelly opened his door. The two stood opposite each other like it was a blind date. "Your nose—you have the Kelly button nose." That's when Serena just lost it. She stumbled the few steps between them and launched herself at Kelly, wrapping both her arms around him like a body glove and just held on for dear life.

Kelly could feel the river of Serena's tears soaking his shoulder. Then the floodgates of his own personal emotional rollercoaster opened like a festering wound. The revolving door that had been his life for the past eighteen years was spinning out of control. Both he and Serena were unable to speak. Kelly tried, but it just made things worse. A second siren rang loud in the distance.

Kelly attempted to pry Serena from her vice-like embrace. She was a strong girl and refused to break her sisterly grasp. "Come on. Really, we need to get out of here," Kelly said in words that could almost be understood. Serena slowly peeled herself off her brother. He started the van. "Where *is* home for you, then?"

"Clontarf. Just get back onto the Wakehurst Parkway, and I'll show you from there. You still haven't told me about those two men who kidnapped me."

"That, Serena—is a man that lost the right to live, a waste of good air and something you can never speak about again." Suddenly, Kelly slowed. "Well, I'll be . . ."

"I'll be what?" Serena asked.

"Hang on a minute."

Wakehurst Parkway merges into Clontarf St then after a sharp right, becomes Frenchs Forest Rd. He continued driving straight into Dalwood Ave, then turned left into Peacock St then right into Redman St. He slowed to a crawl and counted out the house numbers, stopping next to a huge plum tree. The footpath showed the red stains from years of fallen fruit. Kelly leaned over towards Serena and pointed out a home with peeling paint, the cement roof tiles were faded from the constant beating of the long hot summers. The yard looked unkempt and disorganised like no one really cared.

"I lived in this house for a time. You see that plum tree, well it produces the best plums every season without fail. I remember Burt and his wife, Emily. The couple who were the beneficiary of the monthly government cheque. Burt liked to sit on the front porch and throw rocks at the kids trying to steal his precious plums. He'd prefer to see them drop and rot on the ground than share them with neighbours."

"Serena asked, "How long did you live here?"

"Not long. I was a real pain in the arse as a kid. I ran away a lot. That's why I was shunted between so many foster homes—a problem child, my file read. This was the spot I hot-wired my first car, a Fiat 850 owned by, Burt. When I returned, I parked it under the tree. The next morning it was covered in splotches of deep crimson. Mother Nature's own paint job. Old Burt freaked out, and shortly after I was gone. A good result for all."

Serena asked, "How many foster homes?"

"Lost count. It was more than a few."

"You know my home is probably less than five kilometres from here. That's just weird."

"Life is weird. You need to make hay while the sun shines, kiddo." Kelly put the van into gear. "Let's get you home then, shall we?"

"Oh shit, I just remembered something." Serena's frown spoke its own language.

"What is it?"

"Don't get mad, okay. I'm supposed to be away with my girlfriend's parents on a farm down south until Monday. If Mum finds out, she will kill me."

Kelly had to ask. "So, where were you heading off to for the weekend?"

"The party of the year at Wisemans Ferry."

"Are you kidding me? You're just thirteen. Is that why your kidnapping was never reported?"

"Probably," she answered sheepishly.

Kelly looked at his watch. It was 3:15 in the A.M. "What's the earliest you can arrive back at home without arousing suspicion?"

"Later on today will be fine. I could just say we decided to come home early."

"If I agree to do this for you, then you need to repay the debt."

"I'm listening."

"In time. First, I need to do one last thing." Kelly headed back towards the harbour bridge. He took the Eastern Distributor that would lead him to Watsons Bay. He pulled into a small car park next to an all-night chemist. "Wait here, this won't take long." He returned with a plastic container of cotton buds, a set of tweezers, a pair of nail clippers and a pack of Glad sandwich bags. Kelly peeled open a single bag, ripped a few nose hairs out with the tweezers, then dropped them inside, needing to wipe his watering eyes with the back of his sleeve.

Serena cringed. "Yuk, that's disgusting."

"Calm down." Then he pulled out some hairs from his scalp, checking the follicles were still attached. He swabbed the inside of his mouth with three cotton buds, then removed one glove and clipped a nail from his left index finger, and handed the four sealed bags to Serena. "There, that should do it. Take all this, then get it tested for DNA. We need to be one hundred per cent positive, which brings me back to your part of this pact we will make."

"How do you know all this stuff?"

"I watched every James Bond movie ever made. Now listen to what I'm about to say. All that has happened tonight—the kidnapping, the two men, and what happened inside that house..." Kelly paused for effect. He needed to know Serena was listening and understood the implications. "Me and you, brother and sister, maybe or maybe not, well— you can't mention *any* of this to anyone, and that especially includes the rest of the family. Do you understand?"

"No. How can you expect me not to tell, Mum? Bloody hell, Jaxon, Leah and Daniel, all have a right to know you are alive and well. We are your own flesh and blood, for God's sake. This is ridiculous."

Kelly asked, "Those are their names?"

"Yes."

"What if I told you that my life will depend on you keeping this a secret? Not forever, just until I can sort through a few other nagging problems. I might need to go away for a while, and I can't risk the family asking a million questions about their missing brother. Loose lips sink ships. In this scenario, we are all sailing on that same ship."

"Are we in danger?"

"Not if you do as I say. Is it starting to sink in now? I know you're only thirteen years . . ."

"I'm fourteen now," Serena interrupted.

"Sorry, fourteen then. This won't be easy. You need to be strong, Serena."

"Okay, I got it. Leah and I are very close, you know. She will sense something is not gelling. You can't pull the wool over that big sister's eyes, let me tell you."

"I'm sure you can work it out."

The Telecom van pulled over in the Gap Park car park on Gap Rd. "Why are we stopping here?"

"Paying tribute to a small frog. You stay in the van and keep your head down," Kelly answered in a dour tone. He lifted the back door and retrieved the rifle case with the handgun, then wrapped them tightly in a spare pair of overalls. Kelly was betting on the fact the local council may have installed CCTV recently. He wasn't about to take the risk. He pulled down his peak cap and walked the short distance to the fenced-off railing that was The Gap. The sound of the Pacific Ocean pounding away at the bottom of the steep bluff was a stark reminder—this was not a smart place to get drunk. Kelly unclipped the outer case, pulled out the rifle and hurled it as far as he could into the black void. The Heckler & Koch followed the same flight path, and then it was time to do the same with the two boxes of ammunition.

"Good luck to you, Frog. I hope this gift will help you rest in peace, little man." Kelly returned and changed out of his Telecom work gear.

The driver's door closed. Serena asked in a typical teenage fashion. They want to know everything. "What was that all about? Have you just knocked off for the day?"

"Funny girl," Kelly answered while cracking a smile.

"Why can't you just tell me honestly? You always answer with a cryptic meaning..."

"How was your long weekend down south on the farm?" Kelly fired back, satisfied at his quick wit. Serena's silence was almost expected.

Kelly spent the time to drive from The Gap back to the Telecom Depot on Oxford St, listening to Serena explaining how tough her life was with such a disciplinarian mother. Kelly just listened and smiled inside, then asked, "How old are the others?"

"They're all much older than me. Jaxon is thirty-four, Leah is thirty-two, and Daniel is twenty-eight. When Mum was eight months pregnant with me, she grabbed you and left my birth father. My... sorry, our father was a drunk and a violent man who liked to bash his wife senseless. She knew if she stayed, the pregnancy was in danger. The other kids remained with him until each left to attend university. He passed away over six years ago now, and I never met with him. Mum wouldn't allow it."

"Are any of them married—with kids?"

"Yes, yes, and no. Jaxon *was* married with a son now living with his mother somewhere overseas. Leah is divorced with two girls, and Daniel is married with no kids as yet. He lives in Perth now."

"And our mother, what's she like?"

"The word neurotic comes to mind. Mum remarried when I was six. That lasted for five years until he started screwing around. She got the house and a big chunk of money out of the divorce. I think she is happy now after finally mending the bridge with the other three kids. That took some time. She never stops thinking about you. Why can't you just come and say hello to her? She would die if she ever found out I met you and didn't tell her."

"It's just not that simple, Serena. It's all for your own welfare."

"So you keep telling me. I still don't get it, though."

"You don't have to."

From this point on, they both shared a short past that would now culminate in Serena holding on to a secret that could never be spoken of again—ever. She wept openly at regular intervals as she recalled special events in the family's lives—Kelly's family. It sounded weird just thinking about it, but in a nice family way. Kelly completed a U-turn, backtracked two kilometres, then parked the van at the Telecom Depot's main gate with the keys in the ignition. He wiped down the inside passenger door handles, both side and front windows and anything else Serena may have come into contact with. They both crossed Oxford Street with Serena holding her bag like it held the Crown Jewels. Kelly flagged down a bus. He pulled out some loose change. "You stop anywhere near The Rocks?"

"Sure do. You can get off at Circular Quay. From there, it's only a short walk," the driver answered while passing over two tickets.

Serena looked at her brother. "Where are we going?"

"I need a drink, and The Rocks has a few early openers," Kelly explained.

Serena looked shocked. "It's not even six o'clock in the morning."

"I have no doubts you'll learn soon enough. It's been a long night. I need to relax. Why, do you have another party to sneak off to?" Kelly joked.

Serena grabbed his hand, "No, happy where I am right now. Lead the way, big brother."

Kelly looked hard into Serena's eyes, "Yes, and don't you forget it. If I ever hear of you pulling off another scam like you did this weekend, you will find out in a real hurry just how tough I can be. You got that?"

"Well, that didn't take long."

The Spit Bridge is a concrete girder construction with a bascule lift span that opens four times each day to allow boat traffic to pass through this busy and important waterway. The taxi continued down the steep incline of Spit Road before being forced to brake to a complete stop while the bridge slowly lifted for its scheduled 10:15 A.M. opening time.

Serena was looking to her right with searching eyes. Kelly shifted his casual gaze left. Without counting, about a thousand different boats were moored inside their pens. Suddenly, Serena almost screamed from inside the stationary taxi. "Shit, there's, Helen. Excuse me, driver, can you pull over inside that car park?" He grumbled under his breath while creeping out of the line of traffic. "That's my friend, Helen," she explained to Kelly. "Quick, I've got to see her. She'll be going crazy wandering why I didn't meet her, and she might even ring, Mum."

They both exited the taxi. Kelly poked his head through the passenger window, "Just wait here, driver. I'll be back in a minute."

Serena pointed to a two-storey Tudor style building overlooking the shores of Peach Tree Bay. "That's the Endeavour Restaurant, and it's owned by Helen's parents." She moved her extended arm to the left, "You see over there on the other side of that passage of water, that's Clontarf. Sandy Beach is where Helen's brother often drops me off. It's a shortcut to my home, which is only two streets back. Number nineteen Allenby Street."

Kelly pulled out his wallet and slid out four fifty-dollar notes. "Here, take this. Don't forget about the DNA testing and then buy yourself a belated birthday present from me. I must owe you a few by now."

"So this is it, then? I finally welcome you back into my life, and now you're about to leave again. It's not fair, especially the part where I can't tell anyone."

"That's about the crux of it. It won't always be like this, trust me. Don't worry, Serena, I want to catch up with the rest of the family as much as anyone. Just not now, okay."

They both held each other tight in a brother and sister embrace that flowed with the essence of their dissimilar lives.

"All right, you better go now. I think your friend has just spotted you. Remember what I told you—word for word. Take care."

"When will we see you again, Phil? God, this is killing me."

"Probably when you least expect it. Go on, get out of here before I tear up again."

Serena crossed the road. Kelly watched on as the two teenage girls embraced. Helen had about a thousand questions ready for Serena. The first one was, "What happened to you, we waited for almost an hour, and you never showed? You didn't miss much. Ray and Evan are both pigs. I left after just a few short hours and caught the train home. It was a total flop, Serena."

"I'm sorry, but something unexpected came up."

"Yes, I can see that. Who was the hunky-looking guy I saw you hugging? Come on, Serena, there are no secrets between best friends."

Serena thought about her answer. "Oh, he's just an old family friend. It's not what you think. He's more like a brother."

The taxi had no choice but to continue on over the bridge. Kelly knew the road well. The sign pointing right to Manly spanned the four-lane road under a footbridge as you reached the top of the hill. He asked the driver, "Have you got a street directory handy?" Kelly then directed the taxi to turn right across the busy Pittwater Road, then while following his verbal directions, the taxi turned left and right back down the hill. The view back over the Spit Bridge was a spectacular one. Kelly counted out the house numbers. "Nice neighbourhood, - thirteen, fifteen, okay, slow down and pull over to the other side of the road."

Kelly slid into the middle of the back seat and cast an inquisitive eye on number 19. A woman was bent over in the raised front yard with a hose in one hand, and a dog held tightly between her knees as she created a thick lather of soap with her free hand. The golden retriever seemed to be enjoying the bath until she stood erect and slowly stretched her aching back, loosening her grip. Then, in a body-shaking spray of water and shampoo, the stranger dropped the hose.

Kelly was pleading inside. *Just turn around and let me get a good look at your face.*

Gillian Hartman suddenly felt the urge to turn. It was like an invisible love tap on her shoulder, prompting her to face the road . . . so she did. Her shoulder-length brown hair had a natural wave that swung loosely as she pushed her damp fringe to one side from a forehead covered in spots of soap . . . wandering why a taxi had stopped opposite? A strange feeling enveloped her in the form of a warming flush. She felt her cheeks burning. Her stomach pinged with a reminding twinge of pain—the pain of childbirth. Confusion and joy mixed with the emotions of her past actions were percolating internally, and could no longer be ignored. She took one step forward, and then she removed both her gloves and kept walking without breaking stride. She didn't know or care why. Another step, then a third and a fourth. Gillian felt the urge to run straight at this stationary taxi. She yearned for her lost son, asking herself for God's forgiveness.

Kelly tapped the driver on the shoulder. "Sorry, mate. Wrong address, we need to go. Do you know Paddy's Market near Chinatown?"

"Yes, my wife buys fruit and vege's there every weekend."

"That's the one." The taxi pulled away while Kelly forced himself not to look back. He attempted to wade through the confusing but intimate feelings he was currently experiencing, now fermenting away inside his guts—the same ones that never lied. He delved deep inside his own shifting thoughts in trying to dissect the waves of emotion sweeping over him like an invisible cloak of the unknown—being connected to another person's soul without actually understanding what that meant.

As the taxi made its way back towards the city, he made good use of the time to contemplate his next move. Somehow he needed to remove the shackles that were threatening to rip away any chance he had at a life with the family he did not know. Nothing was going to stand in his way to achieve that dream.

Gillian Hartman stood alone on the footpath, slightly embarrassed, hoping the neighbours weren't watching. She felt a bit silly, but also harboured a sense of bitter disappointment. Emptiness filled her heart. She suddenly had the roused feeling to phone Helen's sister just to check her youngest daughter was okay.

Chapter-28

THE TAXI PASSED through Chinatown with a grinding noise vibrating up through the rear floor from a differential that had just about seen its last days. A neon sign read: Loong Hing Wan Tong Restaurant. Kelly had the sudden urge to eat Chinese food—maybe the last supper. He asked the driver to pull over and handed him seventy dollars. "Keep the change, buddy."

A young Chinese kid sat cross-legged in the driver's seat of a three-wheeled motorised rickshaw. "Hey, mister... you want a ride?" Kelly ignored the call. "What about I read your fortune? No bullshit?" That was tempting, but his stomach didn't agree. He found a seat with his back to the wall facing both the front door and the entrance to the kitchen. The only people he hadn't pissed-off so far were the Triads, so he felt reasonably at ease here.

Forty minutes later, he stepped back into the walking-only street. His young entrepreneurial friend was waiting patiently under the 'Welcome to Chinatown' sign with two fire-breathing dragons forming an arch. "I take you where you want to go, Aussie. Cheap-cheap, no worries, *mate*," he rolled off the tongue with a heavy accent.

"You know Paddy's Market, not far?" Then Kelly asked, "How much?"

"You want fortune read, special deal today?"

"Of course I do," Kelly smiled back. "Give me a number."

"Five dollars extra. You pay fifteen. Good deal for you, I think."

Kelly stepped up and inside then leaned into the comfortable seat. He tapped the kid on the shoulder, "What's your name, young fella?"

"My name, Jackie Chan—superstar."

Kelly used this short respite to consider his current predicament and sort through his options, which weren't that many at this point in time. "Chuck a right here, Jackie Chan, and then circle the block one more time, okay."

"No worries."

There were no parked Pontiac's, no strange men lounging on a park bench pretending to read the paper, and no crazy sniper hanging off a tree branch with his scope burning a hole in Kelly's back. The streets looked quiet— almost too quiet. He leaned forward and needed to raise his voice over the buzz of the two-stroke motor "There is a green roller door just down the end of this lane. Drop me off there." Kelly went to grab his wallet.

The kid turned in his seat to face him square on. "You stay still now." He reached into his kit and retrieved a small silver snuffbox, then sprinkled a generous amount of yellow powder into his open palm. "You ready? I read your fortune."

Kelly was hoping he wasn't an apprentice Triad practising his death-by-Anthrax routine. Jackie Chan blew the dust from his open hand towards the back seat. Kelly shut both his eyes and mouth for a split second. He opened one eye first with a squint. A luminous rotating dust cloud formed a perfect ball and just hung, suspended in the air. Then the kid mumbled some Chinese words, and with a pointed finger, he completed a figure-eight through the globe-shaped mist. One ball became four, and then slowly dissipated.

"Beware of the twin-headed serpent. His evil other searches from a broken branch. Fifty-one queen slippers is a sign. Tread carefully when you enter the house of cards."

"That's it?" Kelly opened his wallet and passed Jackie Chan a twenty-dollar note. "Hang around for a bit, and you can keep the change." Kelly was banking on the fact that

Fanny would have left his bike inside and hopefully with both the key and his helmet.

He pulled the green roller door half open and bent down then turned to the young Chinese boy with the thumbs-up signal. His full-face Shoei hung over one mirror, but there was no key in the ignition. Kelly ran his hand under the front wheel guard, feeling the top of the tyre. He did the same with the rear tyre, and still no sign of a key. He couldn't risk going back inside the restaurant. Kelly thought about hot-wiring the bike while pushing it off the centre-stand. The helmet rolled to the ground with a slight jingling sound. He looked inside to see the keyring threaded through the strap.

Kelly started the Kawasaki and felt the pulsating power between his legs. It was almost better than sex, and a bike will never turn its back on a man. He found a phone booth in Darling Harbour and rang Madeleine's number with a half-baked plan in mind. It was almost more of a wish than a plan, but he was running out of options. He'd discarded his old life, that was over. The opportunity to be part of a family—his own flesh and blood, was there for the taking and he wanted it so bad he was willing to roll the dice and go all in.

The phone picked up, "Hello . . ."

Kelly paused, "Maddy?"

"Yes, is that you, Lucky Phil?"

"It's done."

"Are you positive? Is there any confirmation to prove what you're saying? I want to hear you say the words."

"You're an idiot. My word as a man, that's all you're going to get. I need you to talk to your auntie."

"About what?"

"I want her to set up a meeting with the President of God's Garbage and clear my name about who shot their Sergeant in Arms."

Madeleine's conniving mind was working overtime. "It will take some time. Where do you propose this meeting take place?"

"What about Ma's house? No one would dare screw with her."

"No, I've got a better idea. Write down this address, then ring me back in two hours." Madeleine hung up the phone with a satisfied smile. She met the interested gaze of her Italian lover. "He wants an audience with, Ma."

Luca Costa answered with a blank look, "Well, that's not going to happen anytime soon, is it—what now?"

"It's perfect. Don't you see? Kelly will come to us. We can finish this today."

Kelly needed to clear his head and sort out in his own mind all the possible scenarios that could play out if this meeting was to get the green light. He shifted into the left-hand lane and prepared to take the Sydney Harbour Bridge northbound exit towards North Sydney. A thickening cover of black clouds was forming over the northern skyline. The first drops of rain splattered against his visor. Kelly remembered the last time he rode his old Speedwell bicycle and felt the stinging drops of rain on his exposed face. He decided to take cover, stopping his bike on a footpath under the front awning of a milk bar and purchased two muesli bars, a block of peppermint chocolate and a litre of water.

Lightning and thunder clapped over the distant horizon. Within minutes, a shower of marble-sized raindrops, preceded by the accompanying destructive winds, passed overhead, and then it was gone. The sweet smell of rain causing steam vapours to rise off the hot road surface was a mental trigger to appreciate the simple things in life. Like the smell of freshly cut grass. That was a life Kelly felt he deserved. He'd paid his dues, and now it was time to collect. He lifted his seat and placed the litre bottle inside. The Frog's leather satchel was a deadly reminder of the people he was dealing with, and inside was the one thing that could change the status quo in his favour. Take no prisoners and trust no bastard.

Kelly completed a slow drive-by. The house in question was located not far from Chatswood Golf Club on a dead end road called Harnett Place. He did a U-turn and realised Harnett Place split in two. The second spur stopped near Swaines Creek and was very secluded. He parked his bike away from the prying eyes of any local traffic, then pushed his way through a horse's smorgasbord of damp knee-high lucerne until he found the perfect viewing spot from a tall eucalyptus tree.

Totally bored, he ripped open his second muesli bar, scrunched the wrapper into a tight ball and slipped it into his top pocket. He had one more hour to kill before the second phone call needed to be made.

A late-model Range Rover, with heavy tinting, pulled into the brick-paved driveway. The double roller door opened electronically, the vehicle crept inside then disappeared as the door closed. Ten minutes later, a second car pulled up and stopped. The front door opened and out walked Madeleine in all her finery, looking like she was gliding down the catwalk. A short conversation followed between her and an Italian-looking man dressed in a flashy suit. He followed her inside while his passenger moved the car to the other side of the driveway.

Kelly swallowed his last chew when the unmistakable ear-splitting, twin-engine roar from more than one Harley was enough to scatter a sleeping kookaburra perched in the same tree. The Garbage had arrived. Madeleine re-appeared and ushered three patched members through a side gate, still wearing their helmets. Kelly was about to drop back down to ground-level when Maddy walked back out through the same gate. She used a remote to open the roller door, and reversed her Triumph *Stag* out, parking it on the street. Kelly wandered why?

He dropped down from the tree and walked back to his bike. Two young boys could be seen hiking down a trodden path towards the creek. They crossed over a planked walkway with a spoked bicycle wheel in one hand, less the inner tube and tyre. They stopped not far from where he stood. Kelly asked, "What's with the wheel, boys?"

"Yabbies." The second kid emptied a bag of meat scraps, and they began tying the rotten meat to the spokes.

Kelly asked again, "Where does that track take you to? Is there a phone booth up that way anywhere?"

"Yeah, outside the Video Ezy store. You can't miss it," the kid with a missing front tooth answered.

"Can I get my bike through?"

"Depends . . . How good a rider are you?" They both laughed.

"I'll be back soon. Good luck with the yabbies," Kelly answered while returning the smile.

Kelly dialled the number a second time. Madeleine answered. Her tone was decisively different this time. She sounded nervous. "Lucky Phil. It's all set up. Ma is on her way here, she sounds confident this will work. Where are you now?"

"Not far. Who will be in attendance?"

"Just, Ma, the President of God's Garbage, and me of course—plus a person I know you trust." *The first lie.* Madeleine handed the phone over.

"Lucky Phil, it's all cool man. This can be sorted out, but you need to front the president in person. That's the deal."

"Emmanuel? I don't understand. Why are you there?"

"They trust me, that's why, and now so should you. Big Ma asked me to set up the meet. It's safe to come on in, but don't ride your bike, okay."

"Why is that a problem?"

"Just grab a taxi. If the President of God's Garbage hears a piece of Jap-crap pull up outside, he might decide to bounce you just for that. They don't even like sharing the roads with bikes from the same country some of their father's fought and died fighting against, let alone if you were to park next to their Harley's. It's all about respect, Lucky. I can drop you back after this is all over."

"Is Fanny there with you?"

"No, he's not part of this today."

The newly appointed Sergeant of Arms yelled from outside, "Tell that little prick to get his spineless arse over here before we all change our fucking minds."

"Lucky, it's now or never. This is a onetime offer. Never to be repeated. Everyone wants this put to bed so we can all get on with the business of making money."

"Yeah, right? I'll go grab a cab and be there in thirty minutes."

Kelly backtracked the same way he'd arrived. The two boys were in the middle of pulling the bike wheel slowly up from the muddy water with a good haul of yabbies flicking their tails trying to back out between the spokes. "Good job, boys," Kelly shared. "Dear old Mum will be happy. You want to earn a quick twenty bucks?"

The answer was obvious while both kids nodded. "You keep an eye on that bike for me parked under that big tree. Ten bucks now and the same when I return. When I do, I will ride across that little bridge you guys built one more time. You pull the plank after I pass, then both of you skedaddle. Deal?"

"Show us the money first."

Kelly smiled and pulled out a note. "I like your thinking. Spit and shake on it, then it's a done deal, okay."

Kelly stepped out from the cover of the wild lucerne. From this angle, he noticed the branch from a neighbour's tree had been ripped off by the storm and had ended up perched on Madeleine's tiled roof. Kelly looked up at the broken dollhouse window and caught a shadowed glimpse of the curtain swaying. His gut feelings were sending him a clear message—danger lurked beyond those walls. It was like entering the House of Horrors at Luna Park. You knew to expect something, but still almost crap yourself when it jumps out and scares the living shit out of you. He made his way across the road and stood at the front door, all the while thinking about the risk versus reward in throwing that Heckler & Koch into the drink. Right now it might have come in real handy.

Inside the house were seven people, six were scattered under a spacious A-framed pergola in the manicured backyard. Emmanuel and the other two God's Garbage boys were seated and playing poker. The Italians were sniffing a freshly uncorked bottle of Hunter Valley Shiraz while admiring the roses and herb garden. Madelaine was treading a path on the plush pile carpet, moving from outside, then back to the lounge window. The sound of the doorbell prompted her into action. She stood next to Vincenzo and whispered, "Come and see if this is the same car that you caught on the camera at the Venus Room?" She pulled the curtain open. "There, you see. Kelly just arrived in that sports car. Is it the same one?"

Vincenzo felt the pearl handle of his Beretta and smiled with only thoughts of payback in his one-track revengeful mind. He had lost face that night amongst his peers, and for that, there was a price to pay. "Remember our deal," Madeleine reminded him, "not here in this house. It must be a clean kill with no possible chance of finding the body."

Vincenzo just nodded and went to speak in private with Antonio.

Madeleine opened the front door. "Lucky Phil, come on in. Everybody is ready and waiting for you to arrive. They're out the back."

All three men laid down their dealt hands. Emmanuel shifted in his chair and stood. "Lucky Phil, take a seat and let me introduce each person here today."

"I'll just stay standing if that's okay with you?" Kelly answered while taking in his surroundings.

"Up to you," Emmanuel continued. "This is the President of God's Garbage and his Sergeant of Arms." He then turned, "Over here is Vincenzo and Antonio Costa, and Madeleine you have already met."

Kelly eyed off the loose cards. He picked up the small pack they came in and read the label out loud. "Queen Slipper playing cards." He fanned through the deck, then checked all the discarded cards on the table. "Fifty-one, I bet. Did Fanny give you these?"

Emmanuel looked a bit confused, "Yeah, he insisted. Said it would help pass the time. Why?"

"No matter." Kelly faced Madeleine, "I don't see your auntie anywhere. It's not like a blind man could miss her. What's goin' on?"

"Ma has made her peace with, God. Let's all just move on."

"Yeah, and if you look out the window, you'll see a pink pig flying south for winter. With a family like yours, Maddy—who needs enemies, heh? My meeting today was with, Ma." Then Kelly walked towards Vincenzo. "Costa— Vincenzo Costa? Now, where have I only just recently seen that name written? Oh yeah, I remember now, you have a twin brother. I've seen Luca's birth certificate. The firstborn son."

The colour of Vincenzo's olive skin drained of all colour. Antonio stepped in between Kelly and his dumbstruck brother. "Step back," he shouted, then pushed Kelly away.

Madeleine's brain was attempting to assimilate how Kelly was aware that Vincenzo had a twin.

The president swiped his open hand across the table, sending glasses, an ashtray full of butts and the loose cards flying to the ground. "I don't give a fuck how many brothers you have. I want revenge for what happened that night in the car park?" His anger was directed at one man.

Kelly didn't flinch. He looked the president in the eye, "Why would you believe anything I say? You could have asked JC, but I can only assume that small problem has been sorted out by now. The man that pulled the trigger is dead. Believe it or not, it makes no difference today. The only reason you're here is to earn yourself a bigger piece of the drug pie with our Italian friends standing here right now. The same men that harbour a dirty little family secret and the price for that is to take me out."

Vincenzo was enraged. He pulled out his pearl-handled Beretta and pointed it at Kelly. Madeleine stepped in, crying out, "No...no, not here. That was the deal."

"This man is mine," Vincenzo screamed. "He tried to frame me for the murders of nine men."

Kelly turned back towards Vincenzo, "You were just a back-up, Vince, so calm the fuck down. You can't kill a man twice."

The president withdrew a brown-handled .44 Magnum from the inside of his jacket. His Sergeant of Arms bent his arm back over his head and pulled a sawn-off shotgun from a back holster. All Kelly had was a crumpled muesli bar wrapper in his shirt pocket. A Mexican stand-off. Like the Americans and the Russians with both hands on the nuclear trigger, no one was game to fire first, knowing they would be signing their own death warrants.

The sounds of heavy boots coming down the stairs accompanied by a slow handclap broke the awkward stalemate. The seventh person walked through the glass sliding door. "Bravo, bravo. Look what you have all achieved so far? Guns loaded and ready to shoot each other. That's good for business if ever I saw. Mr Kelly, allow me to introduce myself. I am Luca Francesco Costa, and yes, you are right." Luca turned slowly, took two steps forward and placed his face inches away from his twin brother. "I *am* the firstborn son of my dead father. Hello, Vincenzo. Are you surprised to see me still alive?"

Kelly thought about Jackie Chan and wandered if this kid had a future.

Vincenzo lowered his gun, "Luca, I did not know you lived. Father said you died shortly after childbirth."

"Did he now? I was sick for a long time, but as you can see, I did not die. So, where is my gravestone, Vincenzo? Surely you must have visited many times to offer a flower for your dead brother." His words oozed like a virulent poison.

Vincenzo started to quiver. "Luca, you must believe me, I did not know."

"Enough of your lies", Luca shouted. "I will deal with you in good time. Holster your weapon, or do you intend to use that on me?" He pointed towards the president, "That also applies to you two."

"Someone has to die for killing my friend and fellow God's Garbage member," the president fired back. "It is our sacred blood oath sworn by each patched member. A man for a man . . . Surely you know the importance of that being a Catholic?"

"God's Garbage, really? You take The Lord's name and plaster it all over the backs of your filthy jackets. Patrick O'Finlay is dead, as dead can be. Soon his body will be recovered from inside a burnt-out home and eventually identified." He pointed towards Kelly. "You see this man? Your business with him is over. I will now decide your future dealings with the Costa family from this moment on. Don't make me repeat myself."

Antonio stepped forward while running a finger across his heart with the sign of the Holy Cross. He held

Luca's two hands and kissed each one while kneeling. "Oh, sweet mother of God, what is happening here today?"

"All in good time, Antonio. You are another innocent victim in this family dispute."

Madeleine was freaking out. None of this was part of her and Luca's well-laid-out plan. *What was Luca up to?* She struggled to come to terms with the whole situation. She was considering she may be on the wrong end of another double-cross. Madeleine tried to catch Luca's eye. He dismissed the gesture with a return scowl.

"Now, Mr Kelly. You say you have seen a birth certificate with my name on it? Was that a lie to gain you some leverage? If so, you are of no further use to me." He pulled out a Beretta M9. "I much prefer the Italian version over the American knockoff."

"Well, it's nice to be a part of your little family reunion," Kelly replied, "but I came here today for one reason and one reason only. Now with Ma being served up as pig fodder . . ."

Luca cut him off. "You are here to clear your name of a murder you did not commit, and yet you were there. Perhaps you wish to protect the sister you reunited with only yesterday?"

"That was a case of mistaken identity. The only thing me and that fourteen-year-old girl share is the same surname. Still, she is safe now, and that's something."

Luca asked again, "The birth certificate you spoke about? How else would you know my treacherous brother had a twin, and how did it come to be in your possession?"

". . . And all very good questions. I want my life back. Fuck, I haven't even had a life yet. I'm no patched member of a bike gang, and I am definitely *not* connected to any underworld family unless you count a string of foster homes as the Mob. And yet you all want me dead. Fuck the lot of you," Kelly fired back. Attack was his only form of defence right now.

"Don't talk to my brother like that," Vincenzo cried out.

Luca stepped to one side and removed a book he'd left on a shelf. He handed it to his twin brother. "You disgust me, Vincenzo, and bring shame to this family. This was written in the 1840s by an author called, Alexandre Dumas. The title is *D'Artagnan saga.* Perhaps better known as *The Man in the Iron Mask.* This time tomorrow night, you will be escorted by boat back to our homeland in Sicily and dealt with accordingly. Read the book, I think you may find it relevant."

"You can't do this to me. I run the family business in Australia. I am my father's representative. No person will recognise your claim. This is outrageous."

"They will if you can get your hands on that bloody birth certificate," Kelly interjected.

Luca asked Kelly, "What proof do you have?"

"The hospital was the Ospedale E. Muscatello in the province of Syracuse, and was witnessed by a man called, Stefano Elia Paola Costa."

"Our uncle?" Vincenzo was questioning rather than confirming.

"Yes, Vincenzo, dear old, Uncle Stefano. It seems you speak the truth, Mr Kelly. Today might just be your lucky day. Rest assured, you are going to die, but where I come from in Sicily, there is still some honour among thieves. Provide me with this *original* birth certificate, and the best I can offer you is a one-hour head start. There will be a contract put on your head. Fifty thousand dollars buys a lot of guns."

Madeleine had heard enough. "Are you insane? He needs to die. Just take him somewhere quiet, shoot him and get rid of the body... and do it NOW!"

Kelly turned to witness Madeleine's ire and addressed Luca again. "You might want to reconsider your choice in women, Luca?"

"My future bride and new business partner can get a bit excited. The birth certificate—*now*."

"It's somewhere safe with my bike."

Vincenzo interrupted, "He doesn't ride a bike, Luca. He's lying. His car is parked out the front."

Kelly faced Vincenzo, "Mate, how much of that wine have you knocked back? I don't own a bloody car."

Vincenzo walked to the window and pointed at the Triumph *Stag*, "Then what is that parked on the kerb?"

Kelly stood next to Vincenzo and pushed the curtain open. He turned to face Madeleine, "Maybe you want to answer that one sweet-cheeks."

Madeleine ignored the question. It made no difference now with Luca deviating from the original plan.

Kelly laughed at Vincenzo. "Next time you want to be taken for a ride, you clown, Luna Park is open seven days a week."

Luca shouted, "Enough of this bullshit. Your bike, Mr Kelly, where is it now?"

"Not far," Kelly answered.

"How far is not far? I'm losing my patience," Luca growled.

"Walking distance. Send one of these goons with me, and I'll get it right now."

"You have it with you?"

"Yes."

"I'll take him," Emmanuel offered.

"You're making a mistake, Luca," Madeleine yelled with arms waving frantically in the air.

Luca faced Emmanuel. "Go now, while I deal with my twin brother, and don't take your eyes off him. Do you have a gun?"

Emmanuel grabbed the president's gun, still sitting on the table. "I do now. Come on, let's go." He prodded Kelly in the back for good effect. They both headed for the front door.

Vincenzo knew he needed to seize his opportunity to convince his brother to see reason. "Luca, please listen to me. Yes, I was aware I had a brother, but not until my eighteenth birthday. That is when our father told me the truth."

"The truth! And what is that, Vincenzo... the so-called truth?"

"That you were born with polio. Father said you were taken away to be cared for by the Sisters of Mercy Convent until God welcomed you into his arms."

"Let me update you. Our mother was unable to conceive a child, not able to produce an heir. She was tasked with choosing a *courtesan* to bear our father a son. It tore her apart. I was a breech birth, and the affliction you refer to is known as developmental dysplasia of the hip: clicky hips. The nuns cared for me until the money suddenly stopped without notice when I was seven years old. That's when our Uncle Stefano was ordered to place me in an asylum for the insane, and the family all immigrated to Australia. Currently, I am listed as missing, but that small problem will be easily amended when you are returned in my absence. Don't you just love the irony?"

Vincenzo dropped to both knees with his hands clasped in a final plea for clemency.

Luca issued his first order. "Antonio, take his weapon. It is God's will, Vincenzo, an eye for an eye and a tooth for a tooth. One life stops and another starts. I have waited over twenty-one years for this day, and thanks to Madeleine's help, my day of reckoning has finally arrived."

Kelly stepped onto the road and kept walking, "Right now, I just want to punch you in the head Emmanuel, but I know you would beat the living shit out of me."

"You'll get your chance, don't worry. We all do what's necessary to protect the family, Lucky Phil. I have a sick mother in Uruguay, two sisters to put through university and two brothers that are almost unemployable. One day when you have a family, you might understand," Emmanuel replied before asking, "Where are we going?"

Kelly pointed, "My bike is down under that tree."

"That Madeleine, she's a real piece of work, isn't she?"

"She has her good points," Kelly smirked back.

"You dog. Did you nail her?"

"Seven times in the one night," Kelly answered proudly.

"What was she like? A real tiger, I bet."

"I don't know. Nothing to compare it to."

Emmanuel stopped by the parked bike. "You mean, she popped your cherry?"

"Someone had to do it. Better with a woman like that than with a twenty-dollar hooker from the Cross."

"You got a good point there." Emmanuel jabbed him in the ribs. "Maybe that's why you're called, Lucky Phil."

Maybe - maybe not.

Kelly unlocked the seat and passed Emmanuel the leather satchel. Emmanuel opened it and flipped through the two sets of documents. "Just give the Italian both birth certificates. The promissory note with a title deed has nothing to do with him," Kelly said.

Emmanuel asked, "Title deed to what?"

"Who knows?" Kelly showed the old document to Emmanuel.

Emmanuel finished reading and faced Kelly, "This ain't no title deed, it's a promissory note."

"Yeah, like I said, so continue on, Einstein."

"It's a promise to sell the land title that relates to this volume, folio, and lot number for the consideration of one-dollar US upon producing this document to what looks like an Italian company registered in the Cayman Islands."

"Is that right?" Kelly slid it back inside its plastic dust cover and placed the satchel back under his seat.

Emmanuel then said, "You need to go now, Lucky."

"Huh, what do you mean?"

"Hit me, I know you want to."

"Hit you! I was only half-serious."

"Belt me with one of those quick left jabs of yours, then get on that bike and get the fuck out of Sydney. Come on, stop piss-farting around. I need a cover story."

"Why the sudden change?"

"Mad Dog's current hold is under threat. He needs a strong show of strength to reinforce his position. You are that show of force. He won't stop until you're dead, so get on that piece of shit and piss off. Every minute counts."

"Mad Dog?"

"That's the President's name."

Kelly didn't hesitate. He smacked Emmanuel hard on the bottom lip, and it didn't make him feel any better. Emmanuel faked a fall as the sound of two Harley's cranked over. Kelly slid his helmet on and headed back towards the creek. He stopped and paid the two boys. "Don't forget our deal." He crossed the wooden planks, almost sliding into the creek himself, then followed the track back to the road. The two God's Garbage members saw Emmanuel lying on the ground. He got up, still cursing, "Quick, he went that way. Little prick belted me."

Both Harley's flew past the eucalyptus tree, their rear wheels fishtailing on the damp grass. They approached the creek crossing, one behind the other. The young boys only had time to knock out the front support beam, but that did the trick just fine. The president's front wheel made the first contact. Initially, the wheel just wobbled while holding its line. The rear wheel soon followed with a very different result. The heavy bike swayed to one side. The rider tried to power his way out of trouble, which only made it worse. The homemade bridge gave way, sliding sideways, and the Harley T-boned when it collided with the opposite bank, before spectacularly falling into the mud and slime. Seconds later, the whole scene played out again in a perfect action replay.

Chapter-29

CROSSING THE BIG GREY coat-hanger for what was probably the last time bought to the surface a myriad of mixed emotions for Kelly. He thought about Serena, and the disappointment she will feel when her brother disappears out of her life for the second time. And then there was the rest of the family he so desperately wanted to meet.

Kelly had three simple tasks to complete before he planned to head towards Central Station and jump on the next train out of Sydney to leave the city that would both haunt him while also holding a special place in his heart. The afternoon peak hour traffic was slow and tedious and chewed up over twenty-five minutes of his precious one hour head start. He looked at the time as he pulled up outside City Kawasaki. It only took ten minutes to negotiate a price for his slightly used bike. He counted out the $1,900 and slid the notes into his wallet. Next, he needed a haircut. His shoulder-length blond locks were like a walking billboard. Kelly asked the sales manager, "Do you know a barber close by?"

"There's plenty in the city."

"What about out of the city, maybe on the train line?"

"Central has a barber opposite the main entrance. I've been using Berny's for years."

Kelly found the barber. He asked for a number three buzz cut and paid the extra for a clean shave, then left Berny's and crossed the road. Looking up at the big clock in the middle of Central's Grand Concourse, he noticed it was a couple of minutes before his deadline of 5:00 P.M. Kelly found a gift shop and purchased an A4 sized picture frame. He removed the promissory note and placed it inside the glass frame, then slid a small hand-written note in behind:

'*April 1988. Serena, I thought this might look good on your wall. Something to remind you I am real, and I will be back.*

Luv U . . . Your other brother, Lucky Phil'.

He found the Post Office and paid for a Post-it-Pak with some additional bubble wrap. He wrote down an address: No-19 Allenby St, Clontarf 2093, attached the '*fragile - handle with care*' sticker, then passed it back over the counter for postage that same day.

Kelly made his way over to the ticket window and was greeted by a young lady with a purple and orange mane who resembled a stoned parrot. What was once her hair now looked like bird feathers sticking out at odd angles, so it was only natural she would have a matching giant silver ring pierced through her left nostril. Kelly had the urge to pull at it for no other reason than it was there while thinking of how the hell her father stayed sober long enough to have sex with a galah. He smiled after seeing her bloodshot, happy eyes. Kelly could only assume it must be okay to chug-a-lug on a late afternoon bong if you are a government employee.

He enquired about a ticket on the Indian Pacific to Perth in Western Australia, the most isolated city in the world, 3,933 kilometres across the great expanses of the largest continent on the planet. From the Pacific Ocean in the east to the Indian Ocean in the west, and a long way from Sydney.

She answered with a clouded glow radiating from both her cheeks. "The next train heading west is due to depart at seven A.M. tomorrow, and there are only first-class carriages available."

Kelly asked, "What other interstate trains are scheduled to depart in the next hour?"

"All interstate services leave Central before midday. Only local N.S.W country services depart in the afternoon apart from the Grafton, Casino and Brisbane trains which depart at eight P.M. sharp." She directed him to the thirty-six-foot-long sandstone coloured indicator board. Kelly walked over and started weighing up his available options. He found himself checking out perfect strangers with a wandering eye. He considered how someone might carry out his own assassination in broad daylight while in the public domain. The possibilities were endless. He asked himself what his childhood hero James Bond would do, probably smile at his leading lady and whisk her off to the bedroom. Thoughts of Madeleine suddenly washed over him, and that all too familiar painful tug on the heart-strings still brewed inside like a chest cough that won't go away.

Kelly made his way back to the ticket office and purchased a single first-class ticket to Perth. Now he needed to find a safe haven for his last night in Sydney.

Kelly left the station via the western exit, following Eddy Ave before turning right into Pitt Street. He stopped outside a reasonably busy restaurant and flipped through the kerbside menu. Through the glass window, tables were occupied by normal, everyday members of society. They didn't have to put up with the fear and uncertainties of a life dictated by the actions of others', just enjoy each day as it unfolded and try not to annoy the missus. *Lucky bastards.* Kelly had been alone all his life, but right now, he never felt more isolated.

An elderly couple were making a heartfelt attempt at spoon-feeding what looked like a couple of grandkids, the delights of chocolate chip ice cream. Grandma was having a win while poppy looked on with a smiling curiosity, watching the young boy performing some magical artistry with the small bowl of crushed nuts. Nanna looked on in dismay before the inevitable tongue-lashing followed, putting a stop to the creative ambitions of a six-year-old.

The setting sun slowly retreated behind the city skyline, and soon the nightcrawlers would emerge like sewer rats to compete in the never-ending battle for simple survival. Kelly was about to enter the restaurant and erase another hour from the ticking time bomb shadowing him like a cash-strapped undertaker.

In the reflection on the opposite side of the road, Kelly recognised the sleek lines of a Suzuki GT-380 slowing. These were a three-cylinder configuration with a Ram Air System. A nice-looking bike until you turned a corner. Two people wearing full-face helmets and dark visors veered sharply into the transit lane. A woman dressed in a matching sky blue skirt and jacket was walking alone with a stylish ladies' leather work bag hanging at waist height from a shoulder strap. The bike stopped, and the pillion eased off the rear seat then made a grab for the bag from behind. The woman reacted and held tight with two hands. A tug of war followed, with no one willing to give an inch.

Kelly turned, expecting someone to stop and offer some help, and yet wasn't the least bit surprised when none was forthcoming. A bus pulled to a stop blocking his view, Kelly walked back to the pedestrian crossing. The red '*don't walk*' sign was still blinking. He was mad as hell and bolted across the busy road, reaching the fourth lane as cars inched forward through the green arrow.

The attractive-looking lady was losing the battle of strength, but not the battle of wits. She looked determined, and why wouldn't she? With her back bent, and the weight of her entire body pulling against the tightened strap, the buckle let go. She staggered backwards in a half-controlled trip, eventually landing heavily on the footpath, breaking a heel in the process. The guy on the other end also came a cropper and landed heavily against the door of a parked car with the bag now firmly in his grasp.

Kelly covered the last few metres in a couple of strides. He lined this thieving bastard up with precision and aimed his open palm at the stranger's collarbone. The man turned, and luckily for him, stepped to one side. Kelly's well-aimed bone buster missed its intended target, instead glancing off the man's left shoulder. Kelly could see his own reflection beaming back from his tinted visor. He wanted to land the telling blow with a snap kick to his balls and send him into orbit. Suddenly, he felt a world of pain from a clenched fist wrapped around a cigarette lighter, hammering him on the back of his skull. He stumbled forward, breaking his momentum with both hands on the bonnet of an idling car. A women's shoe came flying through the air and collected the rider on his helmet. Kelly needed to take three deep breaths before he could turn and face his new attacker when the pillion swung the leather bag with exacting aim, slamming into the side of his face. That was all the time the team of two needed as the bike sped up down Pitt St then disappeared amongst the peak hour traffic.

Kelly stepped over while rubbing his cheekbone and offered a helping hand to assist the startled woman back to her feet. Now all the heroes arrived and started to fuss about doing nothing but trying to justify their hidden guilt. The lady's skirt was slightly ripped, and she was bleeding where her left hand took the brunt of her fall.

"Are you okay?" Kelly asked.

She stood and brushed clean the front of her uniform, "Little bastards, the cops warned people to be on the lookout. You never think it will be you, but there you go. Thank you so much for stepping in like that." She cast a telling stare at the small crowd, counting more men than women. "Perhaps if I was offered some help earlier, it might have ended differently?" Her raised tone was meant for all to hear.

"So, you're not hurt?" Kelly pressed again.

"I'm fine, it will take more than a couple of petty thieves to put this lady down, let me tell you. Bloody pussies."

"Can I get you anything—maybe a tissue? Do you have anyone to come and pick you up?"

"Yeah, how about my bag, with my purse and all my money? Plus two weeks worth of work and tickets to see David Bowie. Sorry, I don't mean to sound ungrateful, I'm just so angry right now."

Kelly gave her the once-over like any man would or should. Just don't get caught. She was a good-looking sort— really good-looking, in fact. Kelly flirted with the idea for a fleeting second, and then just as quick he mentally retreated. "Do you need taxi fare? I'm heading towards Kings Cross if you need a lift."

"A bit early for the Cross, isn't it?"

"Just looking for a good feed. I know a quiet Mexican restaurant in William St."

"Is that some sort of dinner invitation?"

"No, that's me telling you I'm hungry."

A lady approached with her broken shoe and handed it back. "Thank you." She held Kelly's shoulder while balancing on one leg and slipped the scuffed shoe back on her foot. "I need to get home and ring the cops, then cancel my credit cards. Have you got a car?"

"Taxi, remember," Kelly replied.

"Sorry. I live in Paddington. It's sort of on the way. Are you offering me a lift home?"

"Apparently, it seems I am now. Which side of the street do we grab a cab from?"

"Not this one. We can cross over at the lights. Thank you again. My name is Roxanne, most people just call me Roxy. And you?"

Kelly hesitated, "James, my name is James."

"Are you sure? You don't sound confident. Nice haircut, by the way. Are you a serving soldier or something?"

Kelly ran his fingers through his prickled hair. "A change is as good as a holiday, they say."

The taxi pulled away, Roxanne offered some verbal directions from the back seat. He seemed to understand, which was a first. She turned to face her fellow passenger, "Do you make a habit of coming to the aid of damsels in distress?"

"No, you would be my first. Have you got a spare key to your home?"

"Oh, shoot, I didn't even think about that. My brother might be at home. Otherwise, it's my neighbour if I can find her. Sharyn and I swapped keys in case we ever locked ourselves out."

"You said, brother?"

"Yes, and he's big and strong, so don't go getting any ideas, okay," Roxanne laughed at her own joke. "He's studying an arts degree at Sydney Uni, so he's hardly ever home, anyway. So, you like Mexican food?"

"Some of it."

Roxanne leaned forward and started barking out instructions, "Driver, take the next right into Lang Road, then follow that past Parade Grounds, turn right at Oxford then first lights left into Queen St. The traffic lights at Anzac Parade will take three changes to get through this time of day."

This was a woman accustomed to issuing instructions and having them followed. Kelly took the opportunity to glance sideways and read the logo on her jacket pocket. Roxanne turned, "Are you right there? I know this jacket is a bit tight in all the wrong places," she joked.

Kelly straightened his gaze, "No, I was reading the logo: Hot Property."

"I sell real estate, and I sell a lot of it."

"I'm not surprised," he answered back.

Roxanne turned back towards the front seat. "Just follow this street, my house is the last one on the right driver." She turned to face Kelly again, "Do you enjoy eating lamb?"

"Huh?"

"Lamb, you know, a small sheep. I cook a leg of lamb each week just so I can eat cold meat the next day. Beats your Mexican hands down. A crusty loaf of fresh bread with pickles or chutney, and two slices of Jarlsberg cheese, you can't beat it."

Kelly asked, "Are you inviting *me* to dinner now?"

"I'm asking if you want to share the last of my lamb. Not every man is so lucky, James. It's the least I can do under the circumstances. I might even have a bottle of wine in the fridge if my brother hasn't already drunk it."

Kelly's first priority was finding a safe place to wind down the clock. He planned to crash at the church in the Cross later that night, but they didn't open their doors until eleven o'clock. *This might work out just fine*, he thought.

Roxanne buzzed the front doorbell of her three-story terraced home, which looked like it was halfway through a self-renovation. No one answered. "Wait here, and I'll go see if anyone is home next door."

Kelly sat down on the front step and made a mental map of the immediate area. Rows of the same style houses lined both sides of the street. Parking was at a premium. Roxanne returned with a heavyset man in overalls. "This is Sharyn's husband, Michael." He unlocked the door and reminded her she might want to organise a locksmith. The front door closed, and Kelly followed Roxanne down a long hallway to a kitchen with a breakfast bench. A four-seater table sat alone in a small dining area which led outside to a rear porch.

"Help yourself to a beer. I'm going to change, then start making some phone calls. I won't be long." Roxanne's voice faded as she scaled the two flights of steep stairs.

Kelly opened the fridge door. Inside was a single bottle of Brown Bros Spatlese Lexia, a sweet favourite with the young crowd. One stubby of Carlsberg Elephant beer sat in the inside door, and there was no sign of a leg of lamb. He popped the top and lifted the bin lid. There were no other empty beer bottles, so Kelly opened the back door and looked inside the outside bin. Then he decided to check out the entire ground floor. There was a small office as you passed the front door and a toilet with a hand basin opposite. The toilet lid was down, and the hand towel looked clean and still hung perfectly. Inside the office was the expected desk with a high-back fake leather chair. Kelly shuffled the loose papers on the desktop. There were some real estate brochures and two printed photos of houses for sale.

He could hear the shower running upstairs, so he climbed the first set of stairs. Three bedrooms were all located to the right of another hallway. Kelly stepped through an open door. No men's clothes were lying about the floor. He opened a wardrobe to find it empty. The sound of the shower ceased from above. Kelly opened the second door, and this room was full of empty packing boxes and just regular crap, so he did the same with the last door. There was no doubt about the sex of the person who occupied this room. The smell of perfume hung in the air. Make-up and other personable items lay scattered over a mirrored table. A name tag read: Tracy Cunningham. Discarded clothes were strewn over a made bed, and the wardrobe was full of female clothing. Kelly opened the second door and inside were four other uniforms in varying colours, all sporting the logo: Hot Property. Lime green, rose red, burnt orange and purple. One for each working day. He had a good idea where the sky blue one was.

Kelly had an uneasy feeling. His guts were sending him mixed messages that something was not right. *Why bullshit about having a brother?* Kelly stopped at the second last stair and waited. He could hear Roxanne speaking on the phone. Kelly needed to get closer. He placed one shoe on the last rung and eased his weight forward. These old houses creak and groan like an angry old man. He stopped in his tracks when he heard two words that sent a shiver down his spine—"Lucky Phil." The gig was well and truly up now.

Kelly pushed through the closed door. Roxanne remained seated on her bed with a towel wrapped around her well-endowed body. She tried hard to disguise it, but her body language said it all. She eased the phone back down. Kelly asked one question, "How long do I have?"

She played the scorned woman card. "Excuse me, how dare you come barging into my room like this."

"Cut the crap," Kelly answered. By now, he'd had enough of people's bullshit.

"Don't be like that," Roxanne changed tact like a seasoned pro. She stood, allowing the towel to drop to the floor. "Come on, James, let's start over again, shall we?"

"Let's not. What time do you expect Tracy home?"

"Tracy—who's Tracy?"

"That's it, get inside that walk-in robe." Roxanne raised an arm in anger. Kelly told her, "Don't be stupid."

Then she asked, "Are you going to kill me?"

"What day is it today?" Kelly replied.

"It's Friday. Why?"

"I promised myself I wouldn't kill any woman on a Friday, so, today is your lucky day. Get inside *now*."

He closed the door and wedged a chair against the handle. "How much they paying you? What's my life worth to a woman like you?"

Roxanne started sobbing, "It's not what you think. Patrick O'Finlay screwed me over, and the Costa family captured the lot on CCTV."

"There's that name again. How fucking much?" Kelly yelled through the door.

"They promised five thousand dollars, and the slate wiped clean if I could get you off the streets."

There was a pause. Kelly needed to think on his feet.

"You've got about ten minutes. I told them the back door will be open, and we would be upstairs in the bedroom." Roxanne added, "I'm really sorry. You seem like a nice guy."

"The two men on the motorbike—that was all for my benefit?"

"They had Central Station covered. You were spotted the minute you walked in."

Kelly opened up a curtain and checked the road outside. Then he did the same from the end of the hallway window overlooking the back gate. It was too late to make a run for it from here. He'd be caught out in the open and would make an easy target. Kelly flew downstairs and opened up the cupboard under the sink. He grabbed a squeeze bottle of Draino. Inside the pantry was a bottle of virgin olive oil and a tin of Keens Mustard Powder. Kelly remembered the small 10 x 10-ft-shed out back. He pulled the back door open. A quick search turned up some basic tools, a rake, a short-handled shovel and an old cricket bat. He turned to his right and found a half-full box of brass tacks. Kelly opened the latch and left the back gate ajar, then sprinkled the tacks on the paved footpath. Then he smeared oil over the outside back door handle. He barricaded the front door with the shovel handle just for good measure and prepared for the wait. Ten minutes turned out to be under eight.

The Suzuki pulled to a stop in the rear lane. A man that was well known in Sydney's underworld as a cheap gun-for-hire called Slip the Ding slid off the rear seat. He tapped his rider on the shoulder who then cruised down the end of the lane-way, turned a sharp left to take up a position with an unobstructed view to the front door. Slip pushed open the gate. He stepped through the tacks with his heavy boots, not realising until he heard his own feet tapping on the footpath. Slip lifted one boot to see the thick sole full with the brass tacks. He didn't have time to start pulling each one out, so he kept creeping forward.

Kelly braced himself with both eyes locked on to the door handle. It shimmied slightly, and then it half turned. Kelly took a firm grip. The knob rocked up and down before the door finally creaked open. Kelly held his breath. A man's helmet poked through the open space. Kelly swung hard. The noise of the bat cracking the visor was followed by Kelly squirting the Draino inside the open space. The gunman stumbled to one side with a short-barrelled pistol in his preferred hand. Kelly sprinkled the curry powder over Slip the Ding's free hand and waited for human nature to run its course. Slip raised his hand and rubbed his eyes clean, then started screaming in Italian. "*Fanculo tu. Chi siano tu. Aiuto me per favore—acqua. Acqua, per favour.*"

Kelly understood fanculo translated to fuck, and acqua meant water, "Fat chance of that happening, Giuseppe."

He swung the bat again like a sweeping cricket stroke to the boundary. The gun was ripped from Slip's hand and bounced against the fridge door, then Kelly lined up his would-be-killer for the final blow across the front of both knees. He buckled to the floor. Kelly picked up the firearm and slipped it down the back of his jeans. The assassin was wriggling about on the kitchen floor, still swearing in his native tongue. Kelly released his helmet strap and pulled his helmet and jacket up and over his head. Slip spat at him blindly, so Kelly fed him a tight-fisted knuckle sandwich. The room became silent.

Kelly zipped up the jacket and even squeezed the helmet over his own boof-head. He removed the shovel and edged the door open. The Suzuki was parked, leaning on its side-stand with the rider sitting side-saddle. Kelly fired off two rounds into the ceiling, then counted to ten before making his escape towards the bike at speed with his arms waving. The rider reacted and straddled the bike while starting the engine. Kelly launched himself onto the back of the seat and tapped him on the shoulder while panting like a cattle dog after muster. The Suzuki powered off down the street with the two-stroke motor screaming as the tacho redlined. The bike turned left, then a hard right and accelerated again. Kelly held tight with one hand on the gun.

The lights at Anzac Parade turned amber, and the Suzuki slowed to a complete stop. Kelly stepped off, and power punched the rider in the kidneys then chopped down hard on his right arm. He fell sideways, and so did the bike.

That was soon followed with the rancid smell of burning flesh from the chrome three-into-one extractor scorching a hole through his jeans and then came the delayed screeching howl. Kelly stepped around the opposite side, lifted the Suzuki and rode on through the red light.

The Sydney Sports Ground was bubbling with excited fans lining up at multiple entry gates. The outside sign advertised an ARL game between the St George Dragons and the South Sydney Rabbitohs. Kelly dumped the bike in the adjoining Moore Park, dropped the gun inside a half-full rubbish bin and parted with some cash, then found a seat in the Southern Stand. The newly built stadium was packed for the clash between two foundation member clubs, which suited Kelly just fine. No one was going to take a crack at him while watching a game of rugby league. The Rabbitohs kicked the winning field goal in the dying seconds, and a sea of red and green erupted while standing as one to applaud their winning team.

Kelly found the Rabbitohs merchandise stall, which was named The Burrow. He purchased a red and green footy jumper plus a peak cap with a matching scarf, then dumped both Slip the Ding's jacket and T-shirt inside a bin and melted into the departing crowd. He fell in behind a bunch of thirsty red and green supporters and followed the nice pear-shaped backside of a young woman into the Captain Cook Hotel. Kelly wedged himself into a corner not far from the bar and knocked back five pints of cider. The time flew by, and the crowded pub started to thin out. It was 10:45 and time to steal some much-needed sack time before his scheduled departure the next morning.

Kelly's taxi dropped him off outside the Anglicare Elizabeth Lodge, where he had stayed previously. He was met by an unfamiliar priest who informed him he would now need to locate the Wayside Chapel located on Hughes St. Kelly didn't quite fit the profile of a homeless man, but desperate was a perfect match. He declined the offer of a bowl of soup and was shown to a thin floor mattress and handed a clean pillow.

Sleep was difficult, but obviously humanly possible when he was shaken awake by a bearded stranger who reeked of cheap cask wine and body odour. "Wake up, they're looking for runaways."

Kelly sat up and wiped the sleep from his eyes. He looked at his watch. It read 5:45 A.M. "Shit, runaways, who's looking?"

"Over there, you see," the old-timer pointed with a nicotine-stained fingernail.

Two men with torches were kicking awake sleeping bodies with a photo held in one hand despite the continued demands of the caretaker to leave. Kelly scrambled on all fours through the only other door that led to the toilet block. He opened a window and fell to the ground with a decent thump. He followed Hughes Street and turned right into Victoria Street. An early morning Sydney City Council water truck was spraying the gutters clean. Kelly jumped on the back and hitched a ride to the top of William Street. He stood under the famous Coca-Cola sign and screamed, "Fuck! This is getting bloody ridiculous." He checked the front of his jocks and felt his wallet tucked in tight. Kelly slid it out while looking in both directions for a taxi. He had just over an hour to make his way back to Central.

He started a slow jog down the hill towards the city, which helped jolt him out of the slumber of his forced awakening. The streets were quiet, and the morning was brisk. Kelly could see a uniformed man placing a man-sized A-frame billboard onto the footpath. As he approached, Kelly slowed to a comfortable stride and then ground to a halt ten feet short. At that moment he saw some clarity. Suddenly he was looking at a possible answer to all his problems. He had an epiphany. His heart rate lifted like when you're about to touch an electrical wire and risk a shock, but you do it anyway.

Kelly opened his wallet and slid out his train ticket. Then he felt inside his front pocket for a coin—any coin will do. He tossed the twenty-cent piece high into the air and let it bounce on the pavement. "Heads I do it, tails never fails," he told himself. The coin spun and rolled into the gutter just short of a grated stormwater drain. Kelly bent over and saw the head of Queen Elizabeth II. He ripped the ticket in two and prepared to cut all ties with the last day of his old life.

Chapter-30

CHIEF PETTY OFFICER Simon Morrow flipped the switch on his coffee percolator, then walked casually back and sat down on his steel-framed, vinyl office chair while gazing through the floor-to-ceiling windows of his small and scantily decorated recruiting office. He was repeating under his breath the words, "Forty-nine, forty-nine. Just one more, and I'll finally have that little bastard." Even though he was not required to open his doors until 8:00 A.M., he liked his chances of snaring one of the many passing all-night party revellers as they made their way back to what may be a miserable and fruitless life in a desperate search for a change.

When the majority of Sydney pubs are forced to close at midnight, the Rugby League Clubs call last drinks, and the private parties jostle to drain the last keg of beer, Kings Cross is just shifting into second gear. By 2:00 A.M. the crowds build. Between three and four was like bewitching hour. It was the last chance to hook up with a one-night-stand before returning to life in the suburbs with the opportunity to wake up next to a complete stranger sharing your bed, and hopefully of the right gender. By six A.M. it's just the hardcore drinkers left with the addicts and staff who make a part-time living working the bars and nightclubs.

Like vampires, as the sun prepares to enter in a new day, even the broken-hearted, the gambler on a losing streak, or maybe a disgruntled husband wanting to run from an angry spouse may be searching for a way out. Sometimes it can be the homeless who have reached the end of the road. Each and every category of these victims of the new world of sex, drugs and rock-n-roll was fair game as far as the Australian Defence Force was concerned.

This was a way of life Chief Petty Officer Simon Morrow could not participate in and had no yearning to do so. He was a committed and career Navy man to the core of his bones and lived his life governed by a strict set of rules. He glanced at his watch. It was nearing 6:15 A.M. He started to organise his small desk and prepare his practised speech sprouting the many benefits of a career in the Armed Forces.

The two most successful recruiting offices in all of Sydney were his own Surry Hills location, and the other was manned by his nemesis and arch-rival Staff Sergeant Paul Lidlow near the exit to Circular Quay. His Army rival was a balding man who was vertically challenged. His beady little eyes looked like they belonged on a horsefly through his coke-bottle-thick glasses. But he was good at his job—very good and just quietly, it drove Chief Petty Officer Morrow crazy.

Each month the two competing men had a standing bet. The first past the post to sign up fifty new recruits would be the proud owner of a crisp new one hundred dollar note and free drinks at the local pub for the next four Friday nights. Lidlow had now climbed that mountain on the past three separate occasions. The average number of new monthly recruits throughout the Sydney region was thirty-three. Simon Morrow had been close on two occasions but always seemed to fall short of the line, and Lidlow loved to remind him of this very fact at every available opportunity via phone calls and subtle comments, almost on a daily basis.

Chief Petty Officer Morrow was about to set up the second of two life-size coloured posters that stood at each side of the doorway to entice any prospective fly into the ADF spider web that awaited them inside. He noticed a tall, solidly built young man stop and stare at the poster of a Navy Seahawk helicopter hovering above an ANZAC-class frigate trailing a Collins-class submarine with the Navy training ship

Young Endeavour in the foreground under full sail, all the while gliding through the pristine waters of the Great Barrier Reef at flank speed.

The caption read: *'Where would you rather be right now? Where will you be in eight short years? The Royal Australian Navy needs good men & women—now. Are you up to the challenge?'*

It was one of the most successful recruiting posters Morrow had seen in his four years as a recruitment officer. He kept himself busy while forming a vision of a one hundred dollar note coming his way.

Kelly opened the door and stepped inside. He was almost blinded by the words: HONOUR, HONESTY, COURAGE, INTEGRITY and LOYALTY plastered in big letters above the only desk in the small office.

"Good morning, you sure open early," Kelly said.

"Hello, come on in. Saturday's are a short day, so it doesn't hurt to get an early start." The man stood, walked out from behind his desk and offered his hand. "Chief Petty Officer Simon Morrow at your service."

"Gooday. Kelly, Phil Kelly. How does all this work, then?"

"Do you mean the recruitment process?"

"Well... yeah," Kelly answered, still unsure.

"There are basically three steps. If you were thinking about a career, step one would be a short interview between just the two of us, some personal details and so forth. We don't get people drunk anymore and whisk them away in the middle of the night," he joked before saying. "Have a seat."

Kelly sat down in one of two interview chairs. "What I'm getting at is the timing? If I was to prove to be a suitable candidate, how long until I did get whisked away? I'm guessing it's no coincidence there is a recruiting office so close to Kings Cross. "

Morrow leaned forward while folding both his arms and looked at Kelly square in the eye. "Young man, I won't lie to you. There are times when we can fast-track the process for people who find themselves in, let's say, difficult situations? Let me ask you a straight-up question. Are you, or have you ever taken illegal drugs? If you lie, the first medical will reveal the truth, and you'll be right back where you started. And I'm guessing that's not a favoured outcome for you right now?"

"I don't do drugs—ever. A clear head is all that has got me to this point, trust me."

"Well, are you in some kind of trouble?"

"Not with the cops. I have a clean record."

"How old are you?"

Kelly pulled out his wallet and placed his bike license on the desk. "I turned eighteen in January."

"And family? Do your parents know where you are right now?"

"There is no mum or dad, no family, just me."

"Hmm, I see." *Forty-nine, forty-nine . . .* "What about academic achievements?"

"Like school?" Kelly asked.

"Yes, what level did you reach?"

"I turned up when the fish weren't biting, that's about all."

"Okay, that probably rules out becoming an officer. Are you swinging towards the Navy, Army or the Air Force, then?"

"I like the water, and I'm a fantastic shot."

Morrow smiled and opened a drawer. He pulled out a personal application form. "Mr Kelly, I will make a phone call to the twenty-four-hour clinic across the road. I see you have money to pay for a medical certificate. You come back here with a signed form declaring you are in good health, we complete this application, and I can guarantee you will be on a bus to Melbourne before 0900 hours."

"Melbourne?"

"Yes, HMAS *Cerberus* Training School is situated on the Mornington Peninsula. That's where you will complete steps two and three. If unsuccessful, the Navy offers a free return bus trip back home."

Kelly stood to attention. Suddenly, it was important to straighten his back. "Let's do it."

One hour later, with a smile as wide as the clown face that welcomes you to Luna Park, Chief Petty Officer Simon Morrow made a second phone call. "Winners are grinners, Paul, and it's your shout. Sorry, old mate."

The End

Leaving a Review

Reviews are the lifeblood of any self-publishing author. Please feel free to have your say or add any comments while placing an open and honest review on the page you purchased the book from. Any help is greatly appreciated and does make a very real difference. You can go to my Amazon book page by copying or clicking the following link mybook.to/TheSchoolOfHardKnocks. Thank you.

Other titles available from P.D. Nelson

P.N. Each book is a standalone story and is available in both print and e-book format by visiting: www.pdnelson.com

In order of release.

The School of Hard Knocks - released February 2019.

The Proposition - released October 2019 Available at www.pdnelson.com

The Blurb

To predict a man's future, look no further than his past.

After a smugglers plane encounters a tropical monsoon in the middle of the South China Sea, suddenly it disappears off the radar. As the sole survivor, Jack Kelly's life as he once knew it was about to change forever—and not for the better. With a $100,000 'kill on sight' contract still outstanding, soon he will need a new identity—and it didn't matter whose.

A desperate man will clutch at any straw, and when Travis Chivres receives the timely diagnosis of his wife's brain tumour, time was fast running out to locate his now-missing son to collect on her family estate. Then, while in Bangkok, he meets a man that could provide a possible solution.

Together, can these two complete strangers pull off what sounds like the perfect plan? Will Kelly still end up paying the ultimate price or can he find a way to right the wrongs from a tortured and violent past he chose to leave behind?

The second book in The Man Called Kelly Series is a fast-paced life adventure about one man's journey to reconnect with his unknown family that will keep you guessing until the last page.

The Book of Remedies - released December 2019.
The Blurb

Murder-Money-Betrayal-Treason

After nearly 400 years, the shipwrecked *Batavia* gives up her last secret. A celestial globe. An ancient mapping device. But to what and to where?

Jack Kelly now enjoys his new life whiling away the time as the owner of a 72-ft charter vessel. While on the island of Bali, he meets, Evina Bishop-Joiner, an associate professor with the Smithsonian. In her ten-year quest to locate an ancient artefact, a twist of fate now points to a previously unknown grave-site that could be linked to the sinking of the HMAS *Sydney*.

After being forced at gunpoint by an ASIO agent Kelly once trusted with his life, their search to uncover the truth leads to the already famous Zuytdorp Cliffs. At the same time, three terrorists masquerading as refugees survive a storm at sea to arrive on the very same remote stretch of coastline.

In a country that boasts an honest parliament, will Kelly be able to peel back the layers of deceit cloaked behind the mantle of justice and a fair go for all?

The third book in The Man Called Kelly Series is a riveting, fast-paced historical treasure hunt that should please the action junkies.

Released September 2019. To find out more or to purchase *The Book of Remedies*, you can visit www.pdnelson.com

Acknowledgements

I would like to thank my mother for allowing me to share some intimate details about her difficult life as a child growing up in New Zealand. I never met my grandparents, but she convinced me to follow in her own father's footsteps. As a great storyteller, he was apparently the life of many a party while tapping away on the piano keys encouraging friends to join him in a sing-a-long. "Have the courage of your convictions, find something that makes you happy then turn that into a job," she'd love to say. So after fifty-seven years—I did. Fiction and reality were closely aligned in the early days of my rebellious, runaway teenage years. The inspiration and many of the characters in all my books are formed from my own personal life experiences. Keep your enemies close, and choose your friends wisely.

About the author

Phillip Nelson was born and raised in the Snowy Mountains on the east coast of Australia. At sixteen, with just his Kawasaki Z-900 he left home for the final time with a head full of bad ideas and an attitude to match. The harsh realities of gang life surviving on the streets of Sydney and Melbourne was a steep learning curve that ended the day a whacked-out meth head bikie poked a shotgun under his chin and pulled the trigger. Saved by a dud cartridge, he needed a total re-evaluation of his life—a Plan B.

He spent time working in the hospitality industry, then as a part-time deckhand on a rock lobster boat before becoming a backup drummer in a band until he settled into delivering on-site Workplace Assessment and Training courses throughout Western Australia.

People who live in the Land Down Under are great travellers through necessity, and after continually tweaking with a fifteen-year-old idea for his first novel; Phillip Nelson jumped on a plane and headed to Europe. He now lives in a small, culturally diverse Thailand village with two very spoilt Soi dogs and a pond full of disappearing walking fish. If he hasn't got a rod in his hand, then he is normally writing, and with three books completed in 'The Man Called Kelly Series,' *The School of Hard Knocks* was his debut novel released in 2019.

Contact the author

Email: philnelson@pdnelson.com

www.ingramcontent.com/pod-product-compliance
Lightning Source LLC
Chambersburg PA
CBHW032208190626
46810CB00019B/2272